ALL THE TIME

AUTUMN MILLER

Published by Miller Publishing.

eBook ISBN 978 1916397989

ISBN 978 1916397996

Cover Design: Scott Gaunt.

A CIP catalogue record for this book is available from the British Library.

19.07.22

To my husband, and to all the other good guys out there.

FOREWORD

This book is set in the UK with British characters. Spelling and phrasing may differ.

Liam and Nora appear in the first book of the series, *All The Feels*, so you might want to start their journey there. That said, this is a standalone romance.

Warning: explicit content ahead...

PROLOGUE

LIAM

THE FIRST TIME I met Nora Moretti was impactful. The most absolute, direct meeting of two souls that could ever exist. Yet, there was no semblance of an introduction, not even a name. In fact, she seemed pretty bummed that I was even there, standing within feet of her, watching events unfold like some kind of weirdo.

And it became clear that Nora Moretti didn't need an introduction. She lived her life to the max, gifting those around her with a moment of unexpectedness that left you reeling, chasing her for another hit. She was a drug, one that had me hooked from our very first encounter.

So it should come as no surprise that my first impression of Nora would be ever-lasting. Unshakeable and life-affirming. That she'd knock me off balance in more ways than one. I needed her in my life like the Earth does the Sun, inextricably linked by galaxies, eons and gravitational pull.

Except, there were two obstacles to overcome. One, she had just started dating my brother. And two, I was pretty sure she was still in love with an ex.

CHAPTER ONE

Liam

MY BROTHER IS BRICKING IT. I should feel some sympathy for him but instead, I smother a smile, relishing the sight of obvious tension gripping his body: stiff shoulders; rigid back; a forced smile when he's not grinding his molars so hard I'm surprised they've not shattered.

Normally, he's Mr. Vaguely Uninterested. Mr. I've Got More Important Things To Think About. This detached, impatient man is better than the alternative though. The one I grew up with. As boys we had little in common, something he shared with our sisters too. When he wasn't throwing his weight around, being that stereotypical oldest child who had to beat me at just about everything, he dedicated himself to gainful hobbies and interests, like reading. But instead of locking himself away, engrossed in fantasy novels or thrillers, he got bogged down in really hard-going subjects like the great philosophers of the eighteenth-century, or prison reform in nineteenth-century Britain.

Dull.

While Tom worked his way through the nearest well-stocked library, Fay, Tilly, and I ran wild in the Suffolk countryside, bramble scrapes and ditch-muck covering us head to toe by the time dinner was ready. We'd come indoors, high on fatigue, our muscles so weary we were hysterical from it.

Being older, Tom outgrew us quickly. But it never stopped him from wanting to put us in our place every now and then. To hone that blade of competitiveness until I got so frustrated that I turned to other things to amuse me. Things I became quite good at.

My eyes drift towards his agitated form. It doesn't help that just about all the gathered friends and colleagues here to celebrate his thirty-seventh birthday have already asked him one of two things: *Where's your girlfriend? Is your girlfriend here yet?*

I'm sure he's wondering where his new girlfriend is too. She should be at his side, the focus point of multiple, intrigued stares. Instead, he has to stand here, chatting as if nothing's wrong, all of us burning up with curiosity as to when she'll turn up.

If she'll turn up.

He doesn't have a good track record with women. I really hope he manages to keep this one. I've yet to meet Nora. All I know is that she's medical, and that she's *really pretty.* My brother doesn't use words like *hot* or *she's a ten* or *she's gorgeous.* He finds them too superlative, too pretentious, stating it's all subjective anyway. Tom's all about the understatement, which is odd coming from a published writer, and a professor of literature at a London university.

Personally, I've always enjoyed seeing hot, gorgeous girls, but it's all becoming a little predictable. I want to meet someone who'll keep me guessing.

My oldest sister, Fay, hands me a beer. "What are you doing here all by yourself?"

"Dunno." For some reason I'm in a weirdly anti-social mood. Standing to one side of the room to observe everyone else has been entertaining me for the past few minutes.

Silver balloons idle in corners, weighed down by small, silver blocks. Interspersed amongst the plates of appetisers are shallow vases of flowers. Black-clad staff with trays of champagne, whisky, and bottled beer flit between guests.

My brother pushed the boat out for his birthday this year. I think he's trying to impress a certain, yet-to-be-seen lady.

Good for him.

"He must have it bad, arranging this?" I gesture to the balloons and food.

Frowning, Fay asks, "What?"

"Throwing a party to impress Nora."

Scoffing, Fay imparts, "It's to woo *the Dean*. How do you not know this? He wants to cut his days to devote more time to writing. It's not for anyone else's benefit."

I stand corrected, but then Tom and I rarely talk these days, so how was I to know.

Leaning in, Fay whispers, "Do you think she's stood him up?"

There's only one *she* we're all interested in. "I overheard him tell someone she's been delayed. Won't be long now."

Fay sips from her glass. Earlier today, she got her auburn hair cut at the salon, and it's super shiny. "Let's hope so. Would be a shame if he was on his own for the Big Holiday."

At mention of the Big Holiday, I make a face. Our parents have booked a beautiful villa in France to celebrate their wedding anniversary. Fay is coming with her husband, Tilly with her fiancé, and Tom with Nora. Currently in between girlfriends, I'm undecided if I want to ask an ex along for some friends with benefits action, or just take the week to really relax. It's the first time we've all been away together for about fifteen years, and there's a lot riding on it - hence the naming convention. And my parents have gone a little insane over the details, planning day trips to vineyards and forests and chateaux. To cute villages with authentic, artisanal farmer's markets.

"If she dumps him, at least we'd be single together."

Fay rolls her eyes. "If you don't bring someone I'll keel over with shock."

"I'll bring the defibrillator."

"Smelling salts will do. Unless, of course, you want to ask Lowell along. I wouldn't mind if he wanted to resuscitate me."

Lowell is my cardio-thoracic surgeon friend of many years. "I think this is where I remind you that you're married. And have been for four years."

Two years younger than Tom, Fay is happily child-free, much to Mum and Dad's disappointment. Tilly is their next big hope, especially now she's engaged. But with Tom now seeing Nora, Mum and Dad are hoping for babies on at least two fronts. Sometimes it helps to be the youngest child. Parental expectations tend to have been loaded on to older siblings, those high-achieving first-borns.

"I didn't say it had to be mouth-to-mouth resuscitation," Fay defends unnecessarily.

"Yeah, right," I reply, smirking at her. She's had a not-so-secret-crush on Lowell since I met him at university. Nothing came of it, but we do joke about it. We joke about most things.

"Oh, Liam! How are you, my darling?"

Judith, a fellow professor from Tom's university corners me. Fay grins evilly as she disappears, leaving me alone with the forty-year-old.

Judith calls everyone *darling*, an ingrained habit of the faculty I believe, though not something my brother suffers from.

Fancying herself as a cougar, dressed in a leopard print dress and matching shoes, Judith flirts outrageously with me for the next few minutes. Normally, I'd lap the attention up and indulge in the teasing conversation, but I'm just not feeling it today.

Frustrated, I blow out a breath. Heat smothers my back, the black tuxedo and crowded room all adding to my discomfort. The awkward conversation suffocates and stifles as I eye the doors that lead to the patio and the deep garden beyond. It's not even nine o'clock, but already I'm thinking of when I can leave the party without being rude.

My eyes drift across the room to Tom who's locked in conversation with the Dean. My brother pulls out his phone from a pocket to check the screen before slipping it back again.

Taking that as my cue, I finish my beer and wish Judith goodnight. Deciding not to be so obvious by using the patio doors, I leave the reception room of the swanky Richmond hotel and follow the corridor to the side exit. There's a cream stone path that leads down the side of the gardens, and I take it, leaving the fluting laughter and chaotic noise from multiple conversations behind me.

Trying to shake off my restless mood, I focus on the cooler air and the faintest of breezes. It's a balmy night for early June, a hangover from a scorching hot day where the temperature didn't seem to cool as the day progressed.

For a brief moment, I just inhale and exhale, taking in the gardens, looking at it all critically in case I ever wanted to draw it from memory.

The rear of the grounds abut Richmond Park from where towering oaks loom. Garden lights run parallel to the path, high-lighting a flower-filled border, interspersed with an occasional wooden bench for those wishing to sit and enjoy the gardens. The sky is a deep blue, the sun low on the horizon. Planters overspill with French lavender, and a trio of men nurse tumblers of whisky on a nearby table.

I take the path until it ends in a thick hedge of evergreens, a weathered cedar bench nearby. Noise from overhead has me tipping my head back, planes queuing as they head for Heathrow, lights flashing on their underbellies. It's impossible to make out any stars yet.

An uncommon sound catches my attention, and any thoughts I had to sit and unwind on the bench are forgotten. Leaving the path, I squeeze through a small gap at the end of the hedge and venture deeper into the garden, the lights completely obscured.

A pair of silver heels and a matching clutch are discarded on the grass.

For a second I pause, frowning, wondering who they belong to and if I should turn back. Stumbling onto an alfresco romp by two hotel guests is not high on my list of things to do tonight. But then that sound comes again, a distressed cat meowing somewhere to my left.

Intrigued, I take a few more steps. The tree canopy blocks the sky, and that's when I spot the cream, sequinned cocktail dress hanging by its tag on a tree knoll, glinting and shining like a star in the darkness.

I should definitely turn back, but the meowing grows more insistent. Looking up, I scan the tree looming over me, unable to see anything through the abundant, vibrant green leaves. Rustling sounds amongst the smaller branches, and as I strain to pick out something tangible, I catch a glimpse of something flesh-toned against the bark.

Furious whispered curses reach my ears, bringing a reluctant smile to my mouth. "Come on you stupid cat," the voice continues, clearly that of a woman.

There are a couple of choices open to me: go back to the

party and hope to identify this woman via her dress later, or stay and offer my help.

Meow! Meow! Meow!

"Just a little bit closer. Come on, you moronic fur-ball!"

A squeaky noise sounds, the woman trying to imitate a mouse. That reluctant smile of mine turns into a full-on grin.

Just then, there's a surprised gasp, the branch above my head moving alarmingly. Clumps of leaves sway violently as twigs fall to the patchy grass around me. And then two bare legs dangle through the greenery.

"Shit," the voice grumbles, calm but cross.

"Are you okay?" I call up.

"Oh my god!" No doubt shocked at hearing my voice, her grasp on the branch compromised, the legs drop a little further through the foliage. I stretch out my arms in front of me ready to catch. "Don't look up!" the woman calls, distress coating her words.

"Sorry, but I'm not sure I can look away," I return, moving closer and peering upwards. "You're dangling from a branch and I think I might be needed to catch you."

From this position, and because the woman seems to be hanging precariously on a sagging branch, it's no longer just calves and knees I can make out, but all of her legs now. She kicks and wriggles, struggling to pull herself back onto the branch she's slipped from. Grunts of exertion intermingle with more whispered curses, and I start to strip off my tux jacket ready to climb up there myself, or at a minimum prepare to catch.

Tossing my jacket to one side, I move under the tree so that my back is to the boundary. From this angle, fewer leaves block my view, offering me a better vantage point.

A *much* better vantage point.

The legs belong to a brunette, dressed solely in white underwear, dangling from a branch fifteen to twenty feet above my head, her arms at full stretch.

"What are you doing back here anyway?" she shouts down at me.

The question is so left-field, I laugh. Surely she should be concentrating on not crash-landing? But no, she has time to berate me first. To question my motives. "I'll answer that once you do," I suggest, wondering who the hell this woman is. Is she part of Tom's guest list? Is she a diner or guest at the hotel, wandering into parts of the garden that we're not meant to be accessing?

I position myself underneath her, readying myself. "Drop down! I'll catch you." Her feet are probably ten feet above me. It's doable. Just.

There's a horrified, embarrassed sound. "I'm fine. Please... oh god, don't look. I'm not wearing anything."

"Come on," I encourage, ignoring her concerns. I've seen plenty of women in their pants and bras before - professionally and personally - though seeing one stuck up a tree in her underwear is a first. "I'll break your fall."

Just please don't break my back in the process.

"I'll squash you."

"You don't look that heavy," I counter, wondering if I have time to make an emergency call to Tom and the others back at the hotel. Or if I shout for help will anyone hear me? Perhaps those drinkers out on the patio...

Thoughts are ripped clean out of my head as the woman anxiously calls out, "My hands are slipping! I can't hold on....aarrrgghhh!"

The scream rips through the air as she falls towards me at lightning speed. I only get a second before our bodies collide, her legs slipping through my arms and crashing down the front of my torso. I tighten my arms, clamping them around her more forcefully, but already I know my balance is thrown off. Physics GCSE was a long time ago, and I can't even begin to try and calculate anything to do with mass or velocity or force right now. Instead, I just lock my legs and secure my feet to the ground as best I can, grabbing the smooth-skinned woman before she slips right through my hands to a heap on the ground.

"Oofff!"

"Uurrgghhh!"

But it's not enough. The angle of her plummet from above has upset my equilibrium beyond redemption. I'm pushed backwards, my body reacting instinctively as I bend my knees, knowing I'm going to have to take her down with me. Accepting the inevitable, we fall backwards, my heart in my throat. Both of us cry out as I roll us to the ground as smoothly as I can, holding her in my arms and making sure she uses my body as her cushion.

My arms are like steel bands around her. Flush against my body, I don't loosen my hold until all motion has dissipated, our bodies lying still after rocking and tumbling.

Covered by a delightful lace balcony bra, her breasts are squashed up against my chin and neck. Curly, dark hair frames a shocked face, but it's undeniably pretty. Freckles dust her cheeks and nose, with more sprinkled across her forehead. Dark eyes are wide open in surprise and shock as she peers down into my face, our mouths inches away.

"Hi," she whispers.

"Hi," I reply, bemused. But that's mainly because I'm stunned by the force of my attraction. And I like the way she feels in my arms, pressed against me so closely.

"Are you okay?"

It's at that moment that my back protests, an old injury deciding to rear its ugly head and ruin my night. "Yeah," I say grimacing.

Her hips lift away from my lower stomach, her arms supporting her body weight as she hovers over me and regards me with what I recognise as clinical precision. "Is it your back?"

I nod, unable to find words to describe the pain I'm in.

"I'm so sorry. It was stupid of me to climb up there."

I've no idea where that stupid cat is, but if it wasn't for my bad back I'd be praising it for getting into difficulty; my evening has dramatically improved. Sort of. "If you wanted to jump my bones," I murmur quietly, doing my best to speak through the tortuous pain, "you only needed to ask."

With a quick laugh, the woman scrambles to my side and sits on her haunches. "The spine is a particular favourite," she admits, amusement dancing in her eyes.

I risk a chuckle, pain slicing through my back. "Really? I'd offer you a piggyback but I might need one from you."

"Okay. Let's take a look at you," she suggests, her brow furrowing. She stands, scurrying to her dress and slipping it on before returning. "Can you stand?"

Gingerly, I roll to my side and she eases to a squat to assist me. Embarrassment sweeps through me; I must look like an octogenarian right now.

"There's a bench back this way," she says, steering me towards the gap in the firs and the illuminated path. Barefoot, she helps me to the bench, the patio in the distance void of the earlier drinkers.

"Lie down. On your stomach."

Grimacing, I climb onto the wooden bench at glacial speed and stretch out, my feet dangling over the end.

"This bench isn't the best height to check you over but it'll have to do."

"Not the comfiest either," I add dryly, before telling her about my persistent problem, an old rugby injury from my late teens located in my lower back.

"Can I take a look? I'm a chiropractor."

I chuff, my instincts right about that look of professionalism, but even though I have great respect for all medical professions, this woman looks young, and I want to ensure she knows what she's doing. "Where did you study?"

With my head lying on my forearms, I can't see her reaction - or much else - but I can feel a wave of displeasure ghost across my back.

"South Bank University. I have an MChiro and share a clinic in Pimlico with a physiotherapist. We're next to the doctor's surgery on Moreton Street."

"I know it," I say. I live in Pimlico so I know it's probably a fifteen-minute walk to my flat. "How long have you been qualified for?"

"Six years. So how often does the pain manifest?" I open my mouth to respond but she interrupts with, "Put your arms on either side of the bench. I'm going to assess you now."

I do as she asks, knowing I need to keep my back and neck straight. "Help yourself."

Immediately, her hands start to slide over my body, strong fingers probing and pushing, the heel of her hand a pressure that can only mean imminent results.

"Let me know what hurts on a scale of one to ten, ten being horrific pain."

"Oh, that's reassuring," I voice, catching glimpses of her as she moves positions. "Just what I need to hear." There's a soft laugh, her hands constantly on the move. "Are you sure you're a chiropractor? Maybe this is all part of your ploy to jump me."

"Feeling up crooked-backed men on wooden benches? Sounds like my ideal Saturday night," she deadpans, a smile in her voice. I can hear it. That smile sounds good. "What can I say? For the past thirty minutes I've been clinging on for dear life, waiting for some poor unsuspecting man to come along.

And then *finally,*" she stresses, and I just know she's rolling her eyes, as if I've severely inconvenienced her by my tardiness, "you showed up."

I laugh at that. Or try to.

"So what happened?" she pushes.

"There was an awkward tackle consisting of sudden impact on two facet joints, on either side of my vertebrae."

Her hands focus on my lower spine, trying to find some way under my belt. "Could you undo your belt?"

"Oh, I see how it is," I tease. "First the shirt comes off, then maybe my shoes. What's next?"

"Shut up," she replies, drawing out the words to tell me she's playing with me too.

I sigh out a laugh, enjoying the way her hands feel on me, even if my shirt is in the way. But when I try and move my hands underneath me, I get a bit stuck. How am I meant to do this without getting back on my feet?

"Um, I can....help," the woman offers.

"Sure you can."

I imagine she's rolling her eyes at me again.

Planking, I lift my hips a couple of inches off the bench as her hands come to either side of my waist, rummaging around for the buckle. The fact that she manages to undo the belt without touching my junk is an exemplary feat of dexterity and control. "Your master plan is paying off. No sooner have you thrown yourself at me than the trousers are coming off."

I sense a smile. "I didn't realise I was so unsubtle. I'm going to have to work on my game."

"To be fair, only wearing underwear was a bit of a giveaway."

"Hmm. That's a good point. And the tree. Let's not forget that is the number one way for a young woman to land herself a man these days."

"Literally," I deadpan, to her amused, husky laughter.

"Internet dating is so last century."

"I heard that too," I agree. "It looks like you've found yourself a niche in the market. It could be lucrative for you."

"I think I'll stick to fixing backs, thanks."

I let her work for a bit, wondering who'll break the silence first. Currently, it's the best way of distracting myself, even though her welcome touch sends goosebumps all along the length of my back and arms.

"The thing is, I feel I ought to state that this dress is my favourite, and I didn't want to ruin it. That's why I wasn't wearing much."

"That old excuse, eh?" I reply dryly, thoroughly enjoying her attempt to put me straight. I don't need to hear any excuses for her state of undress. It's made my night. It's turned it completely on its head. "Hmm. Sounds like there's a flaw in your business model. Might I suggest an alternative strategy of simply tripping up and falling at my feet instead?"

There's a throaty chuckle that has my blood heating. "That is a much better option. I actually have a dodgy ankle, so I could very easily do that."

"What's wrong with it?" I ask, interested.

"Don't know. It just gives way sometimes."

"Is it when you're drunk?" I lead. "Do you stumble around, trying to walk in a straight line when this ankle gives out?"

She kneads her knuckles into my shoulder, telling me, "Watch it."

"Hey!" I protest. "You're meant to be making me better, not worse." The shirt gets lifted out of my waistband, but her hands stay above the material. "I think you probably sprained your ankle at some point and you've got chronic ankle instability. You should see that physio you work with and do some neuromuscular exercises."

"Thanks genius. I never would've thought of that." She moves to stand by my head, gliding her hands down my back, looking for tension and knots and misalignment. "It doesn't happen often. Are you medical?" she enquires, changing tack.

The register of her voice is low for a woman, but it's still very feminine, sexily so, with a husk that reminds me of Demi Moore. Listening to her talk and laugh while her hands work my flesh is arousing, but not so bad that I can't keep my dick under control.

I think I forget to answer her because she says, "I need to nudge your joints back into place."

"Really?" I ask, not looking forward to this. But if it means my back pain is gone...

"Ready? Stay nice and relaxed."

"Yeah," I murmur under my breath as she gets into position, leaning over my prone form. I sense her hands link together between my shoulder blades, where she makes a high velocity, quick movement. The resulting clicks in my back sound alarming, but it's just a release of gas in the joints to ease the pressure. Still, it's much louder than when I click my finger joints.

"Ooohhhhh," I groan on an uncertain laugh as something gives. Jesus, that was like nothing else I've experienced.

"How does that feel?" she asks brightly.

"Good," I answer, readying myself for more. Because this is just the start, I know that much, and I suddenly have sympathy for all the patients I've sent to chiropractors to sort out their back problems.

Her body presses into mine again as she tucks herself up nice and close. This time I'm tilted on my side, my knee drawn up in front of me. It's a good job the bench is backless. There's another quick thrust, another part of my back clicking into a better position. I groan another half painful, half relieved sound. "Oh god. I take everything back. You just want to torture me."

I get moved again but in the opposite direction, and, after being instructed to relax again, another series of clicks sound.

"Oh wow."

"Do you think you can sit up? I need to work on your neck."

My stomach bottoms out. I know she's not going to give me a spinal injury - probably - but anxiety still floods my system. But that worry disappears when I find I can move easily. When I sit up, dark, expressive eyes sink into mine before she moves behind my head, her warm hands running around my chin and neck before she strikes like a snake, more clicks registering.

"There we go," she says happily, as another wary laugh tumbles from me.

"Are we done yet?"

"All done," she confirms.

I mentally assess myself, before rolling my shoulders and flexing my neck. "Thanks," I tell her, feeling loose and pretty magical actually.

"It was the least I could do. If you have any other pain, please come and see me in Pimlico. I'll give you free treatment for life because I'm pretty sure you saved my neck back there."

At the bare minimum, she would've probably broken a leg or two, so I accept her thanks and tuck away her offer into my memory. "You're welcome." Standing, I tuck my shirt back in as mystery woman throws quick, daring looks at my hands, especially when they fall to my belt to refasten it. She chews on her lips, her gaze falling away to the ground as if looking for something.

That's when I notice she's still barefoot. "Let me get your things and my jacket."

After retrieving her shoes, clutch and my tux jacket, I walk back to the bench, everything feeling supple despite some niggling tenderness. My back hasn't bothered me for a good while, and I'm glad that I'm not going to be incapacitated for my heroic deeds tonight.

As I approach the woman of the hour, she's crouching down, stroking a ginger cat.

"Is that him? Tonight's culprit?"

"Yeah, little bastard," she gripes good-humouredly, a smile curving her mouth. "Listen to him all happy and purring now. You wouldn't know that thirty minutes ago he was stuck up a tree, yelling at me."

Has it been half an hour? No one seems to be missing me, but I should head back to the party soon, even though I've been enjoying meeting this intriguing woman whose name I still don't know.

Abandoning the cat, she lifts her eyes to mine. Something unnameable shifts inside me as our eyes lock, my pulse skittering. With effort, I drop my gaze, but I end up staring at her smooth, olive-skinned legs. "You're bleeding," I murmur.

"Oh," she says absent-mindedly, inspecting her lower half. "The tree wasn't all that comfy."

Now it's my turn to boss her around. "Sit on the bench, I'll take a look."

"It's nothing," she assures me, parking her bottom on the seat. Her dress rides up to mid-thigh, showing off her strong, athletic shape.

Lights stream across the grass from the hotel windows, and if it wasn't for the illuminated path, we'd be sitting in near darkness now. Instead of passing her the shoes, I drop down to my haunches and look up into her face. The sequins are highly reflective of any available light out here, making her skin luminous and bright. "Let me help you with these," I offer, cataloguing the cuts and grazes on her skin. "You've got quite scratched up."

"Yeah. Last time I'm going to try and rescue a cat."

I reach for a foot as she protests, "I can do my own shoes."

"Well, I have this super supple, bendy back now. Might as well make the most of it."

With my hand gently supporting her ankle, she lifts her foot. Unable to resist touching her just a little, I dust off her sole before slipping the shoe on. I repeat the process with the other shoe, this one a little harder to get on because I think she's resisting, making it harder for me and purposefully trying to push me over.

"Stop that," I scold, grinning.

She's smirking when I look up at her. Her canines are pointy, a cute detail I really love on a woman.

Taking out a handkerchief from my pocket I try and smooth away the bloodstains. "So...are you here for the party?"

"Yeah," she says on an exhale, looking away. "You?"

"Yup. I grew up with the birthday boy."

Her eyes flash to mine. Her body goes rigid. "You know Tom? You're medical, aren't you - a doctor?"

An awful feeling of dread has my stomach sinking, but I nod.

Her eyes flit away again, her body deflating, and I think she's coming to the same conclusions as me. "That must make you Liam Alston," she states. "Tom described you pretty perfectly."

Immediately, I'm wondering how exactly Tom described me. My dimples are unavoidable, so I guess he led with that, but if it wasn't something about my physical appearance, maybe it was my don't-take-life-too-seriously personality. Where that's concerned, Tom and I are quite different.

My eyes find those of the Italian beauty in front of me, feelings of defeat rising. This can only mean one thing: this must be Nora, his girlfriend.

Pushing that thought out of my head, I inspect the blood on

her legs. It's dried now, so there's not a lot I can do except rub her skin raw. So I take a seat next to her, folding up the handkerchief and pocketing it.

"Liam," I venture, holding out my hand, aware of a shadow approaching on the path.

"Nora," she answers, folding her hand into mine. She sounds subdued when she continues, "It's really nice to meet you, Liam."

My stomach feels hollow right now. I'm not sure what to say.

"Here you are," Tom says, his abrupt voice making Nora jump.

"It's really good to meet you too," I murmur, before getting to my feet.

Nora smiles at Tom as he approaches, his expression concerned and a little annoyed. When he leans in for a kiss, it looks awkward.

"What are you doing out here? I've been waiting for you all night."

Smiling brightly, she tells him, "I needed to make a phone call before I came to find you, and I was wandering out here when I heard a cat. Turns out he was stuck up a tree back over there," she says, turning to point behind us. "Liam found me and we started talking."

Tom looks across at me and gives me a chin nod. "Why do you look so dishevelled then?"

I blow out a breath, not mishearing the criticism, or suspicion. Personally, her mass of curls and flushed face call to me on many basic, primal levels, ones I shouldn't be thinking about. "I was trying to rescue the sodding thing and got stuck. The tree didn't like me much."

His eyes skim up and down her body. "You're bleeding."

"Just a little. Your brother tried to help, but it's fine."

"Come inside and get fixed up. Everyone's dying to meet you." Reaching for her hand, my brother tucks it into his as he escorts her to the hotel. Not ten seconds ago that hand was in mine, soft and yet capable, strong fingers grasping mine. "I was worried about you," Tom tells Nora. "And everyone's waiting."

What he really means is that *he's* been waiting, fielding questions.

Inside, Nora disappears to the ladies to tend to her cuts. Before she disappears from view, she looks over her shoulder towards my position, our eyes colliding.

My other sister, Tilly, comes to stand next to me, her chestnut hair in a classy chignon. We've all made an effort tonight. "So that's her?"

"That's her."

Just then, Tom joins us, his mood a little brighter. Easier. Feeling sick, I swipe a beer from a waiter and knock it back.

"She looks nice," Tilly compliments her brother. "Love her dress."

Tempted to say *I love her lingerie underneath it,* I just continue drinking. Riling my brother isn't a good idea when his patience is frayed enough already. And as topics go, it's not one I'd share with him anyway.

"I'll introduce you in a bit. Where's Fay?"

"Loos."

The tension seems to build the longer we wait, Tom falling into his own thoughts as Tilly and I talk nonsense. But then Fay returns with Nora, both of them heading straight for us, clearly having struck up a conversation in the toilets.

"Act naturally," Tilly quips, winking at me. "No interrogations tonight, we can save that for France."

"Is she coming?" I ask Tom.

He nods, before introducing his girlfriend to all of us properly. We while away the next hour or so, getting to know her and vice versa. And although it's enlightening, although I become more and more attuned to her every word, breath, and blink, it's also a bad ending to my night.

I like her, the buzzing static that I felt rippling between us in the garden too hard to ignore. And I'm not sure I want to ignore it, even though I must. Tom's my brother. And no matter what I'd like to pursue with Nora, that can never happen.

At best, we can only ever be friends.

CHAPTER TWO

Nora

TERMINAL 5 AT Heathrow Airport is busy. The modern building has a vast, airy concourse, with check-in machines dotted around the generous space. Holiday-makers walk every which way, pushing trolleys loaded with bags, or pulling wheeled suitcases behind them.

I check the time on my phone, hustling past a family of five. I'm a few minutes early, but I'd rather that than be late. Besides, Tom hates tardiness, or things impacting his precious time, and waiting around for me is clearly not high on his priorities.

Nervously, I head towards the designated spot, keeping an eye out for the others. Not that I'd recognise Tom's parents - Barry and Patricia - but I met Fay and Tilly and Liam at Tom's party, and they can't have changed much in three weeks.

Second-guessing why I agreed to come to France with my relatively new boyfriend and his entire family, is something I'm going to avoid. Normally, I would want to feel more secure in the relationship, with a minimum of six to eight months under my belt before agreeing to fly away with them. What do you do if you're stuck in a hotel room together and you decide you hate each other?

Part of me wonders if Tom and I will last much longer. For me, this holiday will either make or break us. Case in point: I was meant to be travelling to the airport with him this morning, but he called last night to tell me to book a taxi for one. I wasn't impressed, especially when he didn't give me a good reason why.

It only reinforced my growing feeling that we're not all that compatible.

My phone buzzes and I pull it out of my rear pocket, hoping it's Tom.

It's not.

Aaron: ***I hope this trip - and guy - isn't a waste of your time. He sounds like a complete dick.***

Reading the message has me deflating. I suck in a deep breath and let it out slowly, wondering if Aaron is right. We spoke a couple of weeks ago and I filled him in on my new boyfriend, even though my relationship with Tom wasn't all that new and shiny anymore. Aaron's pep talk wasn't the moral booster I hoped it would be. He agreed with just about every criticism I had, with every hole I poked at until it widened into something broad and endless. And he was astonished that I was prepared to give Tom - us - another opportunity.

You'll regret it, he said.

Maybe I will, but I want to try, I replied.

Aaron has been my ex for close to three years. I'm not sure when he started to give me dating advice, the origins of his wisdom coming out of nowhere, but however this dynamic between us evolved it's here to stay. And while most people don't speak to their exes ever again, I can't really escape Aaron. It's just how it is.

After mulling over how to reply, I message him, laughing internally at the rhyme. ***Last chance saloon. Talk to you soon *French flag emoji****

Huge letters suspended from the curving ceiling signpost me towards my goal. A group of five adults loiters under the giant letter B, their outlines sparking memories to life. Red-headed Fay comes into view first. She's with an older couple, who must be her parents, and a man I've not laid eyes on before, no doubt her husband.

And then there's Liam.

Butterflies dance in my belly, and not because Tom isn't here yet, which means I have to meet his parents on my own. I'm also a bag of nerves because as much as I try not to focus on Liam, my eyes keep betraying me.

Chestnut hair, gleaming hazel eyes, dimpled cheeks when he smiles. And boy, what a disarming smile he has, one that makes me feel ridiculously seen and noticed. Like he's smiling just for me.

Why can't Tom look at me like that? At one time he did, but he's so preoccupied with his book that I feel pushed aside.

Casting my mind back to the party when I first met Liam has occupied me for twenty-one days. Naturally, I feel guilty about that - I'm dating Tom. But I know attraction when it knocks you right in the solar plexus, leaving you breathless, clutching at air. And once I learned he was Tom's brother, I realised it was a good thing he spent most of our conversation face down on a bench, unable to see how interesting I found him.

Approaching, I take a slow, uneven breath, my large suitcase rolling alongside me. When I'm about five metres away, Liam turns his head, his eyes slamming straight into mine. Immediately, a smile hitches his bearded face, those damned dimples popping out as I release the handle of my suitcase and take the last few steps towards him. Returning his smile with one of my own, I'm just about to stop when my ankle gives way.

I lurch forward, face-planting into Liam's groin, my face meeting *everything* going on under the soft material of his caramel cargo shorts. My hands grab at his hips as I try and steady myself, but it's too late. My cheek scrapes his inner thigh, also brushing against something soft and long that I really shouldn't be this close to, my mouth wide open on a stalled shocked scream. To cap it off, my knees hit the polished floor along with my dignity.

How. Absolutely. Embarrassing.

"Holy shit, Nora," Liam says, following it with a low chuckle. "You've got to stop throwing yourself at me. This is getting to be a habit."

His hands slide down my arms that are still clinging around his hips, desperate to hold myself up. They hook under my biceps, ready to brace me and help me back to my feet.

"Shut up and help me up," I complain, mortified.

Quickly, my eyes scan over his family, all of them standing there watching. Watching with amused expressions, and quite possibly the beginnings of infectious laughter courtesy of Fay.

Great.

"I'm used to girls falling to their knees but this is the most memorable time by far."

"Very funny," I retort, feeling my cheeks redden. "I told you my ankle gives way sometimes."

He can't stop laughing, the others joining in, his eyes dancing with amusement. "If you say so."

"I did!" I protest, wanting to shove his shoulder like I do my brothers when they're annoying me.

"Are you okay?" he asks in a more serious tone, although his voice is still a rich, deep, soothing baritone. I imagine he's good with patients, calm and reassuring.

"Yeah. Just quietly dying here," I say, noticing the wet patch on the front of his shorts.

Oh god.

Brushing my unruly curls out of my face, I straighten my open-zip hoodie and dare myself to look him in the face. He regards me in a cherishing way. A very friendly, I'm having fun with you way.

"Does this happen often?"

"No."

"What about your ankle giving way?" he asks wryly, grinning at his joke.

I roll my eyes, fighting a smile. "Neither event has ever happened to me before," I state plainly.

Wiping away a smile, he looks me over. The slow perusal of my legs smacks of potency, my body feeling hot and tight and exposed. He skips over my jean shorts to the white tank top, and all I know is that he might as well be running his palms over my skin the way I feel right now.

Grateful for her solidarity, Fay throws an arm around my shoulders. "Way to make an entrance," she praises. "I only wish I had caught it on camera."

"Thank god for small mercies," I reply, giving her a quick hug. We bonded a little at Tom's party, and it's good to see her again, a friendly face amongst the sea of faces still looking at me with curious delight and restrained laughter.

"This is my husband, Sam," she introduces, indicating a sandy-haired guy. Slim-built, dark-framed glasses hide deep-set blue eyes.

I extend my arm to shake his hand, but he pulls me in for a quick hug. "This family doesn't do formal."

"Oh, that's good to know," I answer. "I'm not sure I'm capable."

Patricia folds me into her arms. "It's so lovely to finally meet you, Nora. Tom won't stop talking about you."

I'm not sure how to respond to that, so I just make a face, one that implies he's really sweet but also a bit cringe which makes Fay laugh.

Patricia is taller than I expected. I know she's in her late sixties, her short hair threaded with blonde highlights and natural grey streaks. "It's good to meet you too," I say over her shoulder, returning her hug.

"This is my husband, Barry."

Barry carries himself in a commanding, stiff way, reminding me of Tom. He greets me with a warm smile and a handshake, which I'm relieved about. "Welcome to the family, and our holiday. "

"Thanks so much for having me," I tell Barry and Patricia. "I'm so happy to join you."

Patricia smiles toothily. "We're delighted you could come," she enthuses, rubbing my shoulder. "Let's get checked in while we wait for Tom."

After we wander over to the check-in desks, my ankle feeling a little weak and vulnerable, I check for messages from Tom.

Nothing.

"Has anyone heard from Tom?" I ask the group.

Fay shakes her head. "He's often late," she grumbles. "He can always get another flight. He's left it too late to meet with Tilly."

Hmm. I remember now that Tilly and her partner are driving. It was something to do with not wanting the entire family on the same plane should disaster strike, and wanting to bring loads of booze because the hotel's overpriced.

I text Tom, updating him on where we are. And just as

Barry and Patricia are called forward to a vacant desk, Tom arrives at my side, panting and damp-browed. "You're here!"

"Yeah, hi, hi, hi," he greets his family. He sees that we're next to be checked in and says, "Good timing on my part."

"Apart from the fact that you're late," I point out. I want to ask him why we couldn't travel together this morning. I want to ask what took him so long. Pointing out that I've had to meet his family on my own shouldn't be necessary, but I'm not sure he's recognised that fact. He's certainly not offered any kind of apology or acknowledgment.

Disappointed, I stride forward when it's my turn, Tom accompanying me.

A little later, after passport control and security, I offer to get everyone a coffee.

"I'll help," Liam says, standing. "I know how they take it."

Casting a look at Tom who's busy typing into his phone, I smile gratefully as we head towards a busy coffee chain. Just like his carefree, uninhibited family, Liam is easy to be around. Having spent so long talking to him at the party, I feel like we made an uncommon connection, not least for the crazy way we met. "How's your back? I wasn't sure if you'd be stopping by for a full assessment. I owe you, remember."

"I remember," Liam says quietly as we dodge a couple racing for their departure. "My back's been fine. You might have fixed it for good."

"I doubt that. You need to do some regular strengthening exercises, and have it looked at by a professional every six months."

He runs a hand through his richly coloured hair. "I'll start doing the exercises when you start seeing a physio about your ankle."

"Who says I'm not already?" I rebuff, lying through my teeth.

His answering smile tells me he doesn't believe me. Stuffing his hands in his front pockets, Liam dips his head towards me and says quietly, "The fact that you were on your knees for me not that long ago."

Those nervous butterflies are back again. His teasing comments always seem to come out with a seductive rasp, one that has my blood running fast and loose. This time, I do shove his shoulder. "Thanks for reminding me. I had managed to completely forget that uneventful part of the day."

Reaching the end of the queue, we wait, but Liam looks thoroughly pleased with himself, crossing his arms against his chest. The T-shirt strains at the biceps and I try not to notice, or remember what it felt like to be held by him, even if it was for just a few seconds as we collapsed to the ground under an oak tree.

"It was highly memorable, Nora," he states. "In fact, I'm wondering whether I shouldn't carry all the coffees. I'd hate to see you fall over again."

I highly doubt that. I think he'd love to find something else to laugh about at my expense. "I'm calling a moratorium on all, and any further, comment about my earlier mishap."

"Mishap," he scoffs. "Falling on a guy's dick is never that."

My laughter is low, threaded with surprise. But weirdly, I'm not insulted. Liam has a playful character, one that's really easy to fall into. We just *get* each other. We seem to validate one another. And I know he's not accusing me of doing it on purpose. "You love to shock me," I say quietly, Liam pinning me with bright hazel eyes as he concentrates on my voice amongst the background murmur of a hundred others. "But I would say there have been at least four times in my life when I've had serious dick-mishap."

There's a half smile, the outline of a dimple appearing. "That doesn't sound good. What kind of percentage are we talking here? Just how common is dick-mishap for women in general?"

"High," I stress, as we shuffle closer to the counter. "About a one in three chance."

He raises a brow. "Bad odds."

"Very." It's quiet for two, three seconds before I venture, "Is there a male equivalent?"

"Oh yeah," he states, looking deadly serious. And serious Liam is distractingly sexy. He leans his head closer. Conspiratorially. "I'm not sure I should... be so indiscrete."

"Oh come on," I chide. "I'm not buying this gallantry when all you've done is tease me mercilessly ever since I first met you."

"Fell on me," he amends.

"Whatever," I rebuff, miffed, but finding it funny at the same time. "I didn't realise you had a shy side."

"Not shy; it's more like...traumatised."

I grin. "Oh yeah."

A nod. "Psycho pussy tends to do that to a man."

I laugh out loud, people twisting to look at us. "Wow, you really go big, don't you? There's quite a difference between mishap and psycho."

"Pussy problem?" he offers as an alternative.

"Sounds less offensive," I agree, shuffling forward again. I'm pretty sure the people in front and behind are listening in on our conversation, even though we're leaning in and trying to be as discrete as possible. "So what are the stats on this problem?"

"Also high."

"Meet a lot of psychos do you?"

"My fair share."

"Didn't fancy bringing one to France?"

After meeting Liam at Tom's party, I did ask after him, specifically if he was seeing anyone. Tom told me that he was never really sure who Liam was with, but that if he was currently girlfriend-less, it was unlikely he'd be that way for long.

Knowing his status isn't my concern, but for some reason, I'm very curious. Like stalker curious.

His left eyebrow quirks. "Maybe I'm hoping pussy problems in France are less dramatic."

Oh. He wants to hook up on holiday. Figures. I expect he finds it easy to attract female attention. "Holiday goals. Good for you."

He chuffs at that, his eyes skimming over my face, leaving tingles in his wake.

Handsome doesn't really do Liam justice, and I like to look at a hot guy like everyone else out there. But for me, it's about more than the obvious physicality of a man's body or face. And Liam hits the jackpot on every single thing I have a weakness for. It's about the way he delivers a joke, his timing pure perfection. And his tone is a heady mix of dryness and seductive drawl, not least the deep baritone of his voice as he delivers each teasing comment. And his facial gestures are nuanced but addictive: a wry eyebrow hitch, sometimes made in challenge, sometimes just to fuck with you; an uplift to his sensual mouth when he's amused but pretending not to be, which is undeniably sexy; the way he dips his head towards me to murmur about psycho pussy. Liam is a million tiny interactions and reactions. He is complex and complicated. He's dangerously enticing and easy to fall prey to.

And he's very much out of bounds.

We place our order and I pay with my debit card. Ten minutes later, Tom and I follow the rest of his family towards our gate, each of us carrying a coffee. We find somewhere to sit until we board the plane where, pleasingly, I get a window seat. Tom is next to me, Liam the other side of Tom.

Once we're settled, Tom brings out his laptop, logging in with his password. The sight of it makes my stomach sink.

Outside of his teaching job, Tom writes historical fiction. So far, he's had two books published, but this third is proving difficult. For the past four weeks I've hardly seen him, his mind preoccupied with fleshing out his story. His detachment is a reason why I debated if I wanted to come on this holiday, but I haven't been to France in years, and I haven't been abroad in at least three, so I was keen to grab this opportunity. Plus, when Tom asked me to come with him, we were in that exciting, exploratory zone where you just want to hang out all the time and learn everything you can about each other. And after meeting his siblings at his party, I was really confident about my decision.

But the past few weeks have been lonely. And while I accept that we all need space and time to do our jobs, and I'm trying to be supportive of this intense period where he needs to knuckle down and make good progress, I've been second-guessing my decision these past few days.

"Are you going to do some work?"

"Yeah. I'm already feeling inspired."

"That's good."

He told me he was hoping a change of scene would kickstart his grey matter. Opening up his document, he reads through something on the screen and starts to type. I try and read what he's writing because I'm really curious about his story; he's been very tight-lipped about it other than to reveal it's set in occupied France during World War Two.

Tom turns his head to look at me. "Please don't read over my shoulder. I find it really annoying."

"Sorry," I mutter, feeling young. And while there's a nine-year age gap between us, I've never noticed it as a negative thing until right this very minute. Chastened, I look out of the window, the air stewards trying to capture our attention for the safety briefing.

That's when Tom and Liam suddenly start unbuckling their lap belts and swapping seats.

"Hi," Liam says, fastening the straps.

"Hi."

"If he's going to be boring, he can be boring on the end."

"Hey, I can hear you," Tom replies distractedly.

"You were meant to," Liam drawls. Then he tells me, "He's been like this ever since I can remember."

"A writer?"

"His nose stuck in a book. Usually, it was reading them, now it's writing them."

"I enjoyed reading," I respond defensively, for Tom and for me.

"Me too." He doesn't elaborate any further, and I wonder what his point is. To demonstrate that we can all be readers? To show that he knew when to put the books down and have a life too?

Noisily, the air stewards take their seats as we taxi to the runway. Once in position, the engines roar on either side of the plane, this monstrous, deafening machine held steady by a hair's breadth. Air blasts out of the unit above my head. Anticipation hangs taut and deadly in the cabin as we wait anxiously for take-off.

My heart pounds in my chest, my breathing turns laboured. Concerned, Liam looks across at me. "Are you okay?"

"Oh yeah, she's a nervous flyer," Tom relays, a little too late. He was told to stow his laptop and he wasn't happy about it.

Liam offers me his left hand. "Want it?"

Suddenly, we race forwards, every available unit of horse-power unleashed. The plane bounces as we accelerate down the runway, everything around me vibrating with urgency. I slap my right hand in Liam's and face dead ahead, mild terror winding through my veins. When the nose of the plane lifts, I mumble, "Oh God." The wheels grind, a loud whirring crunch sounding as they tuck away into the undercarriage as we climb and climb, passing through thick, white clouds that obscure the brilliant blue sky and blinding sun above.

Sweat coats my palm; I'm sure that's just what Liam wanted. "Sorry," I laugh, wiping my hand on my shorts as I pull my hand away.

"It's fine. Nothing to be concerned about."

I look out of the window. Concerned. Definitely concerned about how high we are. "Only about two hours to go."

"They'll be along with lunch and booze soon. Might help."

I blow out a breath. "Maybe they could sell me some duty-free now, early, and I could just knock myself out."

"Why don't you try and sleep?"

"Tempting, but I'm not sure I trust you enough to leave you unattended with two boring people on either side of you."

His brow hitches, as does the corner of his mouth. "Shit. There goes my plan to draw on your face with permanent marker."

I shake my head, feigning disappointment. "Knew it."

"I had such a good idea, too.

"I bet."

Furious typing has me leaning forwards to see past Liam's masculine frame, trying to catch Tom's eye. "How's it going?" He either doesn't hear me, or is ignoring me. "Tom."

"*What?*"

"H-how's it going?" I stammer, caught off guard by his brusque reply.

"Fine," he mumbles, clearly not liking being interrupted.

I relax back into my seat, feeling young and foolish again. "Maybe I'll take that nap."

"Yeah," Liam murmurs back. "Maybe I'll join you."

AT THE AIRPORT, Tom and I join his parents in their hire car, leaving Liam to join Fay and Sam. We shove our suitcases in the boot, Barry following sat nav directions as we acclimatise to the weirdness of driving on the right. Huge swathes of countryside drift past my window as I revisit the past few hours. I'm cross with Tom, and embarrassed about my earlier trip. But I can't raise it now in the car with his parents in earshot, so I make idle chit-chat until we reach our destination.

The villa we've rented is one of twelve. Situated in the corner of the vast landscaped grounds of a hotel, there's a small private pool out the back. Each day, we can choose to either self-cater, or enjoy the comforts of the hotel restaurant brought directly to our villa. Plus, we have access to the on-site gym and bicycle hire facilities.

Tom and Barry unload the suitcases, while Patricia and I meander around the five-bedroomed eco villa. Constructed out of sustainably-sourced wood and recycled glass, its green credentials are impressive. Even the sofa material is recycled plastics and fabric. The piece de resistance is the open-plan kitchen/living room, where huge bi-fold doors lead to a pretty patio and the sparkling, mosaic-decorated pool beyond. The cool, blue water looks inviting after a tiring, hot day of travel.

"Which room are we having?" Tom asks as I fluff my hair away from my damp neck. I should tie it back, out of the way.

"Pick one," Patricia tells him, as Fay, Sam, and Liam arrive. "But your father and I will take the one downstairs."

As they get acquainted with the place, I follow Tom upstairs. Two rooms have en-suites, but the other two bedrooms have to share a bathroom. Selflessly, he chooses the smallest bedroom of those two, but in my opinion, it has the nicest view.

From the window to the east you can see the tranquil blue lake, surrounded by a dense ring of pines. I imagine it's inspiring.

"I can't wait to swim in the lake. Or cycle round it."

"...Yeah," he replies. "Is this room okay?"

"Of course."

Underneath the window is a desk and chair. Tom's laptop is already set out, charging. The double bed is dressed nicely in white linens, the walls a pale blue. It's simple and pretty and comfortable.

I'm loathe to spoil his happy mood, but I want to make something clear before we continue with the holiday. "You won't be spending all your time writing, will you? I mean, I'm really pleased you're feeling inspired, but this holiday is about us too, Tom. I've hardly seen you since your party."

"I know. And I'm sorry for being snippy on the plane, but you can't do that. I had a particular word in my head to describe something, and your question distracted me. Even now, I can't remember what I was planning on using."

"...Sorry."

"It's okay. Just...I need silence when I'm writing. I will try to be disciplined while we're here, but when the story comes, it comes. And I need to get it written and saved."

I nod, almost hoping this unspoilt corner of France isn't as inspiring as he hopes it is.

Knock, Knock.

"Hello!" Tilly calls out, peering in past the door. "Nora, I'm so glad you could come!" She walks towards me, hugging me gently, a man trailing in after her who must be her fiancé.

"Hi, Tilly. Good to see you." I'm not sure why I notice it, but her chestnut hair is the exact same colour as Liam's.

"This is Charlie."

Dark-haired, Charlie has a strong widow's peak, his face dominated by a broad smile and a bushy brown beard. We shake hands as Tilly and Tom lapse into a stilted conversation about the journey.

Sam appears at the door, announcing, "Champagne guys, by the pool. Get your swim stuff on! Five minutes!"

Tilly and Charlie head back to their room, closing the door behind them. Nervously, I dig out some clothing options from my suitcase, my mind crowded with insecurities. Is a bikini too revealing? What are the other girls wearing? Is a wet suit too much for the pool?

After securing my hair off my face, I slip into a burgundy two-piece. The top is like a sports bra, with cups to hide any embarrassing moments when the wind blows, or the temperature changes. And the bottoms are quite high-waisted. As swimwear goes, it's sporty and functional rather than for posing in. To be extra sure to preserve my dignity after such an awful start this morning, I grab my oversized poncho towel, ready to throw that on before we join the others downstairs.

Ready, I turn towards Tom who's dressed in navy swim trunks. He's sitting on the bed, flicking through some of his handwritten notes. It shouldn't surprise me that he's disinterested in seeing me naked, consumed by his writing instead of murmuring filthy comments about my body, like what he wants to do to it, repeatedly.

Guys like that exist, I know they do, and I want to find one for myself. But Tom and I don't have that kind of relationship, one where all you want to do is have sex on every surface, all the time. Considering we've been together for coming up to three months, we're nowhere close to that mad phase.

The sizzling stage of our relationship doesn't appear to have happened, or if it did, we lingered in it for forty-eight hours before moving on. And I know I shouldn't compare this situation to previous love interests, but that's where my mind drifts. Some women would label me as inexperienced, but I was in a long relationship, and all I know is that it wasn't like this with Aaron. And recently I've been wondering if I haven't wanted to instigate more sex with Tom because of that.

What do I know? I just know I'm not especially happy right now, with lots of things. And Tom's brother is in this villa, in close quarters for the next week, and he's confusing me even more.

Tom hasn't looked up at me yet. Even if I stood here topless, shaking the girls at him, I'm sure he'd still be engrossed in his work. I've not hugged him yet today, let alone kissed him, so I tell him that.

For a second he looks surprised, as if he hadn't noticed. "Haven't we?" he asks. Then he gathers me into his arms and kisses me chastely on the lips.

It'll have to do.

After shoving on some flip-flops I head downstairs, Tom following with two beach towels flung over his arm. Slowly, we assemble in the kitchen, Sam and Liam each opening a bottle of champagne. When we all have a drink in our hands, the siblings share some sweet, cherishing words to toast their parents' anniversary.

I begin to feel uncomfortable, like an intruder, but Patricia makes a point of smiling at me several times as if she knows how I'm feeling. As if to make sure to include me. But I also feel discomfited because I don't know how much longer I'll be sharing celebrations and milestones with this family. It's like I'm here on false pretences, faking my involvement.

Liam nudges my elbow, winking at me before I nudge him back. I think it was to make me feel included too, but mostly it has my heart mis-firing.

Outside by the pool, the sun is bright. Head-height shrubs between the properties offer privacy, and we back onto deciduous woods.

Tilly checks the water thermometer. "Twenty-three degrees."

"It'll be refreshing," Charlie tells her.

The girls haven't bothered with additional clothing over their bikinis, so once they've jumped in the pool, I quietly strip off my poncho and throw it on a sun lounger. I enter the pool via the curving steps, Sam trying to drown Fay, Charlie splashing Tilly, and Liam sitting on the edge of the pool, watching me with a quiet intensity. Quickly, his eyes drop down my body, from bust to bum, something hot and fierce hidden behind that two-second glance. Then, he turns his attention back to the others.

When the water reaches my waist, I extend my arms and push off, gliding forwards. I want the water to cleanse my mind as well as my skin. Because I need it to help me forget that only one Alston brother checked me out today, and it wasn't the one I'm going out with.

CHAPTER THREE

Liam

DINNER COMES WITH A HUGE DECISION. Do I sit next to Nora, suffering her subtle fragrance of lilacs and summer fruits, or do I sit opposite her, my eyes drawn to hers all night long? Deciding it's safer to sit opposite her, the next forty minutes is just a battle of wills where I tell myself that there are other people at this table that could use my attention, while recklessly ignoring my own good advice.

So many times I sneak a peek at the woman I'm obsessing over to find she's already looking at me. My pulse jolts every time our eyes collide. Mostly, Nora will drop her gaze to her lap or her drink or to Tom at her side, but it's a game I like playing.

My blood hasn't felt this alive in a long while.

Apparently, my brother and her met in Waterstones, both of them browsing the shelves when they reached for the same book at the same time. A conversation ensued, my brother clearly in his element discussing *book things*. Phone numbers were exchanged. A coffee the next weekend followed, a dinner date the next...

Nora is wildly different to his usual type. It leaves me wondering about the longevity of their relationship. That's the only reason I gave myself permission to subtly scan her body by the pool. To slide my eyes her direction whenever I think I can get away with it. Why teasing her, talking to her, holds so much fucking appeal.

Between nine of us, we've already consumed several bottles of champagne and wine, though that's mostly down to my sisters, their partners, and my parents. The patio doors are wide open to enjoy the late evening air. Insects fly around the light fittings, Tilly getting up every now and then to spray them with her industrial-strength bug killer she brought with her in the car.

My parents appear happy, pleased to have the family around them. With all of us leading busy, independent lives, it's been hard to find time for a big gathering like this. Mum's tipsy, laughing hard at something Charlie and Sam are regaling her about. My sisters are discussing a mutual friend's divorce, while Dad's talking to Nora.

Looking across at Tom, searching for something to say to him, I overhear my name. "What's that?" I ask my father.

"Nora's an early riser, like you."

"How early?" I ask her, everyone else's conversations drying up.

"Any time between half five and six."

Fay grumbles, "Oh god. We're all night owls, except for Liam."

"I was saying," Dad continues, "that you'll keep her company on her morning run. She shouldn't go out alone in a strange place that early."

My eyes seek Tom's. A flash of something crosses his face that I've not seen for years, a glimmer of intimidation and threat from an older brother to a younger one. But then he nods, once, like me accompanying his girlfriend is a good idea.

"I'll be fine," Nora assures Dad, smiling politely, just as I say, "Of course." There's an awkward moment where we just look at each other. "If you want some company that is," I tag on.

"I'm training for a triathlon, so it all depends if you can keep up."

I take her challenge and rise to it. "What distance?"

"It's a sprint triathlon, so not far. The swim is just under half a mile. The bike is twelve, and the run roughly three."

"What's the occasion?" Sam asks. "I used to do a few triathlons in my time but I'm a bit out of shape now. The last one was...god...got to be seven years ago."

"Come with us," Nora invites. My heart skips at that because it sounds like she's already decided I'm running with her. "It's one that some of my MChiro colleagues and I compete in every year. It's in Norwich, mid-September."

While Dad and Mum reminisce about a weekend they spent there, Fay consults her phone. "It's still got places," she says, looking at her husband. Then me.

Nora is calling my brother's name.

"What's that?" he asks.

"Do you want to train for a triathlon with me?"

He just shakes his head, looking apologetic. "You already asked me this."

"I know, but it looks like Liam and Sam will join in too."

"I won't have time, Nora."

"Yeah," she says quietly. Then her eyes lift to me. I see hesitation there, but also something I'm not sure I should name, or allow myself to dwell on.

"I'll train with you this week," I offer. My fitness is pretty good. I run regularly but I mainly focus on weights, thanks to Lowell's home gym.

Sam stretches his arms above his head, a wry grin forming. "I'm tempted, but not that early."

"I prefer to go when it's cooler, but we could do some pre-dinner swimming some nights?"

Sam nods. "Sounds good." He looks to me. "You in?"

"Yeah," I agree, reaching for the water bottle and pouring myself a glass. If I'm running in the morning I need to start hydrating.

Since I'm on my own this week I had plans to keep busy and active courtesy of the hotel gym. But combining my fitness ambitions with Nora's is not a problem. She looks like she works out, though I'm not sure us spending lots of time together is a good idea. I mean it is, but it also isn't. My restraint where women are concerned is slim, and with Nora I have a feeling I'm already close to my limit.

"I'm gonna head up," I announce, draining my glass.

"Aww, is it our baby brother's bedtime already?" Fay jibes.

"Do you need me to tuck you in?" Tilly chimes in, grinning. "Got to make sure your favourite teddy bear is snuggled up with you."

I stand, sliding my chair back under the table. "Laugh it up, you two."

Nora grins, her eyes jumping from my sisters to me as we trade more friendly insults. I head her direction, wanting to firm up plans for the morning. "What time do you want to get going?"

"Is six okay?"

"Sure thing."

She smiles. "See you in the morning."

"Yeah. Have a good night."

. . .

AS USUAL, the next morning, I wake at around 0540. Birdsong interrupts the quiet stillness of the villa, my room lit up with sunlight. Not a fan of sleeping in absolute darkness, I didn't bother with the shutters last night.

After pulling on some running shorts and a T-shirt, I do some light stretching, including some that my back will benefit from. Once I've freshened up in the bathroom, I make my way downstairs, my trainers in my hands. Nora is already in the kitchen, dressed and looking energetic, her unruly curls tied back in a thick ponytail.

"Morning."

"Morning."

"It's so weird to see anyone else up at this hour," I tell her, trying not to notice how great she looks in her running shorts.

She laughs softly. "My brothers are both early birds. It's strange that others aren't."

When she says *others*, does she mean Tom? Or other people in general?

I head to the fridge, bringing out some apple juice. "Do you want some?"

"I've got some water, thanks."

I fill up a glass and replenish my fluids. The champagne might've been flowing yesterday, but I didn't come all the way out here to sit around nursing a hangover. I leave that to my sisters and their significant others.

Nora warms up her ankles before stretching out her hamstrings and quads. "Do we need a key? Will anyone else be up when we get back?"

"Doubtful." Deciding to look for a key, I find a spare by the front door. "Here's one," I confirm.

"It can go in my pocket."

Nora holds out her hand, and I place the key in her palm, my fingertips grazing her skin. That small moment of contact has our eyes snagging, Nora blinking rapidly as she turns towards the door, unzipping a tiny key pocket at the back of her shorts. There's a pocket next to it, a bigger one, something poking out of the top because it doesn't fit inside.

I pull on my trainers. "Is that an EpiPen?"

"Yeah." We head outside and close the door. "I'm allergic to stinging insects."

That blows. "I'm sorry to hear that. Have you had to use it much?"

We take the path towards the cars before walking in the direction of the lake. The sun is an unmarred, crisp blue, the birds are singing, and the neighbouring villas are quiet.

"One summer I got stung three times, but mostly I can manage four or five years without needing it."

"That's good. Do you have your phone on you?" Automatically I start to scan her hips and thighs, looking for a rectangular shape poking out of side pockets, but there's nothing except a red smartwatch on her left wrist.

"No. It weighs me down."

"Pass me the key. I'll grab mine."

"It's fine," she objects softly. "Don't carry one for my sake."

For a long second, I just look at her. "I'm a doctor, I can't help myself. I'm also your friend who is here to make sure you not only don't face-plant into someone's groin while we're out running, but also to be sure that if we need an ambulance, I can call one."

A reluctant smile forms, her eyes drifting off towards the villa behind me. I start to walk backwards, along the path we just left. "Chuck it here." Her hands twist behind her back to locate the key, and then she aims it towards my cupped hands. "Be right back."

Indoors, I grab my phone that's still charging by the bed, and am back outside in under a minute. "What even is 9-9-9 in France?" I ask when I jog back towards her. I'd like to know what to do if the worst-case scenario arises.

Nora informs me of the emergency number as we walk to the lake, the water a dark, sparkling blue. It stretches out into the distance, lost behind a pinewood and a deep curve in the landscape, the surface utterly still. To one side of the shore is a cedar-constructed café, with boards advertising drinks and ice creams nailed to the exterior. A twenty metre long jetty extends into the lake, pedalos for hire secured to posts by metal chains. A few people are already up and about, running with dogs along the trail, or wading into the water for a swim.

"Ready?" Nora asks, tapping something on her watch.

"Yeah."

We head off at a fast pace, faster than I was expecting. Stone crunches underfoot as we follow the two metre-wide trail east, running side by side. "How far is this trail anyway?"

"About four miles. I'm aiming for a sub-nine-minute mile today," she confesses, checking her watch. "By September I've got to get close to eight and a half."

Fuck me, that's more than I manage on the treadmill on my best ever day.

"Oh, this is pretty," Nora shares as we start rounding the bend. The view opens up, allowing us to see the lake in its entirety. "A beach," she remarks breathlessly as it comes into view, a crescent-shaped stretch of yellow-white sand. "Oh wow!"

"And a floating deck." I nod towards the wooden construction out in the lake, currently unused. "Perfect for a start and endpoint for your timed swim."

Nora grins excitedly before pulling her gaze back to the trail. Without slowing we pass the beach, both of us aware that we'll be back to visit soon. When her watch beeps, she consults the device and tells me, "First mile. Nine minutes seven seconds."

"Crap, come on. We can do better than that."

We speed up, neither of us really talking anymore as we concentrate on the next mile and hitting our target. When we pass two women walking a pug, I get cross that they slow us down. But it's good news at the next update because we're bang on a nine-minute mile.

Not one for entering into races, I'm not sure about game plans and pacing. If Nora competes in the Norwich triathlon annually, then she's in a much better position to know what's successful. She's probably tried a few strategies over the years, and has her ideal race all planned out. Happy to go with her advice, I ask, "What's the plan for the last mile?"

"Save some in the tank for the last two hundred metres."

"Sounds painful."

She just laughs, which doesn't bode well.

We keep running, my breath coming out hard, my lungs feeling the burn. Beside me, Nora's harsh breaths have my mind wandering in directions it shouldn't be. Is this what she sounds like after a good fuck? Does her body break out in a sweat like now?

Nora glances at her watch again, raggedly telling me, "Faster."

And then she picks up the pace. She's medium height, but her legs seem to elongate in front of my eyes, striding out as she begins to create a bigger gap between us. I push on, my pride at stake. I'll happily let her cross some imaginary finish line first today, but I can't come in too far behind; I'll never be able to look her in the eye.

She counts down the last fifty metres, the expression on her face part pain, part determination. When her watch beeps to signal the distance has been met, she exhales loudly and slows her steps until she's walking and then standing, her hands falling to her hips before she bends at the waist.

"How'd we do?"

"Last mile was eight minutes forty-nine."

"That's great," I encourage.

"Just need to bring down miles one and two."

"It'll come. Christ, that was a fast pace. I can't believe you're not winning the damn triathlon with those sorts of times."

She laughs tiredly, but I can tell she liked my compliment, even if she's refusing to see just how accomplished she is. Catching her breath, she pushes stray hairs from her forehead and looks across at me. I'm basically mirroring her stance, exhausted, thirsty, thinking that I need a double lung transplant.

"You can go running on your own from now on," I wheeze out. "I'm not doing that again."

There's a subdued chuckle. "It'll be easier next time. I'm doing you a favour."

"Pfft. I can think of better favours."

Nora raises a solicitous eyebrow but doesn't ask me to clarify. Which is just as well; the favours I had in mind were NSFW, and that is how I need to view this. As work. A job. It'll be a lot easier if I do.

Slowly, we walk back towards the villa. It's closing in on 0630 but I feel like I've already accomplished lots today. The strong scent of pine invades my senses, a cool wind coming off the water this side of the lake. "So how many of you meet up for this annual event?"

"Six of us. Two of them are in Norwich so we make a thing of it for the weekend."

"Nice. Do you get ultra competitive?"

"Oh yeah," she confirms seriously.

"Who wins? It's got to be you."

There's a dismissive sound. "I wish. We're three girls and three guys, one of whom's an ex actually," she says, catching my eye. Her expression is hard to work out. It's both irritation and heartache. "We get on fine, but Beth, the girl he now lives with and has been going out with for the past three years, was my friend at uni. Well," she hedges, "I thought she was my friend but she basically stole him off me, if stealing boyfriends is even possible. I mean, don't they allow themselves to be stolen in the first place? Isn't that just infidelity, going off with your friend?" She blows out a breath. "We don't need to go over that, except to say that they're together. And I was trying so hard to beat her in that first race, but I hadn't really trained as much as I should've. And in the second race, despite being in the lead the entire time, I stumbled on a pothole, spraining my ankle." She gives me a knowing look, and then, seeing that I'm about to rib her about it, points a finger at me and says, "Don't! I know what you're about to say, but you'd better stop while you're ahead."

"Why, what are you going to do about it?"

"You see that lake? You'd look good swimming in it."

My chest rumbles with laughter. "Do your worst."

Pretending to look like she has a grand scheme up her sleeve, she tells me, "Yeah, I'll keep the push-Liam-in-the-lake card in my back pocket for now."

"You do that."

She pats her arse. "It's there, waiting; don't you worry."

I refuse to check out her arse. Refuse to indulge in the dirty commentary occupying my mind.

As a distraction, I imagine when and how she's going to get her revenge. And then I remember our conversation and how cross she was at being teased. Naturally, I can't let that go. "There's mileage in this, Nora. Lots of mileage about dick mishaps, and I never look a gift horse in the mouth."

"So I'm a horse? Fine, do *your* worst, but ever since that first race, I've never beaten her. This is my year. I can feel it."

"That's the spirit. Who's there to support you?"

"Oh, you mean like watching the race?"

I nod.

"Well, it depends if my brothers can get the time off or not."

The fact that she doesn't reference Tom supporting her, is telling. And I know nothing about Nora's family. As uncommunicative as Tom is for someone who selects a bunch of words for a living, he's only shared that she grew up in Watford, northwest of London.

Through the tall grasses lining the trail, the jetty and café are visible about a quarter of a mile ahead. We approach a bench facing the water, and I gesture for us to stop so that I can do some stretches before I cool down completely. "What do they do?"

"Luca's a theatre nurse. Marco's a police officer. They don't have regular workdays so it's hard for them to find the time. And my parents," she starts, perhaps anticipating my next question, "run their own Italian restaurant, so they *never* get any time off."

After stretching, we continue walking, my mind turning over events. Clear from her impassioned voice, her words coming thick and fast, understandably there's some lingering pain where her ex is concerned. When you break someone's trust there's a lot of unresolved emotion. Surprised and grateful that Nora shared that with me, I wonder if Tom knows. If she can tell me when I've not known her for long, then he must know, surely.

Either way, it's clear that a strong intimacy exists between Nora and I. Tom aside, I know without a shadow of doubt that we're destined to know each other, I just can't speculate on anything more than that. Maybe it will be a simple thing, like chiropractor and patient, even though that idea leaves me feeling agitated and like it's all a huge waste.

I blow out a breath, none the wiser. But I do know that as much as I'd like to be in Norwich to support Nora, I can't. That's for Tom to do.

CHAPTER FOUR

Nora

"ARE YOU COMING WITH US?" Tom might have his nose buried in his laptop, but I still ask the question that's been sitting on my tongue all morning, festering. Being apprehensive about asking your boyfriend a question isn't the norm, but that seems to be the way things are today. At the sight of his cautious face, the plate with the baguette sandwich I made for him gets placed a little too heavily onto the table, the clatter of china meeting wood echoing in the open-plan room.

"How long do you think you'll be?"

The plan is to drive to the nearest town and meander around, poking our heads into shops, browsing the local delicacies for sale and absorbing all things French. So a long old time.

"Depends on how interesting it is, I guess. Two to three hours? I'm sure there's a café with pavement seating from where we can people-watch."

Completely under-selling how long we'll stay in Colmar is

strategic. Earlier, I heard Patricia tell Barry that it might be nice to have dinner there.

Tom takes a giant bite out of his sandwich, chewing awkwardly. His eyes hop from parent to parent, sibling to sibling until they come back to rest on me. "How much do you want me there?"

For a second, I'm speechless. Aware that the others are busy talking amongst themselves, I lower my voice all the same when I say, "I didn't agree to come away with just your family, Tom. You promised you'd take a break too."

"I know, but I can't help that the story is gushing out of me and needs to be written. If I delay, I'll lose crucial aspects of the plot."

"Why don't you just scribble something on paper in the car? You can get down what you need that way."

"I get car sick," he counters.

"I'll type it into my phone for you."

He places a hand on my waist. "That's sweet, Nora, but I need to see what I'm writing. It won't work."

It won't work. Those words sound ominously portentous. We've only stayed here one night, my hopes for the future dwindling rapidly before my eyes.

"I'll definitely come when you visit the chateau. And a walk in the Vosges sounds good, but not a nearby town. I'll give it a miss."

He turns, dismissing me, his hand dropping from my body as he scoops up his baguette.

"Tom, please. This is really unfair on me."

"What's unfair, Nora, is your constant interruptions and nagging."

"I beg your pardon?" I seethe, hurt.

Tom rubs a hand down his face. "Sorry, it's just...I have

deadlines. And I'm behind. My publisher and agent are already on my case, and I don't need you on it too."

"Fine," I grit out, storming outside to the patio and throwing myself into a chair. Enraged, I scowl at the pool, wishing I had my sunglasses because the reflected light is blinding. And the sun is streaming down into our patio area with all the force of its midday zenith.

All I've done since our arrival is remind myself why I liked Tom in the first place. Aside from his obvious intellect and passion for story-telling, I exchanged numbers because he was so different to previous boyfriends, older too. By going outside of my comfort zone I hoped to switch things up a little. To be distracted from my usual negativity.

I'm not sure it's worked.

A large part of me wants to cry, but I refuse to do that. It would only create a scene, and I don't want to ruin this holiday for the rest of the Alstons. They've paid a pretty penny for this holiday, a holiday that has them all under one roof for the first time in years according to the conversation last night, and this needs to be remembered for positive reasons.

And besides, Tom's attitude is only reinforcing everything I've been worried about for the past several weeks. Why did I ignore my usual advice and jet off on holiday so soon into a new relationship?

My traitorous brain hints at a reason I cannot indulge in. And then, speak of the devil, Liam comes outside, passing me my phone. "It was buzzing."

"Oh, thanks," I say, taking it from him to see Aaron's name under a missed call.

"Second boyfriend?" Liam asks, the beginnings of a teasing smile there.

"One's ample," I fire back, my eyes drifting towards the

doors in case I can see Tom. "Aaron's the ex I was telling you about."

There's a cautious pause. "Didn't realise you were still so friendly."

It's a leading question, one I don't really feel like answering. "We're congenial, I suppose. It's only been the past six, twelve months that things have improved between us."

Hazel eyes drift over my face, analysing my expression which I try and keep neutral. Then he offers a sympathetic look, running a hand through his glossy hair which somehow makes my hands feel stupidly jealous. "I think we're heading out now."

"Okay."

As Liam heads indoors, I check my notifications to see if there's a voicemail from Aaron. Not seeing one, I type him a message. ***What's up?***

He replies a few seconds later. ***Just thought I'd check in. How's it going?***

Good. Lovely setting and weather. Eaten my weight in croissants and baguette already.

Inside, I can hear Tom's family moving around, getting organised. I stand, knowing I need to gather my things too.

And Tom?

Thanks to the disagreement Tom and I have just had, his reply has my heart feeling leaden. What freakishly shit timing he has. At any other time, I might've felt more resilient, but I can feel myself tearing up, which is just ridiculous. But there comes a point when you need to cut your losses, and I can feel that time fast approaching. Thickly, I swallow down the mounting feelings of disappointment I have in myself. Of my inability to maintain a long-lasting relationship. How can another one fail before it's barely begun? What am I doing wrong?

Got to go I reply. ***We're heading out for a trip.***

Can I call you later? There's something I need to talk to you about...

The request has my stomach tightening. Despite being on friendly terms, Aaron and I don't talk much, not on our own at any rate, away from the group. Beth didn't like it, and I preferred our communications to be limited to group chat messages. It felt simpler. Easier on my residual hurt and tangled feelings. But recently it's been easier to talk to him, our limited messaging turning more often to the occasional chat.

It seemed to happen organically, but then Aaron was always naturally gifted at weaving his way into a situation or conversation. Not because he was especially charming, but because he just inserted himself. If he wanted something he made it happen, bending the rules to suit.

I reread his question, which sounds very mysterious and I am naturally intrigued. ***Not sure of dinner plans yet but give me a try.***

Chin up. Plenty more men out there who can see you for the treasure you are he answers before I pocket my phone.

Urgh. Why do his compliments make me feel so demoralised? If I was such a treasure, why did he cheat on me with my best friend?

Resolving to ignore him when he calls later on, I head inside to gather my things.

An hour later we're in Colmar, an old medieval town in the northeast of France that's been traded between German and French hands several times over the centuries. The town is a visual feast with the half-timbered burgher houses, all of them painted in pretty shades, shutters fixed to the windows. Potted geraniums adorn just about every balcony and doorway, scrolled ironwork shop signs hanging over the cobblestone streets of the picture-perfect town.

We book ourselves onto a canal tour, Patricia and Barry keen to see La Petite Venise as authentically as possible. While we wait, I buy a round of salted pretzels and bottled waters, my way of contributing to the holiday when everyone refused any money towards the villa.

Liam admits, "That run has made me famished too," as I pass him his snack. We find a free bench, the men giving up any claim to a spot so that Fay, Tilly, Patricia and I can squash on together.

I take a picture of my pretzel before I demolish it, and then I take pictures of the family so that Tom's parents have some happy memories of the trip, even if Tom isn't in them.

"Colmar," Fay begins, "is rumoured to be the inspiration for the set of *Beauty and the Beast.*"

"No," Tilly responds. "Really?"

"It's set in France," I remark.

"I could live here," Patricia admits. "A region renowned for its wine, and with pretty towns like this. Barry," she calls. "Why don't we retire here?"

Standing in his usual straight-backed way, he smiles. "Too much good wine and cheese."

"Why's that a bad thing?" Patricia rebuffs.

Ten minutes later, we head back to the flowery Saint Pierre bridge to begin our tour. The wooden boat putters along the canals, and under wide, stone bridges as picturesque building after more picturesque buildings drift by.

"It's so charming here," I murmur to Liam, sitting next to me on the narrow seat. We're so wedged in, our thighs are touching, branding my skin like he's branding my distracted heart. And his cologne of spice and sandalwood is making this experience so much more enchanting. In this fantasyland, I feel so far removed from my earlier gloomy thoughts, Liam's voice, dimpled smile, and easy laughter helping me forget about his frustrating brother.

"It is. It's better than I thought it'd be."

Gently, Liam takes the phone out of my hand. "Come on. Selfie time."

If possible, we squeeze together even more, my breast accidentally squashing into his left tricep with the motion of the boat. I immediately pull back. "Sorry."

"It's fine," he murmurs, his eyes lingering on mine. Then we pose for the camera, my breathing stalled the entire time. When Liam passes back my phone, he murmurs, "Send them to me?"

I try not to wonder why he wants them, but it's an impossible ask - my mind is fixated on the conundrum. But then I remember that I've not seen him take any pictures of Colmar yet, so maybe this is his way of having some memories. "What's your number?"

He rattles off his digits, and I send the photos, along with others I've taken so far. Interestingly, I note that I only have one picture of Tom, and it's from dinner last night.

As the bridge nears, I gather my rucksack handbag from my sandalled feet and get ready to disembark. Liam helps his mum out, then he turns to offer me assistance too. I reach for his hand, refusing to let my thoughts linger on how good it feels to touch him again. When both my feet are on the small square pontoon, I let go. I thank the guide, trying to get past the new horde of tourists ready for their tour when I'm knocked. It's not a big knock, but at the same time, a heavy-set couple steps onto the pontoon from the longer jetty, making my side tip up a fraction with the weight differential. I try and counter the movement but it doesn't work. All I end up doing is losing my balance and falling into the canal.

Shocked, I yelp, tossing my bag towards Liam as I tip sideways, submerged by cold water a split second later. Spluttering, spitting out water, I break through the surface and clamber onto the pontoon. But I only manage to get my arms on there as I deal with the shock and surprise of my situation.

Liam grabs the waistband of my shorts and pulls me onto dry land (sort of), a large hand wrapping around my buttock and sliding my body out of the water.

"Shit."

"You okay?"

Somewhere, some arsehole is laughing. It's mixed in with some concerned voices, not least from the tour guide and the people who might've accidentally toppled me into the canal in the first place. Once I've reassured them that I'm fine, if not a little humiliated, I tell Liam, "I can't stand."

"Is it your ankle?"

"No. My T-shirt is probably transparent."

His eyes drop down to my chest, not that he can see anything with me lying on my stomach, but then he's twisting towards his youngest sister, shouting, "Tilly, I need your hoodie!"

Tilly rushes over, throwing the item of clothing around my back and threading my arms into it. "Thanks," I mumble, as Liam helps me to my feet. Drawing out his movements, he hooks the two pieces of the zip together and pulls the tab until I'm all zipped up tight. He doesn't appear to be trying to get an eyeful, his green-brown eyes on mine, but his expression is one of blatant sexual intent.

"I've got it," I say, clutching the fabric in one hand as Liam passes me my bag. Gently, he takes hold of my arm and guides me towards safety, the rest of his family fussing around me.

My wet clothes cling to my skin, and I'm sure I'm giving off a righteous stink, but Liam seems keen to make sure I'm okay, steering me towards a bench. "Sit here while we get you sorted out."

Nosy tourists cast curious looks my way, every inch of me wet through.

"There's a clothes shop further down here," Fay says, pointing. "We passed it earlier. Tilly and I'll find you something new to wear. You can't stay like that for dinner."

"Wait. Take my card. If contactless doesn't work, the pin's 1379."

The rest of the family stand around, looking a little lost as to what to do. "Patricia, why don't you all go to the market? Once I'm all cleaned up, I'll come and find you."

"Oh, Nora. I'm so sorry this happened."

"It's okay. There's nothing any of you can do right now, so don't waste time standing around here watching me dry out," I offer.

"I suppose," she says, but I can tell she wants to go to the market. We all do. It's been part of the itinerary.

Liam says, "I'll stay with you until my sisters get back."

"If you're sure."

Liam nods. To Sam and Charlie, he says, "We'll catch up."

As the four of them head off, I begin to shiver. The day is warm, so it must be adrenaline or shock that I'm reacting to. Either way, Liam's arm slides around my back, his body heat sending grateful waves of warmth into my shivering muscles.

"I hope they pick out something really hideous for you."

I smile, refusing to look at that small, sexily endearing hitch of his mouth that I know is there. "Such as?"

"Neon green tank top with orange tassels on, or maybe some bright yellow flowers adorning the décolletage," he states clinically. "And some wide-legged trousers in a complimentary hot pink. That way, people might actually see you coming, and not knock you into a disease-ridden canal."

I think my heart just died a little at his protectiveness, wrapped up in a joke.

"Only if you match," I reply. "There's got to be a neon Mankini for sale somewhere in this place."

He chuckles before looking towards the shop his sisters disappeared into, hopefully *not* buying me neon clothes. As I watch the doorway too, I see Tilly scamper out, hurrying towards me with a towel in her hand.

"They sell these." The blue towel has *Colmar* slashed across both sides, visible as Tilly wraps it around my waist. "This way. The manager said we could clean you up in the staff toilet. Then you can try the dress on we've picked out for you."

The shop is quaint and timber-ceilinged, packed full with clothes and souvenirs. By-passing Fay and the manager, Tilly leads me to the toilet, telling Liam to stay put as she drags me inside.

She locks the door. "Okay, strip."

While I wriggle out of my soaked clothes, including her damp hoodie, Tilly wets the towel under the tap, adds some pump soap to it, and hands it over. She turns her back as I shimmy out of my pants and bra. Scrubbing my skin, I'm aware of the lovely smell that's replaced my stinky Eau de Canal. "This soap smells good."

"Yeah. You should buy some as a reminder of your wonderful time in Colmar."

"Hmm. Maybe."

"They don't sell underwear, but they do sell tiny shorts that you can wear underneath the dress."

A red dress hangs on the back of the door, a pair of black cycling shorts dangling off the hangar.

Once I'm clean - though there's not much I can do about my hair except let it dry naturally - I try on the summer dress, the colour one that generally compliments my hair and skin tone. Knee length, it has a halter neck.

"Can I see?" Tilly asks excitedly.

"Yeah, I've got it on."

Tilly spins, her hair whirling around her head as she comes to face me. "Oh wow, it suits you."

"Thanks. You picked out a good one."

"It supports you too, which I was concerned about."

I skim my hands over my boobs, making sure everything is secure.

"Plus, Tom likes red."

I smile, not aware of his colour preferences. I thought he liked blue but -

"But so does Liam," Tilly adds, handing me the shorts and cutting off my train of thought. "Do you want these, or do they look like they'll give you thrush?"

Flustered from her comment about Liam, because surely she's not chosen this dress for him, I stare at the shorts, digesting her words. But why else would she bring him up if not to hint at something? For a long time, I stare at the shorts trying to order my thoughts. The material looks man-made and totally suspicious. "Definitely a yeast infection waiting to happen," I tell her. "I'll skip."

"Good call."

I gather up my clothes, making sure I've got everything before we exit the small cloakroom and find the others. Feeling transparent, I can barely look at Liam. What will he see on my face? How much can I hide from him? I almost hope he doesn't notice what I'm wearing but he does, though he doesn't verbalise it. Instead, his bright eyes crawl up and down my body before they come to rest on my face.

"Nothing in neon, sadly," I voice, trying not to appear affected by yet another blatant look of arousal from him.

"My sisters have good taste." His eyes wander over to Tilly where they remain for a fraction too long.

No one speaks, a weird, tense silence hanging over us which Fay finally breaks. "Here's your card." She passes it over. "We've only paid for the towel so far. Do you want any cheap flip-flops, or are your sandals still good?"

My sandals are already drying out so I just end up paying for the dress, a bottle of soap, and a fridge magnet with *Colmar* on it.

"Thanks for your help," I tell them all as we make our way to the covered market. Fay confirmed that the others are still there, reporting back that they've already bought approximately twenty kilos of cheese and a case of wine.

Constructed from brick, the market building is a long hall, allowing a view of dozens of stalls in the distance. An array of fish, fresh fruit, breads and cakes, colourful flowers, fat salamis, and just about everything else is available.

When Patricia catches sight of me, she fusses over me again. "Such a pretty dress, not that what you were wearing earlier wasn't lovely, but this is so flattering. I'm sure Tom will be disappointed that he didn't come with us."

I'm pretty sure he's perfectly happy where he is. "He promised to join us when we go to the chateau."

"Good. I don't want him to miss out. I realise his book is important, but I do hope he spends some time with us in France. And you," she tacks on, rubbing my bared shoulder. "Do keep persisting with him," she says quietly, her face worried. "I know he can seem distracted, but once the dust has settled, once he's about a third of the way in he'll relax, mark my words."

Dutifully, I smile, hoping she's right. Wondering if I want to keep dangling like a worm on a hook, waiting for him to show some interest.

There are many things that I liked about Tom when I first met him. For starters, I found his face appealing, and he had a good height, an absolute must. And while he isn't one for wasting time by recounting funny stories or anecdotes, I've enjoyed listening to him share historical facts that he's just discovered. But I don't want to talk history all evening, and at times he was hard to distract. Once, I asked him to just sit and watch a film with me, but he told me he had too much research to do.

Generally speaking, finding time for us has been almost non-existent, so waiting for these hallowed, golden moments when he's feeling more comfortable about his progress will undoubtedly be few and far between. How he found time to go on dates with me is incomprehensible now that I've seen the inner workings of his research process, one that's lasted about four months already. And now that he's committed to writing the book, it'll be another four to six months before it's completed. Do I really want to be pushed to one side for ten months out of twelve? Because the process doesn't stop there; there are edits and meetings and book things to go to. There's no room for a girlfriend in his life unless he *makes* time.

Walking over to a stall selling condiments, jars of pickles, and a whole host of other tempting French delicacies, I start loading up my arms with things to try. After I've paid and made some space for the next customer, I look around for the others to realise they've moved on, leaving me standing on my own by the flower stall. The beautiful flowers are distracting, so I turn to look at them, the young florist calling out something to me. Since I've not spoken much French since school I don't understand the quickly spoken words. In heavily accented English, she tells me, "Choose the flower. Any you like."

"Me?"

"Yes! You."

"Why?"

She shrugs in a typically French way, her lips forming a moue. "You look sad, wearing a pretty dress. The flower make it better for you, yes?"

"It's okay," I say, scanning the flowers despite my words.

"Choose one."

Rose, peony, carnation, lisianthus, anemone....The variety is endless. In the end, I pick a blue hyacinth. The rich fragrance sinks into my body as I inhale, the mesmerising blue-purple of the petals soothing.

"Constancy," the florist tells me. "You will persevere."

I think she's referring to the language of flowers. I'm about to say my thanks and catch up to the others when Liam appears at my side. "Thought we'd lost you."

Opening up the cloth shopping bag, I show him what I've been up to. "Thought I'd try these out."

Mustard, piccalilli, a béchamel sauce, a jar of pickles, and other unknown things are inside. Lips hitched with amusement, Liam peeks at my purchases and then takes the handles from my grasp. "Let me carry this for you."

"Monsieur!" The florist calls excitedly. "You pick the flower too."

Liam looks at me with bafflement, then at the flower in my hand. Casting his eyes over the abundant wares, he asks the twenty-something florist, "Am I picking for me, or for the lady?"

She smiles coyly. "You choose."

"In which case, don't all women love a rose?" Reaching for a single lavender rose, Liam takes it from the silver bucket, nodding to the florist in thanks before handing it to me.

"Thank you," I say, joining it to my shorter, stumpier hyacinth, liking how the colours compliment each other. As Liam walks away, I smile at the florist, wondering if she'll tell me what his choice means. Searching on Google later is an option, but that feels like cheating. I want to hear it from her, like she's an oracle or fortune teller, knowing the course of my life.

Perhaps understanding my reluctance to leave, she smiles conspiratorially, whispering, "Love at first sight."

CHAPTER FIVE

Nora

THE FLOWERS from yesterday sit in a glass next to the bed, one I've commandeered from the kitchen. Naturally, I double-checked the florist's remarks, and according to the website I consulted, she was right.

I'm not sure what to do with that knowledge. Dismissing Liam's flower choice is the simplest and sanest thing I can do, so while I wrestle with that, I think about my constancy with regards to Tom. After all, this is what I need to persevere with. My boyfriend. Or maybe, men in general. Some days, I feel like giving them up. Dating seems like more hassle than it's worth.

Last night, Tom came to bed after one o'clock. Aware that he disturbed me, he kissed my shoulder and snuggled down on his side of the bed. Generally, he doesn't fall asleep quickly, even when it's late. I think his brain ticks over with what's coming next in his book, and how he'll tackle the characterisation, or the next plot reveal.

It consumes him.

He didn't seem too upset about missing my canal dive. And I didn't get one single compliment about my shit-hot dress, nor a single query about our regionally renowned dinner, a *tarte flambée*.

"Do you know what it is?" I asked.

"Tell me," he'd replied.

I described the thinly rolled dough, topped with soft white cheese, onions and bacon lardons. "It was really good," I told him. "But not big enough. I could've eaten two."

He poked me in my stuffed full tummy. "Good thing you're doing all this running."

My watch tells me it's 0551. A couple of minutes ago, I heard Liam moving between his bedroom and the bathroom. The forecast states a cloudy morning, the sun breaking through mid-morning. It bodes well for our chateau visit and wine tour later today.

When I go downstairs, I remember that Aaron didn't call me last night, and I wonder if that was part of his plan. Was he hoping I'd call him instead? Demonstrating my neediness? Trying to evict him from my thoughts, I head into the living room to find Liam stretching.

The warm smile he gives me makes my tummy flip. Even though I knew he'd be down here, my eyes always seek him out, whether that's post dinner, by the pool, or after having showered and changed for the day. And I look forward to our conversations, to the relentless teasing and jokes.

We share a few words, hydrating, before heading out to the lake and running the same route as yesterday. Our overall time is only eight seconds faster, but I'll happily take it.

"When's your birthday?" I ask Liam as we walk back to the lake café.

"December. What about you?"

I side-eye him, hoping he won't take the piss. "October, but soon I'll reach day ten thousand five hundred."

Liam throws me a quizzical look. "You what now?"

A tendril of embarrassment unfurls in my gut. This isn't something I've shared with many people - not even Tom - but I'm pretty sure Liam will appreciate this aspect of approaching life. He seems to enjoy each day, making the most of them. "I'm weird, I know, but I like to look at birthdays a little differently. Instead of just being twenty-eight, I can say I've been on this Earth for over ten thousand days. It sounds so much more impressive, don't you think?" I ask, watching his face morph from confused to quietly amused.

"That's a new way of looking at it."

I take that as a positive sign. "My good friend Ashleigh teases me about it, but milestones aren't just for meeting those decades of thirty or forty or fifty. You can hit others like your twenty-thousandth day. If you live to a hundred, you've been alive for thirty-six thousand five hundred days! That's an insane thought."

"Very," he deadpans, chuckling at me. "Though it makes me sound ancient."

"And wise."

"I'll take it," he replies easily.

A young man is opening up the café as we pass nearby, heading along the path back to the villa. He nods at us, calling out *Bonjour!*

"What made you start looking at significant milestones in days not years?"

Unwilling to share that it was around the time Aaron and me split up, keen to look at our two years together as over eight hundred days instead, I admit, "I'm not sure, but it's got something to do with immortality, and it tricks me into thinking I've lived a long life. A full life. Counting in years just diminishes your achievements in some way, because for many, days are all we have. We don't get many years so we need to make the days count, doing things we enjoy, love, that bring us pleasure. I don't want to regret a single day. I want to cram in as many experiences as possible."

Liam hasn't looked away from me, his expression one of enlightenment and focus. "It's a good way of looking at things."

Pleased at his ready acceptance, I tell him, "Keep an eye out for your twelfth thousandth day. You should plan a big party."

"Is that soon? Let me check my calculator app," he says, pulling out his mobile.

Leaving him to it, I fish out the key from my back pocket and unlock the front door.

"It's close to my thirty-third birthday," he announces, his mouth hitching.

"Yeah. And no one celebrates that in any lavish way. Now you can."

"It's over a year away," he points out.

We head inside, going our separate ways to get ready for the day. When I hear Liam exit the shared bathroom, I head upstairs after my pool swim and enter the steamy, white-painted room.

Except, Liam is still in here, a navy towel wrapped low around his hips. And even though I've seen him semi-naked by the pool many times by now, this feels much more intimate.

Water drips down his glistening chest. His hair is tussled. And the towel is wrapped tight across his groin, giving me a considerably better view of him than his swim shorts do.

I wish I hadn't noticed that distracting, impressive bulge because it's hard to find my voice. "Sorry. I thought I heard you leave."

"I did," he says, smiling in that quietly amused way. "But I realised I left this behind."

He hefts a sweaty running top in his hand.

"Oh," is all I manage in reply, my heart tripping at how boxed in I feel. It's just him and me, in a two point five metre square room, an arm's length apart. And his intoxicating shower gel or shampoo smells especially good this close, coming off his warmed skin.

For a second, we just stand there, my brain scrambled. My mind rewinds to dinner the other night, when I couldn't stop looking at him.

Or him me.

His eyes drop to the towel secured around my neck, the ends draped over my shoulders, resting on my breasts. It's then I remember I'm only wearing my costume.

"Good swim?"

"Lovely. You should've joined me."

The atmosphere tightens and I'm not sure why. Maybe it's this small room, the residual steam swirling around us like a caress. Or maybe it's the implied intimacy of us sharing a personal space, and the realisation that I'm fascinated by the feeling it creates inside me. At how I want to relive this moment, but with a different outcome.

And then I remember that Liam is Tom's brother.

He moves a foot, ready to edge past me for the door. "Next time," he says, his voice low, leaving me alone in the bathroom.

Leaving me to my unhelpful, confusing thoughts.

BY THE TIME the rest of the household is up and breakfasted it's 1030, and as per the weather app, it's a gloriously sunny day. And the whole family is upbeat when Tom stands by his promise and comes with us, getting in the car next to me when we're ready to head out.

"I'm so pleased you're here," I tell him. This is the third day of our trip, and it's the first time I feel he's actually taking a moment to relax and enjoy himself.

"Who doesn't love a chateau and vineyard tour?" he replies earnestly.

I try not to focus on the fact that the destination got his vote, rather than the opportunity to spend time with me, his girlfriend. Maybe I'm dissecting words that shouldn't be picked apart so vigorously, but when you look for cracks in a relationship, sometimes that's all you find. It's like you go hunting for them, allowing them to reinforce all the negativity.

"I hear you," Charlie agrees, tugging at his long beard. "It's why we brought the car so we could get all our loot home."

"At the rate Mum and Dad are buying cheese and local wine, there won't be room for our *own* loot, or our luggage," Tilly responds.

When we pull into the long, winding driveway, passing acres of grounds before we even near the sixteenth-century house, the anticipation is almost too much. When the chateau finally comes into view, I know the pictures on the website haven't done it justice. Grand does not seem an adequate enough word. It's ridiculously impressive, imposing and opulent. Built from pale stone, the proportions are entirely symmetrical. The central stone facade features columns and pediments, served by a beautiful horseshoe staircase. Porticos on either side draw the eye further out towards the rounded towers which frame the house, the roofs steepled and reminiscent of Disney logos. The slate roof is heavily pitched, numerous chimneys and decorative dormer windows spaced evenly along the roofline. A metal weathervane glints in the sun.

After parking and assembling with the others, we walk along the cobble driveway that leads past some pretty fancy-looking outbuildings and approach the incredible staircase. My cream, linen summer dress with buttons down the front doesn't compete with Cinderella's ballgown, but I feel swept away in the moment, imagining myself at a high society ball with aristocrats dressed in doublets, breeches and hose, long, curly wigs on their heads.

I turn to Fay and Tilly, both of them wearing their long, straight hair loose today. "I wish I'd done something elaborate with my hair, and maybe added a beauty spot by my top lip or something. I feel underdressed."

"Especially with these slobs walking at our sides," Fay adds dryly, smirking at her bespectacled husband. "I feel like I'm in the wrong century."

"At least Nora has the requisite curls," Tilly points out. "And impressive cleavage."

We ascend the steps and head through the central facade. Once we've paid up and got our guidebook, we wander around the elegant rooms, marvelling at vaulted ceilings, gilded rooms, and furniture that looks impractical but is the epitome of centuries-old luxury.

"What do you think?" I ask Tom, nodding towards a harpsichord. A red velvet chair is in front of it, complete with gold feet and armrests.

"Show-offs," he quips, checking his watch.

Reflexively, a grin appears; he seems happy today and that makes me pleased. He's put his work to one side to concentrate on himself and his family. On us. Liam has stayed by his parents' side ever since we arrived. In fact, Tilly and Fay also seem to be keeping their distance I notice, allowing Tom and I some time together. But aside from the occasional comment, our conversation is minimal.

"When are we going to get to the wine tour?" I ask, feeling thirsty. And hungry. Breakfast was a long time ago.

"Aren't you swimming later?"

"Yup."

He looks at me soberly. "Then you'd better be careful about how much you drink."

I roll my eyes. "I wasn't planning on getting drunk."

He raises a brow, as if he doesn't believe me. "Just trying to be helpful," he mutters before walking across the herringbone floor to gaze out of a long, broad window. Taking a restorative breath, I follow. From our higher vantage point the parterre looks faultless, the pattern precise and the box hedges clipped to perfection. Flowers bring colour to the otherwise green garden, with a few visitors roaming the splendid gardens.

"This place is immaculate. Must cost a fortune to run."

"Hmm."

"...Shall we find the others?"

Tom nods, and we move through to another reception room, embroidered curtains at the windows, more paintings of important people on the walls.

Standing on the opposite side of the room, Liam studies one of the heavily framed portraits. I approach, stopping next to him to consider the painting too.

"Have you ever seen anyone so ugly?" I ask. Liam's eyes light up but I continue quickly, "In all honesty, I don't think I've ever looked at a painting of someone from two, three, four hundred years ago and found any of the individuals remotely appealing. Is it the hair? The clothes? The inbreeding? I mean, what made them so unattractive?"

Liam's head drops, his body shaking with a deep, rumbling laugh. Then he tilts his face to the side, peering across at me, a double-dimpled smile just for me. Awareness that the rest of his family are throwing us looks, not cautionary, but certainly curious, I bite my bottom lip as if to hold in my words.

"You crack me up. I've always been aware of that thought, buried deep, but I've never actually vocalised it. Or had anyone clarify it so perfectly for me."

"Glad to name and shame your subconscious thoughts," I tell him. "And that I'm not alone in thinking that although expertly painted, people weren't particularly beautiful back then."

"It probably had something to do with all the untreatable diseases and illnesses. The unclean water and lack of antibiotics."

"Thanks Dr. Alston."

A wink. "You're welcome."

"So who do you think had an STD? Let's get a professional's opinion." I point to the painting of a woman in front of us. Her face is chubby, her shoulders sloping, accentuated by a puffy-shouldered lime green dress. Her eyes are small, and although there's obvious rouge on her face, it doesn't enhance her features in any way. It just obscures them.

"By professional, I hope you're referring to my skillset as a doctor, and not as a regular contributor to the spread of STD's."

"Well, now I'm worried. Are there two options?"

"No."

"Never had one?"

"No."

"Me neither. Unlike her, or him," I say pointing to a man in a neighbouring portrait, his tummy straining against his silver-blue doublet. "He's definitely got something nasty."

"Yeah, he's got all of them," Liam asserts. "Hepatitis, syphilis, gonorrhea. Bad time to be around if you liked rampant sex."

My knees almost buckle at how Liam's voice turned gravelly and sex-rough when he said *rampant sex*. "I guess so."

"Especially if you were prone to dick mishaps," he adds in that same sinful tenor, flashing me the smuggest smile before sauntering towards the doors that lead outside.

Stupefied, mad at myself for falling into his trap, I catch up to him and shove his shoulder. "I hate you."

As his laughter subsides, and as my frustrated smile slips away, he looks at me for a few frantic heartbeats. It's that cherishing look I saw at the airport, the one that says he's having fun with me. Allowing myself to indulge in it for only a second, I break eye contact, trying to identify the rest of our party.

In comfortable silence we walk through the formal gardens, trailing after the others. Our strides fall into unison, our breathing synchronised too. It's strange how easily we fall into this duality. Earlier, during our morning run, my thoughts caught on it. But like Liam's comment earlier, it was something I was aware of but hadn't quite put my finger on, voicing it aloud. Except, I can't mention this now that I've realised what's going on - this paired commonality. When Liam glances across at me I have to wonder whether he's picked up on it too.

The sound of bees in the lavender beds fills my ears as we walk past a long stretch of the purple-blue plants. They remind me of my hyacinth, and by default Liam's rose. There's no way he could've known what that flower meant. He just selected a pretty flower. But why that one? A rose. Was he hinting at something? Or was it just a sweet gesture for a friend?

A few minutes later, we arrive at the winery. Row upon row of green, healthy looking vines surround it, falling away to the distance. The building is constructed of glass and wood, so modern when viewed alongside the chateau. Famished, when lunch is served at our table, accompanied by small measures of wine as part of the wine tasting, I devour the salmon risotto and destroy my tarte au citron in seconds.

"Someone's getting ready for a timed swim later this evening," Sam voices, grinning.

"You still coming with?"

"You bet. We all are." I know better than to assume he

means Tom, so I turn to him in the neighbouring chair and ask, "Do you fancy a swim later? You really need to see the cute beach, and the pontoon floating out in the lake."

He scratches at his stubble; he's been too busy to shave since our arrival. "We'll see."

I catch Fay's eye as I turn back to my empty plate, both of us conveying in that split-second glance that we know what he really means: No.

When our plates are cleared away, we're ushered by a member of staff towards a nearby building. Here, there'll be a short talk on wine production, explaining everything we need to know about fermentation, ageing and bottling. But Tom doesn't appear to be joining us, heading off with a different member of staff.

"Tom? Where are you going?"

"Didn't I say?"

"Say what?"

"I've arranged to see their cellars. They own some old presses and barrels from the 1800s. It's good research for a section of my book."

I blink several times as I process his words. As I understand why he really wanted to come on the wine tour and visit the chateau. "You forgot to tell me," I say quietly, aware of the male tour guide listening. When I look at Patricia and Barry they appear to be unaware of his plans as well. Inhaling a steadying breath, I say as sweetly as possible, "We'll see you soon."

"Okay," he replies, utterly clueless as he heads in the opposite direction.

Patricia calls after him, but I don't hang around to listen. Taking out my phone I message my flatmate Ashleigh. It's her day off today so she should be able to talk.

Hey! About to get very drunk on my wine tour! *Wine bottle emoji*

Ash: ***Oooh. Wish I was there! How's France?***

Beautiful and relaxing, though Tom is being infuriating.

Ash: ***Oh. That sucks. What's going on?***

He's not interested in a holiday. Or me, I don't think.

Ash: ***God, why not? Is he blind? Does that mean no holiday sex as well?***

Barely a kiss.

Ash: ***Am loathe to say it but I think you need to consider if this is working for you.***

At some stage, Liam went over to join his Mum. As they return (without Tom), I hear Liam placating his mother. From the odd word I was able to pick out, I think she was having a stern word with her oldest child. At thirty-seven, Tom might be considered old enough to reason with, but he's incredibly single-minded about his work. And while I can commend focus and determination, when you're the one being ignored, feeling worthless and unimportant, I'd rather Tom was considerably less ambitious and thorough.

Tour's about to start. Text later xx

During the tour, I drink every sample, sometimes getting a refill from the handsome French dude in charge of pouring. I really don't care about smelling fruity notes, or tasting earthy undertones. All I care about is how high the alcohol content is and how many more samples we get to try. Tilly and Charlie have boot space available for any wine purchases, but it's not going to serve me any purpose when Tom and I go our separate ways, leaving me unable to collect my case of wine, so I might as well make the most of the experience now.

"Got a favourite?" Liam asks, solicitous and interested in my opinion.

"All of them."

Concerned eyes dance over my features. "I could become a real fan of Riesling wines. Not really had them before."

"Then you don't drink enough wine," I quip, clearly having had quite enough already myself. Decision made, I turn to the host and ask, "Could I have some water please?"

He reaches for a bottle of still water, pouring out several glasses. With amused eyes, he slides one my direction and I pick it up, draining it. Then I tell Liam, "I'm ready to go home whenever the rest of you are. I'll meet you by the car."

I'm not a fan of lying. Who is? This week, it feels like I'm not only lying to myself but to the temporary family I've acquired through Tom, and I'm not pretending to be happy for a moment longer.

CHAPTER SIX

Liam

THE SUN IS low in the sky by the time we head out to the lake. I lay out my towel on the sandy beach, and join the others scowling in the direction of two lads claiming the pontoon we plan on using.

Sam announces, "They need to fuck off."

"We can take them," Nora replies, rolling up imaginary sleeves on her bare arms and setting a faux-fierce expression on her face.

God, she makes me smile. She has butterflies swarming in my stomach, my heart lifting. Ever since her unconventional thoughts on significant dates in our lives, celebrating days not years, I've been unable to think about much else.

Already, I know it's such a Nora thing to say. She's a woman who lives for each day. She rises with the sun, before it. She's physically active, pushing her body to extremes. She loves to explore, trying new experiences at every chance, be that foods, drinks, or just getting involved with new things. And she's an avid conversationalist, asking questions, talking about all sorts of thought-provoking nonsense. Over dinner last night, we debated whether there were more doors or windows in the world. I mean, who needs to know the answer to that? And yet, there we were, putting forward theories and suggestions until we thought we'd won the argument, only for other ideas to be aired.

Doors won, by the way, Nora convincing us that internal doors on appliances and sideboards, wardrobes, and kitchen cupboards were far more numerous than any office building with windows.

It was crazy, but I loved every minute of it. It fed some creative part of me that had been slumbering, quiet and unloved for too long.

Sam chuckles at Nora's determination before flinging his arms out to either side of him, stretching. Nora strips off her shorts and T-shirt, leaving her in a black, functional bathing suit. After red, it's my second favourite colour on a woman, especially olive-skinned brunettes with curves in all the right places, unpredictable conversation, and humour that seems to live with me long after the jokes have been shared.

She's wasted on Tom. Sorry, but it's true.

It reminds me of the times we'd take wintry walks along the Suffolk beaches, Tilly, Fay, and I picking through the washed-up stones, wishing for amber. Every time we went to those wind-swept beaches, I was so sure I had at least five pieces in my sand-ridden pockets by the time I got home. But by then, the stones had dried out, and it was obvious they were just similarly coloured stones, not sought-after fossilised tree resin from millennia ago.

One day, once we'd returned home, Tom dumped all of his finds on our gravel drive, telling me none of his hopeful treasure was any good. But one piece had caught my eye. Picking it up, I held it to the sun and peered through that warm-coloured stone, certain of his luck. But when I showed him what he'd found, he just denied it. He rejected that pretty resin even though my sisters tried to convince him too.

It was right in his hands and he threw it away.

I fear it's a common theme for him.

Sam and Fay's voices rip me back to the present, and I feel every one of the fifteen hours I've been awake. The wine after lunch made me sleepy, but Nora was determined to swim, and I didn't want her out here on her own. With our plans made, Charlie and Tilly agreed to hire a pedalo, acting as our health and safety officers. Sam will swim with us, Fay staying on the pontoon to hold our position and time-keep. Meanwhile, my parents are just along to take pictures and store memories, though my mother seems to be really pushing the Retire to France battle plans with Dad.

Nora ties back her hair, her breasts pushing against the tight fit of her suit. I know I shouldn't be looking at her tits, nor wondering how heavy they'd feel in my hands, or how soft against my lips and tongue as I nuzzled them, but I think about them a lot. And when she wore that halter neck dress yesterday, her braless breasts so perfectly displayed, it was a difficult moment.

I might have taken care of myself in the shower that evening, thinking about my brother's girlfriend.

Fuck, what a hopeless situation. But I know what Nora's body looks like. Feels like, pressed against mine. We get hot and sweaty and semi naked every day. I'm up close and personal with her lush body more often than Tom is. Her eyes have crawled over my chest and abs more times than I can count.

I like the way she looked at me when we ran into each other in the bathroom, the small space between us strained and challenging. Sometimes, I want this holiday to be over with, though other days I want every minute to drag by, prolonging my opportunity to get to know Nora better. To just be with her.

When I glance at her again she's struggling to get her swim cap over her hair. I decide to assist, stretching the plastic as far as it will go. Somehow, I manage to break it. "Fuck."

"Thanks, Superman."

"Sorry," I say, laughing. "I guess you're not so streamlined now."

"It's fine. My hair's tied back, so it's not a disaster." She fits the goggles that were dangling around her neck over her eyes, adjusting the straps. Meanwhile, grateful for her taking some of the heat off my idiocy, I throw the ruined cap to my towel.

Once we're all set, we swim towards the two guys lounging on the pontoon, pretending we're not coming for them.

"I feel like a killer whale," Nora shouts, trying to be heard above our splashes. "I know we're not exactly being stealthy," she drags in a big breath, "but they look like seal pups on a slab of ice, ready to be unceremoniously flipped into the water."

"They're toast," Sam calls. "This land shall be ours!"

Fay starts singing the music from *Jaws*, even though it's the wrong mammal. Sam joins in until the *French?* dudes sit up to watch us approach, their faces a mix of mild amusement and confused wariness.

When we're just a couple of metres away, we tread water, Nora calling out, "Bonsoir."

Guy number one, replies, "Salut," as his friend gets to his feet, telling us, "C'est à toi."

It's yours.

They dive into the water as we either climb up the attached steps on the side, or hoist ourselves straight out of the water. It's tethered to the lake bed to make it easier for us, but Nora seems to be struggling. Naturally, being a true gent, I put my hand on her arse and boost her up.

When her body is clear of the water she twists to look at me. "Oh, it was you," she says, getting to her feet. Using my upper body strength, I hoist myself out of the water, Nora eating up every flex and ripple of muscle as I do.

"So I'll just sit here and time you on your fancy watch," Fay states. "I can see a pedalo approaching dead ahead, so the others are in position."

"I'm going to use this to kick start my training," Sam says seriously. "I'm getting a calling."

Nora and him fist bump. "Nice."

"Remind me how many laps this would be in a pool?" I ask.

"Thirty-two."

Christ, I'm not sure I can swim that far.

"Just do what you can," Nora tells me, noticing my reaction. "Turn back when you want."

"I'll be fine," I lie, knowing I'll be coughing up another lung by the time I've finished.

Earlier, using our collective brains and thinking we were fucking smart, we used Google Earth to help calculate how far away from the pontoon we needed to swim to make it comparable to Nora's race. Factoring in how long it normally takes her to swim the distance, we've identified a corresponding point on the shore that will act as our turning point.

When I check on Mum and Dad at the beach, I can see Dad has the camcorder out, pointed our direction. "Everyone turn and wave at Mum and Dad, please." Dutifully, we all turn, even Nora. And even with the goggle straps digging into her cheeks her smile hits me right in the gut.

"Shit," she grumbles. "Why did I have to have my goggles on for the photo op?"

I smile ruefully. "Dad probably didn't push the right button. It's a safe bet that you got away with it."

She grins as Fay calls, "Okay, ready?"

"Are we racing you?" Sam asks. "'Cos, I'm not feeling too confident."

"Please do," Nora encourages. "Some competition will be good for me, but you're likely to be faster than me anyway, what with your orangutang arms."

"Fuck off," he jests back. "My arms are perfectly in proportion."

"Orangutangs always think that," she responds, throwing him a cheeky smile before lining her toes up with the corner edge of the pontoon.

Grumbling good-humouredly, Sam gets into position at the other corner. I take the spot between them. The increasing pace of my heart tells me I'm invested in this race. For starters, I really want to beat my brother-in-law. Secondly, I want Nora to beat us both.

"Ready? Set? *Go!*" Fay shouts.

I dive in, surfacing at the same time as Nora. All I can do is concentrate on my breathing and the rhythm of my arms as I forge a path through the water. My legs kick furiously, my hands scooping water out of the way. Despite my efforts, Nora is slightly ahead, but Sam's a little behind.

For the next few minutes, I just focus on the same damn thing: breathing, finding a rhythm. As I scan ahead for the pedalo and the turn point, my heart sinks when I realise we're nowhere near the curve in the trail yet. I dig deep, regretting this already. My lungs are shot, my energy depleted, but somehow I carry on a little further. A bit later, fatigued, I stop to tread water, catching my breath as Nora reaches the halfway mark, turns, and starts swimming towards me. When I check on Sam, he's already heading back to the safety of the pontoon.

Weak-armed, I chase after Nora, my technique shot to hell. I was hoping to impress her, and while my body might've caught her eye, my swimming prowess certainly won't.

"Want a lift?" Tilly asks cheekily, as she and Charlie cruise past me, their legs furiously pedalling.

There's no room for me on the stupid thing, and anyway, my pride won't let me hitch a ride. Instead, I struggle on, swallowing more water now than I'm managing to drag past me.

Finally, euphorically, I arrive at the pontoon. I'm a good minute behind Nora but I'm sure she won't give me beef over it.

"About bloody time," she says. "I've been back ages."

"Stop flexing."

She laughs, Sam joining in.

Weary, I clamber out of the water, flopping to my back, half-dead. "I never knew it was so hard to swim that distance."

"It fucking kills," Nora agrees. "That's why the sprint triathlon is enough for me."

"Thank fuck I didn't agree to do it. There's no way I'd make it. Not this close to the event." I look across at Sam, gloating ever so slightly that he gave up before I did. "Where did you go?"

There's a weary laugh. "I hate myself. I thought I'd last longer than that. I guess I'm more out of shape than I thought."

"Just so you know, he says that in the bedroom too," Fay jests, following it with a loud shriek as her husband shoves her backwards into the water. He jumps in after her, both of them splashing each other and clowning around. It's proof as to why they don't want children; they're still big kids themselves. Charlie and Tilly jump in the water too, temporarily abandoning the pedalo.

After laughing at their antics, Nora's attention returns to me. It's a habit of hers, as if she senses me looking at her, watching her. Thinking about her.

She's at the centre of every room for me, every conversation. I'm drawn to her at every opportunity, circling her. When our eyes snag, as they did that first night at dinner, we just smile now, an acknowledgement of how close we are. We've moved beyond awkward eye contact. Now we just ease into each other's company, into any and all shared experiences like it was always meant to be this way.

Strap marks dissect her cheeks. Lines have formed around her eyes. My confession just now might've got swallowed up in Fay's joke, but I wonder if Nora's upset that I won't be joining her in Norwich. The other night, it was kind of implied I would be. And after her admission that her brothers might not be able to support her, I'd like to offer to be there myself; it's extremely unlikely that Tom will be. For one, their relationship, if not over soon, will be by then. Two, he won't lose a day, let alone two, travelling to Norwich to support his girlfriend. The only time he might consider it is if he gets plagued by writer's block.

"You're a fit woman, Nora," I compliment, trying not to check her out as I reference her fitness regimen because there are plenty of ways she's fit. "I hope you beat that shitty friend of yours who went behind your back. And I want your ex to see you triumph, regretting the day he ever thought it was wise to move in on your friend."

Various emotions register on her face, but the moment is shattered when Tilly asks, "Wait, what?" She's climbing up the small steps, water cascading off her body as she joins us.

"I'll tell you over dinner," Nora appeases, pulling her knees to her chest. "I'm getting cold and want to get back."

Getting to my feet, I ask quietly, "Sorry, did I say the wrong thing?"

She shakes her head. "I really am cold."

My eyes drop briefly to her chest, her nipples poking through the wet material.

Fuck, wrong thing to do.

"Right," I say, dropping my gaze to the pontoon. "Are you pleased with your time?"

"Yeah. I am."

Her strokes looked strong. She looked on fire. "Good job." I hold my hand up for a high five, Nora smacking my hand with that inviting smile that keeps me awake at night.

"Thanks for coming with."

"Any time."

And then, with a smirk, she stands, shoving me into the water with her push-Liam-in-the-lake card.

WE ENJOY a late dinner on the patio. Moonlight dances on the rippling surface of the pool. The sky is a midnight blue. Muted laughter from a neighbouring villa can be heard, a light breeze washing over my skin.

"I'm just saying," Mum continues, "that if you want children you shouldn't put it off much longer. Once you reach a certain age it all gets much more difficult."

Resigned, Fay and Sam trade glances. This is an old conversation with the same resolute outcome. With four children, it's clear our parents were keen for a large family of their own, but putting pressure on us to continue that legacy seems unfair. When this conversation rears its head I always feel deep sympathy for Fay. As the eldest daughter, she seems to get a greater load of expectations than Tom, the eldest son. It never surprises me how tough society is on women, and sometimes those pressures come directly from loved ones, the worst offenders about accomplishments women need to make.

"We don't want children though. I'm sorry if that's upsetting, but it's not as if I haven't mentioned this before."

Mum puts on a brave face, looking to Dad for support even though she won't get any. Privately, he might grumble about Fay's stance on this but they can't do anything about it. And anyway, it helps that Tilly and Charlie plan on having at least two, but my parents will have to wait until after the wedding next spring.

"What about you, Nora?" Mum asks.

"Mum," Fay warns under her breath. "That's private."

Using her years to her advantage, Mum makes some unintelligible noises while looking imploringly at Nora. It's hard to refuse my mother when she looks so pitiful and cute at the same time, a sweet-looking older lady, who, underneath the facade is tenacious as hell.

Everyone seems to be waiting for Nora to respond. And I'm not sure why my heart is in my throat, but it is, desperate to know her view on babies and children. The thought of her life evolving, of her bearing children with another man makes me feel…makes me feel…*pissed off*.

Nora makes an embarrassed face, but I note she doesn't look at Tom. Instead, her empty plate has all her focus. "Well, as I'm one of three, I do like the dynamic of large families." Mum visibly relaxes, nodding happily at that statement. "But I would need to have a fully invested partner who would co-parent equally."

Everyone's attention swivels to Tom, who just picks up his wine glass and refuses to acknowledge the massive, monumentally direct statement.

But clearly Mum feels like pushing tonight. "You want children, don't you, Tom?"

"Mum," he dismisses, sighing loudly. God, he can be so abrasive sometimes. I realise the question is intrusive and majorly awkward with your new girlfriend sitting next to you, but he doesn't need to be so rude. "The world doesn't need more mouths to feed."

"I thought writers were all about experiences. How can you write about the fierce love a parent has for their child if you don't live it?"

Around the table, everyone shifts uncomfortably. "Here we go," Dad mutters under his breath.

"I've not personally been attacked by mortars, or been knifed in my belly, but I can write about that just fine," Tom responds. Then he stands, abruptly, his chair screeching across the stone floor. "If you're going to hassle me, then I'm going to do some work."

"Tom," Nora tries. "Stay. We can play that card game I brought with me."

"I've got more important things to attend to," he throws back, heading indoors.

I release a taut breath. "I like the sound of that card game," I say to Nora. Anything to change the mood around here.

"I'll go get it."

Nora heads upstairs while the rest of us clear the table. Despite the noise we make stacking the dishwasher, the angry voices of Tom and Nora drift down the stairs. A couple of minutes later, Nora returns, looking resolute. "Who's playing?" she asks. "I should caveat this by saying I've never played it before. It belongs to my flatmate."

Mum and Dad decline, leaving us *youngsters* to it, while Fay reads out the rules, which are basically to either answer a question, or drink.

Tilly and Charlie line up the wine and gin bottles so that we can easily top up our glasses as the game progresses. "By the sounds of things, the winner is the one without blood poisoning," I quip.

"I wish I hadn't had so much wine at dinner now," Tilly complains. "I'm going to fail."

"You won't if you tell the truth," Nora reminds her. "It's when you want to avoid an answer that you drink."

We start with the youngest first, which is Nora. She rolls the dice and progresses to a space in my colour-coded cards. It means I get to ask the question, and her answer is for me and me alone. "When we first met, what was your most abiding impression?"

Tilly laughs.

"Oh good one," Fay says, leaning in towards Nora for her answer.

Smiling, Nora seems to struggle with her reply. I'm unsure whether it's because she's thinking of a good lie, or because it's too hard to choose a particular thing from all the good impressions I gave her.

Lol.

"Ooh, well, I would have to say it was your easy charm. I was certain I'd damaged you in unimaginable ways, and yet you were so good-humoured about it. Your reaction made it easy to laugh about it all, and for that, I was very grateful."

We share a smile that I'm going to call intimate. It might be stepping dangerously close to eye-fucking, which is really inappropriate, so I look to Fay who is next to roll the dice. She lands on Charlie's space.

"What do I do that really annoys you?" he asks laughing. "Oh, I bet the list is long!"

Fay blows out a beleaguered breath. "Jesus, how long do we have to answer the questions? I think we need to set a limit 'cos these are tricky as hell."

"Get on with it."

"Okay. You eat apple cores which is just weird."

"No it's not! They're tasty."

"Apple seeds have cyanide in them."

"Not enough to kill me, or harm me," Charlie amends.

"More's the pity," Fay teases.

While they bicker good-naturedly, Sam picks up the dice and rolls. He lands on Tilly's space, who asks, "Have you ever trolled someone online?"

"Only the government whenever they waste billions of money, or give lucrative contracts to their mates."

"Totally justified," Fay agrees.

We play for at least another hour, drinking when we don't feel like answering the more intrusive questions referring to sex, or past lovers. But I learn quite a lot about Nora. At eighteen, she had cosmetic surgery on her belly button because it poked out like a *Small willy*. Her favourite band in the entire world is Wolf Alice. The snack she finds most comforting is a Twix; she likes to gnaw the caramel off first and then eat the biscuit base. Her most embarrassing moment, thanks to too much weed, was pissing herself. The most courageous thing she's ever accomplished was surviving a wasp sting at three years old, which resulted in a severe anaphylactic shock. Aside from disliking the word moist, her most hated word for vagina is a toss-up between vaj and minge.

Fay couldn't help but shout out *Moist minge* one too many times after that. It draws the evening to a close, everyone deciding that I should end the game with one last question. Just as I was hoping, I land on Nora's space. She selects the top card from her pile and scans the question. Her mouth parts, but the confidence I saw just before she was about to speak seems to drain away. Almost fearfully, she asks, "What are we doing ten years from now?"

The question is a car crash. It's a drumstick mallet striking a cymbal, the sound piercing through every conscious thought. How am I meant to answer? As a possible future brother-in-law, though that's unlikely? As a man who thinks he might be falling in some way for her? How much do I share with my siblings watching me like hawks? Because I know why my sisters chose that stunning dress for Nora. I'm a sucker for women in red, and they can all see Nora and I are close. It's come up, though not in front of Tom. Part of me wonders if I was ever asked outright, with him in earshot: *What are your intentions with Nora,* and I answered: *To fuck her and keep her as mine for the rest of my life*, that he wouldn't even notice. His head is so far past the fucking clouds he's left Earth's atmosphere.

"I think we'll be good friends. And my back will be very grateful for it."

Her answering smile makes my insides tighten with want. It's accompanied by something like heartburn, or an after-burn at the very least. A reminder that she's forbidden, and I need to accept that.

There's so much more I would wish for, but seeing as I can't have the impossible, I'll gladly accept ten torturous years if it means there'll be more days like these.

CHAPTER SEVEN

Nora

RISING up from the depths of sleep, my eyes flutter open. Tom's hand rests against my back, his breathing slow and deep. Yesterday was spent alone again, even if it was emotionally rather than physically. His family is great, including me so effortlessly in their conversations and inside jokes - even their arguments. Entombed in the villa once again with his work, I joined everyone else for a leisurely bike ride into the nearest town.

The main road was lined with restaurants and cafés, tables set out on the pavement allowing us to watch the world go by. It's a slower pace here. The locals amble, they don't race. We had lunch at one of these restaurants before exploring the church with its dusky coloured stone and tiled steeple. Between us, we must've looked in every gift shop, market stall and retailer in town. I treated myself to another fridge magnet. Liam bought me a Twix.

"It'll melt," I said by way of thanks.

"Better eat it then."

So I did, nibbling off the top layer before I chomped my way through the biscuit underneath, destroying that chocolate bar in under a minute.

"You know those tree cutting machines they have in Alaska," Liam started, that damned teasing smile on his mouth, "the ones that cut, trim and demolish tree after tree in seconds? That's what you remind me of."

"Are you saying I should savour it more?"

Melted chocolate coated my fingers. Slowly, deliberately, I put them in my mouth one by one and sucked them clean. I tried not to be overly sexual about it - it would be inappropriate to give Tom's brother a raging boner - but I made sure to smack my lips together teasingly, licking the corners of my mouth clean of chocolate.

Swallowing, Liam answered roughly, "Savour. Yeah, I s'pose you should take it slow."

"Hmm mmm. Well, when I see something tasty, I just get right on with gobbling it down," I replied, my voice a low husk and full of over-stated innuendo. "Even if I choke on it."

Liam's eyes flared. A muscle in his jaw ticked repeatedly. "Sounds like the dick mishap ratio might be higher than you originally let on," he murmured back, his voice low and seductive, meeting my taunt. "In fact, I'm beginning to think that your tumble at the airport was pure fiction."

My stomach twisted with want. So I threw back: "You're such a moist minge."

As the afternoon drew to a close we sipped *kir royales*, a delicious blackcurrant and fizzy white wine cocktail. Every time I caught Liam's intense scrutiny that afternoon I felt flushed and inconsolable, like I was missing out on something big, and I'm not talking about what's behind his swim shorts. When he wasn't eye-fucking me, he shook his head like he still found our interaction exasperatingly memorable.

The concept of him remembering each and every conversation between us is like a triple shot of vodka to my bloodstream. It excites me, warming me right through to my bones.

We returned to the villa via the same cycle track, the one that connected with the lake trail. As the miles drifted by, I concentrated on all the little pieces I learnt about Liam last night. For some reason, he seemed to get several more of the dirtier questions than anyone else, and he seemed perfectly happy answering them. Or maybe that was because his siblings dragged the answers from him? Either way, I learnt that his first snog was when he was twelve. To a girl named Sarah.

I might hate Sarah.

His favourite body parts are his arms. Having checked them out plenty of times now I can attest that they are spectacular. On a woman, his favourite body part is *A pair of perky, round breasts*.

Classic.

He believes his most annoying character trait is his inability to take things seriously for long, unless he's at work of course. The word he overuses is *fuck*.

That had me very (fucking) intrigued. Personally, it's not a word I would particularly associate with him. Throwing the word *dick* into a sentence is more his style, especially if it's to tease me. So when, exactly, is he repeatedly using this word? Or maybe the question is *where*? Dwelling on that point is a kind of torture; it has my skin heating, my heart accelerating.

He's most proud of becoming a doctor. He refused to answer if he had a favourite sibling, drinking a shot of whisky as punishment, and if he had to bat for the other team, he'd bat first with John Krasinski, mostly because he thinks Emily Blunt is hot, but because John strikes him as a funny guy who's also very accomplished.

And finally, the thing he could *never* forgive would be infidelity.

I went to bed last night thinking about that. And the fact that in ten years we will be friends, which is a good feeling, though it won't be if I'm still constantly thinking about him. It makes me wonder how long someone can love another when there's never been anything physical between them. How far would my personal limit be? Am I falling for Liam?

I don't know the answer to those quandaries. And it doesn't change my situation, waking to a new day with a man next to me who's fast becoming a stranger. A man whose brother I am obsessing over as every day goes by. With every interaction. With every exchange of words.

Rising from the bed, I remove the lavender rose from the vase. The petals have bloomed, showcasing its glorious, delicate colour to maximum effect, and even though I'm uncertain whether it will survive the journey back to London, I hope to dry it and keep it.

Maybe this rose will signify what my personal limit is. Maybe, when I've tired of drying out this rose and seeing it hang from a hook in my room year after year after year, I'll finally know how long you can pine for someone without ever having shared intimacy.

Sharing so many personal things last night during the card game was thrilling and interesting, despite opening me up to vulnerabilities. I didn't lie when I said I found Liam absolutely charming. And he did put me at ease after my tree-tumble, allowing me to find humour in the situation. He's naturally gifted at bringing out the best in someone, because that night, I found some happiness I'd been missing for some time. Verbally sparring with Liam for those twenty, thirty minutes made me feel like my old self. I felt like me.

Naturally, I couldn't admit that aloud, in front of his lovely, albeit shit-faced siblings. What if they remembered? How would Liam respond to my admission? No, it was better to say some of the truth, a compliment I was happy to give, but not all of it. It's complicated enough as it is with Tom.

Downstairs, Liam is already waiting for me. I busy myself getting a drink and rotating my ankles when I hear, "Have you got your EpiPen?"

With my back to Liam he probably noticed that it was missing from my pocket, so I take a spare from my handbag, noticing the outline of his phone in his shorts. "Thanks." Sometimes, he's such a doctor, but I like it. It's nice to be considered instead of ignored.

After we've stretched out some important muscle groups, we head to the lake. The sky is overcast, the lake dark and depthless. We run quickly, Liam's longer strides driving my pace up so that our first mile is under nine minutes for the first time ever. Our second mile is four seconds faster, and our third is better still.

"You're going to smash it come September," he assures me as we catch our breath.

"I hope so. My ego has taken a battering by seeing Beth win every year."

Slowly, we amble back to the villa, cooling down.

"You promised my sisters, and by default me, some info on this tool that fucked around on you behind your back."

"Shouldn't I wait for them, then?"

"No. It's their fault for not joining us."

I smirk. "For most people, this is an unsociable hour."

"But not us," he volleys back, but hushed, like it's our secret. "So?"

"So." I take a deep breath. Being cheated on, being betrayed by the love of your life was a crippling feeling, and even now I still get a few pangs of heartache when I think about them together. About what I walked in on. "I'd been seeing Aaron for about two years. Things were really good. We met at uni and had common friends. Neither of us were clingy, spending time with different people, but I began to notice things. He started to get secretive about his phone; Beth did too. I'd catch them making eyes at each other, looking at their phones as they texted, right in front of me as if I was too dumb to notice. After visiting my family one weekend, I came home early and walked in on them."

"Cunts," Liam growls, the ferocity of his word choice not lost on me.

"Needless to say, I ended it, moving out of his flat to go and live with my true, loyal best friend, Ashleigh, who I've known since school. For whatever reasons, I remained cordial with those cheating scumbags, partly because we were always a group of six graduates who hung out. And worried that I'd be jeopardising the group dynamics by not taking part, I agreed to enter the race when Joe - one of our group - suggested it. But mainly, I wanted to show Beth and Aaron that I was better than them." I sigh. "Which I failed at because I lost, Beth inhumanly fit, and then I sprained my ankle in the second race..."

"I can't believe your friends stuck by them."

"Well, to be fair, they did all ghost them for a while, but after some major grovelling on their part, and because I wanted to prove that I was over him, I reluctantly started to join them socially. But it took the best part of a year. And we don't see them much now that they've moved away."

Liam nods, like he understands. As charming and sweet as he is, I get the impression he's a real heartbreaker. A serial heart killer. It's interesting that he specified infidelity as something he could never forgive, so I ask, "Has something similar happened to you? You mentioned infidelity last night playing cards."

"No, I just find it dishonourable, and I respect women a lot." He laughs softly. "I've got two sisters so I'm protective, I guess."

"I like your integrity," I admit. "Being cheated on hurts, and negative feelings tend to linger."

"Yeah, it's not a feeling I want to get acquainted with."

He looks off towards the lake when he says that, away from me, and my thoughts deviate to his brother. Is that who he's thinking of too?

"Are you still hung up on Aaron?"

The question is a sucker punch, and I blow out a breath. "Not in the sense that I have feelings for him, not unless murderous ones count," I add on for fun. "No seriously," I continue, "because that suggests I do have feelings for him. I just don't like the way I feel around him I suppose. Beth too. Like I'm in second place. Last. Discarded. If our relationship had ended naturally, I would've accepted it if he'd moved on with someone else. But cheating on me with someone so close to me? My good friend? That was super shitty behaviour. I never want to go through that again, nor ever be responsible for putting someone through that either."

I might've said too much. I might be thinking about my growing feelings for Liam while those for his brother are becoming non-existent. Nothing more than friendly, wish you well for the future vibes.

I have to hope it's blown straight over his head. There's no way he can know my feelings for him, ones that divide and replicate like mitosis. And if he did, there's not a lot either of us can do about it. Despite not benefitting from my relationship with Tom in any way, I am nevertheless in a relationship, even if it's for only two more days. And I'm kidding myself if I think there's hope for Liam and I. Hope for something that isn't platonic.

We're forbidden by fate.

Listening to everything I've said, Liam's answer is a simple, "I agree."

Of course, he's in agreement. If I'm not mistaken about our unfathomable connection, we both know we're in an awful situation.

The café comes into view, our time together almost over. Stealing him away from his family has been a guilty pleasure of mine, like a secret date. I'll miss these mornings. I'll miss his easy companionship.

I'll miss him.

TOM IS BEING ANNOYINGLY NICE. Although I should be grateful that he's paying me some attention now, it just feels too little too late. And I can't even blame him for not trying harder; I've hardly been a loving girlfriend, and I've been distancing myself all week.

"When are we heading off for our walk?"

I've just returned from the bathroom. If Tom's noticed that I get dressed and undressed in there instead of the bedroom, he's not mentioned it. Maybe he won't mind when we break up? Maybe that's what he's hoping for.

I check the time on my phone. It's already 0930. "In an hour. Fay and Tilly are making sandwiches. They've already been to the local bakery for a supply run."

"Christ. They're keen."

"You're extra late this morning."

As I place my wash bag on the dresser, Tom tells me, "I stayed up 'til half one, but it was a good day yesterday. I accomplished a lot, reaching a spot in the story that allows me to just regroup and take a breath."

I send him a genuine smile. I want him to be successful. "I'm glad."

"Come here," he says softly. "It feels like I haven't touched you, or kissed you in days."

"That's because you haven't."

His face falls, making me feel like crap as I sit next to him on the mattress. Cautiously, I offer a smile, knowing I can't feed this relationship any longer when all I want to do is starve it. We had our chance, an extended chance. And I'm not prepared to offer a second one. I don't do those.

"Have I been that awful?" When I don't answer, because the truth will hurt, he says, "I'm sorry."

Not wanting to get into a heavy argument again like Card Night, nor wanting to ruin his easier temperament, I keep things vague. "I understand the need for focus. And you're lucky your family is so fun."

"You seem to be fitting right in. Must be why Mum was grilling us about babies."

My stomach drops, my brain screaming at me to change the subject. I all but leap towards the door. "You'd better get ready. Bathroom's free."

"Hang on," Tom calls.

I stop, turning back.

"You seem to be getting on well with Liam."

My pulse trips but I push away my unease. "He's fun."

Brown eyes assess me before Tom looks away, disappointed. It has guilt bubbling under my skin. And even though I've done nothing wrong, it feels like I have. The more I get to know Liam, becoming his friend, the more time I want to spend with him.

"See you in a few," Tom says, gathering his towel.

Downstairs, I help the girls make the last sandwiches, gathering snacks and drinks and filling rucksacks with a split of the provisions. When a freshly-showered Tom descends the stairs to join us, my phone pings.

Ash: *Got bad news. The landlord has given us notice *angry face emoji* *head exploding emoji**

"No," I hiss. And then again for good measure. "Nooooo."

"What?"

"What's wrong?"

I stare at my phone, then look defeatedly at Tom and Liam who have come to stand right in front of me. And it strikes me in that moment that I've barely seen them side by side like this. Shoulder to shoulder. It allows me a split-second to compare them. To imagine them as adversaries, fighting for my attention. My words.

They're so different. Under their keen watch, if I could, I know which brother I'd choose.

"Shit," I mutter. "Our landlord has just given us notice on the flat."

I type out a reply to Ash. ***Seriously? When do we have to be out?***

Ash: *10 August.*

Even though that's roughly six weeks, I rub a hand down my face, thinking about the logistics, the upheaval, the frantic rush that awaits me. Crap. I blow out a long breath, wondering what in hell I'm going to do. I don't have time for this.

"You can move in with me," Tom offers. He takes a deep breath, his chest expanding. And then, noticing Liam regarding me intently, he side-eyes his brother, his molars grinding.

Interesting....

A prickling sensation covers my entire body. The thought of living with Tom, although sweet and potentially a life-saving offer, is a hard no. "Thanks, Tom, but I'm sure Ash and I will find somewhere."

"What if you don't?" A shrug. "We've been living together this week and it's been fine."

I'm not sure it has. "We're on holiday, Tom, so it's a little different," I point out. "But I appreciate the offer."

Clearly not hearing my rebuttal, nor noticing the tension that's rising between Tom and I, Patricia enthuses, "What a splendid idea!" Of course she does, the wannabe grandmother. "You must move in together."

I'm shaking my head, trying to politely signal that moving in is not, and never will be, an option. "I can't leave Ash to find somewhere on her own."

"She can move in too," Tom offers. "I've got a two-bed flat."

"You met her for all of sixty-seconds," I remind him.

"She seemed nice enough."

Feeling desperate, I implore, "Tom, that's really so sweet of you, but I'll find somewhere."

"Think about it, though? If you're really stuck it could be good." He places his hands on my waist, his face earnest. "The offer's open."

Grateful, I smile, before flicking my gaze to Liam. He's been very quiet, just listening while I turn his brother's offer down. "Shall we get going?" I ask everyone. I type a quick message to Ash. ***We'll start looking as soon as I'm back xxx***

I get into the car with Tilly, Fay, and Tom, Tilly typing in the sat nav details while I fasten my seatbelt. Another message from Ash comes through. ***Maybe Richard can put us up?***

Richard is Ash's boyfriend of nine months. It's very possible he'll ask Ash to move in with him, but they won't want me there, cramping their style. And I don't really want to third wheel the new living-together-honeymoon-phase. That would be awkward for me and frustrating for them.

If he asks, you should accept it. Seriously. If you want to, that is. I can find somewhere else.

Ash: ***Let's not jump the gun, Nora Adora.***

There's no way you'd say no if he asked, right?

Ash: ***I would LOVE to move in with him, but I don't want to leave you on your own. Unless of course, Tom offers?***

Making sure Tom can't read my messages, I reply: ***He's asked me. He's extended that offer to you too, but I'm ending it when we land so it's not an option. Sorry.***

I've already explained to Ash that Tom and I have been growing further apart this week. I didn't let her know that I was getting closer and closer to Liam, though she did ask after him. When I told her about my tree mishap, and that Liam had saved me, she could tell I was struck by him. But I was still determined to give Tom and I a proper chance, and I hoped France was it. In reality, all it's done is help me see what, or who, I want out of life, and it's not Tom.

Ash: ***Don't apologise. I'm sorry it's been a rough week for you. Wish I could see you right now to give you a big old hug! *red heart emoji****

Thanks Ash. Talk later xx

When we arrive at the national park, a series of hills covered in vast forests, we decamp from the cars. Tom offers to take the rucksack containing our supplies, so I just stuff my mobile in the back pocket of my shorts and throw on my sunglasses.

The air is beautifully clean smelling, the paths easily navigable as we take the seven-mile circular route.

Fay and I end up walking side by side when Tom falls back to speak to his parents. "This is none of my business, so you can tell me to take a hike -" she rolls her eyes at her pun, "- but when you end it with Tom, please stay in touch. I've really enjoyed getting to know you."

I hang my head before casting an apologetic look her way. There's no point pretending she's way off base. "I'm waiting until the end of the holiday. I don't want to ruin it for anyone, but I can't go on like this."

"I understand. Really, I do. He's been typically elusive and..."

"Distracted," I add, when she struggles for more adjectives. "I half expected it, if I'm honest." I smile bravely. "I saw this week as our make or break week, but it's not all his fault."

Looking back, I can see that I've struggled with relationships ever since Aaron. None of them compare, and I just don't know how to get over the initial hurdle, the sticking it out phase.

Fay nods. "I'm sorry. If it helps at all, he's always been lost in his head. As kids, it often felt like there were only three of us. Tom has always been on the fringes of the family and, well, he's too old for us to change him now." She sighs. "And I'm not saying this because I'm hoping you'll give him another chance, but I think he'll be the bachelor uncle to Tilly's kids. Not because he's too busy screwing around, but because he just lives in a different world to most people. It's a good world, I mean, his books have done well, but it seems to hold him captive over reality sometimes."

My heart aches for Tom, for his vulnerability which leaves him aloof and apart from his family and friends. "He's still young enough to find his person. Maybe he needs to find another writer."

"Yeah," she says, smiling ruefully. "I hope you don't regret coming."

"Not at all. It's been fun, despite...all that."

"It has," she agrees, as we come across another car park, accessed from a different road to the one we travelled. Several groups of people linger around the tables or exit from cars. Fay and I head towards a couple of empty picnic tables, clambering into the bench seats like we're contortionists.

"Hate these things," I say.

"Really?" she asks, laughing. "Why?"

"For a start, you can't get in or out, and if a wasp comes and bothers me while I'm eating, I feel trapped."

"Oh right, of course. That must be worrying."

"It's okay. I'm being dramatic."

Being extra attentive today, Tom places our rucksack of supplies on the table, passing me a drink and my sandwiches before opening up his bottle of water.

"I packed Nora's card game," Tilly announces. "Thought we could play as we ate or walked."

"But there's no booze," I complain, winking.

"If you want to pass a question then you have to sing instead," Fay suggests ironically.

To everyone's surprise, Tom wants to play, Tilly dealing the cards. This time, Liam goes first, landing on Fay's space. "Ooh. A personal one," she goads. "Who's the most important person in your life, and why?"

Hidden behind his sunglasses, his eyes are hard to make out. But there's an endearing smile on his face. "That'll be Nippy."

"Knew it," Fay throws out.

"Surprise surprise," Tilly adds.

"Who's Nippy?" I ask. "A childhood friend?"

Liam smirks. "You could say that. I have a pet."

"My turn," Fay announces, picking up the dice.

Wide-eyed, I latch onto the side of his face. "Really? Don't tell me you've got a puppy? Actually, please tell me you have an adorable puppy and you spend every spare evening making TikTok videos."

Liam chuckles. "Now you've given me ideas, but no, not a puppy."

"Well, don't keep me in suspense," I urge.

"I'm going to make you guess."

I huff, but fire off my first option. "Cat?"

He shakes his head.

"Fish?" I ask, knowing it's unlikely.

"No."

Tom asks Fay a question about her worst body part as I consider more pet options. "Er, gerbil."

"No."

"Hamster, stick insect, snake. It had better not be a spider."

"It's not a spider."

My body sinks with relief. I'm not sure I could like a guy who has tarantulas as pets. "Well, I give up, because aside from a pony, I can't think there's much else to suggest, unless you've taken a leaf out of George Clooney's book and snuggled up with a pig."

Liam snorts, which only comes out sounding like a pig. It makes me crease up with laughter, both of us giggling like school children.

"I'll give you a clue," he suggests. "His name is Nippy, right?"

Oh yeah. "Nippy. Hmm, Nippy. That's not terribly helpful. Unless," I begin, my voice changing as an idea occurs, "you have a piranha fish, but you said no fish so I've still got no idea!"

"It's a tortoise!" Tom says, his voice cold. "You can stop guessing now."

Ignoring his outburst, and a little upset Tom never told me about this - he knows I love tortoises, I'm nonetheless super excited about the revelation.

I look at Liam. "Seriously? And you call him Nippy because he's so fast?" I grin, stupidly happy. "Oh, he sounds so cute. I love him already. I can't wait to meet him." I stop talking, slamming on the brakes at my faux pas. It's almost as if you can hear the tyres screeching on tarmac. Practically seamlessly, I say, "Or see a photo. You got one?"

Bringing out his phone from a back pocket, Liam skims through his photo app, presenting me with a photo of his favourite *person*. He's exactly what I expected a tortoise to look like: grey-brown shell, little legs poking out, a sharp mouth chomping on some fruit. I fire off a string of questions, fascinated. "How long does he hibernate for? Where does he hibernate? Where does he poo? How big are his poos? Does he like being cuddled? Have I mentioned that I want to rescue turtles? Or any sea animal really, but mainly turtles, so I'm impressed about this news, Liam, just saying."

"You don't say."

I shove his shoulder, Fay, Tom, and Tilly watching our exchange.

Then he asks, "What sort of turtle rescue?"

"From plastic. Fishing lines tangled around their necks or flippers - the usual stuff. Occasionally, on my Facebook feed, I get videos of people saving animals in exotic locations, and I want that to be me. Sometimes, I wish I'd studied marine biology at uni instead, then I could hang out on the Gulf coast, or Florida, saving turtles. By the way, I hope Nippy looks like Master Oogway out of *Kung Fu Panda*, ancient and full of sage advice. It's my favourite film."

Liam chuckles. "Of course it is."

"What does that mean?"

He shakes his head. "Nothing, I'm just not surprised." I know he's looking at me, but it's still impossible to see his expression behind his sexy aviators. "It's a compliment," he adds quietly, lifting his eyes to Tom.

When I dare to look him in the eye too, he makes a point of

looking between me and Liam. It reminds me of this morning, when he questioned me about his brother.

I feel like a terrible person, my mood sinking, especially when he says, "Rescuing animals doesn't exactly end well for you, Nora."

"The cat was fine," I remind him.

"But you weren't," he reminds me. "And you broke Liam's back."

"She hardly broke it," Liam defends, gifting me with a conspiratorial smile.

"Come on. Roll the dice," Fay demands.

We play for another ten minutes, and when I'm not thinking about Tom, I go over all the compliments Liam has given me this past week. Most of them have been about my fitness, my ambition to do well in the triathlon. There was one about a dress. But this one felt personal and deep, centering on me as a person and my character. Like he understood me. Like he sees me.

I move along the board, Tilly asking me, "Which skill do you wish you had?"

I raise a brow. "Is this limited to just one?"

"Yes," Liam confirms with parental patience, giving me all of his attention. It makes me think my answer is important, that he's trying to understand me even more.

In the background, I hear Patricia ask, "Do you think we should go?" With our lunches and drinks consumed, it's probably time. I start to gather the cards and dice as Liam prods, "Well?"

"Drawing," I reply. "I wish I could draw, or paint, skilfully."

Liam nods almost before the words are out. As if, somehow, he expected that specific answer. And with my love of animated films shared, maybe that's a given. But for some reason his reaction feels so much more than that. And with his sisters making unsubtle eye contact, it has a question forming in my head.

I wriggle my legs out from under the table, standing, waiting for Liam to get up. When he does, I murmur, “Hey, do you draw?”

Quietly, he says, “I used to.”

CHAPTER EIGHT

Liam

AS WE RETURN to the cars, Tom looks at me with a foreboding expression. It's his *I want a word with you* face. Leaving Nora and Fay to wander off together, aware that Tom and I have barely shared three words since our arrival, I hang back.

"What's up?" I ask.

Generally speaking, Tom and I don't ease into conversation, especially not since I turned eighteen and things took a turn for the worse between us. A massive misunderstanding ruined what flimsy relationship we had, and I've been trying to make things better ever since, like coming to his parties and getting hit on by his colleagues. In fairness, there's been some improvement over the years, but Tom and I will never have the easy, natural relationship that I have with Fay or Tilly. Or anyone else for that matter.

His brow is damp with sweat as he casts a glance towards the parked cars, the others opening the doors to get rid of the heat trapped inside. And then that intellectual gaze is angled back to me. "I like her. Things might be going slowly between us, but I want to see where this goes. Don't think you can steal her away from me."

I blow out a shocked breath. "Seriously? You think that's my plan?"

A careless shrug. He tugs at the collar of his salmon pink T-shirt, the heat getting to him. "You've got form."

Not wanting to dredge up the past, the day layering suspicion, on top of bad feeling, on top of long-held anger, I struggle to bite my tongue. We've never been able to get past Antonia, a friend of his. And while I don't regret what happened, I regret that my brother felt so betrayed by my actions, and apparently still does. "You told me you were friends. That nothing was going on between you."

"I know. And I've hated myself for not being honest. For being closed-off." I blink back my surprise. Tom has never volunteered such candour. "But I can see what's happening here, so I'm saying stay away from my girlfriend."

"I can't help that we get on so well, Tom. Be reasonable." I'm not prepared to ignore Nora out of Tom's (not entirely) misguided fears. I have integrity. I know where the boundaries are and will not go beyond them. Preserving the fragile relationship I have with Tom is paramount.

As he sucks in a deep breath, I change tack. "Has she ever mentioned her ex to you?"

"No."

"The name Aaron doesn't mean anything?"

Frowning, he looks off towards the path we just came down. "Yeah, that rings a bell." His eyes swing to mine. "Though it's you I'm more worried about."

Shaking my head, I warn, "You've no idea what you've got in your hands, do you? If I were you, I'd bend over backwards to make Nora laugh every damn day. If you don't, you'll regret it."

"Why's that?" he demands, narrowing his eyes.

"Just wake the fuck up," I grit out, "before she slips through your fingers."

I head towards the others. Pissed off, I throw my rucksack into the boot of the car, eager to return to the villa, specifically the gym where I can beat the shit out of a punch bag. But the car is still too hot, so we stand around until the AC cools everything down. Meanwhile, Tom throws an arm around Nora's shoulders, her head tilted up to his in surprise. When he leans in to kiss her she stiffens, pulling back after a couple of seconds and whispering, "Not in front of everyone," her eyes fixed on the ground.

It's so much easier to be around them when they're not displaying PDA, and while I shouldn't be annoyed that Tom's finally showing Nora some affection, witnessing it rankles.

Counting down the seconds in my head, I wait, barely hanging on for a sign from Nora. Desperately, I want her to look at me, whilst hoping at the same time that she doesn't. Because if she casts a worried look my way, then I know she feels the same as me. That it's not Tom she wants to kiss but his younger brother. Me. But conversely, I don't want her to incriminate us, to give my brother any fuel for the fire that's already burning through his suspicious veins.

Lightning-quick, Nora's eyes flash cautiously to mine. And naturally, Tom notices, his attention now fully on us and not the multitude of thoughts that normally keep him occupied. Like an owl, his head swivels to me, his gaze keen and sharp.

Fuck.

On the way back, I manage to push aside Tom's behaviour, his plea, his warning. I don't think about my culpability, but instead, dwell on Nora's question.

Hey, do you draw?

I used to.

Since that moment, my fingers have been restless, aching for the compressed charcoal pencils I've set to one side for too long. I never share how sad I am about not making more art, and that's not because my loss falls on deaf ears. It's just that I try not to feed my habit by talking about how much I miss it.

And in the forest, my mind clear of stress, I was able to give it some considerable thought. That is, until Tom ruined my moment of calm reflection.

So it's no surprise that after my morning run with Nora the next day, whilst everyone else still slumbers, we cycle to the town where we had lunch. Where Nora ate a Twix that might've got me ridiculously hard. There's an art supply shop, one I tried so hard to avoid or even look at when we were first here, but it's all I could think about since our return from the Vosges.

With the purchases made, we cycle back to the villa. All the while it feels like I'm being chased, my energy high, my blood skittish. Ensuring my parents are otherwise occupied, I gather the black charcoal pencils and paper from Nora's shopping bag and hide the evidence in my room.

Finding time to use them never seems to come. It makes me fidgety, like I'm withdrawing from hard drugs. Perhaps sensing my disquiet, my inner turmoil, Nora catches my eye and nods towards the stairs. She's not asked me about my answer. About why *I used to* draw but don't now, even as I purchased new supplies. Observing me seems to be giving her enough answers.

Aside from Tom, the family is outside by the pool, enjoying a pre-dinner drink. Nodding towards the stairs again, her eyes darting several times in that direction to hurry me along, Nora turns to my parents and says excitedly, "Barry, Patricia, let's start a list of all the reasons why moving to France would be a great idea! You only live once, after all."

As Nora finds a piece of paper and a pen, I quietly make my escape and head to my bedroom. Taking the supplies out of my suitcase makes me tingly. Anxious and excited at once. Anxious because it feels like I'm doing something wrong, with my parents under the same roof, and excited because I haven't drawn in months, maybe years.

Maybe two thousand days.

I blame Nora for this, her comments about seizing the day striking a chord. It's like she's become my accomplice, my advocate, and it leaves me feeling brave.

For the next thirty minutes, I just doodle, getting accustomed to the feel and weight of the pencil in my hand. Whatever I draw here won't survive the baggage handlers, so it's not as if I have to deliver the perfect rendition of Nora's face. But it's really good to push everything else out of my head and focus on this for a while, my fingers and palm studded with charcoal as I devote my full attention to my art.

A knock at the door has me quickly sliding everything under the sheets, calling out, "Yeah."

Dad enters, scoping out my tidy room. When his eyes land on me it's as if he senses what I was up to. What I'm hiding. "Did I interrupt?"

"No." I stand. "Everything okay?"

"Yes," he rumbles out, his back straight. His all-knowing gaze runs over my hands, and when I see him slouch, I feel like I've let him down. Waiting for his commentary, I refuse to say anything to soothe the thickening tension. Reacting like I've been a naughty boy is hard to shake, but old habits die hard; he's never appreciated my love of drawing.

"We're very proud of you, your Mum and I. I'm not sure we say that enough."

I might joke that, as the youngest, I get away with murder, all my parents' aspirations for their children funnelled into my older siblings, but it's not true. All of us were expected to succeed, and therefore art was never an option. An option according to their parameters at any rate.

"Thanks, Dad. I know."

His eyes return to the black smudges on my hands. For a moment, it looks like he's going to say something, but maybe he remembers that he's said it a thousand times already. That I was steered away from an art degree and towards medicine for good reason, because Look At How Successful You Are! You'd be a penniless artist, at the food banks, unable to buy your own paper and paint if we'd not pointed out your future with heavy direction.

And while I'm grateful for the push towards a steadier income, I still feel like art is a dirty word in the family home. So art, making art, hanging my art on my walls is considered taboo. It's a hobby I couldn't indulge in. A future I could never rely on. And while I love my job, it doesn't provide me with everything I need.

Art is my sustenance.

Dad nods, offering me a sad smile. It makes me wonder if he'd ever apologise for forcing my hand. At this late stage in my professional career, maybe it doesn't matter. "I came to say dinner is coming."

I nod. "Thanks."

"See you downstairs," he says stiffly, leaving the room much the same way he entered. Suspicious, let down. Betrayed.

For a full minute, I stay rooted to the spot, listening to his feet on the stairs as I remain thinking, remembering all the arguments of my youth, before sighing out a defeated curse.

. . .

ON OUR FINAL EVENING, we take advantage of the glorious weather and walk to the lake. Nora is swimming, so naturally I opt to go with her. Fay, Tilly, Charlie, and Sam all decide to hang out with us while Nora and I do a timed distance.

En mass, we swim out to the pontoon and climb on while my parents and Tom look on from the beach. Using Nora's waterproof watch, Tilly times us again. It's another fast swim, Nora's arms slicing through the water beside me as we race for the midway point before returning. It's still a hard slog, but it seems fractionally easier than the first time I put myself through this.

Exhausted, I reach the pontoon a good minute behind Nora who's dragging in lungfuls of air. Beating her previous time by eight seconds, we high five.

"Nailed it."

"No need to flex," I tell her as she removes her goggles.

"I meant you," she points out, splashing me. "It looks like it was a better swim for you."

She pushes up on her arms to lift out of the water, so I slide a hand under her foot and give her a boost. "Better help you out. We both know your arms can't support your body weight for shit."

"Shut up," she says without bite. "Trying to hang on to a tree branch is much harder than getting up here."

With their role in timing the swim over, the others water-bomb each other, shrieking and shouting, so I hoist myself up onto the pontoon, Nora's inquisitive gaze dancing over my straining muscles as I do. "I'm not the one who's flexing," she teases, putting her arms to her sides and fisting her hands, tensing her arm and shoulder muscles in a classic weightlifter pose.

Smirking, I shove a hand through my wet hair and collapse

to the boards, Nora following me down. Evening sun warms my skin as we lie side by side, the others swimming off towards the beach. Together, we just soak up the warmth, relaxing into the shared quiet as we stare up at the crystal blue sky.

Our final few hours together count down in my head. My mind is empty yet full at the same time, full of conversation and questions. I'm not sure what happens after we land in London. Nora lives in my Borough, a short walk away. I want to see her, but I also don't. I want to train with her some more, but I also want to stay well away. Apart from spending some quality time with my family, I didn't hope for much from this holiday, but it exceeded every expectation. Nora made this holiday for me. And even though I'm curious how long her and Tom will survive when we get back, I just want to return to normality, a place where Nora doesn't haunt every room with her smile and her husky voice and her fun conversation. Where I'm not tempted to roll over towards her as I am now, staring down into her alert chocolate brown eyes and her tanned freckled face.

"What?" she asks, pawing at her cheek and nose. "Do I have a bug on me?"

"No."

Looking over my shoulder towards the beach, towards Tom, I can see he's staring straight at us. Watching.

I take a breath, two, my attention returning to Nora. Not sweeping my eyes over her prone form is too hard to resist, so I indulge myself. Stretched out alongside me, gazing up at me with so much expectation, it's like she's a vision from my dreams, ones where we're naked and writhing together. "I, erm, hope your race goes well in September."

Nora blinks several times. "...Thanks. The ankle feels strong, so fingers crossed."

"You're so focussed and determined, I'm sure you'll do well."

Nora smiles tightly. If she's reading my contradictory behaviour right, she'll see this for the goodbye and good luck conversation it is. "Thanks." Another blink. "I've really enjoyed your company, and have been so grateful for your friendship this week. Your encouragement too."

I nod. With a tight smile of my own, I get to my feet and dive into the water, swimming back to the beach, reminding myself that this is for the best.

THE JOURNEY to the airport is uneventful, the conversation between Sam, Fay and I subdued. Last night was spent in the hotel bar, everyone knocking back a fair few units of alcohol. I'm not sure why we didn't think about going there sooner, but I think it had something to do with the lake and the pedalos and the exclusive moments I got to spend with a certain young, off-limits woman.

Small booths and tables were dotted around a black and gold-themed room, crystal lighting hanging from the ceiling lending a sultry air. I got talking to the French bartender, trying to remind myself why creating distance between Nora and I was a good thing. If it meant she gave my brother more of a chance, or another chance, then it was worth doing. He might frustrate the hell out of me, but I want to see him happy. And while I don't think I've led Nora on this week, I can't pursue her the way I want to.

Something was happening between us. Something I had to nip in the bud if it helped their relationship.

"I can't believe you didn't shag the French chick," Sam mutters. "If I was single I would've."

"What the hell?" Fay cries.

"If I was *single*," he stresses.

"I heard you the first time, but it's still not right to say that in front of me."

"All I'm saying," Sam defends, "is that if you're a thirty-one-year-old with a working dick and a hot young woman comes on to you for no-strings-attached sex, you do it. Plus, it's not as if Liam is a stranger to that kind of situation."

"Right here, man."

He twists in the car seat to eyeball me, adjusting his glasses. "Sorry, but you know what I mean. I thought it was a wasted opportunity."

"Maybe his mind is on other things?" Fay murmurs, snagging my eyes in the rear-view mirror.

"Other than Nicole's pussy?" Sam queries, incredulous. "Doubt it."

Fay's eyes sear into mine. She knows it's not Nicole's pussy I've been thinking about.

We drive in silence for a little while, the signs for the airport coming more frequently when my sister reveals, "Nora's breaking up with Tom today."

I try not to overreact, but every muscle in my body tenses. "How do you know?"

"She told me when we were in the Vosges."

Well, fuck. That was well before our swim last night. "Maybe she'll change her mind. That was several days ago." And pointedly, before I told her that I wouldn't be seeing her again, even though the idea of it makes my gut clench and my breathing turn choppy. And then I think about how hurt Tom will be. "Do you think Tom knows it's coming?"

"He'd be a fool to think otherwise. You could tell she'd given up."

"She'll get snatched up by someone soon," Sam remarks. "Women like that aren't single for long."

"Yeah," I say automatically, remembering the lake swims

and morning runs Nora and I shared. With my brother ensconced in his room writing most of the week, it left Nora on her own. And with me girlfriend-less, Nora evened out the numbers. It was like we were a couple, not her and Tom. And that was why I had to say something. Do something. Do a thing that hurt me more than it probably hurt her.

"Last night," Fay begins, "she got a call from an Aaron? I think that's what flashed up on her screen."

Aaron. "Right," I say, hoping for further information.

"She went outside to talk and was gone for a few minutes. Has she mentioned him? Do you know who he is?"

"An ex. She's still friendly with him."

"Told you," Sam chimes. "There's always a guy hanging around, ready to swoop in."

I don't think Nora's interested in her ex like that, but then I recall that there's definitely some residual, unresolved feelings there, maybe even murderous ones.

"Oh, is this the story I never got to hear? The friends who she competes against?"

Scenery whizzes past the window as I relay the details Fay missed out on. And while I can understand why my brother never stood a chance with Nora for his lack of effort, I don't like that she's having private conversations with her ex, especially in light of Sam's comment about a guy ready to swoop in.

Heat swamps the back of my neck as anger surges through my blood, and I dwell on the dynamic between them until we arrive at the airport, my mind in a daze. We go through the rituals of bag check-in, security, and passport control, Nora keeping her distance the entire time. She has since breakfast, and definitely since last night while I chatted up Nicole. Maybe she remembers me saying I might try psycho pussy while out here. Maybe she thinks I shagged the bartender.

Remembering Nora's anxiety about flying, I ask her where

she wants to sit on the plane as we board. "Next to Fay and Sam," she answers.

For a second, I freeze. Why isn't she sitting next to Tom? Does that mean she's already told him? I want to ask the question, but I don't, reminding myself of that distance I've been nurturing.

On the plane, our seating plans get disrupted. Fay and Sam end up next to Mum. Dad ends up with my other sister and Charlie, which leaves me, Tom, and Nora again. This time, Tom keeps his laptop tucked away under the seat in front of him. After take-off, with Nora's hands secured to the armrests with a death grip, which only makes me feel like I let her down, Tom starts talking about all the things they'll be able to do together when his book is written. I feign sleep, allowing them this not-so-private moment, but it's good that he's finally realising what's at stake here. Nora's tense voice and overall lack of enthusiasm tell me she's not enjoying the conversation though.

When Tom starts discussing plans for dinner next week, Nora murmurs, "Tom, I'm sorry to tell you this now, but I can't let you think for a moment longer that we have a chance."

"What do you mean?"

"I told you that this week was for us, to see if we could work, and we don't, Tom. I have really enjoyed getting to meet your lovely family, but our relationship has stalled, despite stating what I needed from you."

"It's just a temporary thing, this book of mine. It'll get easier, and I'll be less stressed and able to take time away from it."

"I'm sorry, but I've made up my mind."

There's a sigh. "Nora, please. I'm sorry, I'll try harder."

"You were meant to give me this week, Tom. And I don't think it was unreasonable to ask you to put the book to one side for a few days."

"I came to the chateau, and for the walk."

"The chateau was for your benefit," Nora reminds him. "And aside from those two things, you rarely participated in our games and conversations in the evenings, preferring to write."

Tom's voice lowers, pleading. "I did last night. I came to the beach and the bar. Please Nora. I'm falling in love with you."

Teleporting out of this plane sounds good right now. Guilt smothers me as I sit here, unable to not listen in. Still pretending to sleep, it's hard to hide the anguish I'm feeling for my brother in this moment, and yet, a part of me wonders if it's true. Does he love her? Or is it a tactic to get her to rethink?

"It's my final decision," Nora says softly.

Next to me, Tom sighs. I get the sense he looks my way, perhaps checking I'm asleep when he whispers, "Is this because of my brother?" It's hard to hear him over the air con and general noise from the engines, but that's definitely his question.

Nora waits for a beat before asking, "How do you mean?"

"I've seen the way you two are together. You get on. Well. But you should know that he's incapable of a proper relationship. Nothing lasts longer than three months."

Wow, my brother really has my back. What a dickhead. And I don't care to admit that he's right; three months *is* my limit.

Nora stammers, "I'm not sure how to answer that."

"A denial would be good."

There's a derisive laugh. "Liam is a lot of fun. I've had a good time with your siblings and their partners, and it's a real shame you didn't participate and join in, but that was your choice."

"Still wasn't a denial."

"Because there's nothing to deny," Nora replies, her voice strong.

The pilot's voice comes through the speakers, updating us

on the flight time and other salient points. Pretending to sleep is no longer a viable option, not unless I'm stone-deaf.

When the tinny-voiced instructions end, Tom tells Nora. "He's a notorious flirt. You'd be one of many."

Dismayed by his assessment of me, it's the way he delivered his criticisms that has my anger rising. Trying to keep the peace between us flies out of my head, that long-held resolve dissolving into smoke. Just as Nora tells him: *I'm not having this conversation*, I punch him in the ribs, much softer than I would normally. It's certainly not the first time I've thrown a fist in his direction, and it sure as shit won't be the last if he keeps this up. Because, what the fuck? Nora looks stricken, and I'm not having that. "Don't speak to her like that, arsehole. And thanks, by the way, for that glowing report."

Scowling, rubbing at his ribs, he insists, "It's all true."

Nora's phone is in her hand, AirPods going into her ears as she toggles to her iTunes by the looks of things. A moment of privacy is appreciated while I chew him out some more. "Don't blame me for your relationship woes," I grit out. "And I wasn't flirting with Nora. I was keeping her company while you ignored her, so why don't you take a closer look at your own behaviour."

Defending myself against his slurs, I comment further on why I normally give it three months, and then we stew in silence.

Then: "Stay away from her."

The warning is so low I almost don't catch my brother's solemn threat. His order.

Fuck him. "You can't make me," I threaten back. "Besides, it sounds like you two are over."

His eyes spit fire as he drags in a long breath through his nose. It's the most emotion I've seen from him in days. After throwing him a hard stare back, I pull out the latest copy of *New Scientist* I bought at the airport and bury my nose in it.

Spending a week together was always going to be a tall order. Personally, I'm glad he was squirrelled away, writing. And if we were going to come to blows, at least it's on the homeward journey, away from my parents who view the holiday as a huge success.

Tom scoots down in his seat and closes his eyes. It means I can glance across at Nora, my view unobstructed.

She offers me a sad smile.

I offer her a sad smile back.

CHAPTER NINE

Liam

THE MAIN DOOR to the surgery is locked when I try the handle, the lights inside switched off. Once again, I'm the first one here. Inside, I disable the alarm and head to my office, dumping my bag by the desk. On the wall are several posters: a detailed diagram of the nervous system, a large-scale image of the anatomy of the heart, and a skeleton.

Since meeting Nora, and her pronouncement that the spine is her *particular favourite*, the skeleton poster has me thinking of her. All. The. Time.

I might need to swap it for something else.

It's been five weeks since we parted ways at the airport, some joke shared between us. With a final look her way I murmured: *I can't wait to meet you again*, because I knew then as I do now that it will happen. And it'll be memorable as always. But right now, we both need space. The only reason I need space is trying to be respectful to both her and my brother, because I plan on moving in on that soon, Tom be damned.

She'll get snatched up by someone...Women like that aren't single for long.

Work occupies me for the next thirty minutes, writing referral letters and checking through emails before I go and make myself a cup of tea. As the tea bag does its thing, my phone pings.

Tom: ***I went round to Nora's last night.***

I rarely get a message from my brother so my pulse kicks out. But I'm also on high alert at the content of his message. ***What happened?*** I ask.

Tom: ***I bought her some flowers and asked her if she wanted to try again. Spoiler alert: she said no.***

Is it wrong that I loose a taut breath? That my body sags in relief? ***Sorry.***

Tom: ***Her actual words were: I don't want to try again, Tom. I gave us a chance but I don't feel that we're compatible.***

Not sure what to say, because me reinforcing her words isn't what my brother wants to hear, I fish out the tea bag from the mug and return to my office.

Tom: ***You get on. Can you speak to her? Ask her to retry?***

A pained noise sounds. Selfishly, I don't want her to try again with Tom. Hanging out with her only magnified all the many ways she and I fit. She's made a cast iron impression on me, and I want her.

We've not spoken since France I reply, proving what a good brother I am.

When he calls me three seconds later, his name blaring across my screen, my body jolts.

"Hi."

"Hey," he replies.

"Look," I begin, taking control, the morning slipping away. "You gave it another go, which is fucking admirable, but it's time to let go. You can't change someone's mind. She can't change her feelings for you."

"I just feel like she's the one that got away, you know?"

Don't I fucking know it.

"Did you mean it when you told her you still loved her?"

"You heard that?"

"Yeah."

A deep sigh. "No. But she would be easy to love."

This conversation doesn't bode well for me. Hoping for a clean break was clearly naïve if Tom is trying to win her back. Moving forward with someone whilst knowing their ex is still in love with them is a shitty situation, especially when that ex is your brother.

Fuck. *Why did he get to meet her first?*

Trying not to notice the heavy irony, I encourage, "You'll get over her," my own bright optimism that involves a future with Nora waning right before my eyes.

We disconnect, my mind distracted. Thankfully, by the time my first patient arrives, my head is back in the game. The day flies by, and when I'm finally done, I get in my car and head over to Lowell's in Chelsea, finding a rare parking space outside his impressive home.

Lowell's days as a cardiovascular surgeon are very different to mine, especially with his unnecessary second job that occupies him on Fridays and into the weekend. For starters he went private, his patient list a who's who of London's preposterously, flauntingly rich. Despite his success, he's yet to settle down, something he doesn't seem to be in a hurry to do anytime soon, though this girl he's been seeing lately, Harriet, has caught his attention.

After knocking on his door, he welcomes me inside, already

dressed in athletic wear for our session in his basement gym. We head into the large kitchen first, where Lowell grabs us two beers from his double fridge.

"Cheers," I toast. "To the weekend."

We knock the green bottles together, taking a seat at the kitchen island to catch up on our week. After my conversation with Tom earlier, the beer goes down a treat.

Soon after, we head to his basement gym. Mirrors line two walls, giving the impression it's bigger than it is, the space bright. I use his bathroom, getting changed into some gym gear I brought with me before I warm up on the treadmill.

Lowell sorts out some music while I flick on the big TV screen on the wall, adding subtitles so that I can read what's going on in the local news.

"Have you hooked up with Wendy again? I meant to ask you last week."

"Nah," I reveal. "Not my kind of woman."

Recently, I've come to like them curly-haired, with a curious mind and a passion for triathlons. Who are unforgettable, plaguing your thoughts at every turn. Ones who make an impression through their quick-wit, engaging conversation, or quirky, unconventional thought processes.

I might have seen Wendy a couple of times before Tom's party, but there's no way she interests me now. "She had some bad habits," I tell Lowell. "And not ones I like to take advantage of in the bedroom."

Lowell straightens from a stretch, chuckling. "Sounds like you're on a barren patch."

"I am," I accept. "How are things with Harriet?"

He makes a face, one that tries to show how cool he is about their situation, but I can tell he's getting more and more invested, which is confirmed when he tells me, "Good. I've seen quite a bit of her lately."

Warmed up, I adjust the speed and incline on the treadmill to something fast and demanding to get my heart working. It's not the same as running around lakes, but it'll have to do. When I glance up, my mouth drops open when I see Nora fucking Moretti onscreen, being interviewed by the local news team. "What the fuck?" I murmur. My hand reaches out for the red stop button, swiping at it without actually looking, but somehow, I completely miss it and misjudge what's going on with my feet at the same time.

I'm spat to the floor at high speed, tumbling backwards and crashing into the weight machine behind me. A fiery heat consumes me, my back erupting in pain. I cry out as Lowell stands over me, looking down at me with concern.

"What the hell happened?"

"What is she saying? On the TV."

"Who?" Lowell's head swivels to the screen. "Her?"

"That's Nora."

Lowell reads out the subtitles as I wallow in agony, trying to focus on her image if not the words. "...a surprise discovery in a bag of vegetables from her local supermarket. Nora, take us through the moment you found the piece of jewellery."

The camera closes in on Nora. She looks exactly as I remember her. Wearing a pale blue blouse and a necklace that dangles enticingly near her breasts, she's a feast for the eyes and my love-sick heart.

"I was preparing dinner," Lowell continues, before switching the sound on so that I can hear Nora's voice through the speakers. He turns off the music too. "And I opened up the bag of carrots ready to top and tail them, when I noticed the ring wedged on the end of a pointy carrot."

A photo comes up on screen to show us what it looked like at the moment of discovery. The image credit says: Nora Moretti.

A hollow ache builds in my chest. I feel like I've been missing out by not hearing this in person. At the moment it transpired.

"An incredible story," the news presenter states, "because it turns out the owner of this antique ruby ring is Sally, who's here with us now. Sally's farm in Lincolnshire supplies supermarkets with, not only carrots, but other vegetables too."

The camera moves to Sally, a middle-aged woman with a big grin and a slender build.

"Sally, you must've been delighted when the ring was returned to you."

"I was thrilled and so grateful. It belonged to my mother, who lost it thirty years ago out on the fields. It's got enormous sentimental value and I can't thank Nora enough for getting in touch with the supermarket to track the grower down."

Nora's smile transcends TV. It reaches right out of the screen and slaps me across the face.

Fuck, I've missed her.

I don't give Tom more than a cursory thought. I've missed out on too much of her already and I don't plan on wasting any more time. Seizing the day, I say, "Pass me my phone, will you?"

Lowell goes to a pleather bench where I've left a towel and my mobile. Phone in hand, I scroll to Nora's number, the weatherman now giving us the short-range update.

My heart sinks when I all I get is voicemail, but I leave a message all the same. "It's Liam. I've fucked up my back. I'm at a friend's, in Chelsea. Can you come over? Please?"

Frustrated, I throw my phone down to the matting and scowl at the TV screen which Lowell has helpfully paused, right at the spot where her lovely smile and pointy canines are flashing at me.

"*That's* Nora?"

I nod, too pained to talk further. Lowell takes pity on me

and heads into the bathroom, returning with some painkillers. He holds them out to me with a bottle of water from a little fridge he has down here too. Grateful, I swallow the meds down.

"You told me she was pretty, except she's the spit of a young Sophia Loren. You must've seen that famous *Vanity Fair* picture of her in the red dress?"

Quite clearly I lied, and I don't need reminding of my very necessary falsehood. "Yeah well, I can't think too much on how beautiful she is because she's off-limits."

"Says who?"

"Me. Bastard me."

There's a delighted, low laugh. "I didn't realise you were a masochist."

"Apparently I am."

Lowell studies me quietly, a little bemused. When I returned from France, I filled him in on my week and what transpired with my brother and his girlfriend. And he already knows about the unconventional first meeting between Nora and I, so I'm sure he's putting two and two together and working out my real feelings about this. "I've got to say it, but she's waaaay out of your league, mate."

It hurts too much to laugh, but I'm unable to disagree with him. And then my phone starts ringing, my heart stilling with anticipation. "Pass the damn thing. I can't reach it."

A name that has spikes of pleasure running through me flashes up on the screen. "Nora?"

"Liam, where are you? You didn't leave an address."

I reel off Lowell's details, grateful to her, relief warming my bones at the sound of her husky voice. And even though I heard her voice on the TV a few minutes ago, it sounds so much better when she's saying my name. "I'll be there in ten. I'm jumping into a taxi now."

"Thank you." I say, hitting End on my phone.

I relay the ultra-brief message to Lowell, who just grins down at me. "Best to leave you where you are then."

"Can't you help me up on that bench?"

"Be my guest," he offers, refusing to help me. "But it's best the professional helps you."

"You're a doctor. I think you have it under control."

"Hearts not bones. And there are no bones whatsoever in the heart, so actually, I'm of little use to you."

It's patently clear he's up to something but I don't have the strength to argue, even though the pain relief is beginning to take effect, my muscles loosening. Lowell unfreezes the TV, adjusting the sound to a more reasonable volume before working on his back and shoulder muscles.

"Don't mind me," I gripe.

"I thought we established that I'm of no use to you."

Time flows, Lowell checking in on me every so often. And then, abruptly, the door knocker sounds four loud knocks. It's followed by the bell chiming, over and over and over. Laughing, Lowell pounds up the stairs. "Someone's keen to see you," he calls down to me from the top.

I wish I had the remote in my hand so that I could put the TV and hear what they're saying. I'm sure Nora is perturbed about heading into someone's basement, even if it's a sickeningly handsome man directing you down the stairs.

Just like the first time I saw her, I'm greeted by bare legs, this time bronzed from a long summer. The sight of her brings a much-needed smile to my face. Then I notice the red summer dress from our trip to Colmar, the one with the halter neck that's both flattering and annoyingly dick-hardening. It looks like she's had her hair done, the curls all layered on top of each other creating a whole lot of hair. A crazy amount of hair.

Craning my neck upwards - I've managed to get onto my

front - I see her face. The tip of her tongue is poking out between her teeth in a happy smile as she comes to stand right over me, wrinkling her nose to boot.

"Well well well, look at what's landed at my feet."

I roll a little so that I can see her better. "Cute, Nora, but technically I was already on the floor."

"If it makes you feel better. I seem to remember you saying you couldn't wait to meet me again. Full of anticipation I think you said," she baits, her voice all sorts of happy smugness. She remembers precisely what I told her, and she's having an awful lot of fun throwing it back in my face. "Is this what you had in mind?"

"I don't recall saying anything close," I lie, failing to hide my amusement. "By the way, I can see right up your dress from down here."

She shrugs, pretending not to care, but I can still detect a thrilling undercurrent running between us. That chemistry I tried so hard to ignore in France is back with a vengeance. It blisters between us anew, and if I wasn't in so much pain I'd be hard as steel for her.

"You've already seen me in my underwear. Besides, from where I'm standing it looks like you're worshipping me."

Lowell watches our back and forth with a shit-eating grin on his face. To be honest, I wasn't sure how our first conversation would go, but this beats all expectations. We're like those inseparable duo acts, sparking off each other, living on the exact same wavelength.

"I'll happily worship at your feet for the rest of my life if you can fix my back," I tell her earnestly.

Nora squats at my side, her voice carrying a hint of empathy. "Do you think you can get up and lie down on that bench?"

I shake my head.

"Okay. Could I borrow that towel?" she asks Lowell, who

grabs it off the bench. She folds it before sliding it carefully under my face when I lie down on my tummy.

"Any questions about my qualifications this time?"

I meet her eyes with mine, a sly smile growing on her face. "I trust you," I say honestly.

"You know the drill," she states, shuffling towards my hips and feeling all along my back. With help from the many mirrors, I watch the way she moves, her concentration solely on my body.

I tease, "How's your ankle? Been face-planting into any hot men recently?"

"Har har. No, I reserve that for special friends."

"Oh?" I ask, purposefully lowering my voice and drawing out that smallest of words. One that often carries the heaviest of meanings. She thinks I'm hot.

"You're never going to let me live that down, are you?"

"Nope," I say chuckling.

Somewhere to the side, Lowell laughs quietly.

"Shirt on or off this time?" I enquire.

"On is fine," she says, shaking her head at me. "Nice and relaxed. Breathe out," she instructs, pressing down on my joints and making me groan in relief. For the next few minutes, I'm carefully manoeuvred, her fingers and the heel of her palms turning me into a glow stick.

"Bloody hell," Lowell mutters, pulling a face. "That sounds so much worse than when you were rolling around on the floor screaming in agony."

Nora chuckles, while I deny everything he just said. "I'll have you know I was a big brave boy."

Nora's smile only gets bigger. "Right, let's try and get you up."

Gingerly, I get to my feet with Nora and Lowell either side of me, ready to offer support. Nora leads me to the bench, directing me to lie down on my back as she casually drapes the towel over my groin. "Just a few more things to check," she warns.

"Do all the bad things, but then maybe I can get a massage at the end of it."

"Maybe you'll get a back that allows you to walk," she corrects.

Thankfully, a few minutes later, her work is done, but it doesn't stop her from telling me off for not doing my exercises.

"Technically, this is your fault," I respond, sitting up.

"What? How do you work that out?"

"Firstly, you ambush me from a tree. Secondly, if it wasn't for you being on the local news, then I wouldn't have fallen off the fucking treadmill."

Low, husky laughter sounds. "I can't help it if you're easily distracted," she says, leaning down to pick up the towel that had fallen to the floor. All it does is showcase her amazing cleavage, my cock twitching.

Did she….? Did she just do that on purpose?

"Thanks for coming and helping me out."

"Chelsea's hardly far," Nora replies glibly. "So, you saw me on TV? It was quite the story."

"Trust you to find a ruby in a bag of carrots."

"Why's that?"

"Stuff just seems to happen to you."

She laughs, her hair bouncing. "Life's never boring."

Those words sink through me, clutching at my soul. I want Nora around me, and I'm determined that she'll feature more heavily in my life from now on.

"Come upstairs," I offer. "Lowell and I were going to order a curry. Stay and eat with us. Have a beer." She's dressed for a night out, no work clothes in sight, and I start to worry she might have plans. It's Friday night, so maybe she was heading out for a date. "Unless you have plans?"

"Nothing I need to rush off to," she ventures. "But I don't want to intrude on your evening."

"We'd love to have you," Lowell adds casually, backing me up. "We insist."

I get a smile in agreement, and as I follow Nora up the stairs and into the kitchen, I feel a sense of calm wash through me. Because one way or another, this woman is going to be important to me, and tonight is the reset button on examining how I make that happen.

CHAPTER TEN

Nora

DINNER WITH LIAM and Lowell goes well. It's clear they have a close, long friendship, both of them taking the piss out of each other when we weren't discussing our medical professions and my short brush with Carrot Fame. They're easy to be around, and it was almost as if from this moment onwards, this very night, that Liam and I seemed to distinguish ourselves as two aligned souls, ganging up on Lowell which didn't go unnoticed.

See? I can be his friend. I can do this. After all, that's what he wanted. That's why he basically wished me well and good luck on that pontoon. It was a goodbye. A marker in the ground that we couldn't stray past. And I get it, I do.

I met him too late.

Seeing him again hurts. Witnessing anyone in pain is a difficult aspect of the job, but with Liam it's not only that. Since France, I've missed him so badly. We were joined at the hip for the best part of seven days, sharing experiences and laughter and a whole lot of bone-weakening eye contact. Depressingly, I think he could be the absolute love of my life, but I was devastated to hear he's never had a relationship longer than three months. A small part of me hoped that we could remain friends after Tom and I broke up, but I decided that would be torturous. I'd want him even more, think about him constantly, and I can't give him my heart knowing we'd be limited to such a short length of time. I have longer relationships with a Netflix mini-series.

On the plane, even with my AirPods wedged in my ears, I could hear Tom and Liam talk, the volume muted. I could pick up the odd sentence or grumble, but not everything. Liam had responded to Tom's jibe with: *Just because three months has been my limit so far, it doesn't mean I'm not capable of more.*

I wanted to believe that, I really did. Remembering his statement had me skimming through photos from the holiday, hopelessly dreaming, toying with the idea of reaching out to him and suggesting a coffee or a film or a drink. Ultimately though, three months is his limit, and as much as I'd love to think I could be the woman to change that for him, I don't have that much faith in myself.

In long term relationships, men cheat on me. And my feelings and thoughts are all wrapped up so tight I can't seem to untangle them, lost in a chaotic ball of wool.

Lowell's phone starts ringing. When he disappears to another room to deal with it, Liam says, "That might be Harriet."

"Oh? Girlfriend?"

An uncertain nod. "Back in May, Lowell and I were in his car when he knocked Harriet off her bike. She wasn't hurt, nothing beyond some cuts and grazes and a twisted ankle..." He pauses to grin at me knowingly. "But he took an immediate interest in her. We were invited round hers for coffee, Lowell bringing cake from Lindt-Werner. We met her awful housemate, Ruby, who'd been refusing to move out for months, and then Harriet basically blew him off.

"He bumped into her at a charity thing the following month and they've been hooking up. If she's calling him, it's a good sign. It seems to be going well."

It's nonsensical, but when I hear about everyone else's brilliant love lives, it only reinforces how rubbish mine is. Wanting to rectify that I ask, "So tell me - do guys prefer the chase or the easy option?"

Liam blows out a considered breath. "Each to their own. I've only ever known the easy ones, but I prefer women that are hard to win over."

"Seriously? Every girl you've wanted has fallen at your feet?"

"You did," he says, a masculine, satisfied smile appearing. "Twice."

"Thank gravity for that."

"Pretend all you like, Nora, but I know a solid ruse when I see one. How's that new business model working out for you, by the way?"

"Highly lucrative. I can recommend it to all single ladies."

"Told you. Falling on a dick is never a mishap."

Searching the table for the nearest thing to throw at him, I come up short. Only knives, forks, and glassware. But his annoying habit of mercilessly teasing me aside - which clearly Tom labels as flirting - it's strange to think how bonded I feel to Liam after such a short amount of time. It's like I was always meant to meet him, know him. He's such easy company, and it must be why I ask the following question, determined to upset the equilibrium.

"Have you got any single friends?"

Slowly, Liam's eyes glide away from a returning Lowell before they sear into mine. "No."

"None at all?"

He faffs about with his mobile, then his glass. "None that are looking to date."

"Oh." That's disappointing. "But you have single friends?" I look to Lowell, hoping he might be able to help me out here, but he just retakes his seat and pours himself another wine.

There's a heavy sigh. "A couple, maybe. But they're no good for you."

"How so?"

"They're not good enough."

I snort. "Can't I decide that for myself?"

"I'd rather you just trust me on this."

It's not intended as a test, or a mark of my trust in him - I don't think - but it comes out sounding like that. Either way, I nod, checking the time on my phone and wondering if I should still head out to catch up with Ash and her boyfriend for drinks as per the earlier plan.

"You ready to move on are you?"

Liam's question makes me frown. "Does that bother you?"

"Not in the way you're thinking. There was no mileage for you and Tom. Emotionally, you ended it before it actually ended."

Impressed with his assessment, my eyebrows hike up. Does Liam understand he's the reason why I could forget about his brother so easily?

He clears his throat. "He told me he visited you last night."

Smiling sadly, I nod. "It's hard to keep turning someone down, but I can't let him think there's any hope."

Talking about Tom is spoiling my mood. It's ruining my reconnection with Liam. "I should meet up with Ash and the others," I say, standing to gather my things. "Thanks so much for dinner."

Lowell comes to kiss me goodnight, letting Liam walk me to the door. "Let's meet up," Liam suggests.

Torn between wanting and needing to keep this professional, or indulging in my Liam fantasy, I say, "I want to see you in my clinic."

There's a beat of silence. Then: "Okay."

"I'll text you," I reply, brushing my lips against his cheek, forcing myself to leave.

SINCE MY TV INTERVIEW, the phone has been ringing non-stop. My regular clients seem to want to come more often, and they've also recommended a friend or two to book in for a tune-up. I shouldn't complain, but the timing is awkward. It's put flat hunting on the back burner, leaving me four days to decide where I'm moving before the landlord starts gutting the place.

At times, I consider leaving London and living somewhere cheaper and quieter. But I don't really want to do that - I love London. I love this part of London too, and it doesn't take *that* long to visit my family. But Watford isn't a commutable distance to my practice, so going home for a month or two while I find time to scour the rental market is not feasible.

Liam is my last client of the day, though really he's not a client in the usual sense of the word. For starters, there's no way I'll allow him to pay; he'll receive free back treatment for life. And if I'm giving this friend thing a go, then I need to get used to spending more time with him. It's not going to be easy, but I've decided that I'd rather he was in my life than not at all.

The gentle-sounding bell of the front door rings. For security reasons, I vet anyone trying to enter the building Salma and I manage. When I see it's Liam waiting at the front door, I buzz him through to the small space that we use as a waiting room. Aside from the four chairs, there's a white, sterile-looking desk where Salma and I will sometimes wait for delayed patients, writing up notes and finishing up paperwork. There's a leafy green plant in the corner by my clinic door, one by hers, and health magazines to read.

Painted in a soft, relaxing green, my room is about four metres square. I have two high-spec tables in here according to need. If I wanted to, I could work in tandem with a colleague while they assessed their own patient on the second table, but most patients want privacy when they're in pain. And to be honest, it's nice to have some space to work in, to step into when I've finished being up close and personal with my clients.

When Liam enters, his mischievous eyes capturing mine, I get that punch in the heart sensation that I seem to get all the time with him. Dark navy jogging bottoms showcase his masculine lower half, a fading charcoal hoodie with a university logo on it covers his body. He starts to take it off, the short-sleeved T-shirt he's got on underneath lifting up over his stomach.

A lovely set of tight abdominals greets me. Again. I've seen them many times now, and every time I peek at them my breathing thins out. Surreptitiously, I scan his torso while his head is hidden under the soft fleece material, but I make sure I meet his eyes when his head pops out from underneath his hoodie.

Liam stretches out on the table. Despite the top he's wearing, the delicious definition of his back muscles is starkly obvious.

Attempting to distract myself from the visual, I mumble, "How've you been?" It's only been five days since I saw him, but I made sure to book him in as soon as possible for a proper assessment after his treadmill stumble.

"Good. I'm taking the doc's advice and doing my exercises."

Placing my hands on his covered back, I start checking out his joints and muscles. "A doctor listening to medical advice - who knew it was possible?"

"I know," he agrees, and I can hear the smile, imagining those dimples beaming my way like they were when he arrived.

"Were you in pain in France?"

"Not really."

Hmm. That's interesting.

The next few minutes are spent on clinical work, giving instructions and making sure everything's good since his accident.

"Did you get in touch with the massage therapists I texted the details of?" Regular massages, in conjunction with the daily exercises, would help Liam achieve a pain-free future. Unless he falls off treadmills that is. But in between those catastrophic, excruciatingly painful times I helped him, he admitted to occasional back twinges and soreness, so he really does need to keep on top of this.

"I managed to meet with David, but I didn't especially get on with him."

"Oh? I thought you got on with everyone." He certainly seems to be easy to get on with. I expected Liam to like everyone he ever met, striking up conversations left, right and centre.

"Nope. I only get on with people I want to get on with. And the woman had a full client list and couldn't make time for me, so I've no idea if she'd be any better."

A stupid thought enters my head and I voice it without giving it the very necessary second thought it deserved. "I can give you a massage."

The offer floats in the room for a long second, and then Liam's raising his head and turning to look at me over his shoulder. His hazel eyes are bright and enticing under the spotlights. Quietly, he murmurs, "Thanks."

To be honest, I expected him to dismiss my offer, to argue with me a little bit. But no - he just gratefully accepts, a small smile hitching his lips as he swings his legs down to the floor. Reaching over his shoulder, he grabs a handful of his T-shirt, and then he's pulling it over his head, standing there in front of me completely shirtless.

My breathing turns thin again.

I must not look, I must not look, I must not...

My eyes drop to his chest, sweeping over the lean muscles of his pecs and skimming down his abs to the waist band of his joggers. His body is a marvel, flat and toned and muscular. The right amount of muscles I like on a man. They're obvious, but don't label him as a gym junkie, even though I know he goes. Ultimately, he has far more important things to do than that, like helping the sick, and finding time to see a chiropractor who might just love her job an awful lot right now.

"Are you getting a good look?" he asks, and the low, heated tone of his voice makes my body clench.

My eyes drift back up to find him smirking, his eyes sparkling. In France, for obvious reasons, I tried not to notice his body, but now I can admire freely. "Having a strong core will help your back," I state with professionalism. "Keep up the gym work." His eyes glitter at me, so I gesture him back onto the table. "Speaking of, how's your gym buddy?"

"Lowell's good."

From a white glossy cupboard, I retrieve the small bottle of massage oil and a fresh towel.

"I think my hands are warm enough," I say softly, coming back to stand near Liam's head. Warmth radiates to every corner of my body as I note each delicious muscle. For the first time, I'm nervous about touching him so blatantly. My job is a tactile one, but generally clothes stay on, and a back massage certainly isn't something I normally offer. In fact, the last time I gave a man a massage was Aaron.

Fuck, why does he have to pop into my head *now?*

I squeeze a few drops of oil onto my palm and rub my hands together, the aromatic, botanical scent of it hitting my nose.

"I'll start at the trapezius and deltoids and all the muscles underneath before working my way down, but let me know what feels good."

"Yeah, okay," he says, my hands meeting his gently rounding shoulders.

Conversation, something I'm pretty good at, flies out of my head. My heart races in my chest. All I can do is try and concentrate on my fingers, and pushing the right amount of pressure through my muscles into his.

There's a deep, very male groan. "Oh, that feels good. Yeah, right there," he husks. And Lord, I feel that sound right in my puss, things tingling down there that have no right to be tingling. I massage out the knots, the muscles feeling looser. And then I work my way down his back, focussing on one side of his body and then the other, digging deep and eliciting more masculine, satisfied sounds.

Those sounds of pleasure have me on high alert, actively listening for more of them. My chest and neck feel overwhelmingly hot right now, moisture gathering between my legs.

"I've been missing out," he ventures, a little sleepy. "I didn't realise massages could be so good."

"Do you mind if I tug your joggers down a little? I just need to get to the lower back a little better."

"Sure," he replies, lifting his hips when I grip the material.

Everything on his body narrows down the lower the waistband travels revealing a trim, tight waist and divots in his lower back. The top swell of his buttocks come into view and I immediately stop. "No boxers?" I ask.

"Not today."

I quirk my eyebrows, knowing he can't see me. He could've said, though I think this is probably just how Liam rolls: unfazed, daring, provocative.

"Just as well I didn't keep pulling," I murmur, my hands smoothing out any tension in his external abdominal obliques.

If I'm not careful, I'll massage his back until my hands turn raw, so I sweep my hands into the hair at his nape, Liam making an unintelligible noise. Then, with some reluctance, I pull my hands away, finished. But I saw that under my palms his body erupted in goosebumps, a shiver running through him. "You feel good. Ordered and loose."

His exhale is long and slow. After a few seconds, he lifts himself up off the table and drops down to the oak laminate floor, his eyes dark and dilated. "You, Nora Moretti, are a fucking god-send."

We share a smile, Liam standing barely two feet away from me, relaxed and very easy on the eye.

"Happy to help. Any time," I add, noticing my voice just got a bit gruffer.

"I don't want to take advantage of you."

I definitely don't imagine Liam's voice being deeper than normal, gravel-rough. "You're not. I offered because I wanted to, as a friend. Not because I feel like I owe you."

"Good. Though it feels very one-sided at the moment - this new friendship thing," he elaborates. "Maybe there's some way I can help address the imbalance."

"Like what?"

"I don't know," he says watching me closely. "How's the flat-hunting going? Do you still need to move out?"

"Oh, yeah."

"How long before you have to pack up your things?"

"Well, to be honest, I'm already packed up. I have until Sunday."

Trying to deviate from this topic of conversation, I pass Liam his clothes before tidying away the used towel and wiping down the bed.

"Got a place in mind?"

"Um, not really."

"What does that mean?"

"It means worst-case scenario I'll move in with Ash and her boyfriend for a few weeks until I can find something that works for me. I've been saving for a deposit on my own place but it's taking longer than I want."

Watching Liam dress shouldn't be so visually stimulating, but it captures all of my attention. Powerful shoulders roll as the hoodie comes over his head, and then he's dragging it down his jaw-dropping physique. Dressed, he leans casually against the table, his arms folded across his chest as I offer him a glass of water.

"Why don't you move in with me?"

I could weep. Weep for the refusal I'm about to give him and the sorrow that will fill my heart as a result, and weep for his beautiful offer to help.

"I'm not sure that's a good idea."

"Why?"

"Come on, Liam. I broke up with your brother a few weeks ago. I doubt he'd be all that happy." I don't say that I overheard Tom's accusation on the plane. That there's maybe something developing between us that Tom was right to be concerned about. Not that I plan on doing anything about it. Especially as Liam seems to want to keep me friend-zoned.

"He doesn't have to know. Anyway, he's still furiously writing his book, so he's a bit preoccupied."

"I don't want to lie by omission."

Liam nods, accepting my tolerances. "How about you move in as an emergency pit-stop. Sunday is around the corner. You need a safe place, and I can offer that. It can be days or weeks, and once you've found a place you like, we can let him know because it was just a temporary thing."

I look off towards the window, privacy glass obscuring the view onto the pavement.

"It's a three bed. You get your own bathroom."

"I appreciate it. Let me think about it?" I offer, my gut screaming at me to accept, my brain admiring my caution.

Grabbing my flask of water, I take several gulps, Liam telling me, "Okay, but there's room for you." He pulls out his phone. "I'll change your name in my contacts to Roomie."

I laugh. "Don't get ahead of yourself." And then a cunning thought enters my head. "Oh, I know! You could invite Harriet's housemate to move in - Ruby was it? Problem solved!"

"Not a fucking chance. If it's not you, it's no one."

The fiercely spoken words cause me to choke on my own breath, my inhale going down the wrong tube. Unsure how to respond to his declaration - if it even was one - I just hack up my lungs, tears streaming down my cheeks.

"Jesus, Nora - do I need to perform the Heimlich on you?" Liam moves behind me, his palm slapping my upper back as I hunch over trying to be discreet but epically failing. My windpipe feels about three millimetres wide as I snatch in strangled breaths. My chest feels tight and my throat raw. It has echos of an allergic reaction, though it's obviously not remotely close. Finished pounding on my back, Liam comes to my side, wiping away the tears staining my cheeks. "Better?"

I nod, unable to find my voice yet. Quietly, he teases, "You're such an attention whore."

"Shut up," I croak.

Smiling, he settles me against the table, opening his mouth to say something else by the looks of things. I cut him off. "Don't tease when I can't fight back," I reprimand hoarsely, my voice even huskier than usual.

"While you can't talk and therefore object, how about we discuss this living with me topic again."

Brushing back my hair from my face, I pin him with a look. The playfulness is all gone now, replaced with something milder. Something earnest. In a moment of weakness I groan in acceptance. "Okay. I'll do it. I promise to get organised quickly."

His jaw works, but I think it's to hide a victorious smile on that beautiful mouth of his. It only draws my attention to his lips, specifically the sharp peaks of the cupid's bow before they curve into his usual, naturally wide, full mouth. And even though I happily look at his dimples whenever they're displayed so beautifully, I don't need any more visual reminders of why this is still a bad idea.

"There's no rush," he says, placing my flask in my hand. Lifting his plastic cup of water, he toasts, "To my new roomie." We sip from our drinks to seal the deal, Liam mashing his lips together, licking them clean of water.

I tear my eyes away from his mouth and gather my things.

After securing the building and locking up, we head north. When we arrive outside my block of flats, Liam and I hug each other goodbye. The first time this happened was at the airport, when we said goodbye for what I thought might be the final time. Afterwards, I analysed whether it was better or worse than a quick kiss on the cheek, and I've decided hugging is much worse.

Because now I know what his body feels like standing up, not lying down. I know how perfectly his body fits to mine. How his arms gather me around him. How his palms flatten against my back and seem to press me into his skin, his muscles, his warmth. I know how his long stubble feels against my temples and cheeks, and how alluring his cologne smells. I know I want to stay in the cocoon of his arms, wallowing in the shared closeness, feeling our hearts pounding in our chests for three simple seconds.

It's so *so* much worse.

His mouth finds my cheekbone, a soft kiss placed there. "See you soon," he says, pulling away.

CHAPTER ELEVEN

Liam

AFTER WORK ON THURSDAY, I take a small diversion and drive by Nora's clinic to see that the lights are off. Surprised, I pull to the kerb and call her number through the hands-free. Recently, I learnt that this is her late night; I thought she'd be with a client.

"Hey."

She sounds surprised and happy all at once, and it makes my blood thrum. "Hey. Is everything okay?"

"Yes, why?"

"I just passed your work and the lights were off. I thought you might have a client."

"Oh, no. They cancelled this afternoon, and I wasn't able to fill it, so I'm home now."

In the background, I hear a door close, and I imagine her in her bedroom with boxes all packed. I've not been to her flat, and now I won't get the chance.

"What are you up to tonight?"

Her voice turns subdued. "Not much. Ash is working late so it's just me here all on my lonesome."

"Do you want some company?"

"You can't come here," she panics. "The place is a tip."

"You really don't want me to see your flat do you?"

"It's nothing personal," she responds, chuckling.

"I think you've got a giant poster of me on your bedroom wall, next to your other favourite Liam - Liam Hemsworth, or maybe that dude out of One Direction." Her laughter barrels down the phone line, making me smile. "Or is it the life-size image of me on the living room wall? That's why you didn't want to move out, isn't it? That's why the landlord wanted it back so badly."

"Damn, how did you know? Once she saw it she was very insistent, it's true."

"Have you eaten? Come round for some dinner." Checking for traffic, I move back onto the road with only one destination in mind. "I'm five minutes away. I'll pull up outside your building and wait for you." I might not have been invited inside, but I know her address.

"Erm, okay."

Quickly, before she has a chance to change her mind, I call out, *Bye* and hang up.

I head for Granger Mansions, dark clouds rolling over the city. It's been thundering and raining on and off all day. I find a space further down the road, and as I'm not sure if Nora will recognise the car, I get out and walk towards her building.

As I approach, she exits the main door, scanning the parked cars. I call out her name, her head instantly jerking my way. Watching her walk towards me with her hair bouncing around her shoulders and a happy smile on her face, fills up my heart with strange emotions. For a second, I start to feel overwhelmed with feelings, thinking that this is how it's always meant to be, me calling out her name and Nora responding.

Wearing a pair of dark jeans and a silver blouse tucked in at the waist, I step towards her and hold her close. Her lilac-scented hair and watermelon imbued skin rushes my head as I lean down and kiss her cheek.

"You look pretty," I say, pulling back.

I've surprised her because she struggles to regain her composure, but I want to tell her all the time how beautiful she is. At how often I think about her.

Her eyes smooth over my shirt, tie, and trousers. "You look very handsome and professional. I think I've seen it all now: tuxedo, work attire, sweatpants, trunks, and," she grins, "a towel."

When our eyes lock, hers are dancing with mirth, and I'm pretty sure they mirror mine.

"Which version's your favourite?" I lead.

"Gotta be the trunks 'cos that means we're back in France, swimming in the lake."

I nod, loving her answer, unable to resist adding, "By that definition, then so's me in a towel."

We share a laugh as we get in the Mercedes and buckle up, heading towards mine. Once we're parked, we head for the lift, and I use the special access card to reach the penthouse. I try not to make a big thing about it, but Nora notices.

"You didn't tell me you lived in a penthouse," she accuses as we ascend.

"Would it've made a difference to you living here?"

If she noticed my living arrangement preference - that she *lives* here rather than *stays* here, it goes over her head.

"No, it's just that when you've talked about your flat, you said it had the best views because you were on the top floor."

"I do have the best views because I'm on the top floor. It's not my fault you didn't equate top floor with penthouse."

Playfully, she glares at me.

When we reach my floor, a bell chimes to announce our arrival like some pretentious arsehole. The doors open, Nora stepping out and looking down the hall with its large mirror and pale wood floors.

"Come on," I say, walking to my front door. The reason I liked this penthouse above all others I checked out is that, firstly, I could afford this one, and secondly, it had a little vestibule out here. I'd rather people didn't come up in the lift and straight into my private space.

Nora follows, painfully quiet. "Let's hope we don't regret this," she murmurs.

"We won't."

"I'm only moving in to spite you."

I smirk at her mock-cross face before unlocking the door. Showing Nora my apartment has my heart galloping away from me. Yes, this is a spectacularly bad idea, but I want Nora in my home. I'd rather burn than never look at the fire, fearful of what damage it might cause if I just dared to be brave. I'd rather upset my brother in my pursuit of her than to have never tried.

Because this is what life is - it's for living, for grabbing every opportunity. Nora told me much the same, so her caution is frustrating. It makes me wonder whether I've misread this. Misread her.

Briefly, my mind darts to Aaron.

"Don't say I didn't warn you when this all implodes," she begins, "and I start blocking your number."

I grin, Nora delivering me her usual knock-out smile. I push the door open, Nora glancing through the doorway and into the place I call home.

CHAPTER TWELVE

Nora

LIAM IS BEING INFURIATINGLY attentive and helpful right now, but as I step through the door into his penthouse apartment my mind stops focusing on how discombobulated I'm feeling. Because holy guacamole! This place is something else. Something I'd regularly see in the property supplements as I flipped through the pages, dreaming, wishing. Fantasising that my salary could stretch far enough for a mortgage on a flat half as decent as this.

My head is a battleground of emotions, my heart pounding with each delicious discovery. There's a pale oak door to my left and right, one hiding a coat cupboard and the other the WC. Beyond, the flat opens up into a wide, deep living space, decorated in blues and charcoals with accents of silver. There's a wood burner with a huge flat-screen TV above it, a massive U-shaped sofa facing it. There are cabinets and other seating arrangements, a sideboard with photos of his family hidden amongst some plants, and a bank of glass behind which is a cute terrace and a view to die for.

Instinctively, my feet take me to the black, aluminium-framed sliding doors. Silently, Liam follows, letting the modern grandeur of his flat speak for him. After he unlocks the doors we step outside, a light breeze ghosting over my body.

"It's south-facing," he confirms as I spin around, trying to determine the location of the setting sun in relation to our view. A glass balcony is all that separates us from a twenty-storey drop to the pavements of Pimlico. Large potted plants act as a screen from other nearby buildings. A table and four chairs are situated to one side, while two wooden loungers face due south.

Liam points out landmarks I'm too disconcerted to work out for myself. "This is beyond gorgeous. I'm so pleased I already agreed to your mad suggestion or else I'd look very shallow right now."

Liam scoffs. "I know you better than that. Besides, I think the only reason you agreed is because of Nippy. Come on," he cajoles, leading me back indoors. "You need to see the kitchen."

"I didn't realise you were so sexist."

A deep-dimpled smile. "A woman needs to learn her place."

I shove his arm, knowing exactly where the kitchen is. It's directly in front of me as I return to the living room, beyond it. Unsurprisingly, it's also impressive. There's a bank of pale units all along a wall with built-in ovens. Parallel to it is a long island with a double sink, allowing a view through the wall of glass where we've just been standing. Everything is cool, sleek stone or composite materials, interspersed with chrome taps and groovy gadgets. When Liam flicks a switch, neon lights appear just under the worktop edge. It's so preposterously trendy I shriek with laughter.

"Oh my god! Can this place be any cooler?"

"I didn't choose the kitchen," he admits. "It was already in when I exchanged contracts."

"But you love it," I guess, to which he just looks reluctantly pleased. "What's not to love," I concur, taking it all in. "Where is the little guy, anyway? I want to meet him."

Liam scans the floors. "Maybe through here. The bedrooms are this way," he says, placing a hand on my lower back and nodding his head in the direction of the hallway. We're basically moving in a line from the front door, right through the heart of the penthouse, and through a door that leads to several rooms.

"Office," Liam says, pointing. "Bathroom." More pointing. "You have the choice of these two rooms. And that door there," he adds, indicating a door that is dead ahead rather than off the hallway, "is me."

Something grey and green, about twenty centimetres long, emerges from behind the partially ajar door that leads to Liam's bedroom. I can't see much beyond some buff-coloured carpet and some furniture, and although I'm burning with curiosity to enter his room and look around, the tortoise has all of my attention.

Dropping to my knees, I reach out a hand to Nippy's shell, trailing my fingers over the rough bumps and shapes of the carapace. "So how old is he?"

"Twenty-nine."

"What?" I stare at Liam as he squats next to me. I hoped he was ancient, but for some reason, I didn't expect him to be this old. "Did I hear you right?"

"I got him when I was four. He was already two. "

A smile hitches my mouth, imagining four-year-old Liam. Is it possible to ache for the guy any more? Even so young he must've been the cutest, especially with those dimples and cheeky smile, wanting the most original pet.

My insides go squishy with emotion.

"He's older than me. That's an insane thought."

I admire the patterns on the shell, finding Nippy's movements so comical. He makes me smile; he makes me want to full-on laugh at how unbearably cute he is, but I settle for watching Liam and him shower each other with affection.

I think my ovaries explode. Watching them together, interacting like old friends makes my heart die a thousand deaths. If he's this sweet to a pet, how loving will he be to his children? His heart would overflow for his own flesh and blood.

Composing myself, I stand, Liam following suit.

"So," he picks up, "you get this bathroom basically."

Trying to ignore the flood of hormones surging through me, I check out the charcoal portraits on the walls. Simple in design, they are still profoundly evocative. They remind me of Picasso's charcoal sketches, the ones of the dog and the penguin. "I love these," I say, moving to stand in front of the one of a young girl, a basket in her hand. A nose is depicted by a slash, the eyebrow and eye a short stroke and a dot.

Three other sketches are hung on the walls; a boy; another girl - but older than the first image; a Labrador, ears up with curiosity.

"Are these yours?"

Shyly, "Yeah."

"Liam," I say, unable to tear my eyes away from his. "They're *incredible*."

"Thanks," Liam says quietly, before he walks to the bathroom and pushes open the door.

"This is Tom as a boy, isn't it?" I ask, not ready to let him just walk away. "Tilly and Fay, too." Liam's eyebrows rise on his forehead, surprised at the recognition. "You're very talented," I praise, but it seems difficult for him to hear.

When I asked him if he drew, he said *I used to*. Why did he stop when he's this good?

Peering into the bathroom, I see a whole load of fitted units, some pale marble, a white sink and other essential stuff. Then I'm shown the first bedroom which is opposite the bathroom. My heart lifts as I scan the room. Bigger than my current bedroom by a lot, it has a fitted wardrobe, a big bed, and a lemon and cream colour scheme. "Pretty," I say, walking to the closet to see it's deep, and more than enough space for my things. A window gives me a north-facing view towards Victoria and Buckingham Palace.

"When my sisters stay over, Tilly sleeps in here."

Sudden, guilty thoughts cloud my head. "Shit, I completely forgot about your sisters. I can't steal their rooms."

"Stop worrying. They can share. Either this one, or," he says, walking out of the yellow room to enter the room next to the bathroom, "you can have this one."

This room is cream too, but with teal accents. With it's own south-facing balcony, it's my preference.

It's hard to work out my feelings. I'm incredibly grateful for the offer to stay here, but I also feel ashamed. Like I'm in second place again. Like I don't belong here and shouldn't be here, taking a bedroom away from his siblings, imposing. Swallowing, my throat feeling dry, Liam comes to stand at my side as I gaze out of the floor to ceiling windows, my head tumbling with thoughts.

"You're very quiet. What's going on in that head of yours?"

"I'm thinking, where will your family sleep?" Tilly lives in Kent, Fay in Surrey, both of them regularly staying over. Does he have an air mat, or maybe a sofa bed somewhere? Perhaps I should have that instead.

"They can all bunk in together. Or if you're feeling really guilty, give up your room and bunk in with me."

I laugh quietly, knowing he's teasing but wishing he wasn't. "I'm thinking I shouldn't have given in."

His warm hand comes to my waist, firm and secure. "You're not backing out. I won't let you."

"This place....it makes me feel... insecure."

He frowns. "What do you mean?"

"Maybe it's more emotional," I guess, trying to work out why I'm feeling so out of sorts. "I don't want to appear ungrateful, Liam, because this is a lovely place and a huge offer, but it feels like I shouldn't be here."

Already I'm talking as if I'm here for longer than the agreed short stay while I get my shit together, panic fluttering along my veins in case Liam notices. But I already know that staying for only a month, say, won't be enough. I'd feel short-changed knowing I could've stayed here for longer, even though I have no claim to it.

Moving in goes against all my pragmatic, rational thoughts, but moving out before I'm ready, before we've maybe had a chance to explore what we seem to be heading for, would be even more non-sensical.

Liam uses the hand wrapped around my waist to direct me until I'm facing him. Being a coward, I avert my eyes, not wanting him to see the raw emotion that's swirling inside me. My hands hang awkwardly down by my sides so I lift them to his hips, hooking a finger into a belt loop.

Normally, we don't touch like this. It smacks of danger. I blame his earlier comment about looking pretty for opening the floodgates, because since then, I've felt his hands on my back, on my waist. I've felt his eyes feasting on me as I wander around his flat, admiring and looking. Liking.

His touch elicits frissons and shivers which I try and ignore. We're meant to be friends and nothing more, and it's the only reason I'm brave enough to reach for him too, even if it's just his clothes, something to hang off.

Trying to be more upbeat, I joke, "Must be getting my period."

"Oh God, you don't get those do you?"

"'Fraid so."

A soft chuckle. "I have two sisters. I know everything there is to know about periods, so consider this is a safe place if you want to weep or rage or mope. Just never ever believe you don't belong here, in this apartment, with me. Because you do." I feel his gaze like I do the heat from his palms, burning through my silver blouse, incinerating it until all I can feel is his skin against mine. "What's really the problem?"

I shrug, looking up and seeing so much kindness and empathy. "Perhaps I'm just relieved." Relieved I have this safe space, this gorgeous home, even if it's temporary. But it also terrifies me because one day I'll have to leave. One day, Liam will have a girlfriend, then a fiancée, a wife. He won't want me living here alongside them, cluttering up the place. And where will I go? Will I have enough money to buy my own flat by then? Will there be a Mr to my Miss to share it all with?

Liam folds me into his body, my chin tucking into his chest as I rest my head against his jaw. It's so effortless, so natural. It's as if we've done this a thousand times.

"You can stay as long as you like. There's no pressure and no limit." I exhale through my nose, wondering if he can read minds. "Come on, we need some wine and some food."

With natural ease, Liam collects one of my hands that idles at his waist and gathers it into his own. It feels so good. So comforting and grounding. Then he's tugging me out of the bedroom and down the hallway into the main room. Releasing me, he opens a wine fridge in the island and selects a bottle. Then he turns behind him to the long bank of units and grabs two glasses. Once the wine is poured, he taps on his phone. A few seconds later, a song by Wolf Alice comes through some hidden speakers.

"I love these guys."

He nods, because he already knows this.

I lean on the island, singing along to *Don't Delete The Kisses*, as Liam grabs things out of the fridge.

"What can I do?" I enquire.

"Nothing."

A packet of fresh tortellini and various salad items sit on the counter, waiting to be prepped. Once the pasta is cooking, Liam says, "I'm pretty nervous cooking for an Italian girl whose parents run a restaurant."

I offer him a reassuring smile. "I wouldn't worry. No one eats there - the food's awful. I bet your version is better."

He shakes his head, amusement painting his mouth.

Before long, we're on our second glass of wine as another thunderstorm roars above us, the terrace lashed with heavy, pelting rain. We finish dinner at the island and head over to the sofa, Liam switching on some side lamps.

When he opens a second bottle, I begin to feel light-head. Training for a triathlon has resulted in a reduced alcohol intake, so I abandon my glass on the coffee table and stretch out on the sofa. Liam does the same, which means we're facing each other in the corner of the U-shaped couch, our heads only a foot apart. My stomach is full, my head woozy, and Liam looks distractingly handsome in the dim light, his eyes twinkly and inviting.

"Thanks so much for having me."

"You're welcome."

"What happens if I fail your trial period?" I lead, thinking about the next few days. "Maybe I should sabotage it," I add on, grinning to myself.

A scoff. "Do your worst."

I laugh, giving my idea some consideration. "Seriously, though. You must've shared a place as a student. What winds you up? What would be the worst thing I could do?"

Liam concentrates on my question, his chin resting on his overlapping hands, our postures mirrored. "Being messy, I guess."

"That's it?"

A shrug. "To be honest, I hate it when girls wander around braless in thin T-shirts. It really bothers me."

I snort, reaching for my wine and taking a gulp. "Interesting that you brought that up, because guys without shirts on are just inconsiderate slobs in my opinion. All those muscles on show for no good reason? So annoying."

"No one wants to feel uncomfortable in their home, trying to avoid staring at perky breasts all evening. I mean, I've got dinner to cook and laundry to do."

"Waltzing around the place in just their tracksuit bottoms accentuating a tight arse and muscled thighs," I continue as if he hasn't spoken. "Are they trying to make me hunger for something other than the dinner they so kindly cooked for me?"

"Being half-dressed does save on all that laundry though."

"True. I could help you with that small pile of laundry if you wanted to provide the washboard abs," I offer selflessly. I've seen his torso, and it is mouth-watering.

A deep laugh rumbles out of his chest, vibrating the air between us. "Don't expect me to wash your tiny lace thongs though. I hate those things."

"Don't worry, I prefer to be naked under my leggings. Stops the VPL."

"That's thoughtful of you," he throws back, stretching out his arm to snatch up his glass. The movement of his Adam's apple when he swallows is distressingly masculine, his cologne wafting over me like a hypnotic drug as he shifts again, replacing his glass. "Because red underwear has a habit of turning my whites pink, and even though I consider myself a modern man, it's not really my colour."

Slowly, his eyes fall to my cleavage. His gaze is just a brush, but it has fire roaring across my skin when he brings his eyes back to mine. There's the softest hint of a smile on his mouth, and I'm suddenly aware of how much I must be revealing, facing him, on my front like this with the blouse gaping open.

"I can see how that would be a problem. As you know, if I *do* wear underwear, I prefer it cream or white." I'm wearing a cream bra tonight, one he probably just got a glimpse of.

Liam's focus does not waiver, the air thickening. "I remember."

Breathing suddenly feels really difficult.

"It sounds like this could work out," I say, my voice frayed. I'd love to fall into the moment and see where it leads because I'm getting so many signals from Liam. "I know what bothers you, you know what bothers me. We've got this."

Reaching for our glasses, we make a toast. "Roll on the weekend," Liam announces, holding me hostage with a potent, breath-taking gaze.

CHAPTER THIRTEEN

Nora

BETWEEN ASHLEIGH AND I, the last few boxes for my belongings are piled up by the front door, ready to be taken downstairs and into Liam's car. I sent him a picture of how much there was to move and he was pretty confident it would all fit.

There was something rather troubling about my entire life fitting into a medium-sized car. Something inconsequential about the small pile of bags, boxes, and odds and sods I've collected over the years. And I know possessions do not maketh the man, or whatever the phrase is, but I can't help but make comparisons. Still, I have my work, and even if my personal life is lagging behind, professionally I am totally on my game.

Casting a last look around the living room to ensure I've not left anything, I lean into Ash for a big hug. We've already said our goodbyes a hundred times, but she still mumbles into my hair, "Don't be a stranger."

"Likewise."

"I want an invite round soon," she demands, pouting at me theatrically. A platinum blonde with grey, alluring eyes, she has a face made for the stage or screen.

"Deal. I hope everything goes smoothly moving in with Richard."

We pull apart, Ash gently pulling on one of my curls. "I'll miss you."

"Now, now," I tease, trying to be stoic. "We agreed no tears." An end of an era it might be, but we will always be friends.

"They're just crocodile tears," she objects. "Secretly, I've been counting down the days until I left you and this shit-hole behind."

"Well, that's good to know, because I'm running out of valuable storage space on my phone. Deleting all our selfies will help."

"Make sure you delete my number too."

"I took care of that already." We share a smile. It's riddled with false bravery and sadness, a bittersweet concoction. But there's also excitement and hope because she's moving on to good things, and I'd like to think this means I am too. "Better start lugging this downstairs. Liam will be here soon."

"First," Ash starts, licking her lips nervously, "I just wanted to say that I know this could be a complicated thing moving in with Liam, but this is the happiest I've seen you in a long time."

"Really?" Her words have me starting an internal analysis of my mood over the past few years. I was definitely down in the dumps when Aaron cheated on me, but I've been in a better place since, haven't I?

"When you met him at that party, you seemed conflicted, but happier. After France, you seemed sad but buoyant. Hopeful I suppose. Positive. Liam is a good influence, and while I can't predict if you two stand a chance, he brings out a good side of you. A side I've not seen in too long." She runs her hand down my arm. "Stop listening to Aaron, Nora. He doesn't deserve your attention nor your confidences about who you're seeing."

Immediately, I bristle. While Ash might not mean to criticise, that's how it sounds. She's telling me I've been foolish. That I'm still too trusting. "I can handle Aaron."

Ash pins me with an unconvinced look. "Aaron's the one handling you."

The words land like a bomb. They have my skin tingling, and not in a good way. "He's not. He's just trying to be a good friend when he was a shit boyfriend."

The answering pause lasts far too long. "Your choice," she eventually agrees. "Just... be careful with him."

"Will do," I mutter, my limbs feeling heavier now. Not only do I have to contend with a sad goodbye, but I have to listen to a reprimand from my bestie.

"Sorry. It comes from a good place."

Blowing out a breath, I admit, "I know."

For the next few minutes, Ash and I trudge up and down the creaky stairs, thankfully with help from Liam when he arrives. In the end, it just makes me pleased I didn't have much to call my own: no sofa, no bed, no sideboard or wardrobe. There is nothing in my room I want to take with me, nothing I have space for at Liam's anyway.

Everything gets loaded into the car, but even being efficient with space, the passenger seat is taken up with the final few boxes.

"I'll walk to yours," I suggest. "I'll find you in the carpark."

"Okay, have you got your new keys?" He eyes my handbag slung over my shoulder. After dinner the other evening, Liam handed over everything I needed to access his apartment. It was a nerve-wracking, thrilling moment. It felt so mature, so final. As if this was my life henceforth and forevermore.

"Yup."

"See you in a bit," he says, before getting in his car and driving off with all my worldly possessions. With a final glance at Granger Mansions, I tilt my head to the sun and pause for a second, soaking up the warmth, just needing a moment to reflect and breathe.

I hope I'm doing the right thing. Ignoring the fact that staying with Liam has the potential to tear two brothers apart, I take another deep breath. The fallout from this could be cataclysmic, and I'm suddenly plagued by guilt and indecision. Just how much am I willing to push for? For it all? Because living with Liam temporarily is one thing, but sleeping with him is a whole other ball game. And while I could dismiss our conversations as banter and friendly innuendo, there are too many instances where we're stepping over that boundary Liam quite clearly marked in the sand.

Has he changed his mind? Because I'm not prepared to jeopardise this tight friendship we have for a measly three months.

My ringing phone has me pulling my mobile out of my handbag.

Aaron.

Swallowing, I debate for all of a second whether to answer. Ash's warning is branded on my brain, and our last conversation - which coincided with my last night in France - was unsettling, Aaron asking me several difficult to answer questions about our time together. I wasn't sure if it was to see how good my memory was, or if it was to genuinely nudge his.

I've known him for eight years, the longest amount of time I've been friends with a guy, and especially an ex. Maybe this is why I can't shake him loose from my memory. Why he seems to take up so much room in my head still. Why I was so offended by Ashleigh's words. When people criticise him, it feels like they're criticising me. It makes me uncomfortable and wanting to take back some control. To maintain some ownership of a new dynamic between us, one that isn't tainted by the past.

"Hello?"

"Hey, Nora. How are you?"

Turning, I start walking slowly towards Liam's flat. "Hi. I'm good. How are you?"

The sound of his voice is annoyingly comforting, even though it makes my heart beat irregularly. It's frustrating that I react like this, with some kind of excited anxiety. It only ever happens when it's just us, talking casually on the phone. I'm not sure why I get so confused about him still because I'm fairly certain I still very much hate him, but I also wonder whether I still carry feelings for him. Complicated ones. Ones that need to disappear, and permanently. I don't like thinking he has some control over me still. That my heart hasn't mended properly, either through blatant refusal, or just because I'm a mess. I want to move on. I want a man who'll devote himself to me and push this idiot out of the confines of my defeated, conflicted heart.

"I just had to call you up and tease you about how famous you are now. What with you finding antique jewellery in bags of veg from Sainsbury."

I laugh softly, silently yelling friendly insults at Joe for sending the link of my interview to the group chat. They've all found it very amusing. "It was surreal."

"Which bit? Finding the ring or being on TV?"

"All of it, but especially the local news wanting to interview me. I nearly turned it down."

"It's a great story to tell your children one day."

The comment has my heart sinking. Maybe I should be able to get over comments like this between friends, ones that look ahead to our deviating futures, but before he went and threw away everything good in the world, I envisioned my child-filled future with Aaron.

"Yeah. I'm going to make sure I make a hundred copies, recording it to flash drives before burying them in time capsules to ensure my face and witty interview-style lives on well beyond my thirty-six thousand days on this Earth."

On the other end of the line, Aaron chuckles. "You looked really good. That's not changed."

Taking his compliment and stuffing it inside the very bottom of a deep, deep bag, I reply brightly, "Thanks. Is that what's prompted the call? To tell me I didn't look like a total hag?"

The pause is thick and dense, a smile I think I hear slowly fading. "I guess, I just needed to hear a friendly voice."

Up ahead I spot a side street, so I turn down it, away from the busy main road and speeding cars. "What's wrong?"

"I've been toying with an idea and I wanted your opinion on it." That strained pause returns, though this time there's no smile in his voice. No breathy exhale down the line. "I'm just...." A tight breath. "...I'm thinking of asking Beth to marry me."

I'm unable to extrapolate a single emotion from the hundreds that swarm me. All my old friends are there: rising resentment; returning self-doubt that I was never good enough; boiling anger at the betrayal; relief, aware that I can finally put him - and Beth - aside; resignation; reluctant joy at their happy news. And deep, profound sadness.

It's an endless cycle of depressing thoughts intertwined with a need for bravery and stoicism. Gathering some words, *any* words, I tell him, "Congratulations. It's about time."

Two years and ten months to be exact.

"...I realise it's probably difficult to hear."

His arrogance is astounding, but I'd be lying if I said I was unaffected. So I bluster out, "It's fine," faking a smile. "We were over a long time ago."

There's a pause. "I regret the way things ended between us," he says sincerely. "I've been thinking about you a lot lately."

Hearing that genuine attrition makes my heart clench. This is what I wanted to hear so many times. I wanted him to regret his actions, to remember that it was me he loved, but I'm not a fool. Once a cheater always a cheater.

A song by Dermot Kennedy comes into my head. It's titled: *Something to Someone.* At one point, I was a big deal to Aaron. I was important. Loved.

I want that again.

"I'm not sure thinking about me is a good sign," I deadpan.

"You're kind of memorable, Nora."

I gnaw at my lip, my heart tumbling and somersaulting. "I don't think you should dwell on the past."

"Nora, just hear me out, because I either ask Beth to marry me, or I break up with her and you let me make everything up to you. There's lots of unresolved emotion between us still. I miss you. I miss our conversations and... we had so much fun, didn't we? And we have a lot of history together, had a lot of good times - "

"You have that with Beth too," I point out.

"It doesn't feel the same."

"At one time you must've thought so," I remind him. "It was why we split up."

"We split up because you moved out. You wouldn't take me back. I had no choice but to stick it out with Beth."

Gob-smacked, my mouth drops open. "Wow, I'm sure she'd love to hear that you settled for her."

"I did settle. I regret cheating on you. It's my biggest regret."

Closing my eyes, I try and bolster my defence system from his words, words that have my heart racing.

"Joe told me that you split up with Tom."

Muttering a curse under my breath, I grit out, "He's the biggest gossip in all of England."

"Europe," Aaron corrects.

"Northern hemisphere," I amend, rolling my eyes and hating how I ease into recognisable, teasing territory with him.

There's a soft laugh on the other end of the phone. The familiar sound has memories surfacing, ones I've kept at bay for a long time. It has the corners of my mouth curling reluctantly. "I'm in a good place right now, Aaron. I can't entertain any nostalgia. You hurt me. You need to let me go. We had our moment."

"Some people get second chances. This can be ours."

"I've got to go," I tell him. "I'm moving into a new place and I need to get on." Refusing to divulge anything more - a woman has to have some secrets - I tell him, "I'll see you in a few weeks."

And then I hit the red button on my phone, ending our connection, wishing it would end the turmoil cycling through my gut. Because as much as Aaron called to float the idea of an engagement, the conversation took an unexpected turn.

The call had an ulterior motive. When I didn't cry on hearing his intentions with Beth, he tried a different tactic.

Ultimately, Aaron wants me back.

THE BOXES of books got shoved in the back of the big closet. A few items have been hung up so that they don't crease. Lying on my bed, I ignore all the other boxes and bags that need sorting out - they can wait until tomorrow. I should probably go and find Liam, even though I kind of want to hide in my teal accented bedroom right now. But I don't really have the option. Tonight, we're at a party.

Liam pokes his head into the open doorway, his eyes darting around the room. Earlier, he offered to help me unpack but I declined. "Did you find the WiFi code?"

"Yeah, thanks," I say, sitting up.

"Still up for a party?"

I'm tired, but spending the evening away from Liam's flat, distancing myself from my conversation with Aaron, could be a good distraction. Plus, I get to meet Harriet, who I'm very curious about. "Yeah. I need to get in the shower."

"Me too."

"Will the water pressure go mental if we shower together?" *Shit.* "I mean at the same time?"

A dark brow arches, the small movement indecent and naughty. "No. If this is the sort of arrangement you had in mind when I asked you to move in - "

I throw a pillow at him. Annoyingly, he catches it, throwing it right back with a huge grin on his face. I dodge the looming pillow, but end up rolling off the bed in a tumble of flying limbs.

"Owww," I grumble, attempting to get up off the floor. The carpet is lovely but not nearly thick enough to soften my fall by much. Liam stifles his laughter, but he can't hide the amusement dancing in his eyes as he leans over me.

It's hard not to picture him following me to the floor, pressing into me with that virile, male body, his strong arms caging me in.

Instead, he offers his hand. "You're determined to hurt yourself."

"Am not."

"If this is your attempt to get out of the triathlon, I'm not having it."

"Why?" I ask, rubbing my arm and hip.

"You're going to smash it. I want you to smash it. Anything hurt?"

"Just a little sore."

Nodding, he eases me to my feet so that I can perch on the edge of the bed. "In which case, I'm gonna get ready. Taxi's booked for seven," he informs me, squeezing my thigh tenderly before heading out of my room.

That gives me two hours, which is plenty of time.

My toiletries are already in the bathroom, along with a pile of fluffy towels, so I just grab my bathrobe and overanalyse every single touch and comment Liam and I have ever shared. Most of the time, I fixate on the night I met Nippy, when I was invited round for dinner and allowed myself to get carried away with the idea of Living With Liam.

That's how I'm going to consider this now, as an event, something worthy of capitals and easily abbreviated.

LWL.

The water is hot and relaxing, my mind soothed as I wash out the conditioner. After I dry myself off, I moisturise every inch of skin, prepping my hair with product to ensure the curls do what I like them to do - though that's a little hit and miss.

After two days of thunderstorms, today has been sweltering, so I wear a pretty summer dress and pair it with some sandals, grabbing a cardigan for later. I'm not normally one for much makeup. Usually I wear mascara to lengthen my lashes, sometimes I bother with some red lipstick, but I make my eyes smokey tonight, adding eyeliner and eyeshadow, really paying attention to what I'm doing.

I'm pleased with the results.

Liam is watching a sports channel when I go in search of him. Through the glass doors that overlook London, late evening light glints off windows and spires, the city lit up like a Christmas scene.

"That view," I say, reaching for a glass of red wine Liam holds out for me. "Does it ever get old?"

Liam doesn't appear to look out of the windows. Instead, he just seems to be checking me out in my black, knee-length dress. He shakes his head. "Not yet."

Looking very handsome in a navy polo shirt and some deep burgundy shorts, Liam runs a hand through his hair as we clink glasses, toasting, "To your first night of many."

If only.

Not long after, we're in the taxi, heading for Albert Bridge. Liam reminds me that Harriet is going to be there tonight, and about six of Jack's current or ex-girlfriends.

"Six! Why does he hang around with them all still? It sounds complicated."

"That's Jack's middle name. I happen to think most lawyers believe they can escape justice, or at least worm their way around the law, but his day will come," he says wryly.

"I hope I'm there to witness it. It sounds like it could be entertaining."

Soon, we pull up outside a Victorian property in Putney. Chatter from the rear garden can be heard out on the street, so instead of knocking on the front door, Liam leads me to the side gate and round the back. Fairy lights are strung up on walls and along gutters and pipes. Giant outdoor pillar candles glow from oversized lanterns. At least twenty, thirty people are here already, an industrial-looking barbecue and caterer set up at the back, smoke drifting across the sweet summer air.

I'm so hungry; it smells great.

"There's Jack," Liam says. "In the blue T-shirt."

I follow Liam's gaze to find Jack heading our way. "I thought I disinvited you," he says by way of greeting, before grabbing Liam in for a back slap hug thing that guys do.

"Nice try. The bouncers at the front door were a bit overkill though." They share a laugh before Liam levels his warm eyes on me. "This is Nora, my very good friend."

Jack leans in to kiss my cheek, and I do the same, blushing at Liam's sweet introduction. "Happy birthday!" I announce, holding up the gift I wrapped up in pale pink wrapping paper - all I had. "This is from us both, though the paper was Liam's choice," I joke. "Hope you like it."

Liam grunts. "I was all out of the unicorns and rainbows one."

Like Lowell, Jack is blond and of a similar height. If it wasn't for the low brow and blade-sharp jaw line, the sparkly blue eyes would tell you that they're brothers. Unlike Lowell though, Jack has a tidy, short beard. It makes me think of Liam's soft scruff.

Just then, Lowell approaches with a young woman who can only be Harriet. She has blonde, straight hair that falls below her shoulders, and I wonder if it's naturally wavy but had a straightening iron through it. Blue-eyed, she's a strikingly pretty woman. She looks at me with interest, her eyes skipping to Liam and then back to me again, but it's a look that is wholly good-natured. Teasing. A little bit mischievous and not at all malevolent.

I greet Lowell with a kiss on the cheek, and watch Liam do the same for Harriet, murmuring, *It's good to see you again* before he introduces us formally.

Gently, Harriet hugs me. "So pleased to meet you."

"Likewise. I've heard all about how you three met for the first time. It's incredible that you're now part of each other's lives."

Harriet smiles, looking up at Lowell. "It is. But I don't think I have the monopoly on meet-cutes," she replies wryly, looking at Liam and then me.

"That's true," Liam agrees. "I've never had someone so keen to know me that they launch themselves at me from a tree."

"Shut up," I say, shoving him on the shoulder.

"And that *dodgy* ankle. Excuses galore this one," he adds. His smile is so big, I get the full double dimples.

But I can't let him know how much I like them, so I roll my eyes, grumbling, "Oh my god."

"But if not for those eventful situations, maybe we'd never be friends."

I look at him then, my heart beating awkwardly, and not only because his voice turned from teasing to honey warm. Not having Liam in my life would be the pits. The end of the world. Ash was right when she said I've been happier since meeting him.

Feeling emotional, I turn my attention to Harriet who seems to understand my predicament immediately, saying, "I need to use the little girl's room. Come with?"

Ignoring Liam's concerned face and the short silence we leave behind, I follow Harriet towards the house and through a huge kitchen extension. She turns to me and says with a small laugh, "I really do need the loo, but it looked like you needed a moment."

Pushing my curls out of my eyes, I nod. I don't want to divulge my secret admiration, nor do I want to give it more consideration than it seems to be taking up already, but I do feel Harriet and I could be friends, especially if her and Lowell are together. And friends share personal things.

"It's hard to have such a good-looking friend sometimes."

"Oh yeah," she says, leading me down a hallway. "And those dimples got my attention while I was coming around after being knocked to the tarmac. I get it," she continues, taking the stairs. "Lowell has special dispensation to use the upstairs bathrooms," she whispers. "It's quieter up here, too."

Harriet is the type of girl who continues a conversation even through a door. I instantly love that about her as she enters a room off the upstairs hallway and closes the door, locking it. "It sounds like quite the predicament," Harriet continues, her voice only a little muffled.

"I've got used to it. Anyway, I like being his friend." Thankful for the barrier of the door and her inability to properly catch my tone, I hope it means she can't see through my bullshit.

"He's good fun," she confirms. "So is this the first time you've met Lowell and Jack?"

"Lowell: second time. Jack: first time."

"I've not seen Liam since he came to mine for cake and coffee, right after the accident," she voices. "You'll have to ask him if he misses Ruby!" she says, laughter sounding beyond the door.

"Oh, I heard about her. Is she still living with you?"

"No, she moved out."

"Do you still see her?"

"Not often. We text most weeks though."

The flush sounds and then the taps, Harriet coming out a few moments later. "I'll wait for you."

"I'm okay. I could do with a drink though."

Back downstairs, we pass through the kitchen, piled high with food items, balloons and presents, including mine and Liam's. Jack still hasn't opened it, which is a shame. It's an apron with the words *I'm grilling the witness* on it, under which is a picture of a barbecue. For a lawyer, it's totally apt.

Outside, we head towards the ice-filled tubs, bottles of various alcoholic drinks chilling inside. Harriet pours us some wine, and then, noticing a guy coming our way says cryptically, "Let's see what the evening delivers."

The guy, Aiden, seems to think he has a chance with Harriet, chatting away non-stop. But then Lowell is there with a hand on her waist, eyes hot and face cross at Aiden. Meanwhile, Liam looks bemused, but the expression is directed at his friend. When I catch his eye he just smiles, offering me a wink.

What's he playing at? What does he know?

Aiden manages to soak the crotch of his shorts with his beer, much to Harriet's amusement. When he asks her to help him out, to get the party games started, Harriet coaxes, "Pour a bit more beer on first."

Liam is grinning, but when I encourage, "I'll help too, if you soak it," his smile drops clean away. Meanwhile, Harriet and I exchange another look, our eyes lighting up. "Yeah," Harriet continues. "We've got to be able to suck it out of the material."

Aiden grins like it's his lucky night. Considering he's Jack's colleague - a lawyer - and that the men we came with are *right there*, he's not very bright.

"Lie down. Close your eyes," Harriet continues, passing Lowell her drink as if she's preparing to get down and dirty. I follow her cue, holding out my wine for Liam. Meanwhile, Aiden is stretched out on the grass, his crotch wet through, his eyes shut and a shit-eating grin on his face.

Click!

Phone in hand, Harriet takes a string of pictures, laughing. "It looks like you're so drunk you've passed out and pissed yourself!"

She shows us the photos while Aiden gets up, protesting. "Hey, I never agreed to pictures."

"Too bad," Harriet states.

"Fuck off, Aiden," Liam tells him. "Go and sexually harass someone else and see how far that gets you."

"That...It wasn't...I never..." he stammers. "My career will be over if you say that."

"Well fuck off then," Liam reminds him. "And stop being a dick."

Aiden heads off, muttering something about spare shorts.

When I look at Harriet, she has Lowell's hands gathered up in hers. They look so sweet together. So right.

In answer to something Lowell says, Harriet tells him, "Women fight off advances from overambitious men all the time." She looks meaningfully at me. "Right, Nora? I bet it's a problem for you, too."

I think I blush. At my two o'clock, Liam frowns.

"True. Some guys aren't easily dissuaded," I say, thinking of Tom. And Aaron. "But it feels like the ones I want to show some ambition in asking don't bother."

Approval laces Harriet's smile. "Their loss," she tells me, clinking her wine glass with mine as the men exchange confused glances.

"Who's not bothering to ask you out, Nora?" Liam asks.

I shrug. "Doesn't matter. Shall we get some food?"

We head to the tables which are laden with huge platters, overspilling with sausages, lamb kebabs, and spicy chicken pieces, some veggie options too. When we've loaded our plates, we head indoors to the salads and condiments and rolls.

"How do you like Harriet?" he asks, casting a glance into the garden where she stands wrapped up in Lowell's arms.

"She's great. I can see why Lowell likes her."

"Yeah, he does," he says, his voice low and considered. I think Lowell liking a woman is a new thing. A big thing.

Back outside, we collect a couple of beers and find some chairs, tucking into our food. August might be hot but the nights draw in quickly.

Even though we're busy devouring our food whilst observing Jack and his friends, there's an unmistakeable frisson between Liam and I. It's not tension, but...awareness. As if a new line has been drawn in the sand and we're both trying to work out who put it there and what it means. From my periphery, I can tell he's glancing at me, questions in his eyes. And when he's busy concentrating on his food, sometimes I cast a quick look at him, wondering what he thought about my earlier comment.

The ones I want to show some ambition in asking don't bother.

Does he know I was referencing him? Even though going out with Liam could be ruinous?

Raucous laughter to the right gains my attention, a group of three men surrounding the birthday boy, along with two girls. I wonder if they're Jack's exes.

"So who's your eye on?" Liam asks, looking over at the group I'd just been watching.

"I just wondered what they were laughing about," I explain. "I wasn't checking them out."

Liam settles back into his seat after dropping a beer bottle down by his feet. "Any of them look interesting?"

My eyes flicker back towards the men. They all look perfectly nice, laughing and joking around, but without talking to them I couldn't say either way. "No," I admit. "Why? Are you looking to fix me up with someone?"

Liam's eyes dance over my features. "No. Just thought I'd try and understand the type of guy you go for. The ones that aren't asking you out."

Nerves flutter in my stomach and I reach for my own beer, avoiding an answer by blowing out a defeated breath. "That's a deep hole I don't feel like falling down tonight," I say, hoping we can move the conversation in a different direction. It's silly really; I'm at a party with potentially lots of single men, but I'm sitting here, with my infatuation, wishing he could read my mind. Wishing he didn't care about his brother. Wishing I had met him first.

Liam sits quietly in the neighbouring chair. He has that contemplative look on his face. One that's part scheming, part analysing. "We should talk about it soon, though," he ventures, turning to look at me.

Dismissing him is impossible. Whether we're acknowledging it or not, we're getting closer, more intimate, broaching sensitive topics like the opposite sex when we've tried to avoid it for so long.

"Yeah, soon," I agree, watching a girl sling an arm around Jack's waist. "Does it make me a terrible feminist if I'm disappointed Jack's exes aren't scratching each other's eyes out yet? I was hoping for some entertainment."

"You're so bad."

"Like you don't agree with me," I throw back.

He wipes away a guilty grin. "To be honest, I was really hoping for some girls wrestling in some mud or something."

"Now who's bad?" His low, deep laughter brings a smile to my face, one I was desperately trying to hide. "Have you ever had women fight over you?"

Liam's eyes find mine. "If I tell you, then you need to be honest when I ask you some questions later."

Bribery. A trade of information. He must be desperate for those answers. "...Okay."

He pins me with a determined look when he says, "At university, a few times."

"A few times?! What happened?"

"It wasn't the same girls fighting over me, it was different relationships at different times with different girls."

"That doesn't paint a better picture, Liam. Is your dick diamond-encrusted or something?"

Shit, did I really just say that? I level a look at my beer bottle full of recrimination.

"Are you asking for a look?"

I smirk, but my heart is *frantic* right now. "Are there diamonds on it? Big ones?"

"That's for you to find out," he says quietly, bringing the bottle to his mouth. I can't control my breathing, because that sounded like an invitation. "That's a thing, isn't it? In Essex."

Recovering my breath, I answer, "I'm not sure it's only Essex boys with glitter-bombed dicks."

A corner of his mouth hitches. "What's it called again?"

"You're the doctor. Haven't you seen any pejazzled penises in the surgery yet?"

A low laugh. "Thank fuck. Pejazzled - *jeez.* I'm not sure I'd be able to keep a straight face."

Our laughter ebbs away when Liam asks, "Do you want to go soon?"

I swallow, my throat parched despite all the beer. That sounded like another invitation. An invitation to check out his anatomy. "To look at diamond-encrusted dicks?" Our eyes catch and hold, a devilish smile inching Liam's cheeks higher, those dimples popping and making my stomach dip and dive. He's not from Essex, he's from Suffolk, and I'm pretty sure there are no crystals or embellishments on his knob. Or rather, I hope there aren't because that's not something I'm into. "I'd like to talk to Harriet some more," I tack on quickly.

That smile slowly drifts away, but the fairy lights reflected in his eyes make them very twinkly. "If she shares anything about Lowell, tell me? She holds her cards close to her heart."

"Likes them mysterious, does he?"

"She's guarded. But not intentionally, I don't think."

I nod, shovelling in some potato salad. "By the way," I say, chuckling, "Harriet wants to know if you miss Ruby."

Liam curses softly under his breath. "She was a trip, but best avoided."

My plate is almost empty when I feel Liam's eyes on me for a long, heavy moment. "How about we give it another hour and go home?"

Home.

That word fills me with undeniable longing.

It's about 2130, and it's been a long day for me with a few clients first thing, and then the move. And the energy I've expended today on emotions and just *thinking* has worn me out. So home, sounds pretty fucking good.

"That gives us time for at least another two beers," I say by way of agreement.

CHAPTER FOURTEEN

Nora

DURING THE TAXI RIDE HOME, I tot up how many units of alcohol I've consumed. Whatever the sum, it's pretty high for me. Coupled with my general tiredness from the day, I feel like the alcohol has hit me harder than normal. Yet, the buzzy feeling in my blood tells me it's been a good day. That I made the right decision by moving in with Liam. And tonight has seen us inching closer and closer, testing some self-imposed boundaries, ones that were meant to keep a safe distance between us.

Wondering whether I should come clean about my brief talk with Aaron earlier is fleeting. It would only be necessary if I was giving his admission consideration. His behaviour was classically selfish, testing the waters before he committed to splitting up with Beth. And I don't accept his argument that I ended things. His behaviour was unforgivable.

I know my worth, and it's nowhere near where Aaron places it.

When we pull up outside our building it's close to 2300. In

the apartment, I kick off my shoes and pad towards the sink, placing my mobile on the worktop.

"Water?" I ask Liam, already getting two glasses out of the cupboard.

"Yeah," he agrees, a bottle of cold champagne in his hand. "I think we should celebrate you moving in though," he suggests, moving my phone to one side so that I can place two extra glasses out.

I smile, making a study of Liam as the cork explodes across the room, landing in a big bushy plant in the corner. His arms are tanned, strong. Prominent veins run over the backs of his hands and along his forearms, before disappearing under the material of his polo shirt at the bicep. I watch the muscle flex as he pours two flutes of bubbles. We're so quiet that the sound of them captures all of my attention, but then Liam is wrapping long, strong fingers around a glass and holding it out for me, his face angled down to mine.

We're close, inches apart. The only light we have is courtesy of the neon lights running along the underside of the worktop. It casts Liam in a strange, complimentary glow, and I wonder if it's the same for him when he looks at me.

"To living together."

"To living together," I echo, loving the simplicity of his words. At what they could promise.

Once we're halfway through our glass, Liam moves away, opening a drawer and bringing out a small parcel. It's about an inch thick and oblong-shaped. "This is kind of an anniversary present."

"A what?"

"It's just over two months since we met, and with you moving in, I think it's worth celebrating."

Referring to an anniversary I didn't know existed feeds something potent under my skin. It blooms, dense and thick like the numerous petals of a peony, the flowerhead heavy and weighted. Those words have me picturing us as a couple, as lovers sharing a special day.

Gingerly, I take the offered parcel, wrapped carefully in gold tissue paper with a silver ribbon. Despite feeling a little giddy from the champagne, I'm delirious with intrigue and happy surprise. I rip off the ribbon and paper to find a tiny book, the spine bound in blue cloth. The cover reads: When We Met #1, but it's the drawing of me below the words that has me seeking Liam's eyes.

They're molten but serious. Hungry but patient.

I look back down at the black-inked image. Facing front, it's a great likeness of me. My hair is a mass of tight waves, my eyes the exact same feline shape. And they hold so much emotion in them, something that looks like tortured desire, and I wonder if that's what I look like when I'm around Liam. The symmetry of my face is starkly obvious too, my nose straight and in proportion, a line down the centre of my face. My mouth is wide, the bottom lip fuller than the top, the peaks of my lips rounded off.

I might have studied every centimetre of Liam's features, but it looks like he's studied mine just as closely.

Placing my thumb in the centre of the pages, at the side, I bend back the book, feeling the tension. Slowly, I slide my thumb down the edge, twisting my wrist as my nail and thumb reveal page after page after page of hand-drawn images in the flip book.

I can't fathom how long this must've taken him. The detail is immense, the story disclosed on the pages exactly as I remember it.

The start is new information though, with Liam in his black tuxedo, walking towards a leafy oak. In the background are some shoes, a dress, a clutch, all revealed over several pages as he nears the rear of the garden. The pages continue quickly, revealing his approach towards the tree and when he looks up. I laugh when I see my legs hanging down from the thick branch, Liam's viewpoint of that night searing into my brain. And then he's under the tree, arms out. Pages fly by, my falling body getting caught up in his arms, and then we slide to the ground, me on top of him, straddling him.

The pages where we stare into each other's eyes seem to last and last, my heart in my throat at the obvious attraction. It has tears prickling behind my eyes, but I carry on, reaching the final pages with Liam alternating between grimaces and dimpled smiles, then the image of me kneeling at his side in my underwear, beaming brightly down at him.

Finished, I go straight back to the beginning again, racing through it and picking up all the pieces my brain was too slow to catch before. But a second view also reinforces every detail I picked up first time around too.

Finding words to express how happy I am, fail me. I'm so in awe of his talent, his skill, his creativity. At his rendering of our first encounter, which when sped through in ten seconds flat looks defining, serendipitous, a love for the ages.

"Liam," I croak. "This is...exquisite. I absolutely love it."

When I look at him in amazement, I'm stunned by the fierce expression aimed my way. But then it's gone, replaced with a quietly pleased smile. His expression alternates so quickly it's like another personal flip book, one which has my brain muddled in trying to keep up. But there's love there, I'm sure of it, or at the very least deep affection, before lust and then earnestness and entreaty.

I know what he's asking.

Stepping into his body I lift my face to his and close my eyes, kissing him on the mouth. Our lips meet for all of a second, but his talented hands coming to rest on the top of my hips keep me in place. I open my eyes, finding his. Barely a centimetre separates our lips as I suck in a deep, ragged breath. And then his liquid gaze drops to my mouth, his head angling down again.

I lift my jaw, our mouths connecting, the kiss soft and slow and treasuring. The only sound is the movement of our arms, of our clothes as we move closer, curling into each other.

My breasts meet his hard body. A soft moan sounds at the back of my throat, the feel of him pressed against me causing my blood to riot and my body to tremble. Quickly, the kiss escalates, my lips attentive and eager, discovering the plumpness of his mouth, chasing the delicious taste of him as my tongue touches his. Strong arms gather me in more tightly and I mould myself to his frame as best I can. A deep groan rumbles from his chest. It resonates through my ribcage, communicating directly to my heart as his tongue licks against mine, sweeping inside my mouth.

Without breaking the kiss, he lifts me, gently dropping me to the worktop as he steps between my spread thighs. He kisses me with his whole body, ravishing my mouth, stroking his tongue against mine in relentless, dizzying movements. Crushed against me like this it's impossible not to miss his arousal, his cock a long, hard bar wedged against my lower stomach. I claw at his shirt, his shoulders, as his palms press into my back and secure me against him. Indulging in his kiss is torture, but I allow it for only a little while longer before slowing it all down and gently pulling away.

My breathing is hard and fast, my chest rising and falling like I've kept pace with Usain Bolt in the two hundred metre sprint. Liam straightens, running a hand through my hair. There's a determined light in his eyes as he watches me carefully, bringing his other hand to my cheek.

"Don't start saying that was a mistake," he warns softly.

I'm not sure if I'd got that far ahead. It tasted of a mistake, but a delicious one, one worth pursuing. But it also tasted of every single bright, brilliant thing in the world. It was pet tortoises and dimpled smiles and quiet laughter that has my heart booming out a joyous reply. It's contagious wit and teasing that has me curious, engaged, and stupidly happy.

Slowly, I run my hands down Liam's chest. I can feel his heart pounding, the tightness of his pecs, the hard slabs of abdominals. "Isn't it?"

"I could never call spending time with you a mistake," he says with conviction.

"What about kissing me?"

"Especially not that."

"I'm not regretting it," I confess.

His chest inflates. "I'm asking. Earlier, you mentioned guys not having the ambition to ask you, but I do. I was trying to be respectful to Tom, but I don't give a shit anymore. I don't care if you want this or not, it's happening. It's already started."

His flip book was a confession.

It's all led to this moment. His patience to understand my feelings. His. My reluctance to make things worse for him. He's been biding his time, and getting me in his flat was his master plan.

Picking up the flip book, I run through it again. "I love this. Thank you."

"I want us to try."

"I know."

"And?" He regards me with heavy intrigue, but it's more like he's trying to read my mind, delve into the deepest recesses of my brain and work me out. Understand how he could ensure my agreement to whatever is unravelling between us tonight.

"I do too, but I'm... nervous. Scared this will end before it starts. Worried about...outside influences."

Our eyes hold. And then I'm distracted by the sudden vibration of my phone alerting me to a message. Both of us turn our heads ninety degrees to its location on the counter, the name Aaron easily read.

Aaron: *Give me another chance, Nora.*

Liam's eyes slam into mine, hurt flashing before it's replaced with something I can't put my finger on. His reaction has me crestfallen, scared that what we were working towards will be snatched away before it's even begun. Ice floods my veins as I drop my gaze to the floor, wishing it would swallow me up.

"Is Aaron the outside influence?"

"To be honest, I was thinking of your brother."

Liam looks mildly emboldened by my comment. "I'm not sure it's him you need to worry about," he murmurs, his voice colder than I've ever known it. He tops up our glasses, asking, "When did he raise getting back together?"

"He called earlier after we packed up the car."

"Were you going to tell me?"

I falter, guilt lashing me. "Not today. I didn't want him intruding."

Liam laughs darkly. "He has shit timing."

Doesn't he just.

Wordlessly, Liam passes me a full glass and I follow him to the sofa. I settle into the seat, kicking up my legs behind me and taking a long, deep breath.

Just then, Nippy ambles past, his feet making slow progress over the rug under the coffee table. His presence helps diffuse the strained tension between Liam and I. Helps dissipate the quiet fears I have that now we're finally able to move forwards, Liam might not want to after reading that message. And I also worry that if we do start this, that it will all be over in three months. That I'll fuck this up like I have every relationship since Aaron.

I gulp down my champagne, my head drumming its own beat.

"You'll have to tell me what I owe for the rent."

Liam dismisses me with a look. A look that simultaneously says I can't believe you're changing the subject, and that is never happening. "That's not happening, Nora."

"I want to."

"Well, I don't want you to. My apartment, my rules."

"It doesn't feel right to live here and not country-bute." Liam looks at me quizzically, then he eyes my almost empty glass. "I mean contra - contribute."

"How sloshed are you?" he asks, stretching an arm across the sofa back.

"Just tipsy. When did you finish the flip book?"

I'm not sure he plans on answering, but then he murmurs, "A while ago."

That means he's been thinking about us for some time, doesn't it? My head rewinds to our first encounters. The flip book said #1 on it. Does that mean there's another? A #2?

"Tell me about your last girlfriend," I demand softly, the cold, fizzy alcohol reinforcing my bravery. "How did it end?"

Liam rubs his bearded chin, like there's an itch. It's such a normal gesture, yet strangely intimate with us sitting so closely. He sighs. "Usual stuff."

"What does that mean?"

"I don't know how to love a woman. How to show them that I care. I often get accused of getting bored too quickly, of not giving relationships a chance. Of not being serious."

Oh. That doesn't sound good.

"...Do you think that's true?" If he dedicates the same amount of energy to relationships as he does friendships, I can't see a problem.

"Some of it, yes."

"I think you can be pretty serious when you want to be. When it's warranted."

He remains quiet, then announces: "I think I might be a bit broken."

"No," I say, disbelieving. "That's not true."

Liam watches me. He opens his mouth to say something but I butt in with, "Is it true that your relationships don't last more than three months?"

Liam skims his hand across his jaw again, watching me carefully. It feels like a trap. Dangerous. Like I'm about to get sucked into something I should avoid. All I know is that I want to feel the rasping brush of his beard against my skin again. I want to be reminded how those lips feel like against mine, his strong, commanding hands on my waist, holding me close.

There's a male groan, like it's all too hard to think about. "Three months is only the limit because I can tell if something is worth pursuing or not. It's not a bad thing to be focused on what I want from a girlfriend. For my future. What about you? Are all your relationships long like with Aaron?"

"No, and this is us moving into dick mishap territory," I warn with a smile. "Since Aaron, I shagged a guy called Harry. Twice. True story."

A ghost of a smile."True story?"

"Very true. A very bad true story. And I saw a guy called Jeremy for exactly seventy days." I sip the dregs of my champagne, turning to face Liam a little more. We hold each other's gaze, and it creates an expectancy, like there are more secrets to share and unearth. Bargains to be made.

"What happened?"

"Neither of them knew how to be a good boyfriend. No-one - no men seem to know..." I trail off. Some days I wonder if I'm being too picky. And I can't help but compare every relationship to the one I had with Aaron. It's not healthy, and it's certainly not been helpful, but that's where my twisted mind goes. Silence cocoons us for a few heartbeats, then I admit:

"Since Aaron, I've ended it with every single guy. I'm kind of broken too."

My words collide into him, and he nods. "He was the only man you've loved," he deduces, his voice solemn.

"Yeah," I say shakily.

Quietly, "What makes a good boyfriend in your opinion? One you can love?"

I sigh, mentally running through all the mistakes and misery that was dredged up at Jack's party and that I didn't want to get into. But the dark surroundings, the intimacy we've already shared, and the proximity of our bodies has me ready to spill everything. "It's not rocket science but it seems beyond the capabilities of every guy I date. Women like their men loyal, trustworthy and caring. Personally, they have to totally get irony and sarcasm because that's what I've grown up on. I want to feel important, too. Pausing the remote control so that he doesn't miss any of the football commentary doesn't count," I divulge, thinking of an ex who watched every footie match going.

"What else do you look for?" Liam prods.

"The list is long," I tease, holding his eyes. "Naturally, we like our men attentive and loving. He has to have integrity. A twenty-first-century man who'll buy my tampons as easily as he does the milk and bread. But most importantly," I continue, my demeanour subdued because this seems like the most impossible ask, "I want a man to enter my life like a meteor impact, crashing into me, burning me up, obliterating every obstacle in his path. I want to be consumed by him, blind to anyone else. I want him to take control of my every thought because I feel like I'm searching for someone who doesn't exist."

I must sound crazy, yet Liam looks at me like I'm making perfect sense. "I didn't feel that with Tom," I say quietly. "And then, there was you." Liam stills. "I was planning on ending things with Tom before his party, but I didn't want to let him down like that. And when I met you..."

His voice is like smoke. "What? When you met me, what?"

Dropping my head, I let my hair cover my face. But that tactic doesn't work on Liam. Placing his fingers under my chin, he tips my face back to his, waiting. "You were perfect. I couldn't believe how lucky I was to meet you, but so unlucky to know you were Tom's brother." I offer a commiserating smile. "France was tortuous."

"I'm glad you took your time in ending things. We might not have met otherwise."

His words are another confession, so I offer one back. "I think I met him in order to meet you."

Instantly, Liam kneels at my feet, his gaze dark as he spreads my thighs so that he can shuffle closer. A warm palm rests on my leg, branding me with a single, claiming touch. Heat smothers me as it trails slowly up my thigh, disappearing under the skirts of my dress where it remains, a teasing, tantalising weight.

"We need to explore this," he urges, his voice a deep, gravelly inducement. "I thought I'd be worried about my brother coming between us, but I'm much more concerned about your feelings for Aaron, the only man you've loved."

Fucking Aaron. He's always in the way, poking his nose into my business. It has me wondering why I allowed him to get so involved in my relationships, casting his opinions around like they mattered. I decide this very second, that until the race, I'll keep Liam my personal secret. That way, Aaron can't poison my mind with his negative commentary.

"I want to try this too, and while I can promise Aaron is not a threat, I don't think I'm clear-headed where he's concerned." That might be the first time I've admitted that aloud, and to myself. "And I'm worried about your own built-in time limit. If all I get is three months, I don't think I want to do that to myself. And I don't want to hurt you either."

Liam makes a study of me, that analytical look returning. I wonder what he sees, what he memorises. All the many intricacies of the flip book drawings prove his eye for detail is astounding. "Then we need to be smart about this. We need to look at this as a trade. You can help me learn how to fall in love with a woman, and I'll treat you so good it'll be me you put on that pedestal, never thinking of your ex again."

Surprised at his deductions that I'm only just coming to myself, my head tilts, waiting for more.

"Let me seduce you, worship you. I'll show you that I'm capable of loving you, keeping you. Your every breath, every thought will be for me."

My heart lurches to my throat, drumming violently. *Seduce me?* Holy hell, that sounds epic. But I'm pretty sure that's already happened. It's been long and eventful, over several weeks, and not least the past twelve hours where we've been practically joined at the hip.

"H-how is that meant to work?" I stutter, desperate for him to show me.

Somehow, he shuffles closer, that hand on my thigh gentling along my bare skin. Mesmerised by his proximity, by his masculine scent, all I can do is stare at him, melting under his smouldering gaze.

"Well, now that you've moved in here, perhaps you could teach me how to be a good boyfriend. One you want to keep."

I bite at my bottom lip, his eyes dropping to watch as I gnaw at it repeatedly. His hand comes up, his index finger reaching out to peel away my bottom lip from my teeth. "Little vampire." His voice is like smooth caramel. "Save those teeth for my lips. For my skin. For my body."

I think I sigh. Or moan. Either way, a little sound, feminine and soft escapes. He's so good at seduction, a side I've not seen of him before, but there it was, plain as day. "I don't think you need any help," I say, hating myself.

"I do," Liam confirms, his voice clear and instructive. "I need you, Nora."

There's an ache in my chest, somewhere deep and inaccessible. It thumps out its painful cry, radiating throughout my body until I feel shredded to pieces. Liam wants to wow his next girlfriend. He wants to know how to love her, keep her. And I'll be his teacher. My breath see-saws through my lungs. "Because you need help locking someone down?"

A nod. That one small movement is like a knife through the fucking heart.

"I've never lived with a girlfriend. Or even a woman. You can show me what it's like to be in an enduring couple."

An enduring couple. Can my heart die more than once? Because it is, repeatedly.

"Nora?" Liam says, distracting me from my thoughts. My eyes return to his, mentally giving myself a giant slap. It sounds to me like Liam means kissing. And sex. Being part of an enduring couple definitely sounds like sex is involved. Images of Liam's body come to mind. I want to feel all of him under my searching palms. His heat, his strength, his power. And yet... sanity prevails. Because I won't get to keep him afterwards. I'll spend hours, weeks, months investing in his ability to last the distance with a woman, of possessing my mind, and yet I won't be the beneficiary.

"Getting a girlfriend is not your problem. Neither is seducing a woman in the first place."

A soft smile. "But if I want to keep the woman I seduce, I need you to show me how."

"And watch you walk away afterwards?"

His attention falls to my empty glass. It's possible my head is spinning a little, but I'm pretty sure I'm keeping up. Softly, he queries, "Are you drunk?"

"No." This conversation is like a syringe of adrenaline straight to the heart. My eyes might feel heavy but my brain is processing a billion pieces of information right now, sifting, interrogating, deducing.

"Nora," he says, his voice laced with dominance. "Keep up. I'm going to fall for you, and you're going to fall for me. Everyone else is irrelevant."

Oh.

"This is a real relationship," he confirms. "We're just not labelling it as one." His warm hands slide from my bare knees all along the length of my thighs with blatant familiarity and entitlement. In this position, the neon lights are reflected in his hazel eyes, making them far too attractive. "You trust me, don't you?"

"I do, but this could ruin our friendship," I whisper, fearful.

"It will enhance our relationship. Make it stronger. Deeper."

I want to believe his pretty words, I really do. Of course I want that with Liam. His words fill me with a longing so broad and vast it's impossible to see beyond them. Around them. To foresee anything remotely catastrophic.

"This way, there's no pressure," he murmurs, his hands smoothing up and down my thighs. And Lord help me - his touch feels so gooood.

Nodding, I place all my trust in him. "Of course I want this, Liam."

His chest expands with his next breath, deep and restorative. His hands come to the spot where my arse meets my hips and he shunts me towards him until I'm barely on the seat. Shocked, I release a quick yelp, not sure where to place my arms. But when his hands settle on my lower waist, I lace my hands around his neck.

Those sparkly eyes sweep over my face. He's so close, our lips barely an inch or two apart. "My good boyfriend sensors are telling me you need to be kissed."

Thump thump thump goes my heart. God, yes please.

Liam's eyes drop to my mouth and stay there for a good few seconds before they sink into mine again. Everywhere he looks is like a phantom touch, everything hot and burning and restless with need. A heavy weight throbs between my thighs and I can't help but wonder if he can sense my arousal, so ably placed between my spread legs as he is, our chests brushing with every inhale.

Slowly, his hands move to my hair, brushing it away from my face until most of it sits behind my shoulders. Gently, he cups my cheeks, his eyes dancing between mine. "You're going to show me how to love you - through my kiss, through my touch, through my body. With my heart, Nora."

Featherlight kisses pepper my cheekbone as my insides melt. Then, slowly, he moves to my other cheek, dusting kisses there too. My body, my mind wants to succumb to every single touch. To his every word that lures me into deep, dark, soul-crushing waters. "You can make me into the perfect boyfriend, tailor-made just for you. I'll be so good to you you'll never want to push me away."

Each promise is delivered in a seductive, velvety baritone, as I wallow in the heady rush of his warm, capable lips that kiss a trail down my neck to the vee of my dress.

I'm so drenched with lust it's almost uncomfortable, my core aching. Slowly, his hands skim along my sides, up and up and up until they reach my breasts. He thumbs my nipples, the dress offering me no modesty or protection from his searing touch. But part of me doesn't care. I feel craven, demonic with need, a fire blistering across my flesh as his thumbs continue to abrade my nipples.

Throwing my head back, I moan like a depraved woman. When Liam's hands cup my cheeks again it's with clear impatience. He tilts my face forwards and I get a split second's warning before his lips meet mine.

His mouth undoes me, his lips a silken caress that repeats over and over. Each pass of his mouth against mine is subtly different, his lips never moulding to mine in exactly the same place or way. When he pulls back, it's only to reposition, to kiss me with cashmere-soft lips from a different angle, as if he has to taste me from every possible direction.

My hands tighten against his back. His palms burn through my dress. Self-combustion feels like a real possibility as his tongue slips past my lips and glides against mine like a brand. A deep groan rumbles through his chest, and I answer it with a moan of approval. Of pure unadulterated arousal. I want him touching me in so many places, and he *must* be a mind reader because his hands come up to caress my breasts. My back arches, pushing myself into his hands. I rake my hands through his hair, feeling how soft and thick it is as his fingers deftly unpick three small buttons at the front of my dress.

He stops kissing me to watch as he unveils me, his lips swollen, his eyes dark with lust. "These, Nora, are beautiful. They could start a fucking riot."

A smile tugs at my lips as he slips the dress over my shoulders. My arms are caught up in the cap sleeves but it doesn't matter. Half-exposed to him, he leisurely fingers the edge of the balcony cups of my bra. It's maddeningly slow, yet erotic as hell, his eyes blazing into mine when he's not following the languid journey his fingers make. Finally, he pulls down the cups, securing them under the swell of my breasts. His fingers trail over my budded nipples, awe and hunger in his eyes. And then he bends down, sucking one into his hot mouth, laving it over and over with his silken tongue.

"Oh god." I moan, my breaths broken. "Liam."

His good boyfriend sensors are sinfully intuitive. All I want are his hands on me, *everywhere.* Kissing his way to my other breast, he sucks the nipple into his mouth, biting and nibbling. Nuzzling. Electricity courses through my body, directly south, where that ache ratchets and intensifies.

"I was gutted not to see you in your wet T-shirt. I had to make do with your swimsuit - which was a great visual, don't get me wrong - but I wish you hadn't been so quick to hide your amazing tits when you fell in the canal."

In Colmar, his eyes did drop to my chest, but I was lying flat on my stomach, preserving my modesty. Delighted at his honesty, I run my hands through his shiny hair, whispering his name.

"I'm here," he answers, his mouth capturing mine, his kiss no longer sweet and blistering, but fast and passionate. Gradually I'm pushed to my back, Liam climbing over me. When his weight settles on top of me I relish every pound of trim muscle, of every place he presses into me. His cock is a hard length against my sparking clit, his arms gathering me against his body as his mouth wrestles with mine, chasing after every kiss, claiming every breath I'm capable of.

His hands are constantly on the move. At my waist, across my stomach, on my bared tits. His mouth hunts after every inch of fevered skin, every erogenous zone that isn't covered by my clothes.

Leaning on his side, an arm braced by my head, Liam's hand lowers to the hem of my dress. With his eyes on mine, he glides his fingers along my thigh. When his hand reaches my pants, he tucks his fingers underneath the material until he's sliding over my mound. When he reaches my pussy his eyes flicker, a breath punching out of his chest.

"*Fuck.* My control is hanging on by a thread."

I'm so wet, my body tightening with pleasure as two fingers push inside and fuck me with slow, unrelenting talent. He feels so good. Faultless. Every single movement is exactly as I like it, a knuckle grazing against my clit and turning me boneless. His head dips, his mouth closing over a breast, sucking and licking until I'm intoxicated on desire, my gasps growing louder with every passing second.

It's not long before I'm peaking, his fingers buried deep as I unravel, Liam working me through two successive orgasms. Each time, I seem to implode before exploding, a vast amount of energy drawn into a tight ball before it blasts outwards. My chest heaves shamelessly, my moans of encouragement and soft cries eaten up by Liam's unyielding mouth.

As the last flutters and contractions fade, Liam withdraws his fingers, only to paint my arousal over my parted mouth. He kisses me urgently, licking me clean and letting me taste myself. He sighs out my name, like I'm so precious to him, before claiming my mouth like it's rightfully his.

My mind empties of every man before him. "There is nothing but you," I whisper. "No one else but you. And your GBS - your good boyfriend sensors - are exceptional." I'm beginning to think he was right about being tailor-made for me. But I can't think about that now. I have an insanely hot man on top of me, grinding his hard dick against my inner thigh.

Reaching down, I slide a hand over his crotch and that long, thick bulge. It has my blood heating to volcanic levels again as I rub his very obvious need. But just as I start to locate his belt buckle, he groans like he's fighting his resolve. Then he rises to his knees before clambering off me.

Our gazes collide. "Not here."

He scoops me up bridal-style and heads for the hallway, bypassing my room and entering the master suite.

I am absolutely heading for emotional disaster here, a reckoning for my heart. But I can understand the reasoning behind his proposal. Neither of us will think of this as dating, our poor track records and outside influences ruining it for us. The next three months will bring us closer, strengthening our relationship. Enriching it.

Labelling it as a trade removes the pressure, the doubts. It'll prevent any fear of hurting each other. Because at the end of the day, we want this to work, and this way we'll succeed.

Laying me down on the mattress, Liam tells me, "From now on, this is your bed too."

CHAPTER FIFTEEN

Liam

VIBRATING WITH BARELY RESTRAINED NEED, I lie Nora down on the sheets. Seeing her finally stretched out on my bed sends satisfied, cherishing thoughts through my head.

Dirty ones too.

I can't believe this is happening, even though our first meeting and each time we've met since smacks of profound inevitability. Instinct takes over, that hungry, devouring beast that lives inside me where Nora's concerned. No longer distracted by how unbelievable it is that she's actually. In. My. Bed. I get on with making the most of it. I crawl over her receptive body, unable to take my eyes off her face, her expression one of lust and acceptance.

Once this happens there's no going back.

Her dress gaps open to her waist, her dislodged bra revealing two perfectly round, full breasts. Quickly, I unbutton the rest of her clothing, throwing the two halves of the material to the sheets as Nora wriggles out of the sleeves.

It leaves her in just a hot pink, sheer thong. Toying with the elastic, I stretch it away from her skin and let it ping back against her hip. The *snap* sounds loud in the quiet room. "Naughty girl."

"For when you do the laundry," she whispers, sending me a knowing look.

I've devoured Nora's body quite a few times already, but it's only ever been with platonic eyes, or at least that's what I tried to do. But now I can look my fill. She's perfect, a mixture of soft, fleshy curves and toned muscle groups that's had my cock engorged with blood for a long fucking time.

"Shirt," she murmurs, reaching for me. I strip it off, tossing it to the floor. Then I get rid of my shorts and boxers. Returning my attention to her thong, I tuck my fingers around the elastic and tug them down her tanned thighs.

Her pussy's bare and pink and all fucking mine.

Covering her with my body, I trail kisses from her neck to her breasts. I take my time tasting each one, rolling my palm across a hard nipple when my mouth is elsewhere. I chase kisses lower, down her ribs and across her stomach, shuffling my body lower and lower down her feminine shape.

There's a small scar by her navel, proof of this surgery she had at eighteen. One day, I'll ask her about that.

The smell of her arousal has my blood pounding, but I skirt her pussy, planting open-mouthed kisses all the way down to her knees. When her breathing becomes too loud and impatient, I tongue my way back up to her sex, tasting the sticky residue of her earlier release on her inner thighs.

Our eyes hold as I settle into the widening space between her legs, Nora spreading them nice and wide.

"There's a good girl," I praise, securing her thighs in my arms. "You know I think the world of you, don't you?"

There's a small frown. "Yes."

"Your mind turns me on, but your body is one I plan on violating often. Remember that when I'm inside you."

"Why? You planning on disrespecting me in the bedroom?" she drawls.

Lowering my face to her pussy, I hold her eye and say, "You tell me," my voice thick with lust.

The amused smile drops off her face as I glide my tongue through her wet slit, her head dropping back to the pillow.

"Fuck, that's good," I husk, lapping up her silky wetness, my palm pressing down on her lower stomach and pinning her to the bed.

She sucks in a tattered breath, her hips tilting as I lick her clit with the tip of my tongue, and then kiss it with teasing, feather-soft lips. I repeat everything, my tongue a long, slow slide through her soft, welcoming pussy. She feels incredible, and I devour every part of her, pushing my tongue deep inside her as my hands slide up her stomach, moulding over her aching breasts.

I play with her tits as I eat her out. Breathy moans fall from Nora's lips as I get my fill, as I stroke my tongue against her inner walls and mercilessly tease her. Her pretty thighs tremble either side of my face, her pussy begins to flutter. And when I move my mouth to her clit, nuzzling and licking, when two fingers sink inside her tight heat and steadily fuck her, she comes with a long, keening cry.

Lightly, I lay my tongue over her pink centre as it rhythmically clenches and spasms, my face covered in her flavour. "I want to bury my face here every damn day."

"I'd be okay with that," she sighs out, running a proprietary hand through my hair.

Amused, I run the back of my hand over my mouth and chin, mopping up her sweetness. Then I reach for a condom from the bedside table. Looking gloriously sex-drunk, Nora devours my every move as I rip away the packet and roll the latex over my shaft.

"I knew you were gorgeous, but I'm not prepared for the full magnitude of you," she whispers huskily.

It's me that can't believe how beautiful she is. That I have her, here, with me.

Crawling over her, I brace myself by her shoulder and take her mouth in a deep, controlling kiss. My free hand massages her breast before I take hold of my cock, dragging it across her entrance until it's drenched with her.

"Liam," Nora begs. "Hurry."

My tongue moves against hers with deep, searching strokes. "You sound hungry for more disrespecting. You ready to get your pussy filled?"

Admiring eyes fly to mine. "You're a dirty boy."

"I'm your dirty boy," I remind her.

Locking this woman down was tougher than I expected. Her reluctance to fuck this up is admirable, but I'm confident of my skills in banishing that fuckhead Aaron permanently from her thoughts.

I'll make her *blind to anyone else.*

I'll take every piece of control she'll allow.

My cock has never been so hard in all my life, blood thrumming through my body in violent, desperate waves. Unable to wait any longer, I notch my cock at her opening and drive myself home. She's so wet that I breach her snug walls with ease, her face relaxing as I seat myself deep. As I pump my hips, relishing every way her wet heat surrounds me, a husky moan sounds.

Jeez, she feels good. I've often imagined what it would be like to have Nora under me. In my bed. Just as I pictured, a halo of dark curls splays out over the pillows. Her generous tits bounce every time I slam home, her soft pussy hot and tight and giving.

Now that I have her, any patience I might possess is out of the fucking window. I ride her sweet body like it's the end of the world, incapable of slow or cherishing. "You get fucked hard tonight," I husk into her ear. "I'm too possessed and lacking in control to go slow right now." Making out on the sofa was foreplay, now I just need to have her. To claim her as mine. I've waited long enough. "You're gonna get wrecked," I warn her, fire blazing down my spine.

Our mouths tangle in long, fierce kisses, my bloodstream flooding with the best fucking drugs in the world. With powerful thrusts, I conquer her every moan and harsh exhale, my cock dragging through her welcoming, warm body and setting my skin ablaze.

"I wanted you the first time I met you," I say, my voice rough. "And I've wanted you every day since. So you'd better take your fucking punishment because I've suffered."

Feeling frenzied, I rail her tight ass, an orgasm spilling out of her which I don't slow down for. Her release has my stomach muscles clenching, my balls tightening. Aware my orgasm is closing in, I try to slow things down, but it's hard to think of distracting things when her body is so responsive. And her expression is one I'm committing to memory as sweat gathers between our bodies.

My mouth falls to her neck, sucking on the pulse point and grazing my teeth against her skin. "Give me another," I demand. "You take my cock so well I bet you can give me five."

She arches, meeting every slide of my cock with a roll of her hips. "There," she gasps. "Oh god, right there."

I coax her body up that steep climb until a hoarse cry echoes off the walls, Nora's release pouring out of her as intense heat smothers my rigid flesh. My orgasm shoots out of me, Nora clenching me dry of cum and draining me of coherent thoughts.

But I know one thing.

"There's more where that fucking came from," I growl, grinding against her clit, pushing in right to the hilt. It has another orgasm rippling out of her, her dewy face contorted in ecstasy.

Stunned, I collapse on top of her as I gather my breath, because *sweet Jesus*, that was insane. Flexing my hips, I tease out the last remaining pulses of her release, Nora sinking into the mattress beneath me. She looks thoroughly worn-out, her hair a wild tangle, her cheeks flushed, her blood-red lips swollen.

She looks exactly as I imagined.

With the level of attraction that exists between us already, I couldn't have imagined our first time any other way. Our bone-deep need lays waste to a scorched earth. Nothing else exists but her and me in this moment, our bodies a fluid, synchronised hunger that only the other can sate. We give and take, a flow of lust-riddled power surging between us that has me feeling so utterly heart-wrecked at how this could go wrong, that I just want to hold her against me until we slowly die, tangled together in the aftermath of our connection.

Fatigued exhales fill the room as I withdraw, pulling off the condom and getting rid of it in the bathroom. Once I'm back in bed, I slide my arms around Nora and kiss her chafed lips, Nora chasing after me as I pull back to ask, "You good?"

"Very. I've never...never felt anything like that before." Rolling towards me, she kisses and licks my nipple, running an explorative hand over my abdomen and pecs. "How I resisted you in France I've no idea, because I knew it would be like this." Smiling shyly, she plants a soft kiss on my mouth. "You're so handsome. Have I ever told you that? And I've been desperate to get my hands on your body."

"It's yours. All for you. Every inch of it."

"I think I got every hard inch," she whispers, grinning at her joke. "In fact, I just need to go and check on things," she adds, easing out of bed and heading to the ensuite.

Even though her things are literally across the hallway, I find a (very thin) T-shirt from out of the closet and wait for Nora to exit the bathroom. When she appears a few minutes later, I rise from the bed and pull the top over her head, dressing her. The T-shirt falls to her hips, and I like how easy and natural it is between us. At how she allows my attention. At how her nipples show through the thin material.

"Come on," I urge, leading her back to bed.

Nora scans my room as if she's seeing it for the first time. The carpet is a pale sand colour, the love seat in the corner a velvet blue. A super king bed, covered in grey and blue linens and coverlets and pillows, dominates the wall as you enter, art and prints and a few of my doodles decorating the white walls. A big bank of glass doors that, although closed now, slide open to reveal the terrace on the other side.

"Do you not have blinds?"

As she climbs under the covers, I point to a control panel on the wall by the headboard. "This turns the glass darker. No one can see in, but if you start going very dark, then we stop being able to see out."

Dulled city lights are visible beyond the glass doors now, Nora muttering, "That's cool."

I get in under the sheets, Nora's hands on me straight away. "I just need to clarify something," she begins, her breath minty. She must've brushed her teeth in the bathroom. "On this thing we're doing."

This thing.

This thing that will mean I adore the shit out of her. That I'll love her stupid. That will have her never wanting to push me away. Those words came from the heart. They were promises, because I will be her perfect boyfriend, tailor-made just for her.

"I meant to ask, is there a time limit on this?"

Nora nibbles on her bottom lip as she awaits my answer. "No. And it goes without saying that this is entirely exclusive. There's no trick here, Nora. We're going all in. I want everything you have to give, for as long as you want to give it to me. And you won't end it with me 'cos I'll be too damn perfect."

She just stares at me, disbelieving."What if you realise I'm not that great after three months?"

"The way I see it we've been going out for two already."

Technically she was with my brother for some of that time, but I can't think about that. With her confession that she was basically emotionally separating from him before his party, it must mean the physical side was non-existent. Or limited. So yeah, that doesn't bother me.

A slow smile transforms her face. There's still reticence there, some caution, but she gets what's happening between us now. "But I want the full three months. If we've had two already I feel short-changed."

"You can have three million months."

I know before she even says anything that she's working out how many days that is. But it's too late, and I'm too weary to give the maths any consideration.

Hiding her smile into my shoulder I take the opportunity to study her dark eyelashes, at how dense they are, curving and long. Her sculpted lips are very slightly apart, almost as if she's still yet to catch her breath. Her cheeks are softly pink, her olive skin dotted with freckles under her eyes and on her forehead. I've never been able to study her so keenly before, but I think I got her features pretty much spot on in my drawings.

In a month's time, I'm going to give her the next flip book.

When We Met #2.

"So you want to lock me down for real?"

"For real."

Her canines are out and very pointy, her palm smoothing over my abdomen as our situation sinks in. "C'mere," I murmur. "I plan on kissing my girlfriend goodnight for a very long time."

CHAPTER SIXTEEN

Nora

I'VE NEVER EXPERIENCED a night like this. Liam's been relentless and unforgiving, pushing my body to new, exhausting limits. And somehow, he finds the energy to kiss me until my lips hurt, swollen red, my nerve endings buzzing.

He's been my boyfriend for all of a few hours, and although he's naturally attentive and sweet, he's also a dominant, dirty-mouthed beast between the sheets.

I should've known.

I'm going to have to confess that I like this disrespecting business. It's a misnomer, because Liam respects the hell out of me when we're tangled up together. When he brings me to another orgasm with his tongue and lips and fingers.

But seriously, the past few hours is everything I hoped for. It's like I'm existing all at once and not at all, caught up in something vast, unfathomable and utterly unique.

Right now, my hair is caught up in his hands, his mouth gorging on my neck and throat. Blistering kisses turn my bones liquid, a fiery heat engulfing me as he suckles my skin from behind me in bed.

A muscled arm snakes around my chest, his hand greedily caressing a breast. At the same time, he chases wet kisses along every available desperate part of me. Craning my head, I seek his mouth. He gifts me his lips for a beat, the kiss frantic and heated. All the while he torments my nipple, twisting, an exquisite ache building that I know will break me.

Pulling up the thin T-shirt, I push his hand under it, wanting his skin on mine. My pussy throbs and aches. My skin feels electrified. Arching my neck, he tongues every erogenous zone, his hard length grinding against my ass and promising me relief.

"I can't...take this much longer."

His hand slides tantalisingly lower and lower until he meets the elastic of my pants. He delves a hand under the seam, his fingers almost right where I need them. His free arm comes around me, a hand curling over my other breast. I give in to every scalding sensation. Every way my body reacts to his persuasive touch.

Assured fingers glide through my slick sex, setting off fireworks. He's barely touched me and yet an intense orgasm rushes out, a million nerve endings connecting his attentive mouth to my pounding puss.

"You need cock, don't you?" His voice is a low rumble, confidant, dripping with sex.

Unable to talk, I nod.

My pants get pushed down my legs and off my feet. Behind me, Liam's hot frame crowds mine. He lifts my right leg and settles it over his hip, opening me nice and wide. "That's it. Spread those legs in welcome."

He slots himself between my thighs with unforgiving self-assuredness and sinks deep inside. The stretch feels good, making me full and satisfied.

"You want me to take you for a ride?"

"Hmm mm."

Mind-bending friction has my eyes rolling back. Raggedly, we move together, Liam's mouth a hot, breathy glide over my throat, his beard a glorious sting on my sensitive flesh. I crook my arm, reaching for his head as we collide together, our kiss messy and ravelled.

His hands can't decide where to hold me. They alternate between my slinking hips, my hair, or my swaying boobs. Now, they've moved to my clit, circling and circling until I feel twisted up with overbearing pleasure. His powerful hips rut into me with fluid, masterful strokes, the hard muscles surrounding my pliant body coiled with tension.

Rising up from deep within, he gifts me two toe-clenching orgasms that have my back bowing and my skin breaking out in a well-fucked sweat. And when he comes, energy rushes out of him so forcefully he shudders against me, his muscles trembling and vibrating as he pumps me full of his cum.

"Fuck," he murmurs, pressing into me as his dick continues to jerk inside. "You feel so good."

My eyes fall closed as I regroup. As I struggle to inhale with Liam's weight reminding me that this isn't a dream. That somehow, somewhere, I must've done a good deed, my reward this perfect man.

No wonder women fought over him, I think to myself, the last strains of my release racing through my veins. "Your diamond-studded dick's the best."

Warm lips press into my neck, Liam fighting laughter. "Whenever I'm inside you, you ask for whatever you want, because I'll give it to you, gladly." And then he threads his fingers through my hair, pulling me in for a blistering kiss, our bodies dirtied and cooling.

"Do you think we can do this all day?" I ask.

"I've got you covered."

I chuckle as Liam pulls out, rising from the bed to dispose of the condom.

The clock reads 0515 which is too early considering the late night we've had. So I tug the thin duvet over me and snuggle down, ignoring the aches and pains in my protesting muscles.

The next thing I know, Liam's arm is draped across my waist, his head tucked in behind mine. His chest rises and falls with slow, steady breaths.

We fell asleep, but I've no idea how long for. The fancy glass at the sliding doors tells me the sun has risen but I can't tell what time it is from my position, and my body clock might be out of sync after a long night.

My mouth feels dry, my head a little achey. Carefully, I get out of bed, Liam's arm flopping to the mattress. I hold my breath in case he stirs, but all he does is readjust his position, his eyes resolutely closed.

I head into the ensuite, using the loo and brushing my teeth before staring at my reflection in the mirror. Despite the lack of sleep, my eyes look vivid, my skin glowing.

It's just as well I didn't unpack everything in the spare bedroom yesterday because I'm going to be putting it all in Liam's closet.

But first, I need to run.

After locating my phone and watch, amazed at how late I slept in - it's 0741 - I go through my morning routine. Nippy ambles out from a spot he was hiding in, keeping me company. His presence makes me so joyful, and I scratch his shell with gentle fingertips which he seems to enjoy.

I text Liam what I'm up to and head out, my keys, access

card, and EpiPen stuffed in the back pocket of my leggings. Distracted by memories of last night, the three miles fly by, my feet eating up the concrete as I run along the river path by the Thames. It's overcast but mild, and I can only hope for similar weather for the triathlon in a month's time.

When I'm back in the apartment, Liam is at the long island, making pancake or waffle mixture, a bowl of fruit and a jar of Nutella out on the worktop. Even though I'm no doubt sweaty and red-faced, he has a delicious double-dimpled smile for me, his eyes skimming over my legs. Shirtless, I admire every inch of him, checking out his buff arms with an indulgent look.

"You look thirsty," he says, his voice a rich baritone. The corners of his mouth curl indecently.

"Parched." I flash him my fangs. "Isn't this a violation of the agreed dress code? Looks like an automatic eviction notice."

"Are you kicking me out of my own place?"

"I can be distracted from making a complaint," I offer.

A low laugh eases out of him as he approaches, his steps slow and predatory. "I'm good at distractions."

My arms go around his neck as he slides his hands around my waist. His mouth slants over mine, his lips attentive and deliberate. The slow and tender kiss has every part of me brightening. Even in quiet moments like this he shakes the ground I walk on, leaving me breathless and disorientated. "I'd have accompanied you."

"You looked so peaceful - I thought I'd let you sleep. You earned it," I say, raising a brow.

"I'm always good for it," he assures me.

"It's an admirable work ethic."

He brushes some stray hairs hair away from my face. "Happy to put the time in where you're concerned."

"Overtime?"

"Double shift, overtime, holiday sacrifice, whatever it takes."

I grin, loving the look in his hazel eyes right now: possessive, serious, addictive.

"I'm surprised you woke so early."

"My brain was too busy to get back to sleep. Plus, I only have four weeks to get into shape."

Liam's eyes flit between mine before he asks, "Anything unclear about what's going on here?"

I shake my head, his hands falling to the waistband of my leggings before he's smoothing the material over my buttocks and hips, pulling them down my legs. "How was your time?"

"I thought the miles went by quickly, but I was slow. By a lot. It's all your fault."

He raises a brow. "I'll be sure to abstain the night before your race."

I pout. Not exhausting myself the night before my race would be sensible, but right now, with him undressing me physically and metaphorically with his expressive, roaming eyes, it sounds like a punishment.

"Let's shower."

I step out of my leggings, standing on the material until my feet are free. Liam grabs my hand and pulls me towards his bedroom. Our bedroom.

"Are you on the pill?"

"Yes." He saw me take it in France, but it's right that he checks.

"How about we get a sexual health screening so that I can ditch the condoms?"

"I thought we agreed we were nothing like those French aristocrats, a safe-harbour for every STD going."

"I trust you, and I know the score with me, but we need the paperwork."

"Okay."

In the ensuite, he turns on the water, stripping out of his

bottoms and leaving them discarded on the tiled floor. Meanwhile, I'm yanking off my running top and bra, wriggling out of my white cotton pants.

After testing the water, Liam steps inside the double-sized shower. A teak shelf is cut into the tiled wall, bottles of shampoo and shower gel stacked to one end of it. Liam grabs one of the bottles, lathering up his hands and then running the soap over my skin.

I've never been washed in a shower before. Pampered so intimately by a partner. As Liam's soapy hands slide easily over my skin and around my breasts I decide I could get used to it. I let him take care of me, and then I take care of him, soaping his strong neck before letting my hands run down his hard chest. I linger a little longer on his six-pack, trailing lower and lower until my hand wraps around his stiff, swollen cock.

He kisses me then, fiercely, dominantly, his hands searching my body. "That test needs to happen ASAP," he grits out. "Hands on the wall. I'll pull out."

Despite the risk, I spin, placing my hands on the large pale tiles, securing my hair over a shoulder. Liam steps up behind me, his body radiating thermonuclear heat. He presses down on my shoulders so that I bow forward, my arse rising up behind me as he notches himself at my centre.

"I need you," he tells me, sinking inside, deep and hard. My arms only just catch myself when I shunt forwards, but I realise that's down to his strong hands holding my hips. Then Liam really starts to move, pulling me on and off his fat cock that's wedging me apart.

"Jesus, you're tight. Fuck."

Dexterous fingers reach around my pelvis and strum my clit, his touch the perfect combination of rhythm and pressure. Heat flows over my skin, everything between my legs tensing and sparking with each delicious drag.

Liam's breaths mingle with mine as skilled fingers work me into a tightly wound ball. His thrusting hips turn ragged, that sharp edge fast approaching until I come, bringing Liam with me. His body tenses, his grip on my hip tightens, pulling out at what's got to be the very last second. And all I can think about is wanting him to come inside me. I want everything of his.

A strangled groan sounds, his hand swiping at the shower control. The water cuts off, his hand flying over his engorged length just once as Liam unloads over my lower back and arse, white ropes of cum lashing my skin.

Emptied, he takes his semi-hard cock in hand and paints letters in his smeared release.

L-I-A-M he writes. I just know it.

"Mine," he whispers territorially, our gaze locking over my shoulder. "Next time, I'm coming over your tits."

Languid, circular movements across my lower back and bottom distract me from making any kind of response. It's weird how relaxing it feels while simultaneously warming my blood. So I just wallow in his undivided attention, his possessive affection.

"You want to wear me inside and out, don't you?"

Spinning, my hands roam over his chest as I whisper in his ear, "My mouth does, desperately."

Groaning, he digs his hands into my hair and kisses me forcefully before turning the shower back on, washing all traces of himself off my skin.

"You know, when you shared that your most used word was *fuck*, I thought you must've gone around stubbing your toe a lot."

Liam's lips hitch. He twists off the water before wrapping a big, fluffy towel around me. "I leave the accidents to you," he remarks with a wink.

"Funny," I return, "but Lowell's treadmill would say otherwise."

"Fuck. I'd hoped you'd forgotten about that."

"Not a chance."

We spend the next few minutes getting dressed, and while Liam only needs to shove a hand through his hair, I need to manage my curls with various types of product. By the time I'm done, my stomach is growling unhappily, but Liam has already made a stack of waffles in the kitchen.

"This looks so good, thank you."

"Hungry?"

"Famished."

We load up our plates with fruit and Nutella, sitting on stools at the island as Glass Animals and *Heat Waves* plays in the background. It reminds me of France, of the long, hot nights when all I could think about was Liam.

Next to a trio of house plants I spy my flip book. Since last night, it's remained out here on the counter. It reminds me of Aaron's message, one that I should probably reply to. Reaching for the miniature book, I flip through the pages again as I rest my stomach from too much food.

The drawings are like a song, each page a heartfelt word or lyric that only leads to one conclusion. This thought occurred to me last night, and in the cold light of day I know I'm not imagining this.

I feel like I'm searching for someone who doesn't exist.

That someone existed. That someone is right at my side, existing.

"When did you realise you were good at drawing?"

"It's something that just grows with you. You just get more skilled at it as you develop fine motor skills and a critical eye."

"But you loved it, which must help," I presume.

"Yeah. I mostly drew to relax."

Lifting my eyes from the book, I try and interpret every single facet of his veiled expression. Because although his words appear to be perfectly normal ones, the delivery of them was strained. "To relax? Drawing like this - perfectly, faultlessly - must be a pretty high maintenance hobby that's meant to be for fun."

He holds out a hand for the book and I pass it over. "As a boy, it got me out of Tom's way. And I have a computer program which helped with this, but getting your face and outline right took me several tries," he confesses. "I had to get you just right."

My heart triples in size. "It's incredible. Do you make them for anyone else? Or maybe your other art?" I enquire, spinning on my stool to look at the large charcoal prints on the walls.

"Art won't pay the bills."

Spinning back towards him, I smile sadly. "Really? That's the only reason why you're not doing more of it?"

He shrugs, looking uncomfortable. "Got a mortgage to pay and patients to see."

"But now, you could do this for fun."

A shrug.

"Did you study art at all?"

"A-level. I...To be honest, I wanted to go to art and design college but I...decided on medicine."

Aside from the drawings and paintings in the hallway and bedroom, there are four other works in the living room. The most accomplished one (in my humble opinion) is an intricate 3D view of London's skyline. It's heavy on the charcoal, lots of it smudged and artfully blended to give density and depth to the buildings and horizon. There's a simple, 2D line drawing of Nippy, and another of a luxury sports car, the sleek lines so accurately depicted it looks like a black and white photograph. The final framed piece is of a tropical beach, gentle waves reaching up the sand, a palm tree adding dimension and focussing the eye.

His work deserves to be seen by so many more people than just visitors to his apartment. Immediately, my thoughts turn to how I could help him find time to devote to his love of drawing. My salary isn't anywhere close to his, but I can contribute in some way to the mortgage - if he'll let me. But maybe there's an achievable, quick win.

"The walls at my clinic are pretty bare. We could hang some in the waiting area and give the patients something pretty and evocative to look at. Your work is very calming. They'd be perfect."

Liam chuffs softly, shaking his head. "It's okay."

"I see some seriously wealthy people, Liam. You should hear some of the stories they tell me. Exotic holidays, private jets, fancy restaurants. My god, one guy told me he had a twenty grand wine bill once, so they'd easily pay a grand or two for an original drawing. You are *good*," I praise, desperate for him to see this. "Seriously good."

"I don't know," he answers vaguely. But I can tell there's some interest in exploring this further. And for someone who's so quietly cocksure, he smacks of low self-esteem where this is concerned.

"Do you have any that aren't hanging up?"

There's a beat, and then a nod.

I slide off the stool and grab his hand, tugging him towards the office. It's the only place they must be. "Show me."

Outside his study, he pauses, looking down at me with a tired expression. "I'm just humouring you, you know."

"I know."

Shoving him forwards, we enter the room, a three-metre long, white desk with an iMac on top against a wall. There's also a printer and a scanner, and other things I don't know the names of. But I can see blue cloth that matches the spine of my flip book, and something that might be used to bind it to the spine. There are stacks of black-frames in a variety of sizes resting against a wall, the walls themselves sparse-looking. An easel is tucked into a corner, and there's a wooden V-shaped stand with plastic folders resting inside, each one holding an original design if I'm not mistaken.

Dropping to my haunches I start looking through the frames. "Are these ones you want to keep or sell?"

"I don't know. I can't remember."

Standing motionless next to me, Liam looks bewildered and uncertain. I pull him down to the carpet and offer a reassuring smile. "If you're humouring me, then you need to tell me which ones I can take to work and hang up. These smaller ones," I say, indicating some around ten-inch squared, "can be a thousand. These bigger ones -"

"Eighteen-inch square, and twelve-inch," Liam advises, pointing to the larger, then the smaller sized frames respectively.

"They can go for eighteen hundred. Would that seem reasonable in terms of the time taken to draw them?"

He blows out an unsure breath. "Some of these need to go in the bin. I wouldn't be happy selling them."

"Why not?" I ask, looking at a beautiful watercolour of a pink, cherry blossom tree. It's framed so he must've thought it wall-worthy. "We need to keep this one because it reminds me of Master Oogway. These are all very good, Liam. Why don't you believe me? What's wrong with them?"

He runs a hand through his chestnut hair, his dimples completely hidden. "I guess when you're told you'll never make it as an artist, you tend to believe it."

My hands still. My head turns to give him all of my attention. "Someone made you believe that? Who? What person thinks these are not exceptional and unique?"

"Does it matter? An old teacher from school who I don't see anymore. And to some degree my parents. They didn't think art would pay me a decent living, and they were right."

"What about your siblings?"

A soft sigh. "They were more complimentary, but they thought medicine was the better route. That it was a more secure job."

I feel lost. Lost on how to unearth his true feelings. "Do you enjoy being a doctor?"

A convincing nod. A firm, "Yes."

Relieved, I ask, "But you miss drawing."

"I do. A lot." He seems to struggle for a second so I wait him out. "Urgh, I feel foolish for saying this but at one point I was going to submit some pieces to be considered by the National Gallery for a prize."

"And the critics stopped you?"

A reluctant nod.

"Let me guess, it was the 3D London skyline."

His eyes flash to mine. "How did you know?"

"It stands out. It's so detailed, I feel like I'm right there, on the street looking at that view with my own eyes. But I love the simpler style you have too, and the watercolours. I love all of these," I say, brushing a hand to my side to indicate the work he's stored here. "Liam," I murmur, moving aside some frames that have surrounded us so that I can crawl into his lap. "Please let me try this. Ash's boyfriend designs websites. I can sell them in my clinic. Sadly, I have to work most Saturdays, though only a half-day, but you could spend those mornings doing something that brings you a lot of pleasure."

"Doing you on Saturday morning would bring me a lot of pleasure."

I get the double dimples, so I feel emboldened and encouraged by Liam's mood. He might be trying to talk me out of this but it's only because he's been swayed by shitty teachers and well-meaning family over the years. Draping my arms over his shoulders I say, "Let's make a pile of art you're happy to sell. If there's interest, we can get the website up. On Saturdays, after you've sorted me out and I've gone off to work with bowed legs and a sore kitty, you can work."

He laughs, gorging on my neck as Nippy enters the room on near-silent feet. "This is a hobby, Nora. It's not meant to be a revenue stream."

"But what if it could be?"

He withdraws his focus from my skin, looking me in the eye. "I don't know what to say to that."

"Could you work a four-day week. Three?"

"Perhaps. I'm not sure I want to. Locums aren't cheap."

If he isn't seeing patients, he needs to pay the salary of a doctor who will. "But if you made enough from your art to pay for a locum, and if it allowed you the chance to indulge in a hobby that you love, that's a win-win, surely?"

A laboured sigh. "You think people want to buy my work. At pretty high prices."

"I think they will, yes. Doesn't Lowell have contacts we could approach? He sells high-end products."

"His clients want Degas and Van Gogh. Not Alston."

I smile. "Fair point, but there is a need for affordable art, and that can be your niche. How many do you have?"

Counting up the frames dotted about on the carpet, he says, "Fifteen, plus I have about forty in the stand over there."

"A gold mine," I state.

"That's not why I want to do it."

This is where I offer to share the bills with him, especially if we're going to be this enduring couple. Even though this topic was broached, that was before his need for additional income to allow the love of a hobby was known. I take in a breath, knowing I'll cycle back to this thought another day. "I realise that. But at the end of the day, you need it to pay its way if you want a four-day week."

Rolling his neck, Liam looks anxious and stressed. So I knead my fingers into the muscles, his low growl of approval running through me, making me shiver with anticipation.

"How about a trade?" he asks darkly, looking up into my face.

Jesus, he loves trades. And to be honest, I'm a big fan of them too. "What sort of bargain are you hoping to reach?" I ask coyly, knowing exactly where his mind is heading.

"You give me a massage, a topless one. Afterwards, I get my happy ending by making you wear me, my name written across your breasts," he murmurs, pinching my nipples with warm, greedy fingers. "Then I'll let you take whatever you want from this room to sell."

Kissing his beautiful mouth is all the answer I need to give.

CHAPTER SEVENTEEN

Liam

WITH MY BACK muscles gloriously supple, and my entire body feeling revitalised as a result of Nora's hard work massaging out the kinks and knots, we spend the next few hours recovering.

With a bowl of sweet popcorn between us, we watch *Kung Fu Panda*. Nora's in the V of my legs, her back against my chest as I lean into the corner of the sofa. When we get to Nora's favourite scenes, she always prefaces it with, *This is my favourite scene.* She says that several times, particularly at Tai Lung's prison escape (which is epic), but it's Master Oogway's death, his passing seeing him swept away in a cloud of pink blossom that has her crying.

As crying goes it's rather elegant, her body barely shaking as tears spill down her cheeks. She doesn't even try and tidy them away; she just lets them drip onto my arms that surround her.

When the scene ends, she goes in search of Nippy, affectionately stroking his shell, cuddling him. It's crazy how much she's bonded with him already. How she accepts him, adores him. I like it very very much. After all, he's an extension of me. He's my life-long friend, and to some degree, as I've pointed out to my mother in order to dodge her constant nagging about grandchildren, a baby surrogate.

Nora would make the best mother.

I blow out a breath, not sure why my mind went there so quickly and decidedly.

Something else to admire is her love of my art, her actions championing a hobby that I've pushed to one side for so many years. Her interrogations had me questioning every decision I've made about making room for art in my life. Getting ahead of myself would be easy, but Nora's enthusiasm is infectious, and difficult to brush away. She heightens my senses, everything feeling brighter, sharper, clearer, better. Every expectation I could ever have is met, exceeded.

When the film credits start rolling, Nora receives a text. Picking up her phone, she toggles to her messages and holds the mobile in front of her. It means I can read the entire thing.

Joe: ***Just spoke to Aaron. He thinks there's a problem with your phone?? Anyway, do you want to borrow his bike? Let him know. Love ya x***

Under my hands, Nora's chest expands before she blows out a breath. I'm burning up with resentment and anger, and I want to make it known that there is no way she is giving Aaron a second chance. But telling people what to do doesn't work. They need to resolve things by themselves.

All the same, it's hard to swallow down my own advice.

"Did you reply to Aaron's message last night?"

Quietly, "No."

"But you will?" She'd better not be giving it, or him, any consideration. Why hasn't she already told him to fuck off? Last night, I wanted to demand she recite their conversation verbatim. In the end, knowing I had the upper hand, aware I had the best chance I was ever going to get of making Nora mine, I pushed on with my own plans, confident.

There's no way she'll take him back.

"I've been a little busy," Nora replies saucily, running her palm over my thigh.

My fuck-sore dick proves how busy I've kept her. "Why don't you text him now?"

Shifting her bottom, she twists until she can see my face. "I don't want him to know about you yet."

Uncertain what to make of that, I raise a curious brow.

"He'll only start to stick his nose in our business. This way, I don't need to respond to any of his messages. I want to ignore him."

Liking her answer, I run a hand over her hair, thinking of what to say. "At least tell him you're not interested."

"What should I say?"

The fact that she's asking for my opinion, that this is a combined response, loosens the tension in my body. "You decide."

Her fingers start to type out a reply. ***As I told you I'm in a good, happy place. Hope you can work it out with Beth.***

She shows me the message, even though I was able to read it off the screen anyway. Once Nora sends the message, she relaxes her body against mine. Then a thought occurs. "Do you borrow his bike? You need to let him know that's not happening."

It's hard not to overlook my dominant tone.

"I use Aaron's spare on the day. It saves travelling with it."

"So how do you train?"

"I used Ash's."

But she can't use Ash's now; she's moved to South London with her boyfriend.

"Can I buy you a new one?" The idea of her using her ex's stuff is distractingly bothersome. It fires my blood to volcanic levels. I want her cutting all ties with him. I want her to lose his number for good.

She leans in to kiss my jaw. "No. A good bike is three grand, at least. I'd rather scuff up Aaron's than mine," she deadpans. "He makes sure it's race fit, and I just turn up."

Yeah, I don't like this one bit. It's not guilt that has him offering a spare bike, one he could've traded in. No, he likes that Nora still needs him, a connection kept alive through the use of his stuff. It's just an excuse to keep in touch, to keep him in her thoughts.

I need to extract him from her mind for good.

"Why don't you want your own?"

"The only reason he offers me a spare is out of guilt, and I'm not ready to dissolve him of that yet."

She's so far off the mark it's almost laughable. And I hate her answer. It only reinforces the emotional entanglement I was afraid of. And now that I know she's not had a serious relationship since this guy, all the others short and smacking of little commitment or emotional investment, I'm certain he's the reason why.

It was obvious last night. She *confessed* it.

She's only ever loved Aaron.

Already, I'm planning six months from here. A year. And I can't have Nora stuck on an ex, or fearful of falling for someone only to be betrayed again. And it's especially hard to avoid Aaron if he's still part of her friendship group, interacting regularly.

"I'd still like to buy you a bike. Perhaps we can look online, see what you like?"

"I can afford a bike, but I'm not a bike enthusiast apart from the triathlon. It's a waste of money."

"Nora," I say, threading some steel in my voice. "You're going to let me buy you a bike. This is what boyfriends do; they certainly don't let you use an ex's who wants back in your bed."

Shocked, she stares at me before dropping her gaze. "I didn't mean to be insensitive."

"I know. But my GBS needs to impress upon you that emotionally, physically, materialistically, you rely on me and me alone. How would you like it if I used a previous girlfriend's car?"

"...I'd hate it."

Point made.

Nora sends a last message to Aaron. ***I'll bring my own bike this time. Thanks for the offer though!***

The next hour is spent on her laptop, looking at bikes and making plans to shop for one next weekend. While we do, at least three messages from Aaron arrive, asking her why she doesn't want his bike anymore, or a variation of the same question.

Eventually, Nora replies, ***I'm buying my own***

He immediately responds with: ***How will you get three bikes in Joe's car? Are you buying a car too and driving separately?***

"Fuck," she mutters. "He's so persistent."

Despite her words, she looks almost pleased to hear from him. And it has me wondering: does contact between them make her feel important? Important to him? Is she secretly happy to receive his attention and focus?

My support team will drive me she reveals.

Who? he demands.

She leaves him hanging, ignoring his question. But this entire situation only reinforces why it's been so hard for her to forget about him.

Just to ensure that guy is far from her thoughts, I send her a dirty text. ***Tonight, I want you straddling my lap, riding my cock until I see stars.***

With a grin, she replies: ***Are we doing it out on the balcony? As the sun sets?***

I snigger at her witty retort, and decide to show her that I mean business. ***I'll strip you first, devouring your cunt until you're a sex-drunk puddle, screaming my name. And then I'll do it all over again, licking through your dripping slit until you're begging for my cock. And when I fill up that sweet, hot pussy of yours you'll moan so hard, desperate for me to fuck you good until you're a whimpering mess all over again.***

Nora stares at her phone, reading, the smile on her face dropping away to reveal unadulterated need. Then she looks at me, her lust-filled eyes raking over me. In the next second, she's tossing her phone to the table, straddling me. "I need you now. And later. I'm super horny."

I take care of my girlfriend, multiple times. Until she's weak-boned and worn out, whispering my name.

Eventually, we busy ourselves by ordering some picture hooks, and I dig out my trusty old hammer as Nora looks through the stand of unframed art I haven't looked through in years.

"Which framer do you use? We'll need to get these ready."

"Once some have sold. *If* some get sold."

"Have some faith, young Padawan." She smirks at me,

tossing her hair enticingly. "We also need to sort out a card reader for payments. Not unless they want to hand over an envelope stuffed with cash."

"I don't have a problem with cash," I say dryly.

A little while later, we take a walk outside, heading towards Battersea Park on the south side of the river. The late afternoon is mild, the place packed with people pottering about, buying ice creams and lattes and enjoying the weather.

Hungry from skipping lunch, we head for a Spanish restaurant on Queenstown Road, ordering a ton of food and sipping a super boozy sangria while we wait for it. Concerned that I've not got to the bottom of the dynamics Nora has with her old uni mates, I ask, "Tell me more about this group of friends in Norwich."

Nora takes a reluctant breath. "Well, Aaron and Beth moved there shortly after they hooked up. It was... helpful actually, not needing to include them in our evening or weekend plans. At uni, along with Floss and Harry and Joe, we hung out all the time. For a while, I lived with Beth and Floss, and the boys lived together."

"Floss?"

"Short for Florence."

Right. "Did Joe or Harry not suspect anything?"

"No. They were away the weekend that I walked in on Beth and Aaron."

"And they're all chiropractors?"

Toying with her glass, Nora answers, "Yeah. Floss is now in Cambridge, Harry and Joe - they're together, by the way - live in Clapham. We normally drive across together."

I nod, thinking about how I need to phrase my next question. "You said that you all just kind of agreed to move on, to accept what had happened, that Beth and Aaron were apologetic about what they did. Based on what you said last night, about him messing with your head, you're not over that. But what about Beth's involvement? How do you feel about her?"

Infidelity is a particular dislike of mine. One of the worst feelings in the world is knowing that you were used and lied to by someone you loved and trusted above all others. And in Nora's case, it was both her good friend and her boyfriend who did the dirty on her. If I were her, I'd struggle with trusting someone after that. And coupled with her hurt feelings still, wanting Aaron to wallow in his guilt for as long as possible, tells me she's not moved on, no matter what she professes.

In my mind, it's possible to cheat on someone physically and emotionally. And while Nora wouldn't knowingly do either, I have a suspicion she's not aware of everything going on in that head of hers. Our brains are remarkably good at adapting, sometimes covering difficult memories or encounters under several layers of protection. And while that's good for our head in some ways, it causes other difficulties that we're not always cognisant of.

For a long time, I've been preoccupied with the fact that she's my brother's ex, but all along I needed to focus my attention on a love affair from further back in her relationship history. And it shouldn't surprise me that it was the longest.

Just then, the waitress arrives with an array of dishes: smoked cod fritters, stuffed peppers, garlic prawns, chorizo thingies, some salad bits...I'm not entirely sure what Nora ordered, but wanting her to feel in control after laying down the law earlier, I left it up to her.

Distracted by the food, Nora doesn't answer my question. So I remind her. "Have you forgiven Beth?"

A frown creases her forehead. "No. Why do you think I want to beat her so badly?" she says quietly, refusing to meet my eyes. "And I just don't see why Aaron should get off lightly. It was just a bike."

My chest kicks out. Mild vengeance is a reaction I can understand, but does the hunger for retribution last this many years? Maybe so. But that's not the only issue here. "Nora, it sounds like you're still exerting some ownership over him."

"What? No I'm not."

"By using his bike you're broadcasting that you still need him. Clearly, he's quite happy to help you out. It probably feeds his ego. It might be why he thinks he can involve himself in your life."

For a split second she looks horrified. "You're wrong."

"Am I? How is it then?"

"You don't get to psychoanalyse me. I'm the one who was hurt. I'm the one who's had to watch them together, loved up, rubbing it in my face. Beating me."

She sounds hurt. Angry. "So you want to remind them both that you were there first, I get it, but is that helping you?"

Irritated, she huffs out, "That's not what I'm doing."

As Nora stews in silence, I eat. The flavours explode on my tongue but I don't especially enjoy the food because Nora's upset. And she's not digging in either, and that is one of the things I love about her. Her appetite, and not the one confined to food, or sex, but to life, to experiences and adventures which I want to gorge on right alongside her.

"I don't understand why you're digging around in my past," she accuses, her eyes dark and sad. But there's vulnerability there, and it's exactly what I needed to see. "I thought we were moving forward. Together."

"Because it's *not* your past but your present. Because I give a shit. Because I'm your boyfriend, not that two-timing prick. Because you need undivided attention, to feel validated and important, and I am offering you all of those things. Together."

Taken aback, she just studies me. We're side by side on a bench seat so she has to twist her hips to face me fully. "I thought you didn't know how to love someone? Didn't know how to be serious?"

"With you," I say gathering up her balled hand and threading my fingers through hers, "I'm deadly serious. I'm the motherfucking meteor, remember? And most importantly, with you, I want to be serious for a very long time. About three million months long. I'm here for you in whatever it is that you want from me."

"I thought that was when you were inside me," she states cheekily, but also moodily. It makes my mouth hitch.

"Either works," I stress. "I won't ignore your wants. In fact, I'll be so attentive you'll be sick of me."

For a long minute, her thumb slides along the outside of my hand, running along a prominent vein. "I didn't realise I was still holding onto him. I thought trying not to talk to him, not sharing things with him, was enough."

Her confession has my muscles weakening with relief. It has my heart aching for her. "It just makes him more determined," I comment. "And I think - unconsciously - you liked his attention."

Her eyes whip to me before they drop away, her expression one of shame. Nora runs a hand over her forehead, pushing curls out of her face when really it's to try and clear her head. To make sense of what she's only just coming to terms with.

"Those texts he sends me outside of the group chat - it's almost like he wanted to keep his hooks in me." She sighs. "God, why didn't I see this?"

I've yet to meet this colossal cunt. I've no idea what he even looks like, but there won't be a shadow of doubt who Nora loves when we go to Norwich next month.

Leaning in, I kiss Nora with firm, reassuring lips. She tastes of salt and red wine, and fruity, exotic flavours. "Do you want me to enter the race too, or is it more helpful to cheer you on, making sure no one's stolen your brand new bike I'm buying you next weekend?"

Nora smiles, one that shows off her delightful, pointy little canines. "Cheering me on sounds good."

"Then that's where I'll be."

WHEN OUR STOMACHS ARE FULL, we walk back through the park, enjoying the green space tucked away in London's steel and glass jungle. The evening is drawing in, the sun a low, dull orange orb on the horizon.

Although we've touched on Nora's dependence on her ex today, I don't kid myself that this is suddenly resolved. But we've made progress, and that's all I can hope for so early on in our relationship.

We stop for a Cornetto ice-cream from the café, ripping off the top and side wrappers and walking to a nearby bin to dispose of them. Wasps buzz around the open sides, so I offer to throw Nora's in.

"I can manage."

"I know you can but - "

An errant football thuds loudly against the plastic side just as Nora's hand enters through the gap. At least ten wasps are disturbed, flying out with angry intent.

"Ow, shit," Nora curses, waving her free hand, swatting at buzzing wasps. "I've been stung. Twice."

My insides hollow out.

Fuck.

I go to grab her handbag but realise she didn't bring one. She only brought her phone, tucked into the hip pocket of her leggings. How the fuck did I not notice? Why didn't I check?

Evading the angry wasps, I steer Nora to a bench seat and lie her down. "Slow, deep breaths." I ask a woman who appears to have been watching our drama unfold to stay with her. And then I run into the café, dialling 9-9-9 at the same time. "Does anyone have an EpiPen?" I shout. "EpiPen! Does anyone have one?" I run to the staff on the tills, frantically yelling out the same refrain. "My girlfriend's about to have an anaphylactic reaction."

Anxious faces regard me, heads shaking apologetically. A mother shoves a bottle of Piriton in my hands. "Will this help?"

"Thanks," I answer distractedly, trying to communicate with the ambulance service at the same time.

Grabbing a bottle of water from the fridge, I run back outside, barging into an elderly lady as I whizz through the door. Yelling an apology, I race to Nora reclined on the hard bench. Hands trembling, I administer as much anti-histamine as is allowed, praying it helps in some way.

As I relay our position and Nora's lack of symptoms to the operator, I keep a close eye on her. I'm assured that a motorcycle paramedic will be with us in four minutes.

"It's okay," Nora tells me, seeing me in a blind panic. "I've had desensitisation therapy."

I'm sure I'm the one meant to be telling her to remain calm. "What hurts?"

"I feel a little dizzy, and a touch nauseous but I'm alright."

She looks a little red around the eyes. I'm so bloody scared I could cry. It wasn't just one sting either, it was two. "Can you breathe okay?"

She nods.

"No tingles in your lips?"

A head shake.

"Any tightness in your throat?"

"No."

"Let me check your tongue," I murmur. Nora opens her mouth and I take a look inside, inspecting her tongue and lips.

There's no sign of any swelling there, nor around her eyes. Next, I plant a hand over her heart, the beat regular and normal.

"I'm so sorry, I should've checked you had your meds."

"It's not your fault, it's mine."

"I'm the doctor."

"And I'm over eighteen, responsible for myself." She cups my jaw. "Please, don't blame yourself, Liam, I won't hear it."

Sometimes, symptoms take a while to develop, and the desensitisation therapy has no doubt been useful. Trying to breathe, trying to forgive myself, I drop my head to her stomach, the operator giving me all sorts of instructions that I've already completed.

Four minutes is an excruciatingly long time. I knew this before this moment, but it feels miserably, horrendously protracted right now. Needing to kiss and touch her as much as possible, I fawn over her, worried, while we wait for the paramedic to arrive.

"I didn't get to eat my Cornetto," Nora grumbles. "The lady threw it away for me in case any more wasps came back."

"I'll fill the freezer full of Cornettos," I appease.

The lady who helped is waiting a few metres away, watching us. "Thanks," I call across to her.

"Anything I can do?"

My mind draws a blank, but then I spy the Piriton. "Could you give this back to the woman inside the café? She was in a pink dress. And here's some money for the bottle of water," I say, rummaging in my pocket for some coins.

"Of course," she says, taking the change and bottle and heading for the door.

"Liam," Nora begins, licking her lips. "I'm sorry if I upset you today, about Aaron."

"You didn't. I just wanted to prod at your emotions a little. To understand what's held you back. I don't want that for us."

"Nor do I."

"We're good," I reassure her.

Thankfully, the sound of the paramedic and the flash of blue lights has me standing, waving both arms in a dramatic cross to get his attention. Quickly, he's off his bike, grabbing his medical bag and administering epinephrine into Nora's thigh.

The call with the emergency services ends as we wait for Nora to respond to the medicine. After offering her some more water, I take a long, anxious gulp myself.

When an ambulance rocks up twenty minutes later, we're taken to Chelsea and Westminster A&E. There are endless tests and consultations, but five hours later, with Nora's health not deteriorating, I demand to take her home.

The female doctor - Dr. Sanchez - replies, "It would be wise to stay the night for observation."

"I'm a GP. I can look after her just fine."

Sanchez looks to Nora. "What would you like to do?"

"Go home with Liam. He'll take care of me."

"Clinically, I can release you. It goes without saying that if there are any new symptoms, or a deterioration in your health, you must come back or call for an ambulance."

Relieved, Nora smiles.

So at close to eleven at night we return home, Nora slumping to the sofa as I get Nippy's food ready and replenish his water supply.

"What can I do?" I ask. "Are you hungry, thirsty?"

Slowly, Nora gets to her feet, padding across the floor towards the sink.

"Let me get that," I object softly. "Take a seat at the island."

I pour two glasses of water, both of us draining them dry before Nora asks, "Will you shower with me? Then I want to get into bed."

Under the water, I cradle Nora against my chest, so grateful for modern medicine that gives people a fucking chance when their body reacts against them. It's why I love being a doctor, why I'll continue to love it.

Not wanting to get her hair wet, we're not in the shower for long, but the warm, soothing water cleanses us of the evening's awfulness.

In bed, I pull her back against my chest, reissuing instructions. "I mean it, Nora. You wake me if there's the slightest tingle. The smallest tightness in your chest or around your throat."

"Thank you for being there today."

"Of course. Did you let your parents and brothers know?"

"I will in the morning."

Six o'clock will be here too soon. "Can you cancel your appointments?"

"My first isn't until eight-thirty so I'll be refreshed enough." She runs a distracting finger over the back of my hand, her touch ticklish and teasing all at once. "Sorry to start off your week so chaotically."

A low chuckle tumbles out of me. "To be honest, I should've expected it. My first twenty-four hours with you have been full to overflowing."

We've clarified what we are, we've fucked, and fucked some more. I've had the best massage of my life and I seem to be picking up an old hobby. After opening Nora's eyes to her ex, and almost falling out over it, she's survived two wasp stings and too many hours to count in the hospital.

Wrapped under my arms, Nora shakes with laughter.

"I would've been disappointed if it had been easy."

"It is with you," she whispers. "Even the hardest things seem easy."

My hold on her tightens, and I kiss the back of her neck. "Sleep. I'll be right here in the morning."

CHAPTER EIGHTEEN

Nora

A FEW DAYS after a shot of epinephrine to my leg and a necessary but frustrating few hours at the hospital, I feel pretty much back on track. But the most telling way to assess my recovery is to push myself with a run. Fears that I've lost speed and fitness over the past few days have been ever-present, even though I wish it were different. But I cannot let my focus waiver.

I cannot let Beth beat me *again.*

Tonight, Liam asked if he could tag along. Having him at my side is bolstering on many levels, not least the additional pace I seem to find when we train together.

"It's just like old times," he tells me, stretching his hamstrings.

"Wish we were in France though. That lake was the best."

"Oh yeah. I'm all for Mum and Dad moving out there. We could stay at the hotel, in one of the suites."

I screw up my face, circling my ankles in both directions to ensure they're nice and supple. "That means no private pool. Even with the lake, I still want the pool."

We head for the lift, Liam pushing the call button. "Of course you do. You have to live every experience twice."

Affectionately, I elbow him in the side, even though I can hear admiration in his voice. "So we'll go back?"

Suddenly, his face morphs into something infinitely more focussed. "I have one big regret about that trip. If we'd been together," he states roughly, coming to stand in front of me and running his fingers along my cheeks, "I would've kissed the life out of you on that pontoon. Had every sweet part of you."

My stomach swoops and dives, remembering the fierce look in his eye on our last night. Kissing him was all I could think about when he leaned over towards me, my insides deflating when he basically brushed me off with a good luck wish.

And I know why neither of us could act on the chemistry coursing between us, but it felt like a rejection.

We enter the lift. "I wanted that too," I admit, inhaling his sandalwood cologne.

"It physically hurt to get up and swim back to the beach without you. Leaving you there."

"It hurt to watch you leave, but I understood why."

"I chose cheating as the worst trait in the card game because I was telling myself all the time, every day of that trip, that I couldn't cheat on my brother. It wasn't just because I was protective of my sisters."

"I didn't want to be that person either," I agree. "But hey, look at us now. It's all worked out."

Liam smiles affectionately as we exit the lift and then the building. Slowly, we jog towards the river, getting warmed up. Recently, Liam has been reading blogs by ultra athletes in the hope to learn more about best practise training habits. Knowing what will give me a competitive advantage seems to be high on his agenda right now.

His support and interest means the world. He's even been swatting up on energy-releasing foods, and footwear brands that might give me an almost indiscernible edge. And it's not limited to that, but supplements and altitude testing and all sorts of other wonderful, improbable things that I really can't devote the time to.

But his enthusiasm, his determination in helping me has not gone unnoticed.

It starts to drizzle. I don't enjoy running in the rain but training schedules don't care about the weather. As I've mapped out a route from previous training sessions, we follow my course which ultimately leads us into Battersea Park. When we hit our distance, we slow down and I check the stats.

Heads bowed over my watch, we can see we've shaved off a whopping three seconds.

Blowing out a long breath, Liam holds up a balled hand for a fist bump. Slowly, we walk towards the nearest exit, heading back to Pimlico whilst planning our first proper weekend together.

"Shall we get dinner with Lowell and Harriet?"

"Oh, no, I'm not sure we can," Liam divulges. "They've had a wobble, and Lowell's not had a chance to set that right yet."

I make a face, sad for them. "That's a shame."

"Yeah."

"By the way," I begin excitedly, somehow forgetting to share with Liam a client's comment this afternoon. "My patients are gushing over your drawings. And when I say gushed, I mean close to losing bladder control."

Beside me, Liam gives me a chastising look, but he doesn't

know how serious I am. "One is even bringing his wife round tomorrow for her opinion. Apparently, she gets the veto on all purchases, but he was very hopeful that she'd agree."

The rain starts to fall more heavily. Our steps turn faster until we end up jogging towards a clump of trees that offer some protection.

"That's good," he answers, bemused and looking rather unconvinced of this genuine interest. The frames only went up last night, Liam and I spending a long time making sure each one was hanging at the correct height, and labelled correctly. With a little push from me, he's given each one a title and created a spreadsheet to keep track of sales. I now have a supply of suitably sized jiffy bags and bubble wrap if people need them packaged for the journey home. It's a good job my office has a secure entry system. And Salma, my fellow renter, will direct any interested parties to me.

"It's not going to take up valuable time, is it? Distracting you from your day and clients isn't part of the deal."

"To be honest, it's been a great talking point. Most people noticed them, especially the ones who arrived early and had to wait."

When I glance across at Liam he appears thoughtful. "Thanks," he croaks, his throat thick with emotion, "for being so invested in my art."

"I'm invested in us," I tell him.

THE DAYS EASE PAST, even though work is relentless for both of us. When I can, I continue with my training, the nearing triathlon leaving me with mixed emotions. It's hard to find the energy for it when Liam consumes me in so many more delicious ways. And I don't just mean physically. Emotionally, there's no room for distractions that I dwelled on so heavily before. Errant thoughts weren't just limited to why I was so hopeless at dating, or finding suitable men to date. They concentrated on whether I'd be married to Aaron by now if he hadn't started shagging Beth. If we'd be sharing a clinic. Who would our children have taken after?

None of those speculative thoughts were helpful, but sometimes I found myself wondering random things about my non-future with him. What would my life look like if we hadn't split up?

I don't wonder anymore. There's no time for that when I have several dirty texts to read and respond to every day.

Liam: ***Tonight, I'm going to flip you in half and sink inside your tight heat, fucking you ragged.***

Liam: ***You rode my cock so hard last night, I get a boner every time I think about it. Just wait until I get home, woman. Your ass is mine.***

Liam: ***Last night, when I pushed inside you, you were so wet. And you took every thick inch so well, that toy too. Just as well we're in the penthouse. The neighbours would be alarmed by all your screams...***

Liam: ***I feel like eating pussy when I get in from work.***

Every day, he reminds me in so many ways that I'm it for him. Every day, I show him that I'm devoted to him and him alone. I'm not sure he needs any signposting from me on how to improve his GBS. He just seems to know my every thought and want before I've had a chance to express it.

And he seemed to find the crux of my problem so quickly. I *did* like Aaron's attention. It *did* make me feel important to him still, and while his suggestion to get back together was one I'd thought of from time to time, I would never have pursued it. Besides, it all came too late.

Aside from a few group messages about training niggles and last-minute hotel bookings, contact from my uni friends is minimal, all of them pushed to the recesses of my mind. There's no time to consider them even if I wanted to. Liam dominates me mind, body, and soul. Spending time with him wipes everything clean, resetting the balance of the world and reinforcing the duality I felt in the chateau gardens as we walked side by side, now mirrored in my new reality.

Life is really good.

Except for the odd occasion Liam's exes call him, wanting to hook up. I could do without hearing those conversations or seeing suggestive messages on his phone. But Liam makes a show of blocking their numbers before tossing his phone out of reach. It makes me think that he's throwing away all those previous distractions, those earlier relationships that he wasn't prepared to devote any time to.

It makes me feel secure.

It makes me wonder if I need to throw away Aaron's number.

By the time the second weekend rolls around I've sold six original Alstons. New pieces are already at the framers, ready to take the empty spaces on the walls. I'm so smug about it that I announce, "Did I mention that I get commission for each sale? I'm pretty sure I did."

"You want commission?" Liam leads, well aware that I never said anything remotely close. "How about you take it out of my body."

It's not a question. It's another invitation, especially when you factor in the sinful-edged voice that accompanied it.

Watching him draw is pornographic. The laser focus, the purposeful way he holds his body, the sexy view of his sculpted back. For the past hour, my libido has been steadily climbing while I watched him work, my back propped up against the wall as I sat on the floor. In between, I attempted to start a new fantasy novel I'd recently bought, and texted Ash about dinner plans.

At first I didn't want to disturb him, didn't want to encroach his space, infiltrating the peace that surrounds him when he's entirely focused. But I was so interested, and when he saw me hovering, peering around the door after my morning clients, he invited me into his office, happy for the company.

Without taking his eyes off me, Liam places his charcoal pencil on the easel. And then he's advancing. The feral look in his eyes has my pulse careening. I'm barely upright before his hands gather me under my thighs and I'm slammed into the wall behind me.

"I thought I was taking it out of you," I remind him, arching into the press of his body.

His mouth descends, his assured lips moving across mine with familiar, possessive hunger. His breath is hot, infused with mint from his tea, and I am lost to a million competing sensations.

"I'm not done disrespecting you yet."

The hard bulge in his groin grinds against my centre. My breathing rockets as his mouth chases mine, our tongues tangling until I'm boneless and panting. I slide my fingers into his thick hair, the strands soft and perfect for tugging.

"Take me out," he instructs, his control gone. I push his sweatpants down, shuffling the material past his jutting cock and slim hips. He slides a proprietary finger over my wet seam, my clit throbbing and pulsing with every delicate pass. Under my skirt, I'm still wearing my pants, but it's obvious how much I need him.

"Look at all this wet," Liam husks, sliding a finger under the lace and slicking it through my sex. I can hear how ready I am. Liam can too, his deep, thrilled groan radiating down my throat as he kisses the fuck out of me.

Pinning me to the wall with his hips, Liam hooks his fingers into my knickers and tugs them down my thighs. Wriggling, juggling me in his grip, I help them down my legs and off my feet. He scoops the material of my skirt into the waistband as I pull at his T-shirt, letting him know wordlessly that it has to go. Once he's ripped that over his head, he takes himself in hand to tease my entrance with the wide head of his cock.

I'm desperate for him, my heart pounding, my skin so tight I could burst out of it.

"Does your kitty need feeding?" With a long, deep thrust, Liam enters me, stuffing me full. My head empties bar one thought, my body singing it out loud.

Move.

He rolls his hips against mine as I hang on for dear life, my back braced against the wall. His movements are relentless, his scent enveloping me as a ball of distracting heat builds deep inside my lower belly.

Somehow, I manage to get my T-shirt over my head, but my bra is a lost cause. Unable to undo the back clasp I just hang the straps over my shoulders and push down the cups.

"You beautiful, horny girl," Liam praises, getting a good eyeful. "Show me everything."

His hips kick up, pounding my tailbone into the wall as he bends to mouth at my neck. He's not remotely careful, just frenzied, jostling me higher up the wall as my breasts rub against his pecs. A line of pure gasoline races directly to my core, a twisting, tortuous pressure building. It has me crying out, a fire burning there.

"You're close," Liam husks down my ear, my body erupting in goosebumps. "I can feel you quivering around my dick."

My orgasm hits me hard, my mind possessed by him. With hypnotic kisses, he fucks me through it until his own release crests, his hips slamming me into the wall and holding me there as he unloads inside me.

"There's your commission," he murmurs suggestively into my neck. "And there's more where that came from."

Slowly, he slides me down the wall until my feet hit the floor, my heart hammering as a smile pulls at my lips. Toying with my hair, he pulls out, my skirt dropping back to my knees. I fix my bra, finding my T-shirt and slipping it back on as Liam dresses.

"While you were out," he starts, dropping to the floor and pulling me down into his arms, "I called Fay and Tilly, my parents too, and told them about us."

My eyes widen. "Really? What did they say?"

"I told them the truth; that I fucked up my back and called you. That we hung out a bit, and that I offered you a place to stay. That you've been here since and that we're together."

"Did they seem... positive?"

"My parents are overjoyed. I'm surprised Mum didn't ask me when I was going to get you pregnant."

"Oh god!" I murmur, burying my face into my hands. "Aside from embarrassing questions from your Mum, I can't wait to see them all again."

"Good. We'll make plans soon. But text Fay."

"Will do. I miss her. I miss them all." I pause before asking the million dollar question. "What about Tom?"

"I want to see him in person when I tell him. Everyone knows to keep quiet until then."

Satisfied, I nod, wondering when he'll get the chance to visit his brother. Wondering how it will go.

I glance at the easel, admiring his progress. Earlier, Liam

talked me through his plans for the four silver birches, one tree representing each season. For winter the tree looks bare and forlorn. For spring, the leaves are budding. Currently, he's halfway through summer, a vibrant green canopy haloing the tree.

It's stunning.

"Do you want to work some more on that today?" I ask.

"Are you going out on your bike?"

I sense that he wants me to, partly to satisfy my need to train, and partly so he can finish his painting. And considering he's spent a pile of money on a new bike for me, I should demonstrate how grateful I am for his gift.

"I ought to."

He nods. "Yeah, okay. You don't want to lose momentum."

Those disinterested feelings I've been getting recently gather more strongly. Not because I want to occupy more of Liam's time, but because I'm caring less and less about momentum. But I keep quiet, happy for Liam's focus which I don't want to ruin.

But soon, I won't have triathlons to train for. In all probability, this will be my last one. Instead of spending my spare time exhausting myself, maybe I'll find ways to expand Liam's sales. There are so many places locally where he could hang part of his collection, either in small galleries, or restaurants and upscale bars.

The opportunity is huge.

Several times I've thought about Liam's long-held ambition to enter prestigious art shows. I recall that the London skyline that hangs in the living room was the piece he was going to submit for consideration.

And he should.

I'd love that dream to come true - to at least make the attempt, something he was dissuaded from by critical naysayers. At some stage, I'll track down his old teacher and show him how wrong he was about Liam's talent.

Destroying a person's dreams, their future, damaging someone's self-confidence is a situation I'm sadly familiar with. Liam is showing me how to overcome that.

Now I want to do the same for him.

CHAPTER NINETEEN

Nora

"WE'RE RUNNING LOW ON MILK," Liam tells me. "I'll pop out and get some supplies."

"Okay."

"Need any tampons while I'm there?"

From my position on the balcony lounger, catching some evening sun, I flash him a smile. "All sorted thanks."

Liam stands, dropping a kiss to my mouth. "Okay. I'll head out. Do we need anything else?"

"Melon and chocolate."

"What kind?"

"Surprise me."

There's a slow hitch of his mouth, one that still sets butterflies off in my stomach. "Done. I won't take keys."

That's code for: *I'll buzz from the main entrance, so let me in.* I also have the ability to call the lift to the top floor via the control panel. The sound of the front door clicking shut tells me

Liam has left, so I just lie back on the lounger, thinking ahead to the coming weekend.

It's race weekend.

It's also when I'll see Beth and Aaron for the first time in a year, my nerves jangling.

Grabbing my phone, I put my hand under my tracksuit bottoms, as far as my wrist, and take a picture. Sending it to Liam, I add a message. ***Hurry home. It's boring without you xx***

When my phone dings with a reply, heat unfurls in my belly as I read the message.

Liam: ***Behave…You have no idea how much I want you right now. When I get home, be ready to get destroyed***

Nora: ***What are you going to do to me?***

Liam: ***I'll have you squirming, writhing, begging for my cock until you're a mewling mess on the sheets. And then I'll fuck you so hard the neighbours will hear your screams this time***

Another message swiftly follows. ***Then I promise to make love to you, all weekend***

Fine, but first, come demolish me I reply.

Blowing out an anticipatory breath, knowing Liam's either going to sprint round the store or give up and race back to me, I gather up our empty mugs and stack them in the dishwasher. Then, I pull out my diary and start looking at my client list for tomorrow, returning a phone call from someone seeking an emergency appointment.

When the control panel by the door buzzes, I eagerly press the main door release. The image of Liam on the camera as he enters the building is a blur, but it has me wondering why I haven't seen that pink T-shirt on him before. Did he change?

Ten seconds later, I hear the call from the lift, so I activate that and wait, my mind turning over.

Moving towards the front door, I start doubting myself, wondering why I didn't study the camera before opening the door. Wishing there was a spy-hole for me to peer through, confirming it was Liam. And when the main door buzzes again at the same time I hear the lift doors opening with that annoying *ping*, when I glance at the camera and see Liam standing on the pavement waiting to be let in, I hit the door release button like Thor slams his hammer into his enemies.

My stomach bottoms out. I've fucked up.

I remember where I've seen that salmon pink T-shirt before.

There's a knock on the apartment door just as the lift doors close. I picture it descending twenty floors, ready to collect Liam. Only one of three lifts serves the penthouse; there are no other options but to wait for it to return to the ground floor.

I switch off the upbeat music, the knock coming again, but louder, echoing in the room. My voice is a strangled sensation in my throat, my heart thunderous as I wait out the enveloping silence.

When Liam buzzes the flat from the lift, I press the *Call* button on the digital panel and steel my spine. Swallowing, I throw open the front door to see a shocked Tom standing on the other side. He looks at me and then behind me, as if expecting to see Liam, his expression turning from shock to confusion to betrayal.

"Hi, Tom," I say gently, knowing this moment was bound to happen. And maybe it's better I get a short moment with him first? "Do you want to come in? Liam will be here any second."

The low hum of the ascending lift is the only sound as Tom takes several steps into the apartment. He looks angry, his jaw tense, his eyes hard. After scanning me from head to toe, I wish

I was wearing more than just a flimsy T-shirt and some fitted jogging bottoms.

"I knew it," is all he says, just as the lift doors ping open.

With my heart in my throat, I watch as Liam strolls out, spotting me by the open door. A slow, sensual smile forms. "Couldn't wait for me to - " His words falter, his eyes flickering beyond me to his waiting brother.

"Sorry. I thought it was you buzzing the flat," I murmur.

"Hey, don't worry. It's fine. Did he upset you, say anything..."

"No. I'm fine," I assure him.

Taking one last look at me, confirming I really am okay, Liam nods.

Tom lurks near the kitchen island, violence rolling off his shoulders as we step closer. Behind me, the front door clicks ominously closed, trapping us inside. Together. For a long heartbeat we gather in a loose semi-circle, the brothers locked in a silent stand-off.

That silence engulfs us, tension coiling around my limbs.

"I didn't know you were coming over," Liam begins, walking to the island and dropping the groceries on the end.

"That's obvious," Tom throws back, eyes on me.

"Don't look at her like that."

"Or what?"

"If you have a problem," Liam threatens, "take it out on me."

Tom demands, "Break it off."

"No."

Tom glances at me. It's as if he wants to ask the same of me, or hope *I'll* end things of my own accord. I shake my head, wordlessly letting him know my decision.

Vibrating with anger, Tom's gaze returns to Liam, and then he lunges, tackling Liam to the floor in a classic rugby move. Shock hits me as he raises his right fist and slams it into Liam's face. In the next second, I'm moving, striking him with a forceful downward motion in the suprascapular nerve of his right shoulder. At the same time, Liam punches him in the stomach before shoving his surrendering body to the side.

Incapacitated, Tom bellows a pained curse. "Fuck," he garbles, winded, clutching his belly. "Where the hell did you hit me?" Subdued, he looks up at me from the floor, his face scrunched in agony.

"A well-known pressure point that stops idiots from hurting their brother."

Liam stands over Tom, making sure he's staying put, but his focus is on me. "Did you get hurt?"

"No."

His eyes drift over me, checking, and then he quirks a brow in question.

"I've tussled with my brothers too many times to count. Plus," I point to my chest, "MChiro. I know all about nerves and pressure points."

A slow smile arrives on his handsome face, his dimples popping. "I shouldn't be surprised. That was...very cool."

I run a hand over his cheekbone, his face swelling. "You need ice. Is your back okay?"

Liam nods, touching his bruised face, wincing. Before he moves to the kitchen to retrieve some ice, he runs a gentle, appreciative hand down my arm.

Wide-eyed, Tom regards me from the floor. "It still really hurts."

"It's meant to."

"Is that what they teach at university these days?"

I chuff. "Maybe not in yours."

Truthfully, I taught my police officer brother, Marco, a few of these moves. Both my brothers were my heroes growing up, doling out practical advice on self-defence. But I often had to use my learnings on both of them when they fooled around trying to see who was superior, their play fights sometimes descending into raging battles, their blood-lust high.

Liam dumps some ice in a freezer bag, wrapping it up in a tea towel and pressing it lightly to his face. Falling into usual behaviours, he's all quiet confidence when he asks, "How about a drink?"

Clambering to his feet, Tom suggests, "Make it a triple."

As Liam pours three tumblers of whisky, two generous measures and a smaller one for me, Tom steps to the island and snatches up a glass, knocking it back in two large gulps.

"Fuck, Liam," he growls, a hand rubbing at where he got hit in the gut. "Didn't I tell you to stay away from her?"

"You did." His eyes seek mine. "But I couldn't."

"It was all you had to do."

"It was an impossible ask, Tom. Nora and I were always going to happen."

Wearily, Tom replies, "You just couldn't help yourself, could you?" He reaches for the bottle of Jack Daniels and pours himself another hefty measure.

I feel like I'm at a tennis match, my head swinging from left to right as the conversation volleys back and forth. "My own brother, fucking my girlfriends. That get you off, does it?"

Girlfriends. What does that mean? The question is pushed aside as I replay the vehemence in Liam's voice. Hearing the absolute assuredness he has in us as a couple.

Liam runs a hand through his hair, shaking his head in denial and disappointment. "It's not like that. I did, and have done, nothing wrong."

Trying to diffuse the situation I say, "I'm sorry, Tom. We both are." When Tom looks at me, it's full of resignation, the fight gone. "We only got in touch a few weeks ago. Liam hurt his back; I helped him."

"I should've dated a check-out girl. Is this why you like her? For free back assessments?"

"Fuck you, Tom," Liam responds, glancing at me for my reaction. He needn't worry - I know that's not true.

"When did this really start? Out in the gardens at my party? In France? Were you laughing at me behind my back as you crept off to fuck every morning by the lake?" His gaze swivels from Liam to me and back again. Then it lands on me and stays there. "Are you even doing a triathlon, or was that all a ruse to spend time together?"

Liam steps next to me, resting a comforting hand on my lower back, as I say, "I realise you're doubting everything right now, Tom, but there was nothing going on before three, four weeks ago. I promise."

Slowly, his whisky disappears. Every other sentence he raises the glass to his mouth and sips. I've barely managed two sips, but it's settled my nerves a little, a small fire raging in my stomach at the cruel assessment. "I've been cheated on before," I remind my ex. We discussed it, before France when we were getting to know each other. And after the trip to the Vosges, he asked about Aaron again, his interest in him renewed for some reason. "You know I won't tolerate cheating from anyone, least of all myself."

Looking schooled, Tom casts his eyes to the floor. "I know," he croaks. "I trust you," he says, eyes lifting to his brother. "It's him I don't."

"Why?" I demand. Did Liam lie to me about cheating on someone? Who are these *girlfriends* Tom alluded to?

Tom settles into a stool on the other side of the island. It diffuses the tension, as if he's calmed, ready to talk reasonably. Liam and I sit opposite him, waiting, but Tom just nurses his drink. I catch Liam's inhale before he shares, "Tom had a friend from school - Antonia. They'd been friends for years, but nothing had happened between them as far as I could understand." Tom and Liam lock eyes. "She'd come over every now and then, and we always had a laugh. I asked Tom if anything was going on with her, and when he said no, we had a three week fling before I left for uni." Tom drains his glass. "I would have left well alone if I knew his true feelings for her."

"You knew my feelings for Nora. Didn't stop you," Tom says quietly, defeated.

"I waited until you were over. Give me some credit."

We could've behaved like teenagers, immature and without hearts, who moved on our mutual attraction while under the same roof in France. Out of respect, we didn't steal kisses or touches, but we could've. There were moments I felt weak, like my resolve might crumble. But now I know why Liam was so determined to be good.

"I'm sorry, but Nora is not someone I can stay away from, Tom."

Tired eyes lift to Liam, the alcohol and tonight's drama affecting us all. "Is she worth falling out with your brother over?"

There's no hesitation. "Yes," he confirms, reaching for my hand and lacing our fingers together. Despite the agony our togetherness must bring Tom, I am bowled away by Liam's fierce determination. By his bold heart.

Memories and emotions rush me:

I'm going to fall for you, and you're going to fall for me. Everyone else is irrelevant.

You won't end it with me 'cos I'll be too damn perfect.

I'll show you that I'm capable of loving you, keeping you. Your every breath, every thought will be for me.

I'll treat you so good it'll be me you put on that pedestal, never thinking of your ex again.

With Liam, my love feels three dimensional, robust and

bright, illuminating everything around me until I'm dazzled by it. Until I'm blind to anyone else. And even though I'm certain I loved Liam before this moment, this day, it's in this moment that everything finally makes sense.

Tom groans, placing an elbow on the counter and his head in his hand. "That might be because I've not been the best brother."

Beside me, Liam stills, his focus shifting from me to Tom. "You mean that grudge you've held for thirteen years? Thinking I did the dirty on you?"

A deep sigh. "Antonia and I hardly spoke after your fling. We still don't."

"You hardly spoke to me either."

A bitter chuckle. Tom rubs at his face as if to clear his head, regarding us sadly, dispassionately. But I know inside he's feeling a million things. He's always been closed-off. Reserved. He often had the appearance of someone who had more important things to take care of, to spend his time on, but I'm not fooled by that stoic face. He's hurting, just as I was hurt. I understand his pain, even if his was unintentional on Liam's part.

"I don't mean to sound preachy," I begin, "and heaven knows I've needed some advice from friends over the years, but sometimes life is one big disappointment after another. The trick is to move on, to pick yourself up and keep going. To right the things that have gone wrong. The biggest regrets people have when they pass is the friends they let go of, the family they didn't spend time with. The work that consumed them. Find some space in your life, Tom, and use it to make yourself happy. I know that you will be."

Quietly, Tom studies me, his eyes drifting off over my shoulder as he contemplates my words.

"Did the Dean give you the extra day you wanted?" Liam

asks, catching on to my thoughts. Now that the summer is almost over, universities are starting imminently.

"He did. Got confirmed yesterday."

"That's good," Liam encourages.

"Yeah," Tom says on a sigh. He offers both of us a commiserating smile. Then: "I could do with a coffee, if that's...alright?"

Liam and I trade a glance, one that says, *That's a good sign, right?*

With a hand busy holding the ice pack to his face, I help Liam make the coffees, Tom watching. Several times I think he's going to speak, and maybe aware of that, Liam lets the quiet contain us, hold us.

Finally, Tom says, "I shouldn't lay all the blame at your feet, Liam." I think that's as close to an apology as Liam might get. "And I'm not surprised about you two. You look good together," Tom murmurs, a brave smile appearing. "I will be happy for you," he tells Liam, "but I really wanted to hit you."

"That's the last time I'll let you, so I hope it felt good."

Liam let him? Maybe he could've blocked that hit, or punched Tom first. But he let his brother take out his anger just once before retaliating. I'm sure he didn't need my help, but I'm a woman of action.

Tom grimaces before it morphs into a guilty smile. "Sorry," he tells me before looking back to Liam. "Maybe I can make up for it."

Liam nods, his eyes assessing. "Yeah, that would be good."

"Do you fancy buying an Alston original?" I ask, smiling broadly at Liam, who just chuckles, shaking his head at me. "Liam's drawing again."

Tom perks up, his gaze sliding to his brother, a quiet kind of admiration there. "Sure."

CHAPTER TWENTY

Liam

"WHO'S GOING to look after Nippy?" Nora asks belatedly, well aware that my usual tortoise-sitter, Lowell, is in Madrid right now, no doubt balls deep inside Harriet.

They made up. A lot.

"Have you forgotten that Fay and Sam are staying the weekend? They're going to see a show and get some dinner."

I turn down the drive to our hotel outside Norwich, a red-bricked, ivy-covered former manor house. The evening plans, which consist of spending the entire night with her uni mates are set in stone. Mingling with her friends doesn't concern me. Meeting her ex, does.

Things have been great between us, but just how much influence does Aaron have over her still? Will I punch him once on his dick face or twice? Will Nora want to take him back when he pleads with her in person?

I haven't wanted to ask about her feelings. After all, why would I invoke his name, bringing him to the front of her mind if she's already pushed him to the back? Aside from my art, insecurity is not something I'm afflicted with. Quiet confidence is a mainstay of my character, as is the ability to see the silver lining. But matters of the heart are a whole different ball game, and there's nothing remotely funny about the mild anxiety that's been slowly circling above me like a hungry vulture.

Nora blows out a breath. "My brain's like a sieve right now."

I park the car, turning off the engine and getting out. Nora joins me at the boot so that we can grab our things, but the bike will remain inside until tomorrow. "There's no way I'd invite my sister to stay without checking with you first. That doesn't sound like the action of the perfect boyfriend," I remind her.

My GBS has been excelling over the past few weeks. If I don't have this woman locked down then I've no idea what else I need to do. Every day, I ruin her for any other man. Every day, we talk about our day over dinner. Every day, she's encouraging me to make time for my art.

I've never felt so fulfilled or happy, but a very small part of me is waiting for the ground beneath my feet to fall away. I might be holding back a tiny piece of me just in case Nora is not as strong as I hope.

And I realise she's occupied with her training, probably pleased I have something to distract me when she's busy, but her focus has me concerned. Will she be this determined for the next two or three years? Five? For the rest of her life? For how long does she need to beat Beth and prove herself invincible to Aaron?

She hasn't told me she loves me yet, and I'd be lying if I said I wasn't concerned about that. Not because I've said those immortal words and she hasn't returned the sentiment, but because Aaron is a looming, destructive presence in our relationship, even if Nora is ignoring his messages and phone calls.

This weekend is a critical, defining moment in our relationship. I feel the tension building like a low rumbling thunderstorm in the distance, creeping closer.

Entering the reception area of the hotel, Nora tells me, "You are the best boyfriend. Ever. I'm just...preoccupied, I guess."

I look her over, wanting to ask so many things but putting them on pause.

Once we're checked-in, we head upstairs to our room. Dominating the space is a handsome king-size bed. The luxury bedding and other furnishings in a caramel and navy colour scheme have Nora smiling brightly.

"This is gorgeous. Much nicer than the room I normally book."

We dump our bags by the closet and collapse on the bed, Nora immediately straddling me.

Her gentle hands slide under my T-shirt and along my stomach. They trail higher, thumbing my nipples which has my nerves firing to life. Pulling her down towards me, I capture her mouth in a kiss that has my cock hard, straining against my jeans. Her arms thread around my neck, her fingers toying with the hair at my nape. It sends my body into shivers, my control shot.

Pulling away from her lush mouth, I grip the hem of her top and rip it over her head.

"Face down, on the bed."

From that moment on we're a symphony in motion, our movements coordinated and well-rehearsed by the fact that we've been together so many times now. Every action is smooth and perfectly connected until I'm splitting her apart. Urgently, I move inside her until she's at breaking point, knowing exactly how she likes it. As her release fractures, I follow quickly behind, every muscle stilling as I unload inside her pliant body.

Eventually, coherent thoughts return. "I thought we were abstaining so as not to ruin your times."

Her race is hours away. I know she needs rest, but then she crawled across that bed towards me with blatant need.

"You said that," she answers.

It has my brow creasing.

I pull out. We don't use condoms anymore, a fact I rather like. The way I see it, if we end up pregnant it's a good thing. "I did? When?"

"After our first night together. My time was lamentable and you said something about abstaining."

Well, shit.

"Are you upset that we didn't?"

Picking up her clothes off the floor, Nora's eyes find mine. "No. Why would I be?"

"Just checking," I respond, wondering how I misjudged the situation.

Nora disappears into the bathroom, returning a few minutes later to join me under the covers. From under the pillow, hidden there while Nora cleaned up, I pull out my gift and pass it to her.

Flip book #2.

"Happy three months." It's only been one at most if you consider Jack's party the beginning of our relationship, but I don't care. Passing this milestone seems important to both of us, something significant.

Nora's drooping eyes brighten. She jack-knifes from the mattress until she's sitting against the headboard. "I've been looking forward to this."

"Was the number one a giveaway?"

A sheepish grin. "A little. I could only hope."

"So that's why you left me to my own devices so often," I tease.

She nudges me with her shoulder. "Thank you." And then she's ripping off the bow and paper, pulling out the small book.

"When We Met #2," she reads off the cover, a small section of an aeroplane drawn on the front, her face visible through the plane window.

With a happy smile on her face, she flips through the pages. Knowing it intimately, I see every expression and close-up action shot like she will.

Inevitably, it starts with Nora at the airport, walking towards me with her suitcase trailing behind her. There's a cautious look on her face before a full-blown, megawatt, killer smile emerges. Wild curls surround her expressive face. And then she's crumpling, falling. Her hands come up, reaching for me, her face twisting in surprise. I've taken some creative license when her face connects with my groin because I couldn't make that out from my angle, but I can show what it felt like, a drawing with her mouth and nose squashed against the goods, and then one of my entire body, as if from a bystander, Nora kneeling at my feet with her mouth on my dick.

Naturally, I include the part where she leaves a significant wet patch on my shorts.

Nora chuckles delightedly as she skims through the entire book, flashing me a mischievous look before starting it all over again. And so our moment is prolonged, with me helping her to her clumsy feet, her cheeks stained pink, her hair hiding a mortified expression. But there was lust there too, so I made a point of adding in several pages where we stare into each other's eyes, our bodies so close together even the profoundly dim-witted would notice intimate, physical attraction.

"I look smitten."

You still do, I want to tell her.

Nora flips through the book a third time. Once she's gone through it carefully, that joyous, amazed look on her face finally fading, she places it in her lap. She turns to look at me, her eyes serious. "I love you, Liam Alston. You made such an impression on me right from the start, but I love everything I've learnt about you. Your wicked, warm sense of humour, your bond with Nippy, your generous, patient soul."

Those words clang through me like Big Ben, but it's with the profound joy and knowledge that Nora loves me. *Me.* That she's uttered words I've been desperate to hear for weeks, words I feared I wouldn't hear for some time, or ever.

Pulling her towards me, I secure her lips with mine and plunder her sweet mouth. My hands thread through her mass of waves as I tell her fiercely, "I love you, too. You amaze me, constantly."

My heart pounds in my chest as I clutch her to me, overwhelmed by every shared word. By her confession, one that I needed her to say first. If I'd prompted it with my own declaration, I'd tear myself in two wondering if she really meant it. If Aaron still hogged her heart.

In the circle of my arms, she feels incredible, relief washing through me. Pulling back, I look into her warm eyes and say, "I've been waiting to hear that for a long time."

Her smile arrives with a soft exhale. "Me too. Your drawings are how you express yourself. I knew as soon as I saw flip book #1 that you had deep feelings for me. I knew on seeing #2 that you loved me."

Palming her face, I kiss her softly on the mouth, tasting her love. It has me buoyed and hopeful that the evening will go well. But my mind is racing, latching on to Nora's words again. "Did you ever doubt that I loved you?" I ask. "Or could love you?"

A timid nod. "It's easier to believe the bad stuff than the good things. For a long time, I've worried that if I let myself fall for someone it would all get ripped away. It's not that I don't trust *you*. It's that I don't trust my insecurities." An embarrassed exhale. "Told you I was messed up."

Aaron put those insecurities inside her head. He made her

doubt how special she is. How wanted she can be. That she's worth committing to, permanently. No wonder she's not entirely pulled away from him; his renewed interest would be confidence-boosting. A kind of vindication.

"Are you worried about facing him again?" I don't need to say his name. We both know who I'm referencing.

"He's the root cause of those problems, so yeah. It's why I've always been so determined to prove myself strong and resilient. To win."

My hold on her tightens; inside she's not strong. Not yet. "Never give the bad things a second of your time. You are so easy to love." There's a faint scoff which has me frowning and wanting to dig deeper. "Is this why you're sieve-brained today?"

Tucked into my shoulder, she looks up at me. "I'm sorry if I seem distracted. Once this weekend is over, I'll be clear-headed, I know it."

I like her fighting talk. Clearly, she sees this as a big, defining weekend as well. "If he gives you any shit, tell me."

"I will. He's not a gracious loser, so don't expect him to be overly nice."

"I can beat those types of guys with my hands tied behind my back. Don't worry about me." For a long minute, I enjoy the feel of her hands gliding over my body. "Are you getting nervous about the race?"

"Not really."

"Because you're feeling confident?"

Nora hesitates. "I'm feeling good about it but... I don't know. These past few weeks I've been wondering why I've been doing all this hard work for what's meant to be a fun thing. Yes, some people take it seriously, and why not? But my ambition is feeling a little less ambitious, I guess you could say."

My arm tightens around her, liking the hopeful response. And I know I encouraged her, reading up on ways to boost her time, but it was only because it was important to her. Truthfully, part of me wishes she'd drop it. "You've been training your butt off."

She laughs sadly. "Beating Beth really doesn't matter like it used to."

The admission has my pulse freezing, but not out of terror. "Really?"

"Yeah, but at the weekends I mainly left the apartment to give you some time to draw. And you have been," she points out. "So it's all worked out because you've sold a total of eleven pieces. Which reminds me, when are you going to get your website set up?"

"Soon," I say distractedly. Richard and I have been working on a simple site and it's nearly ready. I just need to learn how to amend the items for sale or mark them as sold myself, negating the need for Richard's input from here on out - unless I get really stuck. "I didn't realise that was why you left the house for such long bike rides, refusing my company."

"I hardly refused," Nora stresses. "I suggested you draw, and you seemed grateful for the opportunity."

Fuck. How did I miss that? Having been on a self-imposed estrangement from my art for so long, I've hurled myself into each and every chance since. It's become a compulsion, a need that I'd struggle to give up now that I've found it again.

"Thank you for allowing me time for that, but what happens when this is over? I don't want you leaving the flat because you're trying to give me space. I'd rather give it up than have you do that."

Her face softens. "Don't give it up. I'm going to consider being your life model. As long as there's some kind of recompense, of course."

Although I've just had her, heat surges in my groin, my dick hardening. "If it's not commission you're after, it's recompense or distractions. You're a horny little thing, aren't you?"

With an embarrassed laugh, Nora snags my eyes. Quietly, she confesses, "I am for you."

Her honesty has me kissing her. "So you'll be my Kate Winslet of *Titanic* fame?"

There's an amused laugh that is so infectious, I always smile when I hear it. "I'm game. But don't feel limited to just *drawing* me," she purrs, "stretched out on that chaise longue, naked for you."

I'm pretty sure there's a song about a chaise longue and... other things. "You want the big D too?"

Nora's hand slides down my stomach until she's wrapping her palm around me. "Please."

AFTER NORA INTRODUCES me to Joe and Harry, who are staying in the same hotel, we all pile in a taxi and head to Aaron and Beth's house where Floss is staying over.

Fair-haired Joe is, according to Nora, the gossip of the group. Every time he asks me a question, Harry rolls his eyes and tells him to stop being so nosy. I don't mind, but it's clear Nora has avoided oversharing with all her friends lately, not just Aaron. Her silence about our relationship is intriguing, but it's her way of protecting us.

"Did you see the latest message from Aaron on the group chat?" Joe asks.

Nora shakes her head.

"He says he's got some important news to share with us tonight."

"Really? Like what?" Nora queries. "Are we not getting tuna pasta bake like usual?"

Harry laughs. Even I raise a smile.

Joe looks momentarily conflicted. "You know, it could be... that he and Beth are finally, you know.... getting engaged." His voice is soft, almost apologetic. "It's almost three years."

Aaron's message is a test, designed to upset Nora and to make her rethink her refusal. It's not possible to hate this guy any more than I already do.

"I've expected this for a long time," Nora explains, reaching for my hand. "I'm fine with it, really. I don't hold any love for him." Her eyes find mine. "I've found my soulmate."

For a few seconds, it feels like it's just the two of us in the taxi, our eyes dancing as another beautiful confession falls from Nora's lips. Uncaring that Joe and Harry are smiling stupidly at us, I kiss her, savouring every pass of her mouth against mine.

Soon, we pull up outside Aaron and Beth's flat, a conversion in a former factory on the riverfront. In fact, the building is ingeniously called The Riverfront, the brick building a squat, square-shaped eight-storey monstrosity.

When we arrive on the seventh floor, strawberry-blond Harry knocks on the front door of apartment 708. Adrenaline sweeps through my veins. With her hand in mine, Nora offers me a devil-may-care smile, clearly feeling in control right now. But despite our declaration in the hotel room, I know tonight is going to throw up some surprises.

You don't ignore controlling guys like Aaron and expect quiet acquiescence.

A brunette with soft beach waves opens the door, Nora murmuring under her breath, "That's Beth."

When it's my turn to greet her, I do it with a kiss on her cheek, watching as Nora and her embrace kindly if not a little stiffly. My immediate take on her is that she looks sad, or resigned, but maybe that's what she looks like all the time. And I don't mean to sound like a bitch, but I have no clue as to what

Aaron saw in her. She's nice enough looking, but there's no allure. No sparkle.

Floss is a short, dark blonde woman with fake eyelashes and dramatic eyebrows. After greeting me with a kiss on the cheek, I don't miss her pulse those dark, heavy eyebrows suggestively at Nora, elbowing Beth like a giddy school kid who's just met her favourite pop star for the first time.

When Aaron steps towards Nora, he swallows her in his arms, murmuring something into her ear that I'm unable to hear. His eyes lift to mine as he holds her, but I don't rise to the challenge he's basically throwing down.

She loves me, arsehole.

Aaron's a good-looking guy. He had to be really, because Nora is an insanely attractive woman in my eyes. She can set a high bar, knowing she can attract the best to put themselves forward, keen to rise to it. The kitchen lights shine off his jet black hair, his eyes that are trying to provoke me a bright blue. And he's more built than most guys, clearly enjoying the gym. When he finally releases Nora - or was that Nora trying to wriggle free? - and he stands to his full height, I can tell he's about a half-inch shorter than me.

Pushing her curls out of her face, Nora slings an arm around my waist and introduces me. With her friends as our rapt audience, I shake Aaron's hand, letting my lips hitch into an arrogant smirk.

She's mine.

All we need are some guns in our holsters, spurs on our boots, and some disgusting chewing tobacco to bring the standoff to life. He just looks me over like I don't impress him, like his opinion counts for something.

Nora's hand tightens around my waist, pulling me deeper into the flat and away from Aaron. Our bottles of wine get stowed in the fridge, alongside several packs of beer. A round table is surrounded by seven chairs, placemats, and cutlery set out.

"Come to the balcony," Beth suggests, pointing towards the open glass doors, beyond which is a small metal-framed balcony about two metres deep. Out here, the air is cool and welcome.

Aaron mingles, handing out drinks as we take in the view of the river, swans and ducks floating downstream. There are four chairs out here, a pair on either side of the balcony to leave an uninterrupted view of the river from the kitchen. Seeing Nora and Floss engrossed in conversation, Aaron claims one of the two spares. As Beth, Joe, and Harry seem to be happy catching up in the kitchen, I take the last chair, next to Aaron.

He seems easy enough to understand. He's the type of guy who feels important, regularly wanting and needing to remind everyone around him. He sits in his chair with his legs splayed out wide, an arm thrown over the balcony as if to overpower us all with his presence. Except there's no one to talk to but me.

Loudly, he says, "I expect Nora's told you that we went out for a really long time."

I nod. And even though I don't mean to debase Nora, nor belittle what we have, I need to put this guy in his place. "The only way to stop her talking about you is to shove my cock down her throat," I reply, the corner of my mouth hitching.

His eyes tighten, but then he smirks as if he's got the better of me. "She always was good at that."

The statement of fact, that they were together, and that she's sucked his cock in the past, doesn't hurt like he intended. He just raised the odds. "Does that mean Beth was better?"

Aaron drinks from his beer, his eyes flitting around guiltily. He must know he has zero chance. "You sound like a real find, talking about women like that."

"Just pleased you fucked up and dropped the catch of the century, Aaron. I plan on putting a ring on that as soon as."

"You've barely been going out." He's so vexed by my plans that his words come out forcefully. It has Nora twisting her head to look between us, her expression worried.

"When you know you know," I tell him, winking at my future wife. "How are your wedding plans going?" With Nora disinterested, getting engaged is his only option. Other than splitting up with Beth, of course.

"Still to be determined," he lies. "I'd invite you but I doubt you'll still be together."

"Why's that?" I push, wondering if he'll admit to all the messages and probing conversations he's directed her way recently.

"You don't seem to be her type."

"Handsome, rich, and well-endowed?" I ask arrogantly. "I sound perfect."

"She doesn't care about any of that. We were together during our leanest years financially. You clearly don't know her."

"That's where you're wrong. I know exactly what a rare woman I wake up to each morning. I would never jeopardise that."

Scowling, Aaron drains his beer. I get to my feet, saying, "Who knows, maybe we'll beat you down the aisle."

And then I leave him, checking if the girls want a top-up of wine. Considering their day tomorrow requires a clear head and strong physical capabilities, I'm a little surprised by how easily they're necking the alcohol.

In the kitchen, Beth is pulling two large dishes of tuna pasta bake from the oven. Joe is chopping up cucumbers, and Harry is placing garlic bread on a plate. "What can I do?" I offer, going to the fridge and pulling out the wine. "Fill more glasses?"

"Yeah, and then get everyone to sit up please," Beth asks, running her gaze over me.

As I leave the kitchen, I overhear Joe say, "I bet Nora doesn't get much sleep with him around."

I slow my steps, eager to hear their conversation. "She was looking a little tired," Harry agrees, a smile in his voice. "Bet he fucked her senseless in the hotel earlier. He's got that under-the-radar dominant look about him."

"Before race day? No chance!" Beth retorts. "Nora wouldn't do that."

"Never trust a man with dimples," Harry states. "It's a front for a devil in the sack."

Outside, Aaron is leaning against the balcony, facing Nora. It's such a look-at-me stance, his attention solely on her, waiting for her to acknowledge him.

"Food's ready," I announce, raising the bottle towards Floss's glass and filling it. "What about you?" I ask my future bride as the other two head indoors. "Do you normally drink before your race?"

"I stop at two, but I'm debating about even doing it."

Confused, I place the bottle on the floor so that I can slide my hands around her waist and give her all of my attention. I know we touched upon this earlier, but I ask, "Why?"

She shrugs, her hands coming over my shoulders, an empty glass clutched in her fingertips. "It doesn't seem important."

"Why not? You've been working so hard for this." I'm only marginally upset that I bust a lung running with her in France, but none of that matters. I'm more interested to know what's changed.

"I've got you," she whispers in that husky voice of hers, her expressive eyes amber-bright in the evening sun. "That's worth beating Beth a million times over. Aaron could grovel and beg for the next twenty-thousand days and I'd never take him back. I don't need to chase after my misplaced pride. Chase after some sense that pipping Beth to the finish line in a stupid race means I'm better. I love you. And you love me, and I don't need anything else."

I fold her into my arms, laying claim to her lips. I kiss her gently, worshipfully, my tongue sliding against hers, my mouth making a slow, steady exploration. She tastes of crisp white wine and sun-bright days, of dirty sex on moonlit nights.

But....

Pulling away, I lean my forehead against hers as I catch my breath. "If my opinion counts for anything, I think you should do it."

"You do?"

Now it's my turn to shrug. "You're here. You're ready. You're doing it for all the right reasons."

"Might still lose," she muses. "But I guess I might as well. You did buy me a very nice bike," she adds on, smirking.

Playfully, I glower at her. That day, I practically had to sit on her in the shop, muffling her protests as I handed over my card to the sales assistant.

"And you've trained alongside me," she adds on, frowning, realising just how much I've invested in this myself.

"Don't do it for me. Do it for you."

"I'll do it for us," she whispers against my lips.

Dinner is a loud affair, everyone's plates heaped high. When Nora moves onto her third wine of the night, I wonder whether she's changed her mind again. Even Harry makes a comment about it.

"Steady on, old girl. Remember, the alarm will be blaring at 0700 at the latest tomorrow."

"Got a built-in alarm clock," she reminds him.

"Oh fuck. You early risers. I don't get it."

"Best part of the day," I agree.

Harry groans. "Oh, God. You're one of those freaks whose

circadian rhythm is attuned to the rising dawn, or whatever it is."

"Early bird catches the worm," Joe states, looking meaningfully at Nora. "Must work in your favour."

She grins, murmuring, "The early bird catches pythons these days."

He hoots out a laugh, looking across at me. "Knew it."

Thankfully, I don't think everyone heard their conversation, but curious eyes do turn our direction.

"Did you see," Aaron begins, his eyes on Nora, "that Wolf Alice are touring soon. We should get tickets."

Nora's head snaps up. There's a flare of excitement before it's extinguished quickly, her nose wrinkling. "Nah, I've moved on from them."

Briefly, I'm confused, because I know for certain that she still loves that group, but clearly Aaron isn't easily dissuaded. "Too bad. I was thinking of getting tickets that come with a backstage pass."

"I thought you hated them?" Floss asks. "Why do you want to pay thousands of pounds for tickets if you don't like the music?"

Dismissing her, Aaron tries again. "We should visit the local tortoise club before you go back tomorrow, Nora. You liked it there."

"OMG," Joe mutters under his breath, looking at Harry meaningfully. "Desperate much?"

"Liam has a tortoise, so while that might've been interesting, I get to co-parent Nippy for real," she says, smiling affectionately at me.

Yup, my heart just melted even more for her.

For the next five minutes, we discuss Nippy and the fact that Nora now lives with me, Aaron grumpy and non-participative. At one point, I overhear Harry ask Nora what I do for a living. When she responds that I'm an artist, it sends shockwaves through me. Most people would mention my medical profession in a heartbeat, but I like the way her answer sounds. It feels liberating to think of myself as something other than a doctor.

"We've all been waiting patiently but I can't wait any longer. What's this big announcement?" Floss asks, her voice lifting with anticipation. "Is it what we all think it is?" She fills her glass with water as if to toast the forthcoming good news.

Beth's eyes drop to the table. Aaron shifts in his seat, glancing at Nora.

"We're splitting up," Beth admits. "Aaron is looking for a new job - possibly London - but I plan on staying in Norwich."

"No," Floss responds, her mouth open as the shock of the announcement registers. Her eyes ping from Aaron to Beth and then to Nora, where they linger a little too long before going back to Beth. "I'm so sorry. I thought from the message that it was good news. I'm such an idiot."

There are other murmurs of apology, mine included. When I look across at Nora for her reaction, I find she's just sitting there quietly, her eyes focussed on her water glass. Now, I'm pretty sure this won't change anything, but my stomach cramps all the same.

He's a free agent. And he clearly wants her back.

I've got a month under my belt, three if you count the day I met her, but it doesn't compare to eight years of friendship, two of them as a couple.

Thanks to that bombshell, the easy atmosphere we'd mostly been enjoying falters. It's a serious, sad state of affairs, and naturally, everyone is reeling. At one time, they might've thought Aaron and Nora would have a long future, and that got turned on its head. And now another outcome they were all confident in has fallen to the wayside.

The next few minutes consist of delicate, careful questions, enquiring how they both are. When Aaron stands to tidy away the plates with help from Floss, Nora excuses herself to the bathroom. As my back is to the balcony, I can see Aaron follow her down the hallway.

Looks like it's about to kick off.

CHAPTER TWENTY-ONE

Nora

A HAND REACHES FOR MINE, one that used to be so familiar to me. When I realise it's Aaron, I shake his touch loose and enter the bathroom, hoping to slam the door in his face.

I know what he wants to say. *Ask.* He murmured it in my ear when he hugged me hello.

I want you back, beautiful. Beth and I are over.

"Nora, I need to talk to you."

The dejected, pitiful plea to his voice makes me reconsider my escape, so I pause in the threshold and look up at him.

He's still a good-looking man with those bright blue eyes and thick, black hair, but Aaron knows it. And he uses his looks to manipulate everyone around him, trading a smile or a look with a pretty woman to get what he wants from them. Admiration. A boost to his ego. A smile.

"There's nothing for you in London. Not in Pimlico at any rate."

"Is that so?"

I nod. "Did you cheat on Beth too?" I demand.

"You didn't seem interested last time we spoke," he murmurs, looking wounded.

Jesus. Was he manoeuvring me into position, ready to do the dirty on Beth?

What an arsehole.

I can't bear to look at his *poor me* face. As if I'd take pity on him. And how nice for Beth to avoid going through what I did, but it's not like she's come out of this unscathed, so I have some sympathy for my old friend.

Not much though, the traitor.

"I'm sorry you couldn't make it work."

He studies me for several long seconds, weighing my expression and my words. "You were a difficult act to follow. She never stood a chance."

"Flattery won't work, Aaron. I feel like I need to remind you - again - that you chose this."

"I didn't though," he hisses. "If you remember, I told you it was a mistake, repeatedly. I never wanted to end things but you wouldn't give me that second chance."

"This sounds like victim-blaming."

"I'm the victim here," he bleats.

I laugh mirthlessly, astounded at the audacity. "You fucked my best friend behind my back for several weeks. You can't pretend that was a one-off mistake that you regretted. I was the victim, not you."

"You barely gave me a chance to explain. You moved out that afternoon and ignored every attempt I made to talk to you about it. I never wanted Beth like that. It *was* a mistake, and maybe a longer one than it should've been, but you have to believe me when I say I still love you, Nora. I've not stopped loving you."

Agitated by his words, my feet shuffle as I process everything. "This is so long ago now, Aaron. I'm over it all."

Well, *recently* I got over it but he doesn't need to know that. Recently, with some help from Liam I got wise to his antics. His forewarning of an engagement was really to force my hand, hoping I'd declare some long-forgotten feelings for him. He wanted me to protest, to jump at his suggestion of a second chance.

Why my emotions got so tangled up about him I don't know. I hate him.

"Don't lie to yourself. You've asked for my opinion on every guy you've dated since."

"You gave your unsolicited advice any chance you got. Don't twist this."

"Waving your new boyfriends under my nose to taunt me. That's not nice, Nora."

I suck in a breath, racing through memories, devastated by his words. I'm about to refute everything but he steps closer.

"I only told you what you wanted to know. That they had to go. It was your way of telling me you were still interested, letting me point out their faults and how they didn't deserve you." He sucks in a breath. "You wanted me in your thoughts and it worked." His hands fall to my waist, his body closing in. "So here I am, ready to pick up where we left off all those years ago."

Lifting both hands to his shoulders, I shove him back. Air punches in and out of my lungs making me breathless with rage. "Don't touch me. And stop gaslighting me. I remember exactly how often I contacted you first, and it was next to never. It was always you, using information Joe told you and asking me about the new guy I was seeing."

The words fly out of my mouth in a rush before I even realise what I'm saying. But as soon as I hear them aloud, I know that's exactly what went down. Aaron loved to throw shade at any new man in my life, but it wasn't out of the good of his heart.

"You wanted to make me pay for dumping your precious arse, your pride wounded." Didn't he say something along the lines of having to stick it out with Beth? "Destroying any hope of a happy relationship was your revenge."

He shakes his head, looking disappointed in me. Or maybe in himself. "No. It was the long con, Nora. You needed time to get over what I did to you and it was working. We've been closer this past year," he says, his voice low and earnest. "I got rid of every obstacle so that we could have our moment. It's our time again."

I twist away, shaking my head, refusing to hear him. "The long con? Seriously? On who - Beth or me?"

"Does it matter? All you need to know is that I did this for us. I gave you space and time. Finally, you stopped resenting me, sounding happy rather than sad. So you owe me a chance, Nora. The chance you never gave me."

"I don't owe you anything. And in case it's not abundantly clear, I'm with Liam. For as long as he'll have me."

Twin blue flames stare back at me, his jaw gritted. "That guy? He doesn't know you like I do. We've got history, years and years of it. You hardly know him."

Even though I owe Aaron nothing, I decide to share a few precious things with him that I've so far avoided. "I know he makes me happy. I know he respects and admires me. I love him, Aaron, and he loves me. He's the best person I know. Our minds and humour just click. And he's protective; he'd never hurt me like you have. Like this."

Aaron sighs crossly, his eyes pinning me like steak knives. "Offering you a place to stay is just a convenience for him. He's taking advantage of your sweet nature. It doesn't mean anything. It just makes you easy pussy."

His jealous words hit me like a physical punch. It's like I can't breathe, choking on air. "You're an arrogant, vain, narcissistic sociopath, so go fuck yourself, Aaron!" I yell.

Suddenly, Liam is there, arms folded across his chest as he eyeballs my ex with disdainful fury. "You've said quite enough. And Nora has made it very clear that's she's not. Fucking. Interested. So go and console Beth who's crying her eyes out, every disgusting complaint or sorry excuse overheard by all of us."

"Fuck you, Liam. You don't have her best interests at heart. Only I can put right the emotional damage I've caused."

"I've managed that just fine on my own," I state.

"Whatever. Don't be fooled by the nice guy act and his gesture of a place to stay."

Liam takes a step closer to Aaron, his hands dropping to his sides. "There's nothing nice about the way I give her my cock, Aaron." His voice is a low, thrumming rumble, full of warning. An electric jolt zaps my womb in response to the tenor of his words, my body flooding with heat. "It's fucking dirty and delicious. It's no sweet gesture, just hard, relentless fucking. Does that clarify things for you?"

Icy fury grips Aaron's face. His chest heaves so obviously it reminds me of a raging bull, charging for the red flag.

"Stay away from my girlfriend," Liam warns. Reminds him. Either one will do, but it's in that same rumbling baritone that reverberates through every cell I own.

Reaching for his hand, I drag Liam into the bathroom and then I slam the door in Aaron's face. Not knowing if he'll burst in here, I lock it and fall easily into the safety of Liam's arms. A mirror behind his shoulder shows my cheeks are spotted red, my eyes furious, my mouth a hard line.

How dare he.

How dare Aaron con me so unapologetically and pretend it was for my own good.

Taking a deep breath, I release the bitter anger, and focus on the man in my arms. We remain tangled together for several long minutes, neither of us talking. It's unnecessary when Liam's hands gentle over my scalp and through my hair, his other arm tight around my back. It's all the communication I need.

Comfort, love, approval. An absolute, blind trust in each other.

I know he only said those crude, goading words to rile Aaron, and I don't care. I like that Liam is fighting at my side.

"Urgh, I really did need a wee," I admit.

Once that's taken care of, I splash some water on my face and neck, and then we return to the kitchen. I wonder if everyone really could hear every word. Knowing Joe, he was probably hiding behind a wall, recording it all on his phone.

"What a prick," Liam eventually grumbles. "Are you okay?"

"Yeah. I feel liberated."

"I wanted to step in earlier, but could see you had it handled."

"I know; you've never wanted to force your opinions on me."

"It's not just that. I needed you to purge him from your head. Me stepping in wouldn't have accomplished that."

It's taken me a long time to come to my own, necessary conclusions, but they were mine to make. Liam was right. I needed to sever the strings that tied me to Aaron myself.

In the kitchen everyone is getting drunk. There's so much to unpack about the sight that I just laugh mournfully. "What a night."

"Aaron's gone out."

"Beth's in her room."

"I'm glad you diddnn't believe his bullshit," Floss slurs. "What a twisted, manipulativvve knobhead."

Liam retakes his seat at the table, pulling me into his lap. I throw an arm around his shoulders, snuggling into his protective embrace.

"He ruined my plans. I had a surprise for you," I whisper in his ear.

"You did?"

"Yeah. I'm going to have to save it for the hotel though."

His soft laugh gusts over the shell of my ear. "Will I like this surprise?"

"You will."

BEFORE WE LEAVE, I end up consoling Beth. Although she's undeserving of any sympathy, I am but a human, a nurturer of bodies and souls, and Aaron was a shithead to both of us. Fixing a small amount of her pain is something I can't overlook, but that is the only commonality that will exist between us until she can fully heal from Aaron's duplicity. His long con.

As for me, I'm totally over him. It feels cathartic. And I'm over Beth, too. She's not my friend, just as Aaron isn't my friend.

Alongside Joe and Harry, Liam and I take a taxi back to the hotel, the mood a morbid mix of sobriety and wicked fascination in light of the night's events. After saying goodnight, Harry and Joe head up to bed.

It leaves just the two of us.

After instructing Liam to wait for me in the hotel bar, I sort out a booking at reception. Once that's arranged, I find an intrigued Liam at the bar, a couple of glasses of champagne waiting.

I give nothing away.

It's close to ten o'clock. The evening has been tiring and stressful, but I try and leave that all behind me. I've wasted so much energy on my toxic ex, and I refuse to give him any more.

Drinking quickly, I tell Liam, "Wait for my text and then come and find me."

His lips hitch with a devilish smile. His eyes swim with sin. "Okay," he murmurs.

He watches me walk away. I know because I look over my shoulder, finding his eyes on me. Familiar with the layout, I step through the bar doors and turn right, heading down the long hallway and stopping by a water fountain outside the gym. We're at the rear end of the hotel, a quieter location than up by reception, up by the bar. Opposite the gym, there's a short corridor, off which there are four small meeting rooms for hire.

I compose my message. First, I select the picture, a close-up of my upper body in a cropped, white T-shirt. It's pretty much a bra top, with a daring rip at the top and bottom seams. Naturally, the material is wet-through and totally transparent. My breasts are two round orbs, my nipples hard and pink as they strain against the tight material.

I type: ***I'm clean out of Twixes. Help a girl out? xx***

In France, he told me I ate chocolate like those rapid machines that cut down trees, noisily sawing off the branches. And even though I've had him in my mouth many times since then, he's yet to see me dressed like this.

From my handbag, I pull out the scrap of material and wet it under the water fountain, ringing out the excess. After checking the bar doors and that Liam hasn't left yet, I hit *Send*.

Almost instantaneously, I get a *Read* notification.

Ten seconds later, Liam bursts through the doors of the bar. He turns his head to the right, knowing this is the way I came. When our eyes connect, a zing of electricity zips though every nerve ending I own. His breathing looks laboured, his face a mixture of intense rapture and disbelief. "You'd better run," he growls out, stalking towards me with clear intent.

So I do.

With my heart in my throat I bolt for the opposite corridor and head for the last door on the right, slotting the key I acquired at reception and throwing myself inside. I flick on the light switch, dimming it low. I waste no time in stripping off my dress and bra, pulling the cold, wet top over my head and threading my arms through the thin straps.

When I hear Liam's footsteps in the hallway, I stifle a cry of alarm, my pulse a ticking bomb under my skin. With a few seconds spare, I kick the dress away, leaving me in just a cream lace thong and the boob-busting top.

The door gets thrown open. Backlit by the corridor lights, Liam looks like a fierce god haloed by golden light. A volatile energy emanates from him, despite the calm, assured way he enters the space. There's potent violence under that polished, quietly confident exterior, all of it ready to be unleashed on me.

Goosebumps scatter across my skin, my nipples rock hard.

Lust-filled eyes drop to my chest, to the wanton scene I've created for him.

Closing the door behind him, he takes another controlled step closer. He falls to his knees, wrapping his arms around my waist and pressing a kiss to my stomach. "You depraved, beautiful woman. You're going to wreck me with pictures like that."

When he stands, his erection jams into my side. We become a tangle of lips and teeth and tongues as he kisses me hungrily, his mouth quickly following a path to my tits. He cups them with his hands, thumbing my pebbled nipples with simultaneous movements, a crippling ache arrowing straight to my core.

"This is so much better than I could've hoped for."

He sucks me through the material, his lips torturous and unrelenting. My fingers grasp his hair, clutching his head right where I need him, letting him taste every inch of me. The next thing I know, he's ripped the top clean in half, the front sections sagging to my arms.

"I hope you didn't want that."

"Lock the door," I command, handing him the key tucked in my knicker-line.

When he returns, slowly, I sink to my knees, my hands on his belt buckle. It jangles as I unfasten it, my fingers ripping open the button at his fly and tugging down the zip. Musk and heat and man overloads my senses as I paw at his boxers, taking him out and fisting him.

"Ah, fuck."

Pre-cum leaks out of the dusky red head. Carefully, I lick it away, swallowing.

"These curls," Liam growls, gripping handfuls of my abundant hair, "were made for my hands."

Opening wide, I sink down on his swollen cock. It throbs against my tongue, the vein pulsing. My free hand slides up and down the base as I take care of the rest, sucking in my cheeks as I lave and lick the velvety soft skin.

"That's it. Suck it. Make it wet," Liam murmurs, his hands pushing against my head, forcing me down a little bit further with every bobbing movement. When my jaw begins to ache I pull back to suck on the head, licking his slit.

"Enough," he says, lifting me up by my underarms. Quickly, he scans the small room, noting a round desk and four chairs. He turns me so that I'm facing the wall. "Hands on your ankles. Spread your legs."

Blood rushes to my head. Dark hair falls around my face, blocking off my vision. But Liam keeps me standing with his hands on my hips as he kneels behind me and eats me out.

A low, unhinged moan crawls out of me as his tongue sweeps through my wet centre.

"Always so wet for me," he praises, his voice molten. "Such a good girl, taking my cock whenever I need you. My mouth when I hunger for your taste."

He spreads me, making sure no part of me is untouched or inaccessible. The tip of his tongue toys with my clit as two long fingers stretch me wide, fucking me in long, deep rhythmic movements.

It won't take much before I obliterate apart. My need is so tightly strung, so taut and close to breaking point that when his mouth closes over my clit, sucking and kissing, when his fingers pump inside me with gradual, incremental speed and pressure, I almost collapse to the floor with how much I'm feeling.

A ball of energy consumes me, but Liam holds me upright, his mouth and tongue gathering my arousal as it drips down my thighs until I'm clean.

"Stay standing," he growls.

He doesn't get as far as removing his jeans. He just tugs the material a little further down his hips before he's sinking that long, hard cock of his inside me, every part of me burning bright with pleasure.

"Christ, you take me so well. You love getting fucked, don't you."

"By you," I murmur.

"That's right. Only me in here." He thrusts in deep, before running a finger between the swells of my arse. "And here."

Folded like this, the angle is deep. My body feels tiny and tight, my head dizzy. Swaying, I grip my ankles for all I'm worth. Liam's hand wraps around my hip, the other sliding to my clit where he gently strums that throbbing part of me. Our bodies slap together, his muscular thighs slamming into the backs of mine as he slowly fucks me, bringing me to another blistering climax.

It's hard to breathe bent in half, Liam taking pity on me. He pulls out, helping me upright and spinning me in his arms. "I'm going to take my sweet time with you tonight," he murmurs, his voice broken and strained. "I'll be all you see. All you'll feel. All you'll want is me."

"I already do," I tell him, our eyes dancing. He looks so emotional tonight, and it feels a little different between us, like maybe he just needed this final piece of our story to be revealed. To be certain that I'm here and staying.

"I know. I know you do, I heard everything. It was everything I wanted to hear."

I climb him like a koala, Liam boosting me up so that our groins meet. With a free hand, I hold him to my centre, his cock wet from my release. As he lowers me down, he surges up with his hips, thrusting, letting me swallow all of him. Then he walks to the locked door, pushing my back against it.

For long minutes, we kiss as he slowly fucks me, grinding against my clit and bringing me mind-numbing relief. When he comes, it's with a hoarse cry, his muscles tense and straining.

As I try and regain my breath, Liam trails teasing, drugging lips along the column of my throat, lingering on that sweet spot that leaves me boneless.

"Sorry about your top."

"S'okay."

"I need you to buy several more."

CHAPTER TWENTY-TWO

Liam

IN THE MORNING, my eyes flick open. A knot of awareness reminds me of recent events, and I look across at Nora on the neighbouring pillow. Already awake, she's no doubt muscle sore, hungover, and emotionally drained, but you wouldn't know it from the dreamy, happy smile she gives me.

"Love you," she whispers.

"Love you," I whisper back, relishing the moment.

This is the most unprepared she's ever been, but Nora doesn't seem to care about the race anymore. Finally, she's accepted she's a winner just as she is.

I'm reminded of a quote by Marcus Aurelius. *The happiness of your life, depends upon the quality of your thoughts.*

Together, we've worked through some heavy stuff, the events of last night bringing closure. There's one small thing to overcome today, but it feels like no matter the result, Nora will be sitting strong.

That said, I really want her to slaughter Beth today. In the race, not for real. Lol.

Tugging at one of her curls, I lean in for a kiss, asking a question I've wanted to ask for some time. "If I hadn't hurt my back, would you have got in touch?"

A nod. "I thought about reaching out to Fay at some stage, and then you, seeing if you fancied a drink, or a coffee." Warm eyes caress mine. "If you hadn't hurt yourself, would you have called?"

"Yeah. I was going to give it a few more weeks though."

"Do you think it's possible to know someone before you actually meet them?" Nora asks, her voice uncharacteristically subdued. "That's how I feel about you. Like I sensed you, knew you. Knew you were who I was waiting for to piece me back together."

She might have closure, but she's still processing. Still finding it hard to believe she's enough. Wrapping my arms around her more tightly, I say, "Nora. You are all that a man could ever need, and you're all that I'll ever want." My heart swells in my chest. "Don't be scared when I say I want a lifetime with you. I'm just being very clear what I want from this."

"Me too," she whispers.

After getting ready and taking breakfast in our room, we check out. As we head to the car, Nora consults her phone. "I've got a message from Tom. He says: *Good luck today. Hope to see you and Liam soon. Take care, Tom.*"

As we set off for the lake, she types out a reply. "Just telling him: *Thanks. Hope the book is going well.*"

While I appreciate the transparency, I tell her, "I don't mind you texting my brother." It was Aaron I had a problem with. "I don't expect to know who you're messaging or what you're talking about."

"I just don't want you to ever second guess who I'm texting."

"I won't," I reply, finding her hand and linking our fingers.

"This is a relationship built on trust."

"Okay, well, I've blocked Aaron," she reveals. "I'm leaving all this behind after today."

"No more triathlons?"

She shakes her head, my heart lifting. "Nope. Not here. Not with them. I won't rule out competing entirely, though, but I'll definitely do them because I want to, rather than because I feel I need to prove something."

When we arrive at the lake, I unload the bike from my car and make sure all of Nora's equipment is to hand. Race officials direct us to the right location to register and get dressed, hundreds of athletes milling around.

As the minutes slip by we're none the wiser if Beth will turn up. The group chat has been quiet, but Aaron was here, along with Joe and Harry, their race starting a short while ago.

My phone buzzes with several messages. I hunt down Nora by the ladies' changing area, the sky a dull metal grey. She's in a black wetsuit with a zip down the front, allowing her to swim and run in the same attire. Her dark curls are tidied away under a cap, goggles dangle around her neck.

"Hey, I just need you for a second."

It's ten minutes until the start. Nora's bike is ready, her shoes, her drinks, and snacks. A steady stream of male athletes are piling out of the lake now, scrambling for their bikes.

"What's going on?"

I search out the newly familiar faces in the gathering crowd of supporters, as Nora mentions the water and air temperatures.

"Where are we going?"

It takes her a few seconds to believe her eyes, her brothers, parents, Ash, and Richard all in a little huddle. And then there's Fay and Sam, Tilly and Charlie, my parents too.

"Here she is!" her older brother Marco announces.

"Oh my god! What are you all doing here?" Nora cries

excitedly.

"You can thank Liam," her mother, Gloria, says, sending me a cherishing look.

Yeah, her mama likes me.

A week ago, I met Nora's entire family courtesy of a Friday night dinner at the family restaurant. As I expected, the food was excellent. When Nora headed off to the ladies, I made the request, letting them know Nora would welcome the support. At that stage, I thought she was hell-bent on whooping Beth's arse, desperate to prove something, but, things change. Needless to say, they readily agreed, as did Ash and Richard when they came over to visit not that long ago.

"Thanks so much for being here."

"Came up this morning," Paulo, her father shares. "And it's been a good excuse to meet Liam's family," he adds on.

My sisters envelop Nora in a joint hug, Charlie and Sam piling in.

"I'm so happy for you and Liam," Fay tells her. "And for me, 'cos that means we get to hang out."

"Aren't you meant to be watching a show, and tortoise-sitting?"

"We set off early this morning. Like arse-crack of dawn, so you owe me."

They share a warm smile as an announcement comes over the speakers, requesting competitors to head for the small beach from where the swim will start. After waving goodbye to her supporters, Nora walks towards the lake edge, pulling me along with her.

"Thanks so much for inviting them. I've never had more than two supporters, ever."

"My pleasure."

"Now I know why you wanted me to race."

I give her a good luck kiss. "You've got this, I know you have.

I'll be cheering you on, waiting at the end with the others. Good luck!"

She lines up next to Floss, both of them running through some last-minute stretches before securing their goggles. And then Beth arrives. I can only tell because her suit has her name on the back.

Try hard.

God, I hope Nora beats her.

Over the next few minutes, a series of klaxons sound, allowing the swimmers to set off according to their groupings. As a strong swimmer, Nora is in the second wave, alongside her uni friends.

It's only on account of her distinctive red and green cap that I can follow her progress. I wish I was closer. I wish my cheers and shouts of encouragement could be heard over the clammer of hundreds of other supportive voices. But I'm pleased that the transition to the bike appears seamless, Nora slotting her feet into her trainers before she disappears down the road.

Now I just have to wait until she returns her bike to that same spot before sprinting off for the three-point-one mile run. With time to kill, we all get a coffee at the nearby café, returning as quickly as possible and waiting for any sign of her.

I don't get too excited when the first female cyclists return. These are probably wave one athletes, but I crane my neck in an attempt to see past a horde of expectant, curious spectators.

A couple of minutes later, I see her. In reality, she's just a blur of movement as she hands off her bike to an official and starts charging towards the path that will take her around the lake.

I'm anxious for her. Worried about her ankle, worried she'll be disappointed in her placement. But I'm also so fucking proud of her for seeing this through. For racing when she's disadvantaged, but not caring either way.

I chat with Nora's family while we wait out the next fifteen to twenty minutes. The majority of the men have returned now, relief evident on their tired faces as they cross the finishing line. When Harry and Joe ran past I cheered them on, Aaron lagging behind them. When the nasal, distorted voice comes over the speakers again, advising us of the first women returning, my nerves ratchet.

None of them are Nora. But happily, none of them are Beth either.

"I see her!" Fay shouts.

It has my heart pounding. I strain to see further down the course, looking for that red and green cap. When it comes into view, I shout her name at the top of my voice, everyone else in our group joining in.

"Come on, Nora!"

"Go, Nora!"

"GO, NORA! I yell when she's a few metres away from me, desperate for her to hear me. "GO GO GO GO GO!"

There's a huge fucking grin on her face as she runs past, her eyes darting over to our spot. To me. She looks strong, her strides fast and long, her arms pumping as she sprints past two, three other women. It has memories of France surfacing, ones that have my heart bursting. I watch her back until she crosses that line, her steps not slowing.

"Got to leave some in the tank for the last two hundred metres," Marco says, the sentence hauntingly familiar.

"Good girl," I murmur.

Marco eyes me then, and I remember that he's a police officer, deducing men in a single blink. "Be good to her," he tells me.

"I will," I promise.

"Yes!" Luca celebrates, coming up to us and playfully punching his brother on the arm.

"Come on," I say to Ash and Richard. "Let's go find her."

Collectively, we walk to the finish zone, eventually locating Nora among the many returning competitors and supporters. A finisher's medal is around her neck, her arm slung around Floss's shoulders. Quietly, Beth stands at their side.

As soon as Nora sees us she leaves her friends and throws her arms around me instead.

"You did it," I praise. "Fuck, you looked so good out there."

She laughs softly, tiredly.

The question about her placement compared to Beth harasses my thought process. Ultimately, it's not important, but the need to know is crippling. At one point, I might've looked upon her reasons as misplaced, but it took guts and huge mental strength to persist year on year. It was a different kind of strength, I realise now.

In the end, it's Floss who puts me out of my misery. "She beat us all. You flew round that course today, Nora. It's like you had wings."

Nora casts an appreciative glance at her friend, squeezing my hand that's holding hers. I know what she's saying because I've had this thought myself already, but in reverse.

I lift her up. I bolster her.

A dejected-looking Aaron emerges through the crowd, Joe and Harry trailing. They've changed out of their wetsuits and into some jeans or tracksuit bottoms. No one mentions last night's epic fall-out, but when lunch plans are broached, Nora immediately rejects any kind of group activity. "My family are unexpectedly here, Liam's too, so we'll have to catch up another time."

She starts to hug everyone goodbye, except for Aaron. All he deserves is her cold shoulder, and that's precisely what he gets. Anything that needed saying was aired last night.

Now, it's time to look ahead.

EPILOGUE

THREE MONTHS LATER

Liam

SWEAT COATS my palm as the plane gradually descends, Nora's hand held firmly within mine. We're already below the cloud cover, the view outside the window one of holiday brochures and long-held dreams. The Caribbean Sea is a vast, dark blue mass, white caps curling across its surface, constantly changing my view. Closer to shore, a turquoise ribbon of water winds along the sandy cays and beaches. From up here, the island looks green and deserted, a tranquil, tropical paradise perfect for whiling away the next ten days.

But it's not going to be all play and no work. I have some secret plans up my sleeve. For starters, we're spending a large chunk of time with Harriet and Lowell, a stop-off on their months-long honeymoon come sabbatical that has seen them island-hop several exotic countries already, with a two-month tour of South America up next.

"You okay?" I murmur.

"Yeah, just still not a fan of flying."

I squeeze Nora's hand, trying to pass along some positive energy.

Looking back, the past few months have been a whirlwind. For starters, we're both a year older, the days consisting of runs along the Thames with no particular goal, or time, in mind. And when we're not hanging out, my art keeps me busy, seemingly of interest to enough people that I've sold most pieces. It's all thanks to Nora's dedication. She's my cheerleader, my little champion, devoted to my cause. I'm certain the videos of Nippy walking to his *favourite piece of art* and shared on social media have helped.

The same weekend Nora destroyed her ghosts and scored one hell of an epiphany, Lowell and Harriet got engaged. A couple of weeks later, a few friends and family celebrated at a low-key engagement party. Jack was there, and Dylan a good school friend of Lowell's, amongst others. And I met Harriet's friends, in particular, Anna, who seemed to hate Jack on sight. The mutual dislike didn't seem to wane even at the wedding last month, a windswept November day. It's possible the notorious Jack Winters might've finally met his match, a woman who appears resistant to his charm, wandering eyes, and boyish good looks.

When Lowell shared his travel plans for after the wedding, an idea instantly bloomed. What better way to catch up with my friends and combine it with a dream-come-true experience for Nora?

The next hour is spent disembarking in Havana, patiently enduring all the usual nightmares with passport control and baggage reclaim. Once we emerge out the other side of Arrivals, we find the shuttle bus that'll take us to our boutique hotel on Avenida Paseo in central Havana.

We get checked in, then head up to our gorgeous room to shower away the long flight until we feel semi-human again.

When I check my phone, there's a message from Tom. ***Meeting Antonia for a drink later***

After relaying everything to Nora, I send him a thumbs up emoji following it with: ***Hope it goes well. Arrived at our hotel okay***

After the showdown in my apartment, Tom reached out to his old friend, finding that she'd recently separated from her husband. If nothing romantic comes from their reconnection, I can at least be glad that he's tried to repair their friendship. And we're closer too. I feel like my brother isn't bordering on estranged anymore. I like having him as my friend, especially as he's cool about Nora and I.

I text Lowell: ***All showered and freshened up. Where are you?***

A minute later I get a reply. ***Checking out the city. Will be back in an hour. Meet us on the terrace for drinks?***

In the hotel bar, I order two mojitos as Nora and I soak up the sun and read through the travel guide. A plethora of sticky tabs poke out from a large number of pages, highlighting all the sights she wants to visit.

All I really care about is the trip to Cayo Largo.

Drinking always seems so much easier on holiday, so by the time Harriet and Lowell arrive, we're finishing our second mojito. Lowell looks like a different man. It's not the tan or the happy expression, married life clearly looking good on him. It's more that he's left a lot of BS behind to simplify his life. To give it focus.

"Look at this man of leisure," I tease. Wearing a white linen shirt and navy shorts, he looks totally at home in a tropical location. "The tourist lifestyle suits you."

"You should try it."

I spread my arms wide, flashing him both dimples. "I'm here, aren't I?"

He laughs quietly. "As I understand it, if you move to a four-day week it's you who'll be kicking his feet up, day-dreaming the hours away."

"Some of us just have too much talent to contain."

His smile is big as he brings me in for a firm embrace, telling me sincerely, "It's so good to see you. I can't believe you're here, in Cuba."

"Me neither," I admit, enveloping Harriet into my arms now that her and Nora have greeted each other. "You look amazing," I tell her. She looks tanned, her wavy hair loose. "You guys must be having a blast."

We sit, ordering more mojitos and a round of piña coladas too.

"You have no idea," Harriet replies, a dreamy smile appearing as she looks across at her husband.

In many ways, I'm still not over their quick engagement and wedding, but when your soulmate stands right in front of you, you act on it. Having known Lowell for so long, especially during the past five years which saw him particularly broken and defeated, I always imagined a different outcome for him. But even optimistic me couldn't have predicted Harriet.

"I can recommend sabbaticals," Harriet continues. "We've seen so much already and it's only been a month."

"Sounds like the best," Nora says, making a face like she's been missing out. "What are the highlights so far?"

"Everything," Lowell responds dryly. "We've seen so many beautiful, interesting places. Though this is the first time we've stayed in a fancy hotel, so we're really enjoying being waited on hand and foot."

Right on cue, the waitress arrives with our cocktails, Lowell taking the opportunity to ask for some menus. After we order, I bring out the little surprise we brought with us from under the chair, hidden in a thin, cotton bag.

"Lowell asked us to bring you a little something," I say, placing it on the table in front of Harriet.

She casts intrigued, delighted eyes towards me, then Lowell, and then across to Nora before peeking inside the bag.

There's a shocked gasp. A huge smile. Reaching inside, she brings out the slightly squished box with a silver bow around it. "Cake from Lindt-Werner! I knew I married a keeper."

"Lowell said you've been craving their mini cakes." Cakes that he brought round to hers as a peace offering on at least two occasions that I know of.

"Very true. These hold a special place in my heart."

The newlyweds have already been here a full day, but the plan is to combine sightseeing wish lists, which includes the trip to Cayo Largo, a small island off the south coast. Vast numbers of turtles lay their eggs on the sixteen-mile-long beach, and although it's not nesting season, I'm hoping Nora will get her long-held wish to rescue a turtle, or to at least swim with one.

Eventually, the cocktails, jet lag, and ten-hour flight catch up with us. When we retire to our respective rooms, I make love to Nora in our beautiful bed before I collapse under the sheets, dreaming of charcoal pencils in my hand, a naked Nora on a chaise longue, and a very large, brilliant-cut diamond.

Nora

AFTER CHECKING in at our hotel on Cayo Largo, we start our day at the Sea Turtle Hatchery, close to the marina. I'm so excited I'm practically lifting off the ground, a joyous smile on my face. To be fair, I think all four of us are filled with a sense of wonder, though Lowell definitely looks like he's indulging my turtle obsession.

"I can't believe I'm finally here!"

Liam grins happily, popping those dimples at me. I'll never tire of seeing them.

We're shown around by friendly, knowledgable staff. Apart from feeding the turtles with some special food, we're allowed to pet them, the man who runs the sanctuary explaining how to calm them. It's fascinating, and I gobble up every fact he shares.

The centre collects eggs from vulnerable beaches, reburying them here until they hatch. So even though the hatching season has passed, it wasn't all that long ago and I haven't entirely missed out. There are some very young turtles here, alongside some older, sick or injured turtles, too.

It's everything I could've wanted.

"Does it make you miss Nippy?"

He's hibernating now, a special, secure spot designated just for him in the building's basement.

"Kind of," Liam answers. "But I'm used to him not lumbering around the apartment for months at a time."

I'm not. After seeing him every day, it's weird not to see his little legs powering him around the place.

"So," the manager says, "how about we release some on the beach?"

Once we're at the beach, I'm allowed to pick up a young turtle and place him on the sand. Liam records the whole, life-changing experience for me, alternating between my ecstatic face and the tiny creature, ploughing his or her way across the sand, building up muscles and committing this beach to memory for a possible return in the future.

We all get the chance to release a turtle. At the shore, I watch each recent hatchling disappear into the sea, wading out as far as I can in my shorts to catch every possible moment.

When there are no more hatchlings to release, I cry.

With an understanding, commiserating smile, Liam folds me into his arms. "We can come back tomorrow and do it all again."

I hiccup, my chest pressed against his. "Okay," I manage, slightly mollified.

With a promise to return, and after gifting a huge donation, we say our goodbyes to the staff and return to the hotel to change.

A little while later, we reconvene on the beach, a different one this time, one closer to our hotel. The only way to describe Cayo Largo is absolute paradise. The white sandy beaches are deserted, the gentle waters a stunning aquamarine. The visibility of the sea, when you're not being blinded by the reflected sunlight, is breathtaking. And there's so little development here, a bona fide deserted paradise in comparison to many other touristy places.

"Are there sharks?" I ask belatedly, the warm water already up to mid-thigh.

"Somewhere," Liam replies vaguely. His answer doesn't help my frantic heart rate, nor still my restless eyes that are obsessively scanning the sea.

Liam dives under the shallow water, grabbing for my legs. I let him sweep me away, swimming awkwardly as I cling to him, our combined strokes leading us further away from the beach. Nearby, Lowell and Harriet play in the water. They'll be heading on in a few days, but Liam and I will stay a little longer, diving every day in a nearby national park.

By the time I return home, I'll be a wrinkled prune.

"Don't worry," Liam placates. "You're a much stronger swimmer than me so if there are sharks, they'll eat me first."

"Don't say things like that!"

Chuckling, he moulds his mouth to mine and kisses me

gently, colourful fish swimming around us, the sun slowly dropping in the cerulean blue sky.

WE RELEASED MORE turtles into the sea, this time bigger ones that had to be rescued as adults and cared for until strong and healthy again. And adults weigh as much as a horse, let me tell you. Once again, the experience and emotions blew me away, my body a blanket of fizzy tingles as I watched the tagged turtle swim to freedom.

In the afternoon, we laze on the beach again, topping up our tan on some complimentary sun loungers. Lying on my tummy, I look through my emails on my phone. There's one I've been expecting for some time, anxiously waiting as the days passed.

When I see the name of the art gallery in my inbox I suck in a tense breath. My pulse races as I open the message, scanning the words quickly.

Holy shit.

Next to me, Liam dozes. Earlier, I gave him a massage, just like I do at home on a twice weekly basis. Normally, he'll text me, pretending to be a patient and not my boyfriend, encouraging me to take full advantage of the client/patient privilege.

Liam: ***I was wondering if there was an opening available.***

Nora: ***For a massage?***

Liam: ***Do you think you can fit me in?***

Nora: ***For that massage?*** I'd reply, playing dumb. ***I'm sure there's a slot open....to squeeze you in.***

Liam: ***That's very accommodating of you, Miss Moretti. I'll be sure to give you a generous tip.***

Unlike at home, he couldn't have his wicked way with me

there and then, so he settled for falling asleep under the intense rays of the sun.

On the other side of him, Lowell and Harriet are going over their itinerary for the next two to three weeks, well-thumbed guidebooks spread out between them.

I poke Liam in the ribs. "Wake up."

"Huh? Why?"

"I've got something to tell you."

He turns to face me. His eyes are hidden behind his sunglasses but there's an expectant look on his face. "Are you pregnant?"

"...No."

"Oh." Almost disappointingly, he runs a hand through his hair. "What is it?"

"I did a thing."

A dimpled smile appears. "What thing? How am I meant to guess," he says affectionately. "You get up to quite a lot of things."

Forcing myself to just say it, I blurt, "I took three pieces of your art to the National Gallery and submitted them for a prize thing."

There's a beat of silence. His expression reveals nothing. "I knew you were up to something." Two agitated hands rake through his hair as he looks off across the water. "Have they written?"

"Yeah. They loved them."

He falls to his back, deflated. "They always say that."

Part of me wants to draw out the suspense, but I know he must be all twisted up inside, thinking - yet again - that he's not good enough. That his teacher and his parents were right. But he couldn't be further from the truth.

"They've given you a highly commended for the silver birch

trees. And they're going to show your London skyline in their special exhibition."

"What?!" He launches to his feet, coming to sit next to me on the lounger. Immediately, I pass him my phone so that he can read the message directly.

"What's going on?" Lowell calls.

Sliding an arm around Liam's waist, I prop my chin on his shoulder and try and reread the email. It's his good news to share, so I wait for his reaction.

"Oh my god," he says, turning and swallowing me up in his arms, hugging me fiercely. "I can't believe you did that!"

"Are you cross?"

"No. I'm shocked, and surprised but...I'm mainly overjoyed."

If the National Gallery had been anything but positive about his drawings and paintings, then I wouldn't have told him what I'd done. And even though I know nothing about art, the fact that he hadn't submitted the piece he knew was good, his best piece, was a lost opportunity.

"Liam," Lowell calls, waiting.

"You're only looking at an accomplished artist," Liam responds, grinning broadly. "One good enough to hang on the walls of the National Gallery."

Harriet and Lowell get to their feet, scampering over to our position.

"Seriously? That's great news!" Lowell enthuses. "I always thought your drawings were shit but good for you."

Liam busts out a laugh, Harriet and I joining in.

"I'm so happy for you," Harriet tells him, giving him a hug. "Congratulations!"

"Yeah, mate. I'm really happy for you," Lowell says more seriously. "It's well deserved, though I didn't know you'd entered for any prizes."

"Well, that would be down to Nora," he clarifies, turning to me and throwing a tanned arm around my shoulders. "Thank you. Thank you for believing in me," he murmurs, folding me into his chest.

THE FOLLOWING DAY, we're on a boat roughly two miles off the western coast. Somehow, Liam has arranged for all four of us to assist a charity that tracks tagged turtles, monitoring their movements through the months and years.

It's another serenely beautiful day, the boat bobbing about on the gentle waves. With the help of the tracker we know there are several turtles nearby. We just need to wait until they surface to breathe. Therefore, we spend quite a lot of time waiting, or moving between different points. Patience isn't a speciality of mine, but having Lowell and Harriet for company has helped enormously.

"Have you named the turtles?" Harriet asks, as Lowell and Liam peer at the impressive sonar equipment with our host Gonzalo.

I nod. "Yeah, the babies were Derek and Seraphina. The adult was Frank. If I rescue one today, it'll be Ashleigh. I made my friend a promise. Did you name yours?"

"It had to be Dan."

"Of course," I say offering a knowing smile. Harriet remembers her twin brother Dan at any opportunity, and especially on her extended trip, one he would've loved.

When Gonzalo instructs me to jump into the water, I do it without question. We've all been sitting around in our swimsuits and shorts, waiting for the opportune moment as we travelled along the coast. Following his instructions and pointing finger, I quickly spot the turtle, my heart leaping into my throat.

And then I notice there's some fishing net tangled around a flipper.

Worried the turtle will swim off again, I grab it around its wide body, desperately trying to drag it towards the back of the boat where there's a low deck. The turtle, however, doesn't want to come with me, so I'm relieved when Liam dives in to help. Between us, we reach the stern, Gonzalo and Lowell helping to lift *Ashleigh* onto the boat, Harriet capturing everything on her phone.

With a hand on my arse, Liam boosts me up to the swim deck. Gonzalo passes me a knife. "Start here," he recommends, pointing.

Carefully, I slice through the thick rope as the others try and unwind, or pull the cut sections away before placing them in a secure bucket. My hands are wet and slippery, adrenaline coursing through me. The whole process takes longer than I thought, saltwater dripping into my eyes, my body chilled from the water, but the connection is everything I could've dreamed of.

Bit by bit I cut the turtle a path to freedom, Gonzalo checking the female over before she's carefully lowered into the sea. I get in with her, but she doesn't hang around, only on the surface for a few brief seconds before she swims down and away on her search for safety and food.

"Yes!" I shout into the air, my head tipped back. "That was so cool!"

Harriet cheers, "That was amazing!"

Looking on happily, Lowell claps, recognising our efforts. Liam swims out to meet me, snagging my hand as we tread water, grinning like loons.

"This might be the happiest day of my life," I tell him.

He kisses me quickly. Hard. "It's not over yet."

. . .

Liam

AS WE DISEMBARK THE BOAT, our energy is high due to *Ashleigh's* successful rescue. All of us got the chance to swim with turtles today, and it's been a surreal time. While the others return to the hotel, I let Nora know I'll catch up. I need to make a quick stop at the local market.

Nora is in the shower when I enter our hotel room, so I join her, exploring the recent changes to her body. Already her skin has darkened, the tips of her hair bronzed by the sun. Similarly, my upper body has tanned to a deep golden brown, a few freckles appearing on my shoulders and back. After making each other feel good, we dry off and get dressed for dinner.

The other two are doing something different tonight, so I lead Nora out to the beach, the sand under our feet like fine sugar. Out here, a reserved table awaits, the waves lapping barely two metres away from the table legs. The sun dips low in the sky, a soft, warm breeze toying with Nora's hair.

We greet the waiter, the table laid out for two. Lights are secured in the sand, night falling soon. After taking our seats, I order us some champagne, and a bottle of water, our meal choice for tonight already taken care of. After returning from the market, I tracked down the hotel manager, ironing out the details for tonight.

When he heads back indoors, Nora exclaims, "Oooh! We get to eat out here?"

"Tonight, we do."

"How come?"

As nonchalantly as possible, I say, "It's our last night. Thought I'd make it special."

Her face softens. "The others will be bummed."

"Let's save the smut talk until after the main course, shall we?"

Grinning, Nora shakes her head before looking out across the water. "You're so bad, and in this heavenly place too."

"You like it when I'm bad. If I remember correctly, all of our conversations in France teetered on a very fine line between respectable and perverted."

Nora has enough time to smirk at me before the waiter returns with our refreshments, both of us waiting as he pours us a glass of champagne. Leaving the water bottle on the table, he informs us, "I will be back shortly with your starters."

I lift my glass, clinking it with Nora's. "To smut talk."

"Of which you're the master," she adds on, meeting my glass with hers and smiling across at me. It's almost a dare that smile, allowing me to be whoever I want to be, whether that's the doctor, artist, or the dirty-talking boyfriend, the one that's my absolute favourite.

"Any other messages from your family?"

The email from the National Gallery got forwarded to my parents, as well as my siblings. I filled them in on recent events, about Nora's involvement in getting my art seen, about the sales I've made.

They've all congratulated my success, my parents even going so far as to apologise. *I hope you can forgive us,* Dad wrote. *Our intentions were good, but we can see we stifled your talent. Your love for it.*

Reading that made me emotional.

"No. And anything more can be said when we get back," I tell her. Right now, I want to concentrate on her. Us.

She nods, smiling happily at me. At the long-awaited apology I got. The vindication.

"I've been thinking," Nora starts, her brow furrowed in

consideration. "Do you think there are more land animals or more sea creatures?"

"Depends," I hedge. "I assume we're focussing on four-legged mammals and not birds, or insects, like ants and mosquitos."

"Precisely. Furry critters versus wet ones," she says slyly. "I know you're a fan of wet things."

Jesus. And she tells me I'm bad.

My cock hardens, her husky voice turning me on. "The only time I know what's coming out of that mouth is when I've been balls deep and I've spilled down your throat, about to pull out."

"Glad I'm unexpected."

No truer words have even been said about this woman. But instead of sweetness and charm, I lean in over the table, our gaze a searing, blistering meeting of like-minded souls. "A wet pussy is a conundrum, Nora. It's neither land mammal nor sea creature."

Her vampire teeth flash. "Are you withdrawing from the contest? Sounds like you're unable to make a decision."

"Sea creatures. With or without including plankton."

"If you count humans, I reckon I win with land mammals."

"That would be cheating."

"Beg to disagree. We're land mammals, and once upon a time we were all land animals. Very furry, hairy ones."

I blow out a breath. "That's a good point. Men are animals, especially when I take you on your hands and knees, feeding you my cock."

Her eyes flare with delicious interest. She squirms in her seat. I bet if I felt her up right now she'd be dripping wet.

We park our dirty conversation to eat the starters the waiter brings out, both of us famished. When he clears away our plates and has topped up our champagne, he disappears with a nod. We pass the time watching the sun disappear into the sea, the sky a red-purple stain. When the waiter returns with our main meals, my heart pounds in my chest.

Nora stares at her plate, the ripple of confusion on her face quickly doused. Her eyes skip to mine, before we thank the waiter who walks off grinning.

"Don't they peel carrots in Cuba?"

The market-bought carrots are indeed just layered on our plates, unpeeled, unwashed, not topped or tailed, the green roots dangling over the edge of the ceramic dish. I pitch my laugh low, trying to hide my nerves. "Maybe this is the authentic Cuba."

"They're not cooked! Do we just gnaw on them?"

"I guess so."

Killing time, I sip from my glass, watching Nora like a hawk as I do. My skin tightens when she reaches for the top carrot in front of her, lifting it up off the small pile. With a shocked inhale she pauses mid-lift, her gaze fixed on the carrot below.

"Liam." The word is just a breath, an incantation that has my body electrified. Warm, cherishing eyes lift to mine. "Liam, I....There's a...a huge diamond ring on the end of my carrot."

Aside from the lulling waves there is no other sound but Nora's quick, sharp breaths.

"Is there? Pick it up."

The carrot in her hand gets dropped unceremoniously to the table cloth. Trembling, she picks up the carrot with the engagement ring stuffed on one end while I come around, sinking to one knee beside her. Every movement she makes seems painfully slow and measured, like she's committing every millisecond to memory. Her teeth dig into her bottom lip as she slides the ring free.

"Do you like it?" I ask.

"It's so beautiful," she whispers back, unable to stop looking at it.

Even under the glow of a full moon and a few solar lights sunk in the sand, the oval, solitaire diamond glitters enticingly, advertising every one of its four carats. The narrow platinum band has seven tiny diamonds on each flank, adding another half carat.

Taking hold of her left hand, I capture her attention. "Nora, when you know you know. And I've known for a while that I'd make you my wife. Marry me, and make me a very happy man."

Her eyes dance between mine, a wide smile on her face. "Yes! Oh my god, yes."

Shaking, she passes me the ring and I slide it on her left hand. Seeing it sitting there, the echoes of her acceptance ringing in my head, fills me with unbridled pride and joy. Rising up on both knees, I capture her mouth. It starts off all teeth and grins, neither of us able to stop smiling. But then it morphs into the type of kiss that's best had in a bedroom, one that is leading, full of lust and temptation.

"Fuck dinner," I growl.

With my fingers threaded through hers I lead her along the beach, the sea glimmering with moonlight. We walk about two hundred metres, not passing a soul. As the tide goes out at this section of beach, it reveals a sandbank. Right now, it's the size of a double bed, about twenty metres out, and I plan on using it.

"Fancy a midnight swim?"

It's not midnight, but the night sky is deceptive.

In answer, Nora slips out of her dress and cropped cardigan, standing beside me in cream, silky underwear as I discard my polo shirt and shorts. After toeing off our shoes and throwing our mobiles to the small pile of clothing, we wade out to the sandbank that juts out of the water by a good two or three feet.

"It's not a pontoon," I admit. "But it's close."

The water feels cool against my skin, but it only comes up to my waist as we wade across to our destination. Looking over her shoulder for any witnesses, Nora lies down on the sand, holding her arms out for me until I'm settled on top of her.

"Are you happy?" I ask, peeling back a bra strap, then the other until her tits are bared.

"Desperately. I love you so much."

"I love you too."

Bending, I suck a pert nipple into my mouth while massaging her other breast. Eager hands rake through my hair, and I picture the ring on her finger, heavy, sparkling, announcing her as mine. I switch to the other breast, biting the budded nipple gently, making her gasp. Her arms come up behind my head, pushing me against her as I suck the swells of her breasts, leaving small hickeys behind.

Her hands drop to the waistband of my boxers, tugging, her sweet lips fastening to mine. I sweep my tongue against hers, tangling them together as I wriggle out of my wet boxers. Hooking my fingers into her cream thong, I pull it down her tanned thighs, Nora helping any way she can.

My heart thrashes in my chest, a wild hunger building as my lips hunt hers. And then she lifts her pelvis, chasing after my cock, rubbing it against her slick, wet pussy.

Words about her being a mythical sea creature get lost to oblivion as she writhes underneath me, eager for me to be inside her. So I slot myself home and plunge inside. Ferocious heat envelopes me, a low, sexy moan forced up Nora's throat as I bottom out.

"This pussy, Nora. Fuck, it loves my dick."

Nora clenches around me, igniting every nerve ending I own. Flexing my hips, I pulse inside her a few times, wanting to savour the moment.

Encircling us, the calm, still sea gives the illusion that it's just Nora and I in the world, joined, loved, cocooned on our little island of sand.

My mouth finds hers for a slow, exploratory kiss, both of us transmitting our emotions. She's liquid in my arms, moulding her body to mine. When her first orgasm washes through her, her back arches, her inner muscles rippling fiercely along the length of my cock as she chants my name over and over.

She pulls her mouth away, her chest heaving as she snatches at air. Hooded, depthless brown eyes regard me as she rakes her nails up and down my back.

"I've just realised," she says, breathless. "We've passed three months."

"That's right," I tell her, nuzzling her neck.

"We made it."

"I didn't doubt it." We're that enduring couple. I'm the man who'll love her so hard she'll never want to let him go. A lone tear drops down her cheek as I start to move inside her again. Wiping it away, I plant a kiss in its stead. "I told you I'd lock you down."

She laughs, her eyes transmitting oceans of love. "I'm so happy."

"Me too."

It's hard not to dive into her when she's so tight and hot, her body hypnotising mine until I'm driven by pure animal instinct. Her knees come up either side of my shoulders, her feet locking behind my back. With a hand wrapped loosely around her throat, we slide into a perfect rhythm. Every muscle I own is locked tight as I fuck her into the sand, my knees slipping, digging deep holes either side of her hips. It constantly changes the angle, but the position must be favourable if Nora's tightening grip on my arse, and her breathy moans are anything to go by.

"Faster. Harder."

I pound into her, lost to the moment. When she begins to flutter around my cock, I know she's close. But so am I, a prickling heat rushing down my spine and pulsing into my groin. Her second time hits her hard, stealing my breath with its intensity. It causes my release to barrel out of me, our bodies sweat-slicked as I fill her with my cum.

Thinking about our future, I murmur, "When can I fuck a baby into you?"

Tenderly, she lays a series of individual kisses on my mouth, each one full of love. "On our honeymoon?"

I smile against her ravaged lips. "A honeymoon baby sounds good. How soon can I get you down the aisle?"

A low husky laugh sounds, her head dropping back into the sand. By now, the crystalline material is everywhere, and especially in her dark hair splayed out underneath her. "You don't hang around, do you?"

"Not where you're concerned."

"I guess we should wait until Lowell and Harriet are back."

"True. Or they can just fly back. I'm not waiting long."

Gentle fingers glide through my hair as I pull out, lying down next to Nora and cuddling into her. Despite the dark sky, it's warm. "We get to tell them before we part ways."

"They'll be thrilled."

Admiring her ring, Nora asks, "Do you think we can stay here until sunrise? I think that would be pretty romantic."

Chuckling, I tell her, "That's about seven hours away."

"Oh, well perhaps we can hunker down on a sun lounger over on the main beach, sleeping on and off until it's time. I want to live every minute of this. I want to enjoy my carrots for carats moment."

"Yeah," I murmur, loving that idea, imagining a new flip book.

My stomach grumbles, Nora giggling into my shoulder.

"Perhaps we should go and see if we can rescue our dinner."

We brush ourselves down and collect our wet underthings

before crossing to the beach hand in hand. Thanks to the receding tide, the sea barely reaches our knees.

"Do you remember the flower you gave me in France?"

"Of course. A lavender rose."

"Yes," she says, eyes bright.

"It means love at first sight," I admit.

We reach our pile of clothes, Nora staring at the side of my face until I turn towards her. I lace my hands around her waist, pulling her groin against mine.

"How do you know?"

"That it's tied to the clothes rail in a spare room, drying out?"

"Not that, but, okay, you found out, but did you know what the rose meant when you gave it to me?"

I smooth a hand over her hair and then gather up our clothes. "Yes. I read a lot as a kid, remembering a few random things." I help Nora step into her dress before I pull my shorts on.

"So you knew it meant love at first sight?"

"I did." Softly, I kiss her cheek, then the other, Nora unable to form words. So I spell it out for her. "It was a message for you, for us. I wanted you to know that we would find our moment, our time. To wait until our reason for being on this earth revealed itself. We were destined since you jumped my bones in Richmond, Nora, and you know it. We just needed some time for the stars to align."

A slow, mesmerised smile spreads across her face. Her palms press against my chest, my heart thumping against the flat of her hand. "Maybe that's why I chose a flower that represented constancy. I was hanging on for us." Her hands wrap around my neck. "I can't imagine my life without you."

I fold her into my arms, tucking my chin against her temple. "That's one thing you'll never have to worry about."

The End

Want to know what happens on the chaise longue....? Want another surprise? (No - it's not a baby.)

For Bonus Scenes, click the link below, or type it into your browser to download.

https://BookHip.com/RFBLFJX

ACKNOWLEDGMENTS

Thank you so much for taking a chance and reading this book, or any book of mine. I hope you loved Liam and Nora's story.

Thanks to a sport injury, just like Nora, I have a dodgy ankle. So far, I've avoided 'meeting' new people by falling on them, but I bet it's happened to someone somewhere.

A few years ago, a woman from Shropshire found her long-lost ring growing on the end of a carrot in her vegetable patch, having lost it in her garden years before. I don't know why this story stuck with me, but it seemed a plausible and fun plot line for Nora to find one of her own.

Thank you to Scott Gaunt for my beautiful cover design.

Thank you to Ami for your editorial input, and your keen attention to detail. I do use 'really' a lot!

Huge thanks again to Susan for Beta reading. You star! And your thoughts on how I could shape the story were much appreciated.

Thanks to Mary, Arlette, Charlotte, Emma and Jess. I really appreciate your commitment to the contemporary romance world I've found myself in. Your support and encouragement means the world.

Big thanks to the book lovers and bloggers out there, the Bookstagrammers, the Booktokers and book tour peeps who are sharing the love for this book. THANK YOU.

If you've left a review, thank you too.

I couldn't do this without a very understanding husband who supports me in so many ways. Love you.

And of course, big hugs to my sister and to my parents, for always being fully supportive and encouraging. Love you too.

ABOUT THE AUTHOR

Autumn Miller writes steamy contemporary romance with complex characters.

A resident of Norfolk, England, she studied French and German at university in London, working in marketing upon graduation where she rarely used her languages. However, her love for linguistics and language will crop up in her novels, mostly because she thinks accents and the ability to speak another language is rather sexy.

During her university years, Autumn lived in Germany, travelling extensively. Having spent many holidays in Europe, and with friends and family from all over the continent too, it's inevitable her stories are influenced by this close connection.

Apart from reading and writing Autumn doesn't get up to much, but walking a shiny-coated black dog and ferrying the children to rugby, cricket, hockey and netball fixtures occupies quite a lot of her time.

If you'd like to reach out, or be part of her ARC team, then please get in touch. She'd love to hear from you.

For updates on books, giveaways etc then follow her at:

Facebook Page: @AutumnMillerWrites

Instagram: autumnmillerbooks

Twitter: @AMillerWrites

Email: autumnmillerauthor@gmail.com

Goodreads: Autumn Miller

Amazon Author Page: Autumn Miller

TikTok: @autumnmillerbooks @authorazmiller
BookBub Autumn Miller

Website coming soon.

ALSO BY AUTUMN MILLER

If you haven't read book 1 in the Hard-Won Love series, take a look at Lowell and Harriet's story here.

All The Feels

I have a standalone, one-night stand turns to enemies to lovers pregnancy book. It involves university student, Rose, and hot doctor, Callum Maddox.

Stranger Love

I have another series of standalones in the Rags to Riches series. *Marrying the Heiress* is first, involving a marriage of convenience, enemies to lovers angst, and lots of twists.

This is followed by *Loving The Bad Boy*, a fake boyfriend romance set in the upper echelons of the peerage.

Marrying The Heiress

Printed in Great Britain
by Amazon

10325371R00194